PENGUIN BOOKS

The First Time We Met

D1430020

The First Time We Met

PIPPA CROFT

PENGUIN BOOKS

PENGUIN BOOKS

Published by the Penguin Group

Penguin Books Ltd, 80 Strand, London WC2R ORL, England

Penguin Group (USA) Inc., 375 Hudson Street, New York, New York 10014, USA

Penguin Group (Canada), 90 Eglinton Avenue East, Suite 700, Toronto, Ontario, Canada M4P 2Y3
(a division of Pearson Penguin Canada Inc.)

Penguin Ireland, 25 St Stephen's Green, Dublin 2, Ireland (a division of Penguin Books Ltd)

Penguin Group (Australia), 707 Collins Street, Melbourne, Victoria 3008, Australia
(a division of Pearson Australia Group Pty Ltd)

Penguin Books India Pvt Ltd, 11 Community Centre, Panchsheel Park,
New Delhi – 110 017, India

Penguin Group (NZ), 67 Apollo Drive, Rosedale, Auckland 0632, New Zealand
(a division of Pearson New Zealand Ltd)

Penguin Books (South Africa) (Pty) Ltd, Block D, Rosebank Office Park,
181 Jan Smuts Avenue, Parktown North, Gauteng 2193, South Africa

Penguin Books Ltd, Registered Offices: 80 Strand, London WC2R ORL, England

www.penguin.com

Fist published in Penguin Books 2014
001

Copyright © Penguin Books UK Ltd, 2014

The moral right of the author has been asserted

Set in 12.5/14.75pt Garamond MT Std
Typeset by Jouve (UK), Milton Keynes
Printed in Great Britain by Clays Ltd, St Ives plc

ISBN: 978–1–405–91702–5

www.greenpenguin.co.uk

MIX
Paper from
responsible sources
FSC® C018179

Penguin Books is committed to a sustainable
future for our business, our readers and our planet.
This book is made from Forest Stewardship
Council™ certified paper.

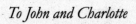

To John and Charlotte

Acknowledgements

Before I mention the awesome people on both sides of the Atlantic who helped me with this book, I'd like to apologize for listening to their advice and then going away and ignoring some of it!

That said, I'd like to give a huge hand to International Man of Mystery – Mike V – Americans, Debra R and Karen M-A, and horsey people, Nick Robinson, Jane Lovering and Jane Ford, as well as Nell Dixon and Elizabeth Hanbury.

At Penguin Books, Alex Clarke and Clare Pelly have literally made my dream come true by publishing this book – thank you to them and the whole Penguin team (especially Charlotte Brabbin in editorial).

As for my editor, Clare Bowron – you truly rock, Clare, and you know why.

I hesitate to mention my agent, Broo, because, like that perfect bar on an idyllic beach, I want to tell the world how amazing she is but I'm not sure I want anyone else to discover her . . .

Families are the most important characters in any book and mine have had to put up with a lot over my writing career, so Mum and Dad, here's a massive bouquet and a hug for everything you do.

To my daughter, the newly minted Dr Charlotte PhD, who's been an inspiration to me in so many ways, I hope you have as much fun reading this as I did writing it.

Finally, to my husband, John, who has not only encouraged me to live my dream, but made it possible, you are one in a million and ILY forever. x

Chapter One

Michaelmas Term

'Here you are then, Miss Cusack. Wyckham College.'

'Um . . . thanks, Roger.'

My voice sounds heavy with sleep as the driver lowers the tinted screen that has separated us since we pulled away from the parking lot at Heathrow. I must have dozed off because the last thing I remember was being surrounded by stationary cars on some four-lane motorway that led out of the airport. My heart had sunk into my Ralph Lauren flats as I'd watched the factory chimneys belching smoke into a pewter-coloured sky.

And I'd thought: So this is *it*? I had to fight tooth and nail to get here and, even if I end up hating the place, there's no going back.

Two hours later, we're finally here. I push the button and the rear passenger window whooshes down. Instantly, cold rain spatters my face and I know the make-up I reapplied in the 747's washroom will have to be touched up.

The hell of the motorway has melted away, replaced by a Jacobean building four floors high with a grand entrance lodge at the centre. Just down the street I can see the Bodleian Library and the Sheldonian Theatre, guarded by grotesque stone heads. I've checked them out a hundred times on the internet and imagined standing before them them more times than you could believe, but seeing them in the flesh makes my pulse race.

Roger appears at the limo door, holding it back like I'm royalty. He shoots a knowing smile at me from beneath his peaked cap and I hope he's not going to doff it or anything.

'Shall I unload your bags, Miss Cusack?'

'That would be perfect, thanks, but, *please*, call me Lauren.' I know this is probably pointless, because I tried it as soon as Roger greeted me in Arrivals.

'Yes, Miss Cusack.'

Russet leaves swirl around my ankles as I swing my legs out of the car to avoid the pooling water in the gutters. Naturally, I wanted to take a cab from Heathrow, but my father said the car was 'non-negotiable' and when Dad uses that phrase I may as well try to pull the moon from the sky. The uniformed chauffeur I can just about handle; the limo no, but Dad didn't seem to care that I would arrive looking like a crack dealer rather than a grad student.

Roger is back with a huge black umbrella. 'I think you'll find this useful, miss.' His thoughtfulness is just in time because the rain has already begun to soak into my Calvin Klein jeans and the fitted jacket I bought for a White House garden party this spring but never got to wear. Would you believe I changed outfits *four* times before I settled on something that would take me from transatlantic flight to Oxford grad student? In the end, my mother actually sat on the driveway in the Cayenne, tooting the horn until I officially Left the Building.

Rain drums on the umbrella as I take in Wyckham. The facade is the colour of ochre, crumbling a little in places but I have to admit it looks pretty. In spite of the deluge, I'm itching to get out my watercolours and capture the scene, but Roger has the trunk of the limo open, and in less than thirty seconds people have to sidestep what appears to be the whole autumn/winter stock of Louis Vuitton. Anyone would think I'd immigrated to Oxford permanently, not come for just one year, and while it looked great as the flight staff checked it in Washington, here I have to admit it seems a little showy next to the battered suitcases and cardboard boxes of the other students.

Roger lurks by the kerb, a little red-faced after unloading my stuff. 'I'm afraid I'll have to move the car, Miss Cusack. There's a traffic warden over there and I don't want a ticket. I'll find somewhere to leave the limo and walk back to help you move your bags into college.'

I flash him the Lauren Cusack smile, the one that finally made Dad give his blessing to me doing my master's at Oxford and not in the States. 'No, really, it's fine, thanks. I'll handle this from now.'

'Whatever you say, miss, but shall I at least go into the Lodge and find someone to help you with your luggage?'

'I'm good, but thanks. You go now.'

He hesitates, but then nods. 'As you wish, Miss Cusack.'

It crosses my mind to correct the Miss Cusack one

last time, but I decide to make a tactical withdrawal. Instead, I dig my wallet out of my new Kate Spade tote and hope twenty pounds will be enough. In Washington, I'm an expert at tipping. My ex, Todd, once told me I should get an honorary Master of Gratuities, which, take it from me, he didn't mean as a compliment.

'Thank you very much, miss.' His eyes widen somewhat as he pockets the twenty, and half a minute later the limo nudges into the stream of traffic, leaving me with my luggage mountain for company.

Telling myself that the fluttering in my stomach definitely *is* anticipation, I check out the students swarming in and out of the lodge and wonder how I'm going to get my things inside before they're soaked through.

It's only then I realize Roger left his umbrella behind. Call it serendipity because the rain is almost horizontal now, with mini leaf tornadoes dancing round my legs. People swirl around me and the smell of exhaust fumes fills my nostrils as a bunch of vehicles pulls up alongside the kerb.

There aren't any other limos, but a young guy in a mud-spattered Range Rover is fighting it out with a Jaguar over a gap that I'm sure wouldn't hold a rickshaw. Just when I think the Jaguar will win, the Range Rover takes it, slotting inch-perfect between the tail and nose of the two parked cars.

I'd really love to see who the speed king is so I step forward to get a better look as a dark-haired guy unfastens his safety belt, opens the driver door and jumps down. Damn! My umbrella chooses the wrong moment to blow inside out, and by the time I get it under control he's striding towards the Lodge. All I get is a back view – but *what* a back view. Despite the rain and wind, he's in a deep-blue polo shirt that shows off a fabulous set of guns, and shoulders that look like they could carry the weight of the world.

He disappears through a gate set in the Lodge's oak door. He seemed about the right age for a grad student, or maybe a little older. Either way I already hope I bump into him again. Not that I'm here to hook up with anyone; it's too soon after Todd and I split up and the last thing I want to do is screw up my master's by getting involved with someone new. Still, it sure would be great to see if his face matches up to that physique . . .

The screech of bicycle brakes sets my teeth on edge.

'Whoaaa!'

The shout is followed by a crash as the rider clips one of my bags and swerves, wobbling dangerously, then the girl manages to stop her bike from falling over.

'Oh God, I *am* sorry.'

'Me too. I'm blocking the sidewalk.'

'And I shouldn't have been riding on it, but the roads are packed with fuck-wit parents today.' She pushes her long dark-brown hair out of her eyes and rearranges her pink wrap round her neck. With a brief smile, the girl cycles off, her hair and pink wrap flying behind her.

Whew, I think, that was a close shave, but at least I haven't killed anyone on my first day.

Rain falls heavier now, wetting my face and bags.

Somewhere in my tote I have the new student notes they sent me . . .

There was nothing for it but to leave most of my luggage on the sidewalk while I dashed into the Lodge and picked up the welcome pack, the keys to my room and directions on how to find it. When the porter suggested I get a trolley, it took me a couple of seconds to realize he meant one of the wheeled carts parked around the edge of the quad. It's now piled high with my bags as I bump it over the uneven flagstones towards the staircase that will be my home for the next year.

I love the rich colour of the Jacobean stone, which is blackened with the grime of age here and there. I guess they have as much of a problem with pollution in Oxford as in Washington, and why wouldn't they? To the left of the Lodge, opposite the steps that lead up to the Great Hall, there's an archway with roman numerals painted above it. This must be it.

A skinny guy who looks about twelve passes by and I take the chance to ask him: 'Hi. Do you know which floor room ten is on?'

He grimaces. 'Top, I'm afraid.'

Through the archway I see a twisted wooden staircase. 'Oh dear.'

He glances at the trolley and back at the stairs. 'Want a hand?'

'Please don't go to the trouble for me.'

'It's no problem.'

'If you're sure, that would be great.'

As we shift my bags from the trolley to the foot of the staircase, my eye is caught by a board hung on the wall inside the archway. It lists the name of each occupant by each room number, freshly painted in copperplate letters: STAIRCASE XIII, ROOM X: L. CUSACK.

'L. Cusack', plain and simple. Not little Laurie (grandparents), or 'Sugar' or 'Honey' or 'Baby' (my parents and Todd too. Need I say more?).

Even with the help of the geek, it takes an age to drag my bags up to my room and a phone call meant my helper had to leave sooner than he thought. I'm hauling the last of my stuff into the room when a face I recognize appears at the top of the staircase.

It's the cycle girl, the pashmina still draped around her neck. 'Oh, hello again!'

I smile, a little awkwardly. 'Hi . . . I'm glad you're OK.'

She scrunches up her face in embarrassment. 'Don't worry about it. I'm always falling off my bike and there's no damage done. I should have known better than to ride down the pavement that close to college, but the roads are so busy at the start of term, and some of the driving is crazy.'

I think back to the Range Rover vs Jaguar duel and know what she means.

'I had to leave my bags on the sidewalk because my driver had to go before he got ticketed.'

'Wise move on his part, not so easy for you.' She glances at my luggage mountain and her pretty face lights up. 'And now it looks like you're on my staircase.'

'Yes, if my bags don't cause the floor to collapse.'

She laughs. 'I doubt it. The beams have survived five hundred years of parties so I think they can cope now. You don't plan on having any wild parties, do you?'

I'm not sure what the response to this is, but from the glint in her eye and her air of mischief I think we may have different ideas of wild. 'Well, you never know . . .'

'I do hope so; this staircase needs a bit of livening up, judging by the people I've seen hanging around so far. Right bunch of northern chemists and maths nerds, from what I can tell. I'm Imogen Hawthorne by the way, but do call me Immy. Imogen is such a fogeyish name.'

Well, I rather like it, but Immy it is. 'Lauren Cusack.'

'So you're L. Cusack. Are you a fresher? Oh God, I hope you're not a chemist or a maths nerd . . .' She gives me an intent look, checking out my outfit. 'Although I have to say I'd be amazed if you were.'

Fresher. It sounds so weird being a Freshman again, though it's also perfect because a fresh start is exactly what I wanted. I can be anything I want to be here.

No, I'm not a maths nerd or a fresher. I'm a post-grad, doing a master's.'

'What in?'

'History of Art and Visual Culture.' My heart seems to expand as I say the words out loud, but I try to make my reply matter of fact. Everyone here is smart – everyone's here to study; maybe this is as much of a dream come true for them as it is for me.

Immy smiles. 'Lucky you. I'm a Geography finalist. That's a capital offence here. Freddie insists I spend my whole time sharpening my colouring pencils.'

8

She doesn't explain who Freddie is and I don't like to ask, especially as I get the feeling I'll hear all about her significant other – or others – soon enough.

'I came up a couple of days ago because I have Collections tomorrow and I needed to do some revision.' She nibbles her lower lip and I wonder if she's nervous despite her apparent confidence. She switches her focus to my bags. 'Um, do you want a hand with your stuff?'

'You mean the small European luggage republic?' I say, conscious of the bags teetering on the trolley.

'You do seem to have rather a lot, but I suppose you've come to stay for the whole year. It is allowed.'

'I know, but I still think I may have over-packed.'

'You can never over-pack. I once took eyelash curlers and a bikini on a field trip to the Isle of Skye. I know my tutor thinks I'm a lightweight, but she wears brogues and has a beard so I don't really think she's qualified to comment.'

'Brogues and copious facial hair are exactly how I imagine an Oxford tutor to look,' I say.

'Then you won't be disappointed.' There's a twinkle in her eye, as my dad would say, and a naturalness and warmth that makes me feel Immy might be fun to be around.

'Want to come inside?' I ask.

'Yes, why not?'

My bags seem to fill every nook and cranny, and boy does my room have a lot of nooks and crannies. It's crammed in under the eaves, with sloping ceilings and beams. There's a single bed against one wall and a desk under one of the windows set in the sloping roof. The armchairs and night stand are battered, and nothing matches, as if it was bought from a thrift store. In fact, my master bathroom at home is bigger than the whole room, but I don't care.

After squeezing past my stuff, I manage to get one of the casement windows open.

Four floors down, the flagstones of the college quad frame a lawn as pristine as a golf green. There's a tower opposite with a bell inside it and the sun has finally broken through a break in the clouds. The way the light falls on the spires, which are shimmering in the haze, puts me in mind of a Turner painting I saw at the Met. Even the weak autumn rays feel warm against my skin as I lean out a little to get a better look at the lead-lined battlements that skirt the college roof.

It's so beautiful and so exactly what I've been dreaming of that I have to swallow a lump in my throat.

'Can we go out on to the battlements?' Maybe my voice sounds a little croaky, but Immy doesn't seem to have noticed, or else she's a good actress.

'Officially? That would be a serious breach of college health and safety rules. Unofficially, oh yes, but don't let anyone catch you doing it or you could get sent down. Fire hazard, you see. So you like your room?' she asks.

I swing round. 'I love it.'

From Immy's indulgent expression, I get the feeling she thinks I'm easily pleased. It may be de rigeur for her to live in a place that was built four hundred years ago and where some of the world's most famous art treasures and architecture are only hours away; for me, it's the fulfilment of an ambition. Sure, I've been to France and Italy with my parents before, and to London a couple of times on vacation, but actually living here in Oxford for a year, on my own, is a whole new ball game. If I want to, I can jump on a train or a plane and be in the Louvre or the Uffizi or the Rijksmuseum all within a couple of hours, with no one to answer to or have to tag along with.

However, I'm not sure Immy would ever understand the battle I've had to get here and how much it means to me.

She throws open a set of double louvre doors, revealing a dimly lit closet. 'You've got a washbasin and wardrobes in here . . .' There's a knowing sort of smile on her face as she turns back to me '. . . though I don't think they'll be enough for all your clothes.'

This, I can't deny. 'Guess I'll have to get a storage unit . . . Um . . . where's the bathroom?'

Immy beams. 'Oh, you're in luck there. There's a loo right at the end of our landing.'

In luck? 'Just a loo?' The word sounds weird in my accent, but I suppose I'd better get used to it.

''Fraid so. All the showers and baths are in the basement.'

'You mean four floors down? I thought most of the colleges have ensuites these days.'

'Most of them do, and most of Wyckham does, but that's the price you pay for having a room in the Front Quad. College hasn't got round to doing them yet and there's no use me pretending they're anything but rank. Marlborough was a palace compared to this.'

OK. Reality check. Wyckham may have some of the 'finest Jacobean architecture' in England, an 'incisive' History of Art tutor and one of the 'liveliest' graduate communities in Oxford, but the thought of heading down to some dungeon in my robe to take a shower is not appealing or romantic. Then again, they surely can't be worse than some of the bathrooms I've survived on summer camps.

'I guess I'll manage somehow,' I reassure Immy, who looks genuinely concerned for me or maybe already has me marked down as a pampered East Coast princess.

'Skanky bathrooms are one of the delights of college life, along with many others like essay crises, exams and tutors who think you're an airhead. But you're probably ultra-conscientious and naturally brilliant so you won't have to worry about that.'

Conscientious? Yes, who wouldn't be? Naturally brilliant? No. I had to work like crazy to get my *summa cum laude* at Brown and I already suspect this course will take everything I can give it and then some. 'To be honest, I'm expecting the course to be pretty demanding.'

'I bet it won't be that bad . . .' Immy heaves in a sigh. 'I got put on academic probation last term because I failed a second-year paper, but they've given me another chance. If I do OK in the Collection, I can carry on with my final year.'

She sounds breezy enough, but I suspect she's putting on a brave face and I feel sorry for her. Maybe my earlier guess about her being nervous was right. 'Sounds like a whole heap of pressure.'

'It's my own stupid fault. I've been too busy enjoying myself to settle down to work. That's the trouble with Oxford, Lauren. There's so many things to do here that are so much more fun than working that it's easy to get distracted. And, um . . . I think there will be plenty of people hoping to distract you.'

The wry smile on her face says she means guys. The image of the Range Rover guy slides into my head again and I wince inwardly. 'Trust me, I won't get distracted. I want to focus on my master's and then I want to work in an art auctioneers like Sotheby's or Christie's in New York. This is my big chance.'

Immediately I realize I've committed that American sin: being earnest and enthusiastic. 'But I can maybe fit in the odd party around my trips to the library.'

Immy gives a tight smile. 'Great. As for work, I have absolutely no idea what I'm going to do with a crappy second in Geography and that's if I make it to actual Finals.' Biting her lip, she picks up my racket bag. 'Do you mind if I take a look?'

'Be my guest. Do you play, then?'

'I can get the odd ball back on a good day.' She unzips the bag and peers inside. 'Oh my God. Are these what I think they are?'

'An ounce of crack cocaine and an automatic weapon? Yes, I got away with it this time.' I try a joke because I'm a little awkward about what she might find in my bags, not that there's anything illegal, but I can guess her reaction.

She pulls out my favourite Head MX Pro and the custom-strung Wilson that Todd insisted on getting for me last summer, telling me it would improve my power and spin, even though I told him it was all wrong for my game and would give me tennis elbow. Immy strokes the handle of the Wilson. 'Wow. This is serious kit. You *have* to join the college tennis team.'

'Thanks. But I'm probably not as good as the rackets might lead you to believe.'

She attempts a forehand, which is some feat in a room this size. 'Oh, I only play to check out the fit men.'

Seeing that classic grip and technique, I don't believe her and I'm tempted to admit I only play so I can wear the outfits, but, being British, she might think I'm joking. However, finding out Immy is a tennis fan like me shoots her up another notch in my estimation.

'I'd love a game if the weather holds, but, to tell the truth, I like dancing even more,' I say.

'Dancing? There are a few clubs in Oxford, but they're not up to much. You'll have to go to London for a really good night out. Fabric's cool, though Rupert loathes it . . .' She says it without looking at me, still distracted by the Wilson. So there's a Rupert as well as a Freddie? Immy seems popular and I can see why. She has that classic English Rose look: kind of Bond girl meets the St Trinian's movies.

'I didn't mean clubs. I mean I *do* like clubbing, but what I really love is classical dance. I did ballet at home in the States.'

Immy's face crinkles with amusement. 'So did I. For

about five minutes. My ballet teacher said I was like a pony in a tutu so Mum gave in and bought me one. A pony, that is.'

Picturing her in a tutu brings a smile to my face. 'Is there a good dance studio in Oxford?'

'Bound to be and we're only an hour from Covent Garden if you want to go and see the real thing.'

'I would *love* to. We didn't have time when we came over to London last year and seeing the Royal Ballet is top of my to-do list while I'm here.'

Immy finally lays the racket down on top of the bed. I've hardly used it and when I know her better I might let her try it out. After all, Todd will never find out now and, anyway, he can go to hell if he does.

'Um. You're not related to John Cusack, are you?' she asks out of the blue.

I smile. I've had this one before. 'Sorry, unfortunately not.'

Immy shrugs. 'Well, it was worth a try.'

It's on the tip of my tongue to say, Yes, but my dad is a little bit famous in his own way and I have actually met John Cusack at a fundraiser for a kids' cancer charity that was hosted by my mother. And Michele Obama was guest of honour and Hillary Clinton dropped by. But I don't say any of that stuff because I genuinely don't like name-dropping and I don't want to play the Pushy Yank on my first day.

Being reminded of my parents makes my stomach twinge with guilt because I haven't called them yet. My cell phone has been switched off since I boarded at

Dulles and I really should have phoned as soon as I landed at Heathrow, but locating my bags took up all my time, then looking out for Roger . . . In the midst of angsting about it, a huge yawn takes me by surprise.

'Sorry. I didn't get much sleep on the flight.'

Immy pulls a face. 'Poor thing, you look knackered. Um, that is you look great considering you got off a plane a few hours ago, but I bet you'd love some time to unpack.'

'I ought to freshen up before dinner.' My palm itches. I *really* need to phone my parents. 'What time is it?'

'Seven, but everyone starts meeting outside at about ten to. Do you want me to call for you on my way to collect Freddie?'

'That would be perfect, but I wouldn't want to take you away from your friend.'

She waves a hand dismissively. 'Freddie won't care and I can see him any time. Treat 'em mean and keep 'em keen, I say. What about if I pop round at quarter to seven?'

'If you're sure.'

Immy smiles. 'I am. Now I *absolutely* have to do some revision for this Collection on Monday and, please, if you see me getting too lashed at dinner, feel free to stop me, won't you? I don't want a hangover the size of Wales in the morning.'

Immy says, 'Ciao,' as she skips out of my room and across the hall to her own. The moment my door shuts, I could slap myself round the head. Damn, I forgot to ask her the most important thing: what on earth is the dress code for tonight's 'Formal Hall'?

Chapter Two

It's six fifty and we're rammed into the vestibule out-side the hall, the buzz and sense of anticipation building by the minute as if everyone's waiting for aliens to mate-rialize. Immy has gone to speak to Freddie and I'm on my own – apart from two hundred others that is, all of whom seem to know each other. I can hardly hear myself think for the noise of air-kissing and laughter – some of which reminds me of mules braying. My nose wrinkles, the combo of fragrance and cooking smells making me feel faintly nauseous.

After Immy went, I called home and got Dad before he left for the office. 'So I don't have to get the embassy to get you out of a British jail yet,' he'd joked. Hearing my mother's gasp in the background, I'd laughed. 'No, Daddy, not yet . . .'

I tug my finger from the strand of hair I'm twirling. I tend to do it when I'm nervous and Todd said it drove him insane. Then again, he said that a lot of things about me drove him insane. Do you know he actually sent me a memo listing all the things he thought were wrong about me? And that was *before* we broke up. Now, just the thought of it makes my stomach clench, even though there's four thousand miles between us. The split with Todd is one of the reasons I'm so glad my application to Wyckham was accepted. The day I'd got the email from Professor Rafe saying he was 'very impressed' by my college report and essays, was just about the happiest of my life.

I smooth a non-existent crease from my dress. In the end I'd solved the what-to-wear dilemma by hanging up four outfits off the doors. I did my hair and make-up, put on a robe and kind of hovered by the window, hoping to get a look at some early birds on their way to the Great Hall. A few people went past en route to the bar, I think, just enough to let me see the code was kind of cocktail meets quirk. The guys were in suits or jackets and the type of pants that my mother insists on calling 'dress slacks'.

I left getting changed as long as I dared and was applying a coat of lipgloss when Immy rapped on the door. She's making her way through the crowd to me now, rocking a shabby-chic look that I envy but could never pull off.

'Hi there. Sorry about that. I'd hoped to find Freddie but he's late as usual.'

Her pale-green printed shift really makes the most of her curves and her hair is piled on her head in that 'just fell outta bed' way the guys love. After checking out the girls in the quad, I decided to go for one of those artfully messy low ponytails that I hope looks sophisticated but not too 'done'.

'Is this OK?' I whisper, glancing down at my claret dress. 'Only I could be imagining it, but some people keep looking at me.'

Immy breaks out the megawatt grin. 'The guys are probably staring because they want to shag you; the girls and the gay men will be lusting after your dress. Is that a Donna Karan?'

'Uh-huh.'

She blows out a breath. 'I love the colour. It's fabulous.'

Although I appreciate the compliment, I half wish I'd chosen something with sleeves rather than this cold-shoulder design with the cut-outs. 'Thanks. Is yours vintage?'

A delighted smile lights up her eyes. 'Well spotted. It's one of Granny's better gifts. She wore it when my grandfather proposed to her at the Ritz and she let me have it on my eighteenth.'

'I think the print is beautiful and the pearls are perfect with it.'

Immy touches the white beads at her throat. 'These are Granny's too. I do have new knickers on, though, as it's the start of term.'

Now it's my turn to laugh as the tension eases a little, but there's no time to relax because the grand doors to the hall open and I'm literally swept inside with the crowd. My jaw drops yet again. The hall is huge and lit by candles, with a high roof supported by oak trusses. Stained-glass windows with coats of arms line the walls and there's a massive painting at one end that looks like a Reubens to me, but has to be a copy or after his style. There's no way an original would be left on display without security.

'Quick, let's get a table near the fire.'

Great idea, I think, as my fingers begin to turn blue.

We hurry along the aisle between the tables, past the huge stone hearth where a group of College Fellows huddles, dressed in their academic gowns.

'Oh, look, there's Freddie and Rupert. Now you can meet them.'

Immy throws her arms round a guy who's so tall he has to stoop to accept her kiss, and when she's planted one on his lips, he seems amazed at the attention. He sticks out a hand awkwardly towards me.

'I'm Freddie.' He turns red to the roots of his hair.

'Lauren,' I say, trying not to laugh.

'Now, where's Rupes got to? Rupes! Rupes! Come here!'

A well-built guy in a tweed jacket detaches himself from a group and saunters over.

'Hawthorne. How the fuck are you? How was your vac? His voice is lazy and upper-class, like Alan Rickman in *Sense & Sensibility*.

'Not too bad I suppose. I spent most of it hanging out in Rock until Daddy dragged me home to do some work. What about you?'

'Ibiza mostly, shame you never made it over – I'm setting up a club there.' He rakes a hand through a sandy thatch of hair. I guess he's kind of good-looking, maybe like I imagine a young Doctor House to be, but with more charm.

He narrows his eyes as he finally spots me and looks me up and down from top to toe. Why do I get the feeling I'm being sized up like a polo pony?

'Who is *this*?'

Immy grabs my arm. 'Lauren Cusack. New master's student. Her room is on my staircase.'

'Hello, Lauren. I'm Rupert de Courcey.' He holds out his hand.

'Good to meet you, Rupert.'

He raises a bushy eyebrow. 'You're American.'

I grit my teeth as he grips my hand. Why do some guys think that mashing a girl's bones signals they have a big dick? I resist the urge to rub my mangled fingers and flash him a smile. 'Yes, so it seems.'

'Excellent.' His eyes light up like he's scented a fox, but he stands back so that I can take my seat on the bench first. 'Be careful how you get your leg over,' he says.

Everyone around me sniggers and I roll my eyes. It's not easy lifting my leg elegantly over the bench seat, but I manage and he slides in beside me, the tweed of his jacket scratchy against my bare flesh. Wow. That cologne is powerful. I'd really prefer not to have him as my neighbour, but there's no way I can wriggle out now and he's Immy's friend so he can't be so bad.

The buzz in the hall quietens and one of the Fellows calls out something unintelligible in Latin.

'Grace,' Rupert hisses in my ear.

'Thanks, I worked that one out.'

'Clever girl. Now, let's get stuck into the wine.'

Grace being done, the hall erupts with the noise of glasses clinking and plates clattering. The waiting staff carries in the first course, smoked salmon with a salad. I ought to be starving after my flight, but I'm too excited to eat much. Immy picks at her fish too, but Rupert has demolished his portion and has moved on to her left-overs. Her eyes sparkle as she chatters away, obviously in her element among her gang of friends, both guys and girls. I'm used to striking up conversations with all manner of people on social occasions, but this grand hall, the accents and the sheer confidence of almost everyone around me, have foxed me a little.

Immy picks up the Sauvignon bottle and turns to Rupert. 'Where's Alexander? I thought he was coming to the welcome dinner.'

'I could tell you but then he'd probably have to kill me. Fuck knows.' Rupert refills his own glass with claret. 'Maybe he's at some spooks bonding session or shagging Valentina.'

'Really? I thought they split up ages ago!'

'So he says, but who knows with Alexander and, frankly, who cares?'

'Now, now, Rupert, I thought you were friends.'

'We are, but all's fair in love and war, isn't it, Lauren?'

All this gossip has flown way over my head and before I can get in a reply Rupert winks and carries on. 'What kind of a name is Cusack anyway? Sounds Irish to me.'

'My dad's grandfather was from County Cork.'

'So you'll be visiting the old country while you're over here.' The smirk tells me he's no true fan of the Emerald Isle and I imagine Dad's face.

'I've no plans to.' Keep it polite, Lauren.

'Good, I'd hate you to be away from Oxford for long.' He holds up the bottle of red. 'More wine?'

'No, I'm fine.'

Before I can put my hand over the top of my glass, Rupert sloshes claret into it, spilling some on the table. 'You've only had a sip. Fuck, I hope you're not going to be one of those puritanical Americans who thinks it's a sin to let alcohol – or anything else remotely enjoyable – get past your lips.'

Freddie grins from opposite us. 'Rupert will cure you, even if you are.'

Immy reaches across me to swat Rupert's arm. 'Don't be such a prat, Rupert. Lauren, ignore him.'

'I'm trying,' I say, summoning up a smile.

'So is Rupert.' Immy holds up her glass and giggles. 'I'll have some more of the white please, Rupes.'

Despite Immy's efforts, it's obviously American-baiting season, and the barbs continue throughout dinner. No, I'm not 'packing heat', I don't have a shrink and I'm not hoping to 'pull' Prince Harry while I'm here. Well, my mother secretly hopes I will, but that's her problem and I'm certainly not letting that out.

The waiting staff have brought platters of cheese and more bottles. That's four courses and I've lost count of the bottles of booze. If this is going to happen every night, I am going to *have* to go for a run tomorrow and I'll take up Immy's offer of a game of tennis. Is it too much to hope there's a decent health-food store nearby?

I was prepared for the Brit humour and ready to take everything with a hefty pinch of salt, but I can't help thinking I'd rather be washing dishes in the kitchen than spending time with some of these people. I guess

I'll get used to it, after all I survived a sorority house at Brown, but some of the baiting has a sharp edge to it. Everyone seems fair game and especially me.

Rupert glares at the waiter as he places a bottle on the table. 'Ah, the port. About bloody time too!'

I see the waiter's lip curl in contempt but Rupert either hasn't noticed or is too drunk to care, and is it me, or has he moved closer? His voice is slurred as he speaks and he shifts his butt even closer to mine. 'Did anyone ever tell you have a fantastic set of . . . teeth?'

'Not often.' My tone is icy but Rupert seems immune.

'Bet you'd love to see my stately pile. It's huge,' he says, raising his voice loud enough for his friends to hear. Roars of laughter ring round the table, but Immy stares at her hands. I get the feeling she'd like to slap him down but doesn't want to take sides.

I smile sweetly. 'It's probably not as impressive as you think it is.'

'Oh, mia-oww. Laurel has claws.' He paws the air and growls.

'It's Lauren.'

He leans close to my ear and whispers. 'Whatever. I'd love to feel those claws in my back.'

As I suppress a shudder, Immy chirps up, clearly trying to change the subject. 'Lauren's from Washington you know.'

It's a nice try but Rupert's straight back in there. 'And do you know the president personally, Laurel?'

I lay my napkin on the table and treat him to my sweetest smile. 'As a matter of fact, I do.'

So that's how you silence a table full of braying toffs in one second flat, but I almost wish I hadn't because, a, it's not quite true and, b, this is the kind of bragging I despise.

Immy's eyes are as wide as saucers. 'Oh. My. God. You mean you *really* know Obama?'

Warmth rises to my cheeks and I'm half wishing I hadn't gone down this route, but Rupes did ask for it. 'Well . . . my father does. He's a Democrat senator and my mother and I have met the president a couple of times.'

'What's your father's name?' a tiny little guy opposite pipes up. I think Immy said he was a cox for the rowing Eight.

'Bill Cusack. I don't expect you'll have heard of him.'

The cox beams. 'I certainly have. I'm doing PPE,' he says proudly. I have no clue what PPE is but I sense an ally. 'He supported Obama's latest gun-control bill,' he adds as the others stare at us. 'And he's a massive advocate of Obamacare.'

I reach out to my new ally with a smile. 'That's my father.'

'You didn't say your dad was a politician,' Immy whispers.

'Well, it can be a conversation stopper.'

'I think it's really cool – and you've managed to shut Rupes up. Well done. He's not that bad, you know, not all the time. And I think you've made an impression with him.'

Right now, I'd like to make an impression with my foot on Rupes' butt, but Immy's right about one thing:

he's gone quiet, which has given him more opportunity to drain the bottle of port. Finally, as the conversation moves on to what people did in the vac, I feel the tension in my muscles ease and hope I might get through the evening after all. Immy persuades me to try a glass of port and I rather like it. Kind of sweet yet tart, like cherry pie.

What the . . . ?

Rupert's hand is on my knee. My skin crawls and nausea rises in my throat as his clammy fingers slide up my thigh. Then I feel his breath against my ear. 'I may have died and gone to heaven. A Yank who's beautiful, bright *and* well-connected, even if it is to a Democrat dynasty. You're a triple threat, Laurel.'

He belches and the alcohol fumes almost knock me out. I try to edge away, but we're so packed into the bench, I can't get out of his reach. I should knee him in the balls but I don't want to draw any more attention to myself. Oh my God, his fingers have reached the hem of my panties. That's it. I've had it with the lot of them.

I leap to my feet and my elbow 'accidentally on purpose' knocks the port glass flying into his lap.

'Fucking hell!' A ruby stain spreads over Rupert's crotch as I scramble off the bench.

Immy's mouth is open in shock. 'Lauren, what's the matter?'

'Ask your douche of a friend!'

Rupert leaps up with a roar. 'For fuck's sake, I only bought these from Jack Wills this morning!'

'If this Jack Wills is as big an asshole as you are then

I'm glad I spilled wine down his pants.' It comes out as a shriek and the whole hall has fallen quiet, but I don't care any more.

Immy stares at him with contempt. 'You total shit, Rupert. Please, Lauren, wait . . .'

Any other time, I'd appreciate the sympathy, but I throw off her hand on my arm because moisture is pricking the back of my eyes and I refuse to cry in front of these people. 'Just leave me, *please*.'

By the time I get out of the hall, the tears are pouring down my cheeks. I tried, I really did, but apart from Immy and a few others, they're a bunch of snobs and creeps, Rupert most of all. Why did I think this was a good idea?

Leaning against a wall, I gulp in the cool air and it helps a little, but it's raining *again* and my dress is getting soaked. I've only been here a day and I already hate the weather and the people. So much for my big dreams of sophisticated independence when I can't even handle a welcome dinner!

In my head, Todd's laughing at me, clucking his tongue with his 'Poor little Lauren, I told you you'd be better off staying home.'

No. I will *not* give up so easily. The Cusacks don't quit. My father taught me that and, after knowing the mountain he climbed to achieve what he has, I know I can handle a pack of snobby Brits.

I wipe my hand over my eyes and hope my nose isn't snotty like a little girl's. I have to get back to my room and calm down, but I know I'll be soaked if I run there in this deluge. A few yards away I spot an archway and some steps leading down to what I think are the college cloisters. Maybe I can shelter in there until this downpour eases.

I run towards them and I skitter under the arch, but my heel slips on the wet steps and I miss my footing. Tumbling through the air, I let out a shriek before my breath is knocked from me as I slam into a solid object.

Curses echo around the cloister, mine and another's, and by some miracle I'm not splattered over the flagstones yet, thanks to two hands gripping my upper arms like a vice.

'Christ! What the fuck do you think you're doing?'

I have no breath left after hitting that chest. It's as solid as the stone walls around me.

'Getting . . . the hell . . . out of this . . . place.'

My chest still heaves as I look up into two ice-blue eyes glaring down at me under eyebrows bunched together in a frown.

'Fine, but could you possibly manage to get the hell out of it without breaking other people's necks?'

My breath leaves my body again as that voice curls round me like silk and resonates in my chest like the deepest note of the piano. His voice alone is enough to turn my mind to mush. My smart, Ivy League-educated, supposedly critical mind . . .

'Get over it. You look fine to me,' I say, pushing away his arms.

In spite of my words, my pulse rate spikes as I take in the dark brown hair and those quarterback shoulders. I *know* him. He's the guy from the Range Rover.

He can't be that much older than me, but there's something behind those eyes that makes me think he's lived much longer and seen so much more than I ever have or will. He glares down at me as if I've committed a crime.

'You've been crying,' he says.

'No, I have not.' But damn, my hand brushes over my cheek as I deny the obvious.

'Yes, you have. Your eyes look red and your face is wet.'

'So my contacts are irritating. Is there a law against it?'

His nostrils flare slightly. 'Of course not. Wait.' He pulls a clean white square from the pocket of his suit and his voice softens. 'May I? There's a lash in the corner of your eye. I don't want to smudge your mascara any more than it already is. Tilt your head up, please.'

It may be a request, but the way he says it there's no room for negotiation. I tilt and my heart thumps like a road drill. Reaching out, he dabs at the tear tracks on my cheek with his handkerchief. I know I ought to feel patronized but it's such an unexpectedly tender gesture from this granite-hewn guy that I don't want to stop him. As his fingers brush across my damp skin, there's a tightening low in my belly that I can't mistake for anger or nerves. As he touches me, my skin prickles all over and not in a bad way.

'Just relax,' he orders, and I'm in no position to disobey with my gaze turned skyward. I feel the cool of metal softly graze my cheek and realize he has a ring on his little finger. This close, he smells of freshly laundered linen. No cologne, no booze, just cool and clean and composed.

'That's it.'

There's a moment where I don't think I will ever be able to move again, then I glance down and the eyelash is the tiniest thing on the tip of his little finger. And there's the ring. A gold signet ring like my grandfather used to wear.

'Thank you.'

'A pleasure.' His expression doesn't match his words, but he adds, 'That didn't hurt a bit, did it?'

If he says it doesn't hurt, I guess it doesn't. And it *really* didn't and, damn it, my nipples have decided to stand to attention. He must know that too because the wind is blowing through the cloisters and has pasted my damp dress to my body like shrink wrap. I feel naked before him and throw my arms around my chest, not that it's any kind of protection from a gaze that seems to penetrate my flesh and bones.

A smile flickers over his face and for that brief second his austerely handsome profile is transfused with warmth. My God, he is *beautiful*. Scary but divine. What is he doing here at Wyckham?

'Don't look so scared. I don't bite.'

My brain is blasted with thoughts of what that mouth could do to me . . . what *am* I thinking? Either I'm still jet-lagged or the dinner port was laced. Nothing else could account for my wild swings in reaction to this man.

'I have to go.' My voice sounds small and unconvincing, even to me.

He folds his arms and even the beautifully cut suit can't hide those guns. What the hell is he studying here? He's different to the other students. Like he stands up straighter, like he has an inner calm. Rupert's gang have got chutzpah in spades, but this guy seems to have an inner confidence that runs through him like a seam of rock, rather than clipped on like a showy facade.

'You've said that already. Are you going to carry out your threat or are you all mouth?'

There's no answer to that question and, anyway, the chimes of the chapel clock ring out and the guy lifts his wrist to check his watch, his mouth twitching in irritation. 'Now *I* have to go. Don't kill anyone on your way back to New York.'

It must be a sign for me too, because alarm bells are going off loud and fast in my head and my body.

His footsteps ring out on the flagstones as he strides off and I get that monumental rear view for the second time today. He *can't* just go like that, not with my every sense leaping around like popcorn in a pan. I don't even know who he is.

'I'm not from New York!' I call after him.

'Boston, then,' he throws back.

But he's still putting the yards between us. He *must* look back at me but I have a horrible feeling that this guy backs down for no one.

My next shout bounces off the walls. 'Not Boston!'

Still he carries on walking, his footsteps ringing out

in the cloister gallery. Then he stops and the quiet is so palpable I can almost taste it.

He turns round and walks back towards me.

Trying not to exhale in relief and triumph, I throw my arms around my damp and shivering body in triumph. He's close enough now for me to look right into those mesmeric blue eyes.

'It's Washington,' I murmur through dry lips. 'I'm from Washington.'

His mouth twitches in a concession to a smile as he gazes down at me, and there's a heartbeat where I think he may kiss me. Is it possible to melt through solid stone? I wonder.

'Congratulations,' he says, 'and you might find it useful to know that you aren't wearing contacts.'

And that is *it*. Turning on his heel, he marches away faster than before and I know there will be no third chance. That magnificent back disappears through the arch at the other end of the cloisters and I'm alone, with only the chilly autumn wind slicing through my dress and the memory of his fingers against my face.

What am I thinking? He's as sexy as hell, yes, but as I come back to earth I'm angry with myself for reacting to him so powerfully. As if to reinforce that fact, I hear footsteps as Immy and Freddie hurry down the long cloister gallery, their faces concerned. I try to dismiss the guy from my mind but all I know is this: for the second time in twenty-four hours, my world just changed for ever.

Chapter Three

'Well, Lauren, I'm absolutely delighted to have you here at Wyckham.'

Professor Rafe Stanford, my tutor for the next year, peers at me over his steel-rimmed glasses. The first thing that strikes me about him is how young he looks, almost boyish, even though I know he's well past thirty. His smile is wide, almost too big for his lean face, but at least he seems friendly. It's my first meeting with him and this time it's not a proper tutorial, more a 'get acquainted' session.

It's Monday morning and I've calmed down a notch since my encounter with Granite Guns in the cloisters on Saturday evening, though the memory of that ice-chip gaze and his touch on my cheek kept me awake until the chapel clock chimed midnight. I never thought I'd sleep again until I woke up Sunday noon with the sun streaming through my window and Immy hammering on my door, asking if I was still alive.

'Tea or coffee?' asks Professor Rafe. 'I'd offer you a glass of wine, but the sun's a long way from the yard-arm, isn't it?'

'Um . . . I suppose it is. Tea would be good.'

'Darjeeling or Earl Grey? I have some of those

dreadful fruit-flavoured things too, if you really must. Some Americans seem to like them.'

What I'd really rather have is a glass of iced water in view of the fact that it's inexplicably now a warm, sunny day outside, however, 'Earl Grey would be good, thanks.'

As the professor pours boiling water on to a tea bag, I take a sneaky survey of his rooms. There seems to be only one room, actually, but it's a lot larger than mine and the walls are lined with a collection of art-history books that I'd kill to own. More books are piled on occasional tables, in the corners and at the sides of his desk. There's a deep-buttoned leather sofa and two tub chairs, both cracked with wear, one of which I'm perched on.

There's also a bed, which, judging by the rumpled covers, has seen some use overnight. The prof is a little rumpled too in his battered cords and wrinkled check shirt. When he pushes his black hair back from his temples, there are glimpses of silver-grey.

'Here you are. Apologies for the mug.'

I probably wouldn't have even noticed the mug he handed me unless he'd drawn attention to the picture on it, but now it's impossible to ignore. It's one of the Austrian painter Egon Schiele's nude self-portraits. I'm not a great Schiele fan and I have to say he doesn't look too happy with his face screwed up, his legs apart and his penis hanging down like a limp flag. Well, it's certainly *different*, though I can't say I'd like to take my tea out of it every day.

The prof plumps for a seat on the sofa and gives an encouraging smile. It's not the greatest Earl Grey I've ever had, but that's fine and it gives me something to do with my hands. He stretches his arm along the back of the sofa and crosses one leg over the other.

'Your essay and references from Brown were really very impressive.'

Without warning, an image of the guy from the cloisters slides into my mind.

'Is your tea all right?'

I deposit the mug hastily on the side table, blowing on my burning fingers. 'Oh yes, thank you.'

I'm not sure whether I'm thanking him for the tea, the compliment or for bringing my mind back to the reason I'm here: to have the benefit of a world-famous tutor's undivided attention. In addition to the seminar programme at the History of Art faculty, Professor Rafe had told me he'd be giving me lots of one-to-ones when he called to say I'd got the place.

'So, have you decided on the subject of your optional course and dissertation topic yet?'

I have, but I'm a little apprehensive about voicing them. Professor Rafe seems charming, but I still get the feeling he's going to take me apart piece by piece at some point, like a tiger dismembering a gazelle. I try to remind myself that this is a good thing and what I've paid out tens of thousands of dollars for.

'Um. I've been considering a variety of options.'

'You don't have to decide right now, of course. I was simply interested to hear what turns you on. Academically speaking, of course.' He flashes me a smile to let me know he's joking. I *think*.

'Let me know later today if you can, so I can prepare my tutorial plan for you. I expect you know that the first term is a taught programme. I'm going to focus on giving you a rigorous training in methodology so you can go and do further research.' He peers at me over his glasses again. 'That is, if you're sure you'd be suited to an academic career. Not everyone wants to hide him- or herself away in a dusty institution and, I must say, it would probably be a waste in your case. That is, you probably have far more interesting options open to you.'

'I had thought of curating a gallery . . .' Perspiration breaks out on the small of my back. Immy told me that boilers get fired up at Wyckham on the first day of term, whether it's frosty or still seventy degrees outside. It must be eighty in here, at least, and Rafe's face is quite shiny.

'There you are, then. Now, shall we make a date for our first proper tutorial? Then you can tell me your final choice of course and I can notify the course leader.'

We spend the next twenty minutes talking about the course and my interests. I'd forgotten quite how indulgent it is to spend so long discussing my subject with someone who's as passionate about it as me, and far more knowledgeable. Rafe is exactly what I'd hoped for intellectually. I could even grow to like the cord trousers and tweed jacket, but does he really need the elbow patches? Maybe he does, if he spends most of his time poring over documents on his ancient-looking desk. He must have chosen the darkest corner of Wyckham for his rooms.

And why does it have to be so damn *hot* in here? The radiators ought to be glowing; they're pumping out so much heat I can barely breathe. I've already taken off my jacket and I'd love to get rid of my sweater but I only have a tank on underneath and, besides, there's no way I'm going to take anything off in front of Professor Rafe. Not that he'd say anything, he's probably too polite, but . . . Whoa, the room just turned in front of my eyes.

'Are you feeling unwell, Lauren?' Rafe leans forward, his eyes full of concern. At least I think it's concern because my eyesight isn't functioning that well right now.

I shake my head, and then regret it as that light-headed feeling seizes me again. 'No . . . No . . . I'm OK.'

'I'm worried about you. You look rather pale and it *is* very warm in here. Maybe you have a temperature? Can I get you a glass of water? Or perhaps you ought to take off your sweater?'

'So Professor Handy's been at it already? I wish I'd known you were seeing him this morning – I'd have warned you first.' Immy pulls a face as we queue for the coffee machine in the grad-student centre. She saw me as I walked out of Rafe's rooms feeling as if I was about to spontaneously combust.

'It was so hot in there I almost passed out and he kept patting my knee like I was a little girl. And then he

37

put his arm round me and asked me if I needed to lie down!'

'The creep. As for hot, that's probably because the bastard keeps his radiators on full when he does one-to-ones with female students. Unless they're lesbians of course, though he has even been known to try and "convert" them.'

A thin trickle of brown liquid sputters into the cup. 'You mean he hits on the students a lot? Surely he could be fired for that?' I'd like to think Immy is wrong about Rafe's intentions and that I misconstrued the signs; I want to keep my relationship with him totally professional. If he's going to come on to me, I'll have to deal with it somehow.

Immy collects her latte from the slot. 'He *could*, but this is Wyckham, darling, and he's more likely to get a rap on the knuckles and told not to get caught. The Master adores Rafe since he brought in that massive endowment from one of his old students. Besides, no one has actually complained to the college about him yet and some of the girls fancy him. And he's a bit of a sleb since he did that series for BBC4.'

'Really? I must have missed it on BBC America.' I place a cup under the slot and press the button.

'Lucky you. The whole thing was about the female nude in Renaissance Art, but it's an excuse for perving at sixteenth-century tits if you ask me. Besides, the Master's worse than anyone. When Rupert smashed a skylight in the library roof, he threatened to take him out into the quad and have him whipped.'

My jaw goes slack. 'Now I *know* you're joking!'

She raises an eyebrow. 'About the whipping, yes, that sort of thing went out about three hundred years ago, but the Master *does* fancy Rupert. He told one of the postgrads that he'd love to give Rupes a good seeing-to, but he's got no chance. Oh fuck, I forgot the sugar.'

While Immy fetches some sugar for her coffee, I sink into a sofa by the window that overlooks the quad and reflect on Immy's warnings about Rafe and the Master. I'd have thought that Wyckham had shrugged off that decadent image decades ago, but it seems to be very much alive and well. It's not only a culture-shock thing – it's so alien to the way I've been brought up and my vision for my future. It would be naive of me to think I can dismiss my own background – and I wouldn't want to – but Immy's world, like Rupert's and the cloister guy's, well . . . it would be so easy to get seduced by it. And that's so not what I'm here for.

Outside the leaves on the lime tree are turning wonderful shades of yellow, russet and brown. It's a picture of peace and tranquillity that should calm my racing mind and remind me why I'm really here. The morning sunlight is soft as it falls on the college buildings, bathing them in a golden glow. I really should paint it, especially as I managed to unearth my watercolours from one of my bags yesterday afternoon. After Immy woke me up, we went out for brunch at Georgina's in the Covered Market – along with half of the student body, it seemed, because we were queuing down the stairs for twenty minutes to get inside. When we finally

39

got a table, I got the chance to find out more about Immy's family. Her younger brother, George, is at Marlborough and from the way she talks about him I can tell she loves him to bits even if he does drive her insane at times.

Although she's been here two years and seems to have tons of friends, I'm not sure she's got any really close girlfriends. Behind the jokey, party-girl facade, I think she lives on the edge, and her work worries really bother her. She's told me she'll probably move to London after her degree and see what's going on there. Her parents bought her a flat in Chelsea as an investment and maybe she feels she owes it to them to do well, or at least complete her degree. I suspect she doesn't 'need' to work.

I guess I don't need to work either . . . My parents are in the fortunate position of being financially secure – you'd probably even say wealthy – but I can't even *imagine* not wanting to have a career in art.

'Hi, sorry about that. There was no sugar by the machine so I had to grab some from the buttery. Can't stomach JCR caffeine without sugar.' Immy flops on to the sofa.

My nose wrinkles up as my own coffee hits the back of my throat.

'Cat's piss?'

'It's better than Rafe's tea. I don't have Earl Grey very often, but, man, his version tasted weird.'

Immy rips open a packet of sugar and dumps it into

her cup. 'That would have been the Rohypnol . . .' she says.

'Ah, that must have been it. Next time I'll stick to water.' I wince at the coffee again. 'Immy, do you happen to know a good whole-foods store?'

'Me? Are you kidding? Well, actually, there's a big health-food place on the Plain. Oscar practically lives in there trying to starve himself to keep his weight down for rowing.'

I remember Oscar. He was the cox who'd heard of my dad. I liked him, but the thought of my unscheduled exit at the welcome dinner brings heat to my cheeks. Immy must have noticed because she's nibbling her bottom lip with her teeth in that nervy way again.

'Lauren . . . I know we talked about this yesterday, but I still feel bad about Rupert. Are you OK?'

'Fine.' I summon up my brightest smile even though I am so sick of saying this when I'm not fine, but I don't want a reputation as a drama queen. 'Why do you feel bad? He's the one who stuck his hand up my dress.'

'Please don't judge him by Saturday. He can be a total twat, but he was completely hammered. None of that crowd is too bad when you get to know them, but I feel guilty because they are my friends. I introduced you to them and I should have warned you.'

'You're not responsible for your school friends.'

We've already had this conversation over our hot chocolate and croissants in Georgina's yesterday. Turns out Rupes, Oscar et al were at Marlborough with Immy.

41

Not Freddie, though, he's the latest in what sounds like a long line of faithful lapdogs.

'Rupes is . . . Rupes, and if it's any consolation, you could take it as a compliment that he's singled you out. He's always had a weakness for the blonde athletic look since we had a Californian housemistress in charge of our mixed house at school.'

Even allowing for the fact that I'm from the opposite side of the States, the idea of Rupes having an American wet dream over his housemistress makes me gag on my coffee even more.

'I can see I haven't convinced you. Look, a few of us were planning on going to the Turf tonight. Why don't you give them another chance? Not every guy at Wyckham is a git.'

And how. Much to my irritation, with myself and him, the Cloister God has rarely been out of my mind and it's been on the tip of my tongue to ask Immy who he might be. There can't be many guys with that kind of presence – or that physique – at Wyckham and, if I described him, I'd bet my Wilson racket she'd know who he is and yet . . . there's no way of asking about him that won't instantly alert her to my unhealthy interest in him, and surely I'm bound to be unlucky enough to bump into him again sooner or later.

'Please come. I promise you won't be disappointed and the Turf is a bit of an Oxford institution. All medieval nooks and crannies and stuff. Not that I'm assuming that because you're American you like old places. That would be a horrendous cliché.'

42

This brings a smile to my lips. 'Assume all you like, and on this occasion I don't mind being a horrendous cliché even though I still have tons of unpacking to do and I have to get some reading done before my first seminar tomorrow.'

Her face lights up. 'The unpacking I can understand, but you have all term to do that. It's just that I shouldn't tell you this, but Rupert feels genuinely bad about touching you up.'

'*Genuinely?* Wow. I'm grateful.'

Immy rolls her eyes. 'He did say he'd like a chance to show you he isn't a complete and utter twat. His words not mine. He does actually really fancy you; the insults are his funny way of showing it.'

'You see me laughing?'

'Come and have your last glass of Pimm's before summer deserts Oxford totally. Oscar will be there and a couple of the girls, and maybe even Alexander might deign to grace us with his presence.'

If Alexander is anything like Rupes, I may have to pass, but her voice is so wheedling I can't help softening. I really like Immy. 'I'll think about it.'

Ten minutes later, I have ceased thinking about whether or not to go to the pub because as we're walking through the archway from the back to the front quads, the Cloister God is striding from a staircase on the opposite side to us, a document wallet under his arm.

Immy pauses in the shadow of the arch. 'Well, what do you know? Alexander *is* in town, after all. I did wonder if he'd actually bother to turn up.'

The brick that's suddenly lodged in my throat turns out to be an advantage because my garbled response sounds like I have as much interest in seeing Alexander as I do in the mating habits of stick insects. *Alexander* . . . I can't believe he has a name, that he's actually flesh and blood – which says a lot about the level of myth that I have built around him since I arrived at Wyckham. I need to calm down, but how can I when he strides around the college quad in jeans and a polo shirt, looking so hot he might set the whole place afire?

And he's going to be at the pub tonight.

'Mmm, and he's looking rather delicious, if I say so myself,' says Immy. 'Not that I'm interested. No chance there and I'd keep away.'

'Why?'

'Because he's loaded and a marquess's son. I'm upper-middle class at best.'

I laugh. 'Tell me you're joking.'

'Yes, I am. Alexander wouldn't care about anything like that, but I still wouldn't go there. Where Alexander leads, a trail of shattered hearts follows.'

Shattered hearts? Now why am I not surprised at that? He is sex on legs, titled and wealthy, and a lot of women must find that hard to resist. I'm not going to be one of them, but I am intrigued enough to know more about the man.

'A marquess?' I say, trying to sound bored.

Immy's eyes gleam with mischief as I collect my jaw from the cobbled flagstones, and I wonder if she suspects I might fancy Alexander myself.

44

'One day he'll be the Marquess of Falconbury and heir to a massive estate, but for God's sake don't mention it to him. He does actually have a courtesy title, Earl of somewhere or other, I can't remember, because he never uses it and he'd probably be furious if he thought I'd discussed it with anyone. He's plain Alexander Hunt in college.'

'Really? What's he doing at Wyckham, then?'

'A master's in International Relations.'

'Right.' I make my next question super casual. 'So did you guys go to high school together?'

'Oh God, no. Alexander went to Eton like his father and his father before him. He's Rupert's cousin.'

'Cousins? You mean the same blood runs through him as Rupes?'

A puzzled frown creases her brow and I'm worried she suspects something. 'Yes, I suppose it does. Does that bother you?'

It's not the fact these guys have so much DNA in common that bothers me. It's more that they share the same 'world owes me' attitude. 'No. It's . . . um . . . none of my business and I don't care how big an estate this Alex has –, titles don't impress me.'

Immy winces. 'It's Alexander, darling. Don't ever let him hear you call him Alex. He hates people shortening his name.'

So he's *furious* if anyone mentions his title? He *hates* mere mortals daring to use his nickname?

He bends to tie a shoelace that has dared to unravel, his shirt straining over his shoulder muscles. Then he marches off again, not glancing to left or right, like he exists in his own universe. It's the same single-minded demeanour I saw when he stole the parking space and thundered into the college on my first day at Wyckham. Wow, he really does think he owns the place.

I make an exaggerated show of shifting my attention from Alex – sorry, Alexander – to the chapel clock, though it kills me to tear my eyes from that magnificent physique. 'I should get back to my room. It's breakfast time in Washington and I might catch Daddy before he leaves for the White House.'

Ouch. I wish I hadn't said that because it sounds like I'm trying to pull rank on Alexander and I am so not. Or maybe I am? Ever since I arrived in Oxford I've been behaving, not so much out of character, but differently. It's a strange place, it's natural that my defences should be up, but I don't really like some of the things I've seen and the ways I've reacted. I don't want to be obsessed with some guy, especially one like Alexander; titled, over-privileged, arrogant – he's going to be another Rupert, and maybe one with even more wealth and power and influence, expecting everyone to do his bidding.

Alexander's tight butt is disappearing into the shadows of the Lodge. I swallow hard, but he doesn't seem to have noticed us. We're obviously not on his radar today, maybe no one ever is, and now he's going to be at the pub tonight.

'So. Shall we meet in the Lodge at eight unless you've changed your mind?'

Her expression is pure innocence and I think it's genuine. I drag my eyes away from the Lodge and shrug nonchalantly. 'Sure. Why not?'

'Awesome. I'll call for you at half-eight. Wear something warm on the off chance it's pissing down.'

'Pissing down' doesn't come close to the biblical deluge as we dash through the streets and down a cobbled alleyway leading to the Turf Tavern. With the olde-world street lamps sputtering and fog wreathing round the college walls, I half expect Jack the Ripper to lunge out of a dark corner. I really must get a bike; Immy has suggested the cycle store next to the Covered Market.

I'm so glad I wore my leather jacket and DKNY ankle boots, not the suede pumps I'd originally planned. Even in the boots, I skitter over the wet cobbles outside the inn with all the grace of a giraffe on stilts. Immy's skinny jeans are soaked and her hair's a bird's nest, but she's giggling as we push open the wooden door of the pub and into a fug of steaming clothes, loud voices and ale fumes.

A bellow reaches us over the top of the general hubbub and we shoulder our way through the crowd to the bar, trying to dodge guys spilling beer on us from their pint glasses. Immy orders a couple of glasses of mulled wine and we plunge into the masses again, threading a path to the rear of the pub, where guys are ducking under beams. At the far end, crammed around an impossibly small table obscured by glasses and bottles, is Immy's crowd.

I recognise Freddie, tiny Oscar and a couple of girls who I hadn't spoken to much but were friendly enough. Chun's a medic whose family live in Shanghai; the other girl, Isla, is Scottish and has the cutest accent. Best of all, there's no Rupert, which makes me want to do a little dance of joy. And no sign of Alexander, which makes me want to beat my head against a wall because, no matter what I told Immy or what I told myself in the privacy of my room earlier today, I've been dying to check out what he's like with his 'tribe' around him. Will there be girls fawning at his feet and batting their eyes at him?

Looks like I'm not going to find out yet, but the old Cusack training kicks in again and I stick on a 'so happy to be here' face. I feel like Lizzy Bennet when Wickham fails to turn up to Bingley's ball. Yeah, and look how he turned out . . . the biggest disappointment in fiction.

'Come on, squash up and make room!' Immy orders.

Surely we're never going to fit in, but somehow a minuscule patch of bench appears at one end of the group.

'Do you want to sit there, Lauren? I'll sit on Freddie's lap.'

Freddie grins and I perch my butt next to Oscar, who's possibly the only guy I ever made look like a Munchkin.

'Sorry,' he says, pushing his glasses nervously up his nose as my leg bumps his skinny thigh. 'Sorry.'

'Don't worry about it,' I smile reassuringly. Immy told me that Oscar wants to be a Member of Parliament, but he's so shy I can't imagine he'll ever survive five minutes in the cut and thrust of politics. I've seen the shit my dad has to put up with and the thick skin he's had to grow. Making it to the Senate must have been tough enough, without the added disadvantage of being partially sighted. I really don't know how he did it and my heart feels as if it's expanding when I think of him now.

Calling on all my experience of international diplomacy, I work hard to make sure the next hour is incident free. All the time, I'm twitching in my seat and checking out the door to the bar, hoping Alexander will grace us with his presence. No one else seems bothered that he hasn't turned up. In fact, no one so much as mentions him and I daren't utter his name, since I'm supposed to a, have never spoken to him before, and b, be completely unimpressed by his unmentionable title.

Around the table, the banter's flying back and forth faster than a Murray–Djokovic rally. OK, there's a little Yank-baiting, but I'm holding my own. Oscar's an intriguing guy when he gets on a subject he's passionate about and it's good to get to know Chun and Isla better. Immy has visibly relaxed, possibly now she knows I'm not going to freak out and leave, and I've even been persuaded to try a 'half' of the local ale. Not that I think I'm going to finish it, because, apart from being lukewarm, it tastes like someone peed in the barrel.

When Immy declares she needs the loo, I take the chance to go with her and when we get back to the table, I see we have guests. It's Rupes with two other guys, one blond in a Regency-style cravat, if you can believe it; the other in an old school tie.

'Oh fuck.' Immy takes my elbow as we get near the table.

'What?'

'That's Gideon and Piers. They're in the same drinking club with Rupert and they're a pair of complete spanners.'

The tool allusion goes slightly over my head, but I detect it's not complimentary. I knew the evening was going too well. Immy lets out a sigh. 'We'll have to try to pretend they're not here.'

As a statement, I know it is wildly optimistic as soon as it's left her lips. In minutes the conversation descends to Neanderthal levels as Gideon and Piers start telling jokes about lighting their own farts, 'epic chundering' and initiation rituals that mostly seem to involve objects being pushed up other guys' anuses – for 'a laugh' apparently. Maybe the chundering has something to do with the anal penetration . . . I don't ask. When Immy whispers that one of them is studying politics and the other nuclear physics, I fear for the future of the free world.

How did these boneheads ever get admitted to Oxford? Then again, how did Sarah Palin get to run for VP? Or Russell Crowe think it was a good idea to be Robin Hood? Whatever, these guys make Rupert look like an intellectual, and incidentally he appears to be ignoring me for now, which is about the best compliment he could ever pay me.

As the noise levels in the pub and around our particular table rise to a new level, my Cartier tells me it's ten thirty and I'm ready to bail out. Faculty classes start tomorrow at nine thirty and I don't want to start the term looking and thinking like an extra from the *Walking Dead*. Will Immy be offended if I leave? She's been so kind to me that I don't want to abandon her. I glance at her, biting her nails since Freddie left to have an 'essay crisis'.

'Immy, I think I'm going to get back to college.' I have to raise my voice above the shouting and raucous laughter. There's movement at the end of the table as I catch the other girls' eyes and they start to slip on their coats. 'I don't want to leave you here, but I can walk back with Chun and Isla if you want to stay.'

'Oh . . . well, it's not last orders for half an hour, but I suppose I ought to get back too, not that I'll sleep much. I get the results of my Collections tomorrow.' Immy pulls a face and I can't tell whether she's disappointed or relieved to have the excuse to leave.

I throw her a sympathetic smile and cross my fingers inwardly. 'I'm sure you'll be just fine.'

'I hope so. OK, shall we go?'

Groans and whistles come from Gideon and Piers as we get up en masse. They're standing at the end of the table, pints in their hands, alcohol stains down their shirts. Piers is swaying a little like he's on the deck of a yacht. I don't mind people enjoying themselves, truly, but why do some guys have to get completely wasted? Todd could be a total shit when he was drunk; actually he turned out to be a total shit when he wasn't and I doubt Gideon and Piers would be any less offensive if they were sober.

'Aww . . . The ladies are leaving.' Their voices are slurred.

'They need to be tucked up in bed by eleven.' Rupert's words seem general, but I suspect they're directed at me.

'I wouldn't mind tucking them up,' Gideon slurs.

'Don't leave this early, ladies. The night is young.'

Immy rolls her eyes and tries to walk past Piers, then shrieks, 'Hey!'

My God, did he grope her ass?

'Do you really have to be so predictable, Piers.' Immy sounds brave, but I can tell from her stiff back that she hates him touching her.

He edges closer, reeking of booze and cigarette smoke. 'What's your problem, Imogen? Don't you like male attention?'

'I have no problem with male attention; I do have a problem with gorillas.'

'Oh, touch-y-y. You're not a rug-muncher, are you?'

'So your parents spent all that money on your education for you to come up with that gem?' I ask.

He snorts, spraying me with spittle. 'Just a little joke. Why do so many American girls have to be so uptight?'

'Why have so many British men undergone frontal lobotomies?'

As he glares at me, his eyes hold something almost feral behind the drunken glaze, but I'm not scared. I've dealt with creeps like him before at Brown, frat boys who thought they were God's gift to women while secretly hating and fearing us. The only difference is his accent, but I don't want us to turn into free entertainment for the evening and I can see Oscar, Chun and Isla twitching nervously, unsure whether to intervene.

'If you don't mind letting us past, *gentlemen*?'

'Shall I, Gideon? Shall I let these totties past?'

Totties? Is this the twenty-first century? I actually laugh at this.

Gideon sneers. 'I don't know, Piers.'

Losing patience, Immy pushes Gideon's chest and my heart sinks as his eyes darken with fury.

I keep my voice calm. 'Boys, I can appreciate that a request to move out of our way may take up a great deal of your brainpower, but I'd hoped you might have comprehended my meaning by now.'

'You're wasting your time, Piers. I crashed and burned with her on Saturday night. Leave it.' Rupert's arm is at Piers's elbow, his voice bored. I *think* he's trying to defuse the situation, but it's not helping.

Piers's face crumples in mock hurt. 'Gideon and I had rather hoped Lauren would be keen to develop the Special Relationship back at our rooms. Now, it looks like I'm going to spend a long lonely night with only the thought of you boys to keep me warm. Boo hoo.'

Immy holds her hand to her ear. 'Hear that? It's the sound of the saddest song being played on the world's smallest violin.' She sniggers and in unison we try to push past Piers and Gideon, as Oscar leaps up from his seat, stung into action.

'Stop being such a pair of tits. You heard them, now fuck off.'

It ought to be funny, this tiny little guy squaring up like a terrier taking on two pit bulls, but this is turning nasty and I hate seeing anyone bullied. With one hand, Gideon shoves Oscar back into the table and a bottle smashes. His glasses fall off and shatter on the tiles.

What happens next is all over so fast, I barely have time to breathe.

Chapter Four

One second I'm inches from Piers's face, the next someone grabs my arm and pulls me aside while the whole pub erupts in flying glass, a sickening crack and lots of hooting and girly screaming. When I look down, Piers is on his back at my feet, surrounded by shattered glass, blood pouring from his nose – with Alexander towering over him.

'When a woman tells you to get out of her way, you obnoxious cunt, you get out of her way. Now is that clear?' He barely raises his voice, but his words silence the bar. His shiny brogue prods Piers' thigh. 'Speak up, I can't hear you.'

Piers burbles, propping himself up on an elbow as he stares at the red liquid trickling down his shirt from his bloodied nose. Bile rises to my throat at the sight of it.

'You've broben by fucking node, you bastard.'

'You should be grateful this girl didn't kick you in your tiny balls.' He reaches out his hand and pulls Piers roughly to his feet, shoving him at his mates. 'Now get him out of here.'

You can almost smell the testosterone and feel the tension crackling in the air. Rupert and Oscar have quietly moved behind Alexander like the Three Musketeers while Piers and his boorish friends bristle with hurt pride and venom. A couple of bar staff try to weave their way through the drinkers. We've become Oxford's latest spectator sport. That's what I hate the most: once again I'm the centre of attention when all I wanted to do was fit in here. Does it have to be so hard to blend in?

Piers clutches a handkerchief to his nose, as Gideon throws an ill-advised 'You're not worth it, you shit,' at Alexander before bundling Piers out of the rear door of the pub. As for me, I'm shaking like a leaf inside, all indignation on the surface.

Rupert shakes his head. 'For fuck's sake, Alexander. Do you have to resort to willy-waving to impress a girl?'

'You can piss off, Rupert. I didn't see you stepping in.'

'Why bother when you'd waded in like a tank battalion?'

Alexander brushes glass fragments from his rugby shirt as if they were cookie crumbs. 'Why don't you settle up for the damage with the bar staff? I'll sort it out with you later.'

That comment is sheathed in silky menace and Rupert curls his lip but does as he's told, reduced to a hired lackey. I know what he's thinking, what they're all thinking – Immy, Oscar and the rest – as Alexander gestures to a corridor that leads to the pub bathrooms. The hubbub is rising again, but strangely enough everyone is giving us some space. I ought to walk out of here now, but I find myself doing the same as Piers and Gideon and Rupert.

That is, dancing to Alexander's tune.

His voice is calm and oddly soothing as we face off in the corridor. 'I'm sorry about that. Are you OK?'

I don't need his apology because I'm not some shrinking Edwardian lady, but I'm also human and when Alexander touches my arm, the contact is electric. Then I spot the skinned knuckles and the spots of blood on his shirt. *He smacked a guy in the mouth for me.* Well, this isn't the Stone Age and I don't need to be presented with a sabre-toothed tiger and dragged by the hair to his cave. He's just as bad as the rest of them.

I take a step back, as much to back off from the idea of being carried to his lair as to show him my indifference to his boxing skills. My back brushes the wood of the door.

'You know, I – we really didn't need rescuing,' I say, refusing to be fazed by that intense gaze.

A ghost of a smile touches his lips. 'Again?'

I know he's referring to the cloister incident and the memory of it makes me prickle with indignation and lust all over again. Over his shoulder, Immy, Rupes et al have their eyes on stalks, desperate to check out what's going on. Then Alexander shifts his position slightly so that his back is between me and them, shielding our conversation from view. He smells and looks incredible, and the bloodied shirt both repulses me and connects with some deep-rooted primeval need.

Suddenly I realize how skilfully I've been manoeuvred into place and my heart pitter-patters. Well, I'm not intimidated and I'm not impressed. So unimpressed, a jolt of desire for him shoots right through me.

'Um, Alexander . . .' Wow, that name sounds weird on my tongue, like I agreed to try a new food for the first time and I'm not sure I like it. I'll have to take another bite to be sure. 'Alexander, I do appreciate you thought you were helping me . . . us, but I didn't ask you to hit that guy for me. We were in control of the situation.'

He shrugs and his mouth turns up at the corners. 'Whatever you say.'

'Please, don't patronize me.'

'I wouldn't dream of patronizing you, Ms Cusack.'

'How do you know my name?'

He taps his nose. 'That's on a need-to-know basis.'

'OK. If you want to play it that way, it's fine. *You* need to know this, though: thanks for saving me from Piers, but you were wasting your time. Now, if it's OK with you, *Mister* Hunt, I'm going home.'

'You can play it any way you like with me.' Those ice-blue eyes slam down a challenge that's laced with provocation. 'And, as for going home, it's a very long way to Washington.'

He looks so unbelievably sexy that momentarily he's robbed me of words, but I snap to my senses. Alexander Hunt is trouble, in every single sense of the word, and I have to get away from him before I *can't* get away from him. That built, lean frame is still blocking my way and the scent of fresh clean sweat and testosterone makes me twitch with desire.

'I heard what happened over dinner last night, by the way. I hear that Rupert has finally met his match,' he says.

'I hope I never match Rupert in any respect.'

His eyes are bright with amusement. 'I admire a woman who can hold her own and I so rarely meet one.'

'I find that hard to believe. And now . . . um . . . if it's OK with you, I'd really appreciate it if you could let me past.'

Static crackles in the air between us. Never mind the real fight I witnessed, we're shadow-boxing with innuendo and the effect on me, at least, is as powerful as any aphrodisiac.

'I never mind any reasonable request.' He steps aside, his hand held out. The moment hangs in the air between us; if he asks me to stay, I won't, because that is what this Alexander expects me to do. I'm not about to be manoeuvred or manipulated or intimidated by any guy, not even one who makes me tremble with lust.

'Much obliged to you,' I say, imitating his cut-glass accent. As I stroll past his open hand towards Immy and the girls, I have the satisfaction of glimpsing the frustration on his face, and this time it's me who turns my back and walks away.

Chapter Five

So much for being fresh into classes. I only had a few hours' sleep after last night's encounter with Alex so there was no chance of me missing my first seminar at the faculty; I was awake at six a.m. Somehow, I managed to get back to my room last night without too much interrogation from Immy. It was still pouring down so we had to run, and Freddie made a booty-call to Immy so I headed straight for my room.

I don't need any more drama on my first day.

This morning we had an ice-breaker meeting with the other master's students on my course, then it was a full-on intro to the course, punctuated by lunch. There's a wholefoods cafe near the faculty where I grabbed a quinoa salad with some of the other grad students. Then it was back to work.

We get three exam essays at the start of Trinity term – but as that's not until next June I won't start stressing about it yet. This term 'all' I have to worry about is two extended essays on my specialist subject.

Whichever way you look at it, I've more than enough on my plate, so what do I go and do? Waste far too much time and energy trying to fathom out Alexander Hunt.

I step out of the Faculty of Art History into the weak rays of afternoon sun shining on the facades around me. In contrast to the austere grandeur of the colleges, the faculty is a sixties building shoehorned into the narrow streets near the centre of town, yet it encapsulates all that I love about Oxford. Where else would you get a brand-new bar and sixties brick building next to a Victorian church and a medieval college? Even the names are like something from a novel. I mean, Penny Farthing Place?

I grab a photo of the street name on my iPhone, wondering if I can work it in as part of a collage.

Back at college I resist the urge to collapse on to my bed and, instead, pull on some running shorts, a tee and my Nikes and head out into the streets. I'm not the serious kind of runner who runs till she throws up and beats herself up if she doesn't get a PB every time. I'm more the 'plug in the headphones, have I managed twenty minutes yet?' kind. I'm in dire need of a workout because my head is reeling with new experiences, and my feelings in respect of Alexander Hunt are so conflicted that not even Kofi Annan could reconcile them.

Immy told me that the Parks are a great place to run – not that she ever does – so that's where I go, jogging through the iron gate and into this lush expanse of meadowland. Narrow paths criss-cross the lawns and I take the one that leads down to the river, a blur of green all around me. I thread my way under the willow trees, now turning yellow, batting away tiny bugs as the 'yeah yeah yeahs' jostle for space in my head with the Gustav Holst I downloaded after I noticed the blue plaque on his house next to the Turf.

I know I'm running too fast too soon and will pay for it, but I'm high as a kite on new experiences, both Oxford- and Alexander-induced. A glance at my watch gives me the excuse to stop and take a breather. I've been out twenty minutes already and I need to get back, shower and change for dinner. It looks like I can run a little further through the parks past some nets I think are for cricket, and back along the street to Wyckham.

Ten minutes later, perspiration running down my neck, I put in a burst of speed in the final sprint towards college, miss my footing on the kerb and crash to the sidewalk.

I. Am. Not. Going. To. Cry.

Not out here in the street, even though my elbow feels like the skin has been taken off it and my ankle is throbbing so hard I may throw up. Except I have to get up because I'm lying in the road like one of the speed bumps they have everywhere here in Oxford. A bike swerves to miss me as I try to get to my feet and fall back again. Crawling back on to the sidewalk is my only option, but even that hurts. My butt must have taken some of the force because that's aching like crazy too.

The worst thing of all is that people are coming to help.

'Are you all right? That was a nasty fall.' An elderly lady, in a velour tracksuit, peers down at me.

'I'm . . .' *sick of saying fine.* 'I'll be OK.' Turning my grimace into a brave smile, I make another failed attempt to get up.

'Let me give you a hand. That's a nasty graze on your elbow.'

It probably is, but I'm more concerned about my ankle, which doesn't seem to want to function any more. I don't think it will support my weight, that's for sure, and I don't want to grab this lady's hand and bring her down on top of me.

'Here. Put your arm around me.'

I know that voice and it isn't the old lady's. Before I can protest, before I even know I don't want to protest, Alexander's hand is in mine, pulling me to my feet. His arm is firm round my back as I balance on one foot. Why does he have to come along now?

'I'll take care of this now.' He throws a smile at the old lady, a smile like he's never given me or anyone so far, and my heart does a triple Salchow. Is this smiling guy the real Alexander? Or simply the public version?

The lady seems relieved. 'I'll let this young man look after you. I'm late for my salsa class.'

'Thanks anyway,' I say as she hurries off. I could be bloody-minded and throw off his arm, but I'm in no position to flounce off anywhere. My ankle really hurts and my elbow's skinned raw and pin-pricked with tiny spots of blood.

'Careful.' His grip on my arm tightens as I wince and, despite the pain, I'm aware of the tickle of the hairs on his bare forearms brushing against my flesh.

'I'll be OK. It's not far to college.'

'With a sprained ankle?'

63

'I think it's just twisted.' I grab him for support as I try to place my sole on the sidewalk and half collapse.

'If you're hell bent on limping back to college, at least let me strap it up for you.'

'Really, I'm . . .'

He raises both eyebrows, and I realize I've gripped his arm so tightly, there are nail marks.

'Thanks, but how are we going to get back to Wyckham?' I have visions of us arriving in the Lodge like we've been tied together on some freshers' pub crawl.

'We're not going back to Wyckham. I live here.' I follow his finger to a house across the street, the centre of an elegant stone-built terrace that I took for a university building.

'Oh, I see.'

'Come inside and let's take a look at you.'

From the kitchen across the hall, there are dull thuds as drawers open and close. I'm lying on Alexander's sofa, wearing Alexander's rugby shirt, with my injured foot propped up on Alexander's silk cushion. After I'd limped up the steps on his arm, he left me in the sitting room with a bag of frozen peas round my ankle while he fetched some tape.

As I sip the iced water he brought me, I hear the chirrup of a cell phone and his deep voice answering 'Hunt'. Even though it's wrong, I strain my ears to hear what he's saying, but the kitchen door slams.

So this is Alexander Hunt's lair and I have to admit it looks remarkably civilized for a caveman's. Of course, he has to live somewhere, but I'd assumed it would be at Wyckham. Is this his place or rented? If he's only here for a year doing his master's, I guess it's rented? Judging by the cornice mouldings, picture rails and ornate ceiling roses, the house is mid- to late-Victorian. The decor is a mix of contemporary – all beech wood and plain lines, though nothing too self-consciously cool – combined with funky rugs on the bare boards. There's an eclectic mix of modern prints on the walls, but nothing stand-out, and no family photos from what I can see from my sofa, so I assume it's not his own place, or definitely not his own stuff.

It's still his *home*, though, and I'm alone with him in it.

'Sorry about that. I knew I had some tape somewhere . . .'

The glass is halfway to my lips as he enters the room. Now it's his turn to pause as we stare at each other across the room. In his hands are a pair of scissors and some blue sticky tape. My throat dries up. Now that I'm not in agony, my senses have space and time to react to him properly. He has on chinos, a shirt with the sleeves rolled back and shiny shoes, all of which fit him like they were made for him, which, now I know his background, they probably were.

He is even taller than I remember, six-two at least, and lean yet built. If he's in the army, then of course he's going to be fit, but, still, he looks hot.

He also recovers faster than I do.

'May I?' he asks in that clipped voice that's a notch up from being rude. Am I totally misreading the signals here or is there static crackling between us as he sits on the end of the sofa, without waiting for my reply.

He lifts my foot from the cushion and into his lap. I cringe at the mud smear and wet patch on his silk cushion and am horribly conscious of my bare legs.

'I'm sorry, I meant to take off my Nikes.'

'I'll do it.' His glance is brief, his voice curt and the tension between us is as taut as a high wire. Does he regret asking me inside? Does he feel the sparks arcing between us – or from me to him? Does he want to jump off the sofa and run away, like I do, because he's so frightened of what might happen and how he might feel if it does?

He's unlaced my shoe and he's gently easing it off my foot. Despite his care, my foot is sore, but I'm too transfixed by the strong fingers encircling my ankle to mind. His nails are short, square and clean, but his fingers are a little calloused.

'OK?'

'Mmm.' As he slides my sock over my foot, I am so glad I got a pedi before I left Washington.

'This may hurt a bit.'

'It'll be – ow!'

He glances up, his mouth tilting slightly, then resumes his exam of my foot as I try not to dig my nails too hard into the sofa cushion. Underlying the pain, I'm in heaven and hell as his fingertips prod my sole and swollen joint.

'Ideally, you should keep the ice on it for half an hour before I strap it, but this should keep it more stable and comfortable.'

Half an hour. In here with him? I'll self-combust.

He holds up the tape. 'This is vet tape. We use it for the horses, but there's nothing like it for sports injuries.'

OK. I suppose I can cope with being treated like a pony in this instance. He rolls the vet tape round my lower calf and the ball of my foot. I find it hard to tear my eyes away from his fingers as he does it, then I become conscious that his hands have come to rest on my ankle.

'Do you do a lot of running?' he asks.

'Does it look like it?' My attempt at Brit self-deprecation was a bad idea because he has a wicked gleam in his eye as he secures the tape.

'I won't answer that.'

'I run a little at home, to keep fit but mainly to de-stress,' I say, shifting my bottom on the sofa. Suddenly, I can't keep still.

He tears off the tape and he could move away now that his job is done. Instead, he strokes the blade of my foot almost idly and his mouth quirks in a smile. 'And are you stressed now?'

The touch of those strong fingers up and down my foot is more erotic than sex itself and he asks me if I'm *stressed*?

'Um . . . No, I'm doing just fine.'

He looks at me intensely, as if he's daring me to glance away first. 'Are you sure because you seem a little flustered. Maybe it's delayed shock. You did hit the ground *very* hard back there.'

I try not to gasp as he probes my ankle, gently but firmly.

'Can you feel that?'

'Yes.'

'Are you sure?' He massages the sole of my foot. 'I'm only checking that you've still got feeling down there, of course.'

'Trust me, I can feel it.' I'm unable to tear my eyes away from that arrogantly handsome face. He runs his fingers lightly along my sole. I don't believe in reflexology but something definitely connected a lot higher up just then.

'I had my first day of classes today,' I blurt out, frantically trying to change the subject.

'And how was that for you?' His mouth twitches into a smile as I brace my hands on the sofa cushion.

'Pretty full-on, but amazing . . . They sure throw you in at the deep end here . . .'

His eyes are still on mine as his hands move to my calf, kneading the sore muscle. I am struggling not to take off into orbit from the sofa.

He strokes my calf gently with his fingertips. 'And do you find yourself out of your depth often?'

'I . . . um . . . er . . .' I can't think of a single answer to that question. 'I had to decide on my specialist area,' I say in desperation. He rests my foot on the cushion again and gives me the Alexander Hunt deep penetrating gaze. 'Really? And what *is* your specialist area, Lauren?'

Please. Do not say my name. Hearing those syllables in that cut-glass accent, no matter how much I've scorned his aristocratic credentials, is driving me insane. 'I . . .

um ... it's called Women, Art and Culture in Early Modern Europe.'

He raises his eyebrows. 'Really? That must be *very* stimulating.'

His fingertips skate over the tape to where my flesh is bare. I hitch a breath as they make little circles on my shin. This is not a necessary part of the treatment. This is beyond the call of duty.

'More than you could ever imagine ...' My head drifts back against the sofa arm and I can't help but slip a little lower down the couch.

His hand glides over my knee and stops in the middle of my thigh. His palm is warm and a little rough. I can't help shifting my hips as his hand moves higher to the skin below the hem of my shorts. I have no need of his shirt now, the temperature seems to have risen by ten degrees in a few minutes.

'How about this?' His voice is lower, as if he senses the deep, matching sensation spreading through my core.

'That's ... ah ... very ... stimulating too.'

'Purely in an intellectual way, of course?'

Now I am glad of his rugby shirt because my nipples are prodding my tank top.

'Of course ...'

'How about this, then?' There's a raw edge to his tone as he slips his fingers under the edge of my running shorts. I try not to moan out loud as he slides his hand ever higher, playing with the lace of my panties. Any second now, I know he will slip his finger under the edge of them. With my eyes closed, I slide even further down the leather sofa until my bottom butts against the solidity of his thighs.

'Alexander, please . . .' Hell, *why* am I saying 'please'!

He has moved without me realizing and is now kneeling beside the sofa with me in his arms. Every nerve is alive and screaming as his lips meet mine, gently at first then, as I respond, he claims my mouth with a fierceness that wipes away any resistance I had.

His tongue pushes inside my mouth, exploring, and I devour him. I want him inside my mouth, inside me. The muscles around his spine and shoulder blades are firm through the cotton of his shirt. He is solidity, uncompromising, maddening.

Sparks of desire shoot through me and I buck my hips upwards. He pushes his hand inside the rugby shirt and under my tank, flattening his palm against my abdomen. His fingers brand my skin, and I start to pull his shirt from the waistband of his jeans. Half-crazed with lust, I want to have his skin on mine and I want it now.

The phone rings from the other side of the room and I tense. Alexander presses on, pulling aside my sports bra to close his fingers gently around my breast.

'Wait!'

'What for?'

I can't answer him because I can't answer myself. *Why* do I hesitate?

'Your phone . . .'

'Ignore it.' His voice is gravelly and impatient, but all I can think of is the door slamming as he took the other call. A call he didn't want me to hear, a call I shouldn't have heard because I shouldn't be in his house, on his sofa with his hands all over my body. He glances over at the phone on the side table, buzzing like an angry swarm of wasps, and his eyes cloud with anger and frustration.

'You should answer it. It might be someone important.'

'I don't care. They can wait.'

Through my clothes, my hand closes over his. 'Like everyone does for Alexander Hunt?'

The phone sounds even louder to me now.

He pulls his hand from under my top and swears under his breath. 'Will you go away?'

'What? Your caller or me?'

'I think you know what I mean.'

'Yes, I think I do.'

He rakes a hand through his hair in frustration and gets up. He towers over me as I shuffle up the sofa and swing my legs on to the rug. I'm left asking myself, did that really happen?

'We both know what we want so why wait? At least I *thought* I knew what you wanted, but clearly I'm wrong.'

'I got here three days ago, I've only met you a few times so if you were expecting me to leap into bed with you . . .'

He blows out a tiny breath of derision. 'I hardly think you're in a position to leap anywhere right now.'

I watch him struggle to hide his irritation under a veneer of politeness, but it's too late. I now wish I'd never run past his house or even heard of him. I'm damned if I'm going to stay here any longer explaining why I won't have sex with any man who snaps his fingers and expects me to fall at his feet. Actually, I *did* fall at his feet . . . But I'm not going to dance to his tune, no matter how much I want his body and I'm definitely not naive enough to mistake the chemistry between us as anything other than lust.

'Maybe not, but I can still walk out of here and that's exactly what I'm going to do.'

He nods. 'Of course. I'll get the car and drive you back to college.'

Gritting my teeth, I manage to stand on my injured ankle. 'Don't trouble yourself. I can walk.'

'If you think I'm going to stand and watch you hobbling down the street, you're mistaken. Wait here.'

'No, you wait!'

Ignoring me, he marches out of the sitting room. In the past few minutes we've gone from scorching the sofa to freezing it solid.

Well, Immy told me he's a heartbreaker and I already know he's ruthless and treads on anyone who gets in his way. No matter how much my body tells me I want him, I'd need to know a lot more about Alexander Hunt before I'd even think of jumping into his bed. Actually, no, it's far better to know nothing about him at all and keep a wide berth.

There's a rattle from the hall as the front door opens. I pick up my iPod from the side table where he left it.

He stands in the doorframe to the hallway, keys in his hand. 'Ready?'

With a nod that's as curt as his 'ready', I hop towards

him and, without asking me, he takes my arm to help me down the steps.

Five minutes later, the Range Rover stops outside the front of Wyckham. Our conversation during the drive has been non-existent, the atmosphere brittle with confusion and frustration on both sides. Ignoring the scowls and toots from other road users, Alexander double parks at the entrance. In seconds he is at the passenger door with his hand out.

'Be careful,' he says, helping me climb down to the sidewalk. I take his hand for the minimum time possible.

'Thanks.' Then, 'What about your shirt?' I ask, now I'm safely back on terra firma.

'Please, keep it.'

'I'll get it laundered and bring it back.'

His mouth twitches proudly. 'That won't be necessary.'

'I know it's not necessary, but I'd like to do it all the same.'

He shrugs. 'As you wish.'

'I *do*.' I am surprised at the firmness of my voice and maybe Alexander is too. Horns blast from the street behind us and his eyes narrow in irritation. 'I have to go.'

'I know.'

Yet he does *not* go. He hovers by the door, his blue eyes intent on mine, and my body betrays every rational thought I had about ignoring him. Despite everything that has passed between us and all my better

73

judgement, I still want to feel his naked body next to mine. And damn it but I'm compelled to break the silence, to explain myself and I have no idea *why*.

'Look, Alexander, I don't sleep with a guy because he snaps his fingers. If you knew me better, you'd realize that.'

'I've never met anyone like you before.'

The look he gives me is icy and fiery all at once. It burns into me and I don't know how to reply or whether I want to believe what he just told me or not. I want to believe it a lot – and that's exactly why I won't.

'I should go now.'

'I'll call you.'

'Sure you will,' I mutter, and he can make of that what he likes. I don't even know if he heard it because he's dashed round the front of the car and is about to climb into the driver's seat, ignoring the queue of shouting, hooting drivers. In a few seconds, he executes a U-turn into the traffic and is gone.

Despite his shirt, I shiver as I limp through the Lodge and drag my aching body up the three flights to my room. Now that the adrenaline and endorphins have ebbed away, my bumps and bruises have begun to throb and I'm suddenly as exhausted as if I'd run a marathon. And the first thing I do when I close the door on the world is to rip off his top and toss it into the darkest corner of my room.

Chapter Six

Three days later Alexander's shirt lies in the same place. He hasn't called, of course, and I'm annoyed that I even entertained the possibility that he ever would. The fact that he didn't take my number is no excuse. He could have got it from Rupert or Immy, but he hasn't, and I'm not going to waste another second thinking about him. There are way too many other interesting places to visit, things to do – and people to meet – in Oxford, to spend my time on Alexander Hunt.

However.

No matter how hard I try, in my fantasies – and there have been some since Tuesday – I took that leap into Alexander's bed.

Enough. I've not even told Immy what happened between Alexander and me – not that anything *did* happen. It's not that I don't trust her to be discreet, I *do*. It's more that I can't cope with the interrogation that would follow and the fact that she'd make far more of our brief encounter than it deserves.

I've seen her every day after my classes, and she's introduced me to some more of Oxford's institutions: dinner at Brown's and cocktails in the Duke of Cambridge with its legendary hot bar staff, not that I noticed them much. We were also meant to squeeze in a game of tennis on the college courts this afternoon, but my ankle is still too sore.

Somehow, Friday evening has come round and we're sitting in a dark corner of the Eagle and Child in St Giles – another Oxford institution and the place where Tolkien and C. S. Lewis used to meet and read out their works. I feel as surreal as Alice in Wonderland or Lucy when she found herself in Narnia.

We're celebrating because Immy has scraped through her Collections and is free to complete her final year. She's returning from the bar, but instead of our drinks she waggles her phone, a grin on her face.

'You are so not going to believe this.'

For a second, I think she's going to say that her call was from Alexander, but why would that be? There have now been a whole three days of nothing between us, despite his remark about calling me. I could curse myself for even giving him a second thought and I'm mad that I checked my pigeonhole this morning to see if he'd decided to go the snail-mail route and drop a note in there. It seemed ironic – and also a warning – that all I found was a bunch of circulars about the Speculative Fiction Society (scary), a badger cull (horrible) and some evangelical group warning me about the dangers of promiscuous sex (hilarious). There was also an invite to some upcoming USSoc grad events, which could provide an interesting contrast to Rupert and his Hooray Henry friends.

Now, Immy is popping with excitement. 'Well, don't you want to *know*?'

I have to smile. 'You want to tell me and I have no objection to hearing it.'

'Oh, stop it, Lauren!'

'Sure I want to know and you better tell me before you burst.'

'OK. Right. So . . .' She pauses for dramatic effect. 'Are you doing anything tomorrow evening?'

'I was thinking of going to a USSoc intro party?'

Her face falls. 'Oh, fuck.'

'But . . . I'm always wary of "expat" events and I did come to Europe specifically to immerse myself in a new culture and get away from my fellow Americans, much as I love my country . . .' Her face brightens and I really shouldn't tease her. 'So if you've got a better idea.'

If she could, I think she'd actually hop about in glee. 'How would you like to go to a ball?'

'A ball? Sounds awesome.'

'It is, indeed, awesome. One of my old friends from Marlborough called. She's at Oriel and she's been invited to a winter ball at Rashleigh Hall. Jocasta can't go because her boyfriend has broken his ankle and she wanted to know if we would like to go instead.'

'I'd love to come, but what about Freddie?'

She waves a hand airily. 'Oh, he's going on his older brother's stag do. Rupert will be there, though, and Oscar maybe if he isn't knackered after being on the river.'

'Rupert? That's a mixed blessing if ever I heard it.'

She laughs and then there is a moment when neither

77

of us speaks because there is a big gap in the conversation that I realize is an Alexander-sized gap. One of us has to fill it and it turns out to be Immy.

She pretends to fiddle with her phone. 'I suppose there's a chance Alexander might put in an appearance. He was at Eton with Jocasta's brother, Hugo.'

'Oh, really?' I take refuge in the dregs of my Diet Coke.

'He's bound to have been invited. He generally gets invited to everything, though he rarely turns up of course.'

'Of course.' I try not to show I am disappointed by this, or to actually *be* disappointed. Because I am *not*.

Immy goes on. 'Then again, Hugo *is* a friend of his, Rupes is definitely going and it's a private party, so he might be there, especially if there's the chance of a game.'

Briefly, I have visions of Alexander and Rupert tossing a rugby ball to each other across the dance floor. Then a vision of Alexander naked in a communal locker room, towelling himself down. I give myself a mental rap on the knuckles.

'What kind of game?'

'Poker, of course. Alexander loves playing it.'

'What for? Castles? Small republics?'

'Gosh, no, although rumour has it that he did once win a polo pony in one game.'

'You're kidding me, right?'

She shrugs. 'Actually, no. Oscar told me about it a while back. But don't get your hopes up. I haven't seen Alexander all week. Have you?' She glances up at me, eyes wide with innocence.

'No. Why would I?' It's fortunate that the pub is so

dimly lit because otherwise Immy would see the red in my cheeks as I utter what is plainly a bare-faced lie.

Immy tuts. 'I don't believe you.'

'I've no interest in whether he turns up at the ball or not, but it has crossed my mind that I haven't seen him around this week.'

I am not going to lie any more – it makes me look and feel as if I'm protesting too much where Alexander is concerned and Immy deserves my trust. 'To tell the truth, it was outside his house that I twisted my ankle on Tuesday. He strapped it up for me.'

Her eyes are wide again, but with surprise. 'Alexander Hunt asked you into his *house*?'

'Sure. He had to fetch an ice pack and some vet tape for me.'

She squeals in delight. 'Vet tape!'

Oh, hell, what have I started now? 'He, um, said it was the best thing for sports injuries and that he'd used it on his horses.'

Immy's shriek attracts the attention of some of our fellow drinkers.

'Immy, *please*.'

Her face is mock solemn. 'And, pray, what happened after he'd done his Nurse Alexander act?'

And? Should I tell her that he kissed me and had his hand inside my shorts and that we were on the verge of having sex on his sofa? No way. We may have got to know each other pretty well in a short time, but I'm not ready to share that info with anyone.

I shrug. 'He drove me back to college.'

79

'So,' she says, leaning forward. 'Let me get this straight. Alexander Hunt carried you into his house, laid you on his sofa, strapped up your injured ankle and brought you home in the Range Rover and you say it's *nothing*?'

'He didn't carry me into his house and I didn't say he'd laid me on his sofa.'

'But you *were* lying on it?' Wow, Immy could work for MI6.

'Sitting, actually. I had no choice.'

Immy snorts. 'Do you have any idea what you're saying here?'

'That I fell over outside some random guy's house? That he taped up my foot? Is that such a big deal?'

'It is when Alexander Hunt is the random guy in question!'

I shrug my shoulders. 'So?'

'*So*, he's incredibly choosy about his women and a huge catch and when this gets out half the girls in Oxford will have the knives out for you.'

'His women? Hey, I'm deeply flattered to be one of the chosen few – I don't think – but there's no need for anything to "get out". I'd hate people to get the impression I set out to "hook" Alexander or something, which incidentally makes him sound like some huge great fish that I've landed.'

Immy wipes her eyes and I see her mascara has run where she's been laughing at my horrified response. 'I know you haven't set out to get him and that's probably half the attraction with him – not that you're not gorgeous and glamorous, of course.'

I roll my eyes and Immy smirks mischievously. 'And he also totally cannot resist a challenge.'

That figures. 'And I suppose he rarely gets any opposition?'

'What do you think?'

'That he needs a reality check. He may be wealthy, titled and I'll admit he's pretty good-looking – but I'm not that shallow.' But am I? I'm thinking, because deep down there's a part of me that is, damn it, very flattered by being singled out by Alexander. And another part that's annoyed for *being* flattered.

'I don't think for a moment you are, and actually you're probably driving Alexander insane by not taking his bait. So, after he dropped you off at college, did he say anything else?'

'Like what?' I study my fingernails as if I'm about as interested in the topic of Mr A. Hunt as the shipping forecast.

'Like seeing you again,' says Immy.

'I . . . um . . . kind of got the impression that he *might* contact me again.'

She frowns, suddenly serious. 'Did he actually *say* he would call you?'

'Well, yes, he did.'

She blows out a breath. 'Did he say exactly when he'd call?'

'No, and I haven't seen him around college for the

past few days either, not that I've been looking out for him.'

'Hmm. I wonder if his mysterious absence may have something to do with his military work.'

'The military?' I shake my head as small but telling details slot into place, like a few things Rupert said at dinner and the way he waded into the fight. 'So he's in the army?'

'Not sure it's the army, strictly speaking . . .' She lowers her voice. 'Rupert hinted to me that Alexander's in the special forces, but he's not supposed to spread it about.'

'Special forces?' Momentarily I'm thrown off kilter. 'He's a marquess's son and now he's in the SAS?'

'I don't know for sure that it's the SAS and I'm not sure Rupert does. He might be embellishing the facts. He's hardly the most discreet man in Oxford and there's no way Alexander would trust him with any detail, even if they are cousins.'

'Alexander doesn't seem old enough and how will he find time to study for his master's if he keeps disappearing off campus to do all this stuff?'

'He's almost twenty-six and I think he was in Afghanistan before he came here, but I don't know the details. As for disappearing off all the time, I can't imagine the Master or his tutors would be thrilled about him being away so much during term time, but then Alexander doesn't play by the normal rules. Of anything . . . Look, Lauren, I hate pouring cold water on things, but I'd tread extremely carefully where Alexander is concerned.'

'You mean he has a girlfriend?'

'Not now . . . not as far as I know, though he's so bloody secretive, you can't tell for sure. There *was* someone but it's totally over now and, whatever you say about Alexander, I don't think he'd ever lead a girl on. I'm only suggesting you go into this – and him – with your eyes open.'

'Thanks for the warning, but I've no intention of going anywhere with Alexander. He's hot, I won't deny that, but I'm not into all that macho, stiff-upper-lip posturing and I can see that he's a player.'

'I didn't say he was a player, more that he's . . . well . . . difficult to get close to.'

'Don't worry, I already put crime-scene tape round him. Besides I want to concentrate on my studies. Did I tell you that Professor Rafe is trying to organize a trip to the Klimt Museum in Vienna?'

She raises an eyebrow. 'No. Really? Does he plan on inviting anyone else along or is it just you and him?'

'Ha ha.' I may laugh but I must admit I haven't seen any notices about the Klimt trip on the faculty notice board.

'He mentioned it when I bumped into him on my way back from the faculty. I'd stopped for a hot chocolate in Georgina's while I checked my emails on my iPad.'

'Rafe was in Georgina's?'

'Yes. He came in after me.'

'*Quelle* surprise.'

'Don't look at me like that. He's entitled to drink in a cafe and that place does have an arty bohemian vibe.'

'Of course it does, Lauren.'

'Stop it!'

Though I join in her laughter, I can't suppress my uneasiness that Rafe might have stalked me to the cafe. Then I see her laughing eyes, and realize Immy's teasing me, and it's pure coincidence he walked in there.

'Tell me more about the ball,' I say, and her eyes light up.

'It's a masked ball,' she says, barely able to conceal her delight. 'Take a look at this.'

She scrolls through the Rashleigh Hall website on her iPhone.

'Wow. That looks fantastic. But *tomorrow*?'

'Yes. It's very short notice, but there's no way I'm going to miss it.'

'What's the dress code? Black tie? Cocktail?'

'Noooo. White tie for the guys and full-length glamour for us. I've got a few things I could wear already, but my parents have treated me for passing my exams so I was thinking of getting something new. Jocasta said that *Tatler* might be there and I would *kill* to be in Bystander. What about you? Haven't you got anything in your luggage mountain?'

'I brought a few cocktail dresses with me. I've got an Alexander McQueen dress at home that would be perfect.' For a nanosecond, I think of having it couriered over on the night flight then think better of it as Immy's eyes widen.

'Oh my God. Really?'

I laugh. 'Yes, my parents took me to New York to

choose it for my twenty-first but there wasn't any more room in the luggage for it and I wasn't aware I'd need a mask.'

She laughs. 'In that case, be ready at nine tomorrow. We're off on a rescue mission.'

'To London?'

'Sadly no. There's no time for that because we'll need to get our hair and nails done in the afternoon, but worry not – I know the perfect place.'

I am ascending the steps of Rashleigh Hall, holding up the most divine dress I ever owned. I say 'ascending' because plain walking would not do justice to The Dress – a full-length silk column that's subtly draped at the front, but cut so low at the back it skims the base of my spine. As soon as I spotted it on the rail at the store, I knew I had to have it, even though it's more daring than anything I'd usually wear. Immy looks sensational in a full-skirted cobalt dress that's a perfect foil for her brunette hair, which is styled on top of her head like a Grecian goddess.

After the store arranged to deliver the gowns and matching masks to Wyckham, Immy and I parked the bikes in the racks and grabbed a cab to a boutique spa in the countryside, which is owned by one of her cousins. We got our hair done by the spa's head stylist, who Immy says is from some TV makeover show, and squeezed in mani-pedis, just in time to make it back to Wyckham to do our make-up

Holding our skirts above our ankles, we finally reach the top of the steps. I've been to formal events at the

White House and a couple of embassies, not to mention high school and university proms, but this is different. There's an air of fairy tale about Rashleigh Hall, accentuated by everyone around us wearing masks. They make it tricky to see but add to the mystery.

Flames flicker from metal baskets arranged along the edge of the steps, casting shadows on the ground and warming my skin as we pass. The October evening is chilly and dark, of course, because it's eight o'clock now, but I'm so excited I don't even mind the wind blowing the leaves around my skirt and chilling my bare back.

We got a cab to Rashleigh Hall, which rests in its own estate a few miles out of Oxford. I have to say that the website doesn't do it justice. The grand facade is in the baroque style with a series of huge columns ranged across the front of the house and a vast classical portico above the door. Apparently the architect was inspired by a design for the Louvre, which seems kind of appropriate.

'Is this a public venue?' I ask Immy as we pass through the doors into the huge reception vestibule. The mask, a silver affair that matches my dress, cuts down some of my peripheral vision, yet even so I can see the vivid colours of the painted ceiling three floors above us. The buzz of excited chatter overlays the sounds of a string quartet playing Vivaldi's 'Winter' as waiters glide around with trays of champagne and canapés.

'It's owned by one of Jocasta's relatives, some earl or other, but he rents it out for photo shoots and weddings. These places cost a fortune to run these days – you have to make them pay.' Immy lowers her voice, her black-feathered mask fluttering mischievously. 'But it's a shed compared to Alexander's place.'

I give a little laugh in reply because, truth to tell, I'm not comfortable that Immy may think I am interested in Alexander for his wealth and title. Money, even old money, holds no real appeal for me although I'm well aware that life would be a whole lot tougher without enough of it. The thing is that my great-grandparents started off in life with hardly a bean and worked their way up by succeeding in business. OK, my grandpa was well-to-do by the time my father was born, but he always instilled the work ethic in Dad, who passed it on to me. Not that he needed to, because as far back as I can remember I wanted to succeed on my own terms. That's another thing that bothered me about Todd: he never really took my passion for art seriously.

I certainly don't need to hang on to the coat tails of some aristocrat now, even if he does turn up.

A waiter hands us glasses of champagne as we're sucked deeper into the marble vestibule. The room is full of men in white tie and girls in glamorous dresses but my eye is drawn to the artwork. A huge portrait of an aristocratic young woman, dressed in white with a blue silk sash, dominates one wall. I'm sure it's an original of a copy I've seen at the White House.

'Immy, have you checked out this amazing Reynolds?'

She sips her drink then murmurs, 'No, but I've checked out some pretty stunning talent. We seem to have made quite an entrance.'

She nods at a knot of guys a few yards away, who raise their glasses to us.

'Do you know them?' I ask, sipping my fizz, acting as if I haven't noticed them.

'No, but I might make closer acquaintance with the tall one in the dark purple mask. He's completely hot.'

As I check him out, a curly-haired guy in a kilt smiles back at me then nudges his purple-masked friend. 'I do believe they may be coming over . . .'

Immy giggles. 'Good. I knew you and that dress would be a major attraction.'

'Hey, I think the word you used in the store was "elegant".'

She finishes her fizz and swipes a canapé from a tray. 'It *is* elegant, and it also makes the most of your assets. Now, let this nice man top up your champagne and let's see how we can wangle seats next to the Purple Pimpernel and his Scottish friend for dinner.'

It's past ten thirty now, dinner has been over a while and there's still no sign of Alexander. I gave up scanning the room hours ago and now I don't care if he's flown off on a mission to Mars. I *really* don't care because I'm being whirled around the floor by the boy in the kilt. There's a disco starting in one of the other rooms, but Immy and I thought it would be a laugh to try out the Scottish dancing in the grand ballroom. The band is playing a reel which is *wild* and has the whole dance floor shrieking and hooting with delight. This Angus is a doctor-friend of Rupert's who has entertained me over dinner and I could not resist when he pulled me to my feet. It's almost impossible in the dress and hardly anyone knows what they're doing apart from Angus, but it's a blast.

The fiddle player stops and we come to a halt, breathless and laughing. The room is spinning a little as I stop. With the endorphins kicking in, not to mention wayyy too many glasses of champagne, I don't really mind when Angus puts his arms round my back for the slow waltz the band has struck up.

'Do you mind.'

There is only one man who makes his questions sound like orders and I don't even need to turn round to know whose hand is at my elbow. What I am not prepared for is the sight of Alexander Hunt in full military dress uniform.

Chapter Seven

Still dizzy from the reel, I wobble on my heels. Angus has stepped aside as Alexander fills my vision. I want to hate him, but I'm too pole-axed by his sheer physical presence.

He isn't quite the tallest man in the room, he just seems as if he is. In the uniform, I swear he stands up even straighter. He's wearing tight-fitting black trousers like riding jodhpurs, and a short red jacket with claret lapels and cuffs over his white shirt and bow tie. He faces me, and it's then I notice two tiny badges of airplanes on the lapels. It's as if every eye in the room burns into us as he settles his hands either side of my waist.

Angus, arms folded, lurks at the side of the floor and I feel guilty. But not *very*. In fact, overwhelming desire comes closer to my feelings right now, though I would rather die than let Alexander know it. Some of the people around us are waltzing properly, but we're in our own little universe. His breathing quickens as he rests his fingers on my bare back, and though it's the lightest of touches I feel as if he's scorching my skin.

I'm desperate to distract myself from a fierce urge to press myself against him. 'That was pretty abrupt . . .'

His lips curve in a smile of triumph. 'It was.'

He pulls me a little closer, and my breasts brush against the cloth of his jacket. My senses are alive to every tiny movement of his fingertips on my skin and to the sensuous way my dress clings to my body.

'Don't think this changes anything . . .' I challenge him to look away first, but his gaze is rock steady, his eyes burning into me with an intensity that takes my breath away.

'Oh, I wouldn't dream of it.'

He seems to inch a little closer and now we're barely even moving to the music while everyone circles around us. His breath is warm against the nape of my neck, making every pore tingle deliciously. I close my eyes briefly, revelling in the hardness of his chest against my breasts, knowing I should break away, but losing the battle, and before I even know it's happening our mouths meet in a hot, deep kiss.

It's so unexpected it almost knocks me off my feet and it's a second before I respond. When I do, there's no holding back, I relish the taste and texture of his gorgeous mouth. His hands slip lower down my back to my bottom, pulling me tight up against him. There's absolutely no doubt of how he's feeling about me and every inch of my body zings with desire.

Even when our lips finally part, I don't want to open my eyes and face the world but, gradually, I become aware of the buzz of voices in the room. The music has stopped and there's only the two of us now. Everyone else is leaving the dance floor, some of them glancing over their shoulders at us while others watch us from the sidelines.

We're the centre of attention, but Alexander keeps his eyes on me and takes my hand in his.

'Let's get out of here.'

Maybe it's my dress that makes me almost trip over my heels or maybe it's because my legs are watery, but I'm struggling to keep up as he pulls me across the vestibule towards a door beneath the grand staircase. Maybe I catch sight of Immy and Rupert as we exit the room, but most of the faces around me are a blur. I know I've had too much champagne and that I'm crazy to allow Alexander to whisk me off like this, but any common sense I had flew out of the grand sash windows of Rashleigh Hall when he marched on to the floor.

A guy calls out to him from a fug of cigar smoke as we pass. 'Alexander!'

'Not now.'

'What about the game later?' he shouts.

Alexander's reply is almost feral. 'I said, not *now*.'

So there is a game later and I wonder if I am part of it, a stake to be played for and won because what Alexander wants he gets. I don't care right now and, anyway, I'm more than equal to any challenge he cares to throw at me.

We shoot through a library, stopping at a panelled door on the far side. Finally, he releases my hand.

'And what's this?'

'Somewhere we can talk.'

He takes a key from the pocket of his trousers and inserts it in the lock. The door opens, he steps into the black space and flicks a switch. The room is bathed in a muted, almost green, light.

'After you,' he says, as politely as if he's letting me go ahead of him in the lunch line, though his hungry look makes me feel as if I'm about to be devoured.

Immediately my senses tell me that this place looks, smells and feels different to the rest of Rashleigh Hall. The ceiling is lower, giving it an air of intimacy, and the walls are panelled with dark oak and painted a rich red above the dado rail. Mahogany chairs and deep-buttoned sofas line the walls, which are hung with hunting prints. All of this is cast in shadow, in contrast to the billiard table that dominates the room, the green baize cloth lit by a suspended chandelier.

The place has such a consciously masculine feel that I can almost hear the soft hiss of gas lamps and smell the cigar smoke in the air. It is so obviously designed as a retreat from the world, a place where no lady would have ever set foot unless she was invited for a very specific purpose.

That image both excites and repels me; like so many aspects of Alexander Hunt and his set do. The door closes with a soft click as he locks it and the rest of the world no longer exists. The band music is so faint that I have to strain to hear it, and only the distant pulse of a bass line reminds me that, yards away, several hundred people are dancing and partying.

As he approaches, the key is outlined in the pocket of his trousers, which sends a tiny shiver through me. My heart feels as if it is trying to escape from my ribcage at the realization that I am locked into a small room with Alexander. There is no escape now for either of us and I'm not sure how I feel about that. My reaction is to retreat deeper into the room, stopping by a chaise. I want him badly but I also realize I've walked – or rather waltzed – right into his hands.

I run my hand over the leather of the chaise, cooling a palm made hot by his firm grip on it. 'Is this a private room?'

'Yes, it is.'

'How did you get the key?'

He crosses towards me and my stomach flutters a little. 'I know the family.'

Moving away from the sofa, I rest my hand on the billiard table. 'Ah. Of course you know the family. Do you know everyone?'

'Only the people I need to.' As he sits down, the fabric of his trousers strain over his thighs. Throwing his arm along the back of the chaise, he spreads his legs wide and I'm mesmerised by those long legs encased in tight black trousers.

He allows his gaze to drift down my body from my head to my feet. It's a slow, deliberate assessment – everything he does has a purpose – obviously designed to unnerve me and, of course, it does. 'How's your ankle, by the way? I noticed you were able to manage a reel with Angus.'

'You know, it turned out not to be as bad as I'd first thought.'

'My treatment must have worked wonders, then.' His deep voice is silky smooth and sends shivers through my body.

'My powers of recovery must be better than you expected and maybe the damage wasn't as bad as you thought in the first place.' I throw him a triumphant glare, but, as if my body wants to prove him right, my ankle throbs on cue, followed by a few places higher up.

'In that case I'm delighted to be wrong.'

'Is that a new experience for you? Being wrong?'

'Not new, but certainly unfamiliar.' He uncrosses his legs, making space for me on the sofa. 'And why don't you sit down, *please*.'

No other man I've ever met could make the simplest of words sound like an invitation to get naked. He angles himself towards me, and I notice that his face is tanned, like he's been caught out in the sun, even though the skies have been grey in Oxford since he left. Perhaps Immy's theories about his absence having something to do with his army work are right. Perhaps he also looks a little tired underneath the sunburn and that, inexplicably, makes him seem almost human and even hotter.

'I'm sorry I didn't call you,' he says.

I shrug. 'I think you may be confusing me with someone who cares whether you call or not.'

'Oh, really?' He seems amused, and when his knee nudges mine through my dress my thigh tingles. He's a tall guy, well-built rather than bulky, yet he seems to take over any space he enters. I clasp my hands together in my lap. 'So have you been anywhere nice while you've been away?' I ask.

'"Nice" is not the word I'd use, but I have been out of town, as you might say.'

'Out of town?'

His laugh is brief and ironic. 'In a manner of speaking.'

Is it me or has he edged closer? My chest rises and falls a little faster and I'm seized by an urge to wipe the smug expression from his arrogant lips with my own. He brushes an imaginary mark from his trousers. Unhelpfully, the gesture draws my attention to the muscles in his thighs.

He frowns. 'Forgive me for saying it, but you seem very tense . . . I can understand it if you're angry with me for not calling you, but it couldn't be helped.'

'Like I said, I'm not bothered.'

'Good, I'm glad that's clear between us. You see, I *had* thought you might have wanted to see me again, but now it looks like I misread the signals from you. I'm only human, despite what you, may think.'

'I don't think anything about you, Alexander.' Fifteen–love to me, I think.

'That's most unfortunate because I *do* think about you.'

Fifteen–all. Actually, damn, I think he aced that game. 'Oh.'

'However, if I've genuinely never crossed your mind in the past few days and you've *absolutely* no interest in me whatsoever, then perhaps I should give up thinking of you at all.'

My fingers are warm and when I glance down I find he's taken them in his.

'If I *had* thought about you . . .' My voice falters because his thumb is circling the hollow of my palm in a way that looks innocent yet feels like the prelude to something intensely erotic.

'In the event of that slim possibility . . .'

'*Very* slim . . . oh . . .' His jacket brushes my bare arm and shivers of sensation dance through my body. '*If* I – ah – had thought about you, I suppose I might – just *might* – have been wondering where you had been, *but . . .*'

'You haven't given it a second's thought?'

'Not even a nanosecond's.'

He gives an exaggerated sigh that has my hackles rising. 'In that case, I won't have to disappoint you by saying that I can't tell you anyway. You'll have to trust me.'

'Trust *you*?'

'Is it really *that* hard?' He leans so close to me that there's only the silk of my dress between my skin and his thigh. Suddenly, the impulse to press my mouth to his again is almost overwhelming. It's as if some drug has been injected into my bloodstream that's stolen away my inhibitions. I can't blame the champagne. It's the wickedly sexy gleam in his eyes, that seductive voice, the whole incendiary package that is Alexander Hunt.

'Why don't you try me?'

'I haven't been in Oxford because I've been . . . *working*. Do you remember the phone call I took while you were in my house?'

I feign an interest in a hunting print on the wall. 'Possibly.'

'That was work saying I had to leave that evening. I didn't know when I'd be back.'

I hardly trust myself to speak anyhow, because I know I'm still a little high on the champagne and a lot high on Alexander's sheer physical presence and the intriguing prospect of finding out more about him. Not, of course, that I want him to know that I'm remotely interested in any aspect of him.

'So do you have to go off on these jaunts often?' I ask, trying to keep my voice on the polite side of bored.

'I never go on "jaunts",' he says, imbuing the word with thinly disguised contempt. 'As for having to disappear off in the middle of my course, that shouldn't happen at all. We should be keeping term, of course, according to the college rules.' He hesitates and his mouth tilts in a maddening smile. 'But I don't like to play by the rules, as you've probably worked out by now.'

'Ah ha. I get it now. You're a rebel. That explains everything.'

'A rebel?' He gives a soft laugh. 'I hardly think so, but if that's the way you like to imagine me then I can live with it.'

The way I like to imagine him? I almost hate the guy, but I want to wipe the smile off his smug, gorgeous face with my mouth even more. And I swear he opened those long legs even wider, leaving me in no doubt that he's as turned on as I am.

'So, you have a sabbatical for a year?' I ask in what I hope is an aloof kind of way.

'Of sorts, and hopefully I won't have to go off too often from now on.'

'How long have you been in the army?'

'Since I left Oxford the first time. I did my first degree here after I left Eton and then I went to Sandhurst.'

'Ah. Sandhurst. Of *course*. The officer training college.'

'Well done.'

'I'm not entirely ignorant of British history and culture, whatever you may think.'

He shakes his head. 'On the contrary, I'd never make that mistake. I suspect your knowledge extends to some very esoteric fields.'

Actually, I have the feeling that compared to Alexander, in some fields I'm a complete novice, and does he *have* to look at me in that 'scorch your panties off' way? 'But military academy . . . that sounds tough,' I murmur, saying anything to cover the rogue blush that's started at my chest and is rapidly rising up my neck

He gives a wry smile. 'It wasn't a holiday camp and at times I'd have given everything I owned to be anywhere else, but I survived, as you see, and now I love my job.'

His row of medals draws my attention. No, I can't tease him about those, because I know they don't hand them out like candy to just anyone. I'd love to know what he's done to get them, but I'd rather rip out my fingernails than ask him. He'd only give some flippant reply anyhow.

'So, *what* are you? You turned up in the uniform tonight, after all. Can you tell me or will you have to kill me?'

He regards me levelly, only for a second, but it seems a hell of a lot longer. I feel as if he's weighing up his opponent and deciding on a course of action. My blush heats my face, but to my relief he glances down at his chest with a sigh of resignation. 'I've been to a mess dinner with some colleagues, straight from, well, from where I was earlier today.'

'And these?'

Before I realize what I'm doing, I reach up and touch one of the tiny airplanes on his lapel with my fingertip.

'The Paras. I'm a captain in the Parachute Regiment.' Pride adds a richer texture to his voice as he says this and he can't help lifting his chin a little. So I've found his true passion. Not his degree, not his estate, but the army. For some reason, I'm shivering inside, but I still can't resist teasing him.

'So, no guarding Buckingham Palace in a bearskin? I thought you might have been in some kind of Guards regiment.'

His tone turns icy. 'I'm sorry to disappoint you.'

I drop my fingers from his lapel, aware I touched a raw nerve. 'What makes you think you've disappointed me?'

'People make assumptions.'

Wow. That was spiky, but I won't back down now. 'So, it's Captain Alexander Hunt, but that's not all, is it?'

'Immy must have told you about the rest by now. I'd be amazed if she hadn't.'

'She said your father's a marquess although, frankly, that means nothing to me.' He laughs softly and it's clear my remark has amused rather than offended him, but he continues with faultless politesse.

'Actually, it means precisely nothing as far as I'm concerned too. Other than the fact that, by an accident of birth, I've been extremely fortunate. Or perhaps not, depending on how you look at it. My father wants me to leave the army and learn how to run the estate properly.'

'And you don't?'

He looks at me as if I've gone crazy. 'Of course not. I want to carry on in the service. I'm not ready to swap the uniform for tweeds and a wax jacket and spend my days poring over accounts books and meeting land agents. I'd rather die.'

My skin prickles at the vehemence in his voice. 'You don't mean that.'

'Perhaps, but I'm not going back to manage Falconbury until I absolutely have to.'

I notice there's no mention of a mother, which must mean she left, or worse, and he has a thorny relationship with his father from what I can gather.

'Well, if it's any consolation, when it comes to family expectations . . . I can understand those. I love my parents to bits, and they've always had big aspirations for me, but . . .' His thigh bumps mine through the confection of my skirt and I can hardly keep still with him so close to me. Whether he likes it or not, I have to edge away.

I get up and cross over to the billiard table and pick up a ball because I need something – anything – to distract me from his sheer animal presence.

'So your parents didn't expect your aspiration to involve flying halfway round the world to get away from them?'

I am so surprised at this insight that I laugh out loud. 'No, they didn't. Like you, I suppose I deliberately went against their expectations. My mother is a wonderful woman, but I think she envisaged me at least being in the same country; she said she couldn't really understand why I couldn't do my master's in the States. My father thought the same, but he might have been more worried that something would "happen" to me. I had such a hard job to make them accept I was coming to Oxford.'

'Well, I'm very glad you chose Wyckham or we'd never have met.'

'That's luck for you,' I say lightly.

'Oh, I don't believe in luck, Lauren, and by the way . . .' His gaze flames me from head to toe. '. . . have you any idea how fucking sexy you look tonight?'

Any words stop in my throat. How can I reply to that?

'That dress is . . . something else, and at the risk of getting my face slapped you have the most amazing breasts in Oxford.'

'Only Oxford?' I murmur as he gets up slowly and deliberately from the chaise.

'Perhaps I could extend it to the whole county. Your bottom is pretty sensational too. I'd go so far as to say it's the most spectacularly pert arse I've ever seen.'

Frozen in position, I'm trying to crush the ball to

powder. Alexander lifts up my wrist, opens my fingers and takes the ball from me. He drops it on the table and it rolls across the baize until it bumps the cushion with a soft thud. We're so close now you couldn't slot a business card between us. The next thing I hear is my intake of breath as he pulls me tight to him. My back bumps the edge of the table and he takes my face in his hands, tilts my chin upwards and kisses me.

It's a slower, more considered kiss than the one on the dance floor. Maybe it's because we're alone now, or it's quiet, but I'm alive to every sensation. His mouth is warm and he tastes bitter-sweet from the whisky he must have been drinking with his army buddies earlier. It's a gentle kiss at first, but quickly becomes harder, insistent and greedy. I can't help myself; I crave his body under my hands. As we kiss, I tug his shirt out of his trousers and slip my hands beneath the cotton.

It is the first time I've felt his bare flesh beneath my fingers and I feel almost faint with lust as my hands settle on the smooth skin of his back. The bunched muscles tense and ripple as I press my fingers against them. There's intense pleasure in his sigh when I slide my hands higher to the ridges of his shoulder blades. His response makes me dizzy with power. The tiny down hairs on my neck rise and my skin tingles as his tongue explores my mouth. His fingers drift lower, stroking the bare flesh between my shoulders and my whole body tightens with desire.

'Oh . . .'

The rasp of a zip is loud in the quiet room. Cool air

whispers across my back as the side of my dress opens under Alexander's guiding hands. He runs his knuckles from the nape of my neck to the base of my spine. Any lower and he will reach my panties . . . It's only the pressure of his chest against mine which is stopping the front of my dress from slipping down.

A shiver wracks me as he pulls the front of my dress away from my breasts. My inner muscles clench almost painfully as his hungry gaze travels slowly up from my now bare breasts to my face.

'You're beautiful.'

He lowers his head and his lips close around my nipple. My sigh of pleasure feels as if it's coming from a place deep inside me that's been buried for a long time. I have fantasised about him touching me like this, kissing me and undressing me. I've fought against those fantasies and now – the flesh-and-blood reality is beyond anything I'd imagined. He flicks his tongue over my nipple and it puckers instantly in response. Then he alternates the flicks by blowing softly on my breast until I squirm with pleasure.

'Not going too fast for you this time?'

My fingers dig into his back so hard I must be hurting him but I don't care. I'm selfish, abandoned, and reckless. 'I'll um . . . ah . . . let you know.'

'I'm sure you will.'

The table digs into me as his mouth comes down on mine again, stealing away my reply. My breathing quickens as he presses his pelvis into mine, leaving me in no doubt of how aroused he is. When he nips the soft skin on the top of my shoulder I whimper out loud with pleasure. He instantly then soothes the place with his tongue. It didn't really hurt and the remedy makes my knees feel soft and the inside of my mouth tingle deliciously. He kisses his way across my décolletage and down to my cleavage, leaving a trail of fire.

Then he stops and looks into my eyes. 'You have far too much on, Miss Cusack.'

'You think?' My voice is ragged, my resistance in shreds.

It's a second before I realise what is coming next because Alexander has sunk to his knees in front of me. He slides the dress over my bottom to my feet, slowly and deliberately, teasing me. Only my panties, and there's not much of those, protect me from the full force of his gaze.

He stands up, shrugs off his jacket and tosses it on to the floor. It's my turn to devour him now as he pulls off his bow-tie and unbuttons the top of his shirt. Those trousers leave nothing to the imagination and I can see how much he wants me. I want him too, my nipples are like pebbles and my muscles clench in anticipation, ready for him. Shamelessly, I run my hands over his backside, revelling in the hardness of his glutes. He needs no further encouragement and his hands cup my bottom, lifting me up on to the edge of the billiard table. Under the baize cloth, the slate bed of the table is hard against my body. From outside the window, there's a shriek and laughter . . . and I am almost naked, lying on a billiard table in a stranger's house, with Alexander

Hunt above me, looking at me as if he wants to devour me whole.

He hooks his fingers into the side of my panties. My damp panties . . . I want him to take them off; I want him inside me. I've never wanted any man to make love to me like I want Alexander to, *but* –

He's in a hurry, pulling down his trousers.

Without warning, my body tenses as I think of how I have ended up here. We've had one proper conversation in our lives, I don't know a thing about him and I've let him strip me naked. The dance, the private room, the locked door, the careful lowering of my defences . . . was it really that easy for him to wear me down?

What Alexander wants, Alexander gets and now I am one of his conquests.

And, yes, he's given me a glimpse of a different side to him, but did he share it because it was one more way of getting me where I am right now?

A scream from outside pierces through the quiet then a cork pops and the sash rattles. People must be right under the window. They can't see us *but* . . . Alexander is above me, trousers and shorts down. Oh *fuck*.

I grab his wrist as he starts to slip my panties over my hips.

'What's the matter?'

'Stop!' I struggle onto my elbows. 'I don't think we should be doing this.'

'You don't think *we* should be doing this?' His jaw-line hardens, but he lifts me up from the table until I'm sitting, painfully aware of my nudity. 'Why not?'

Oh, shit. How did I let things get this far? This situation, this Lauren, is not quite *me*. It's not only the champagne. I don't know myself tonight otherwise I'd never have let Alexander manoeuvre me into this situation.

'It's a bad idea. Terrible, in fact.'

His hiss of frustration cuts through the air. 'For you or me? It didn't seem terrible half a minute ago.'

'For both of us, trust me.'

He sneers. 'Well, thank you for your concern.'

I open my mouth, shut it then shake my head, knowing he wouldn't understand me if I tried to explain why I have to leave. If I let him make love to me, I'll be lost, another of Alexander's conquests, and, boy, I made it so easy for him. He snapped his fingers and I dropped my panties. But that's not the real reason. The real reason is that I wanted to make it easy for him; I wanted to be conquered and after Todd I vowed I'd never feel that vulnerable again. And I sense – no, I *know*, that Alexander is ten times more of a threat to me than Todd ever was.

'Wait. Let me help you.'

'No. I can manage.'

Ignoring me, he lifts me down off the table to the floor where my dress and his mess jacket lie tangled in a heap like two casualties of war. My face is burning as I wriggle my panties back up my thighs and snatch up my dress from the rug. I tug it over my chest and struggle with the zip.

Then I make the mistake of catching sight of my face in the mirror on the wall.

Oh God. Are those my cheeks flushed with booze and sex? My lipstick smudged like I applied it in the dark? My hair half down like I got dragged through a hedge backwards?

Alexander's face appears behind me, his expression unfathomable, buttoned up as tight as his waistcoat. 'I hope you're not regretting this.'

I can't give him an answer. 'I should go now or Immy will guess what I've been doing.'

'I doubt that will be too difficult.'

Oh shit. Does everyone know that I have been fucking Alexander? Except I haven't.

'I'll unlock the door.' With no more than that brittle comment, he produces the key and turns it in the lock. I hover by the door, my only aim to get out of here before anyone sees me; to sober up and try to make sense of what just happened.

'Wait. Don't run away.'

'I'm not running.'

'That's not the way it seems to me.' There's a sharp edge of irritation back in his voice as he blocks the way to the door.

'I *don't* run away.'

He folds his arms. 'Really? Prove it, then. Walk out of here with me and fuck what anyone else thinks.'

Oh, the bastard. He *must* know that I would never back down from a challenge like that. Now I'm caught between the Devil and the Deep Blue Sea; I either do as he wants or I prove him right.

'I have absolutely no problem walking out of here

with you but first', I reply, 'it might be a good idea to zip up your dress properly.'

I've been so focused on getting out of here I haven't even realized. The brush of hands on my skin as he draws up the zip awakens my senses again and when he drops a parting kiss on the back of my neck I want to scream with frustration.

He locks the door behind us and I give a silent sigh of relief that the library is empty. Maybe no one will, after all, know we were in there because, no matter how cavalier Alexander is about anyone guessing, I really want to keep our encounter private while I calm my raging emotions. He may think the world can go to hell and be able to cast off the snide remarks and innuendo, but he's been born to it; he has a hide as tough as a rhino. I don't find it so easy, no matter how confident I may sound.

The music ramps up in volume and the shouting and laughter are louder as he follows me through the book-lined room to the outer door that opens into the vestibule. At the door I hesitate, knowing that I will have to face Immy and the rest of the guests. Will what we have done be written on my face?

Alexander twists the handle and the light and noise hit us. People dash across the hallway, girls giggle on a padded bench, a guy is passed out next to them and a couple are entwined under the stairs. A uniformed butler opens the front door and Rupert, drinking from a bottle of champagne, walks in. My stomach tenses sharply. Was it him underneath the window? Was he spying on us? I tell myself that not even he would have sunk to that, but then he catches sight of us and his mouth turns up in a triumphant smile.

I wish he didn't hang out with Alexander so much. Just because they're cousins doesn't mean they have to be friends. Yet the ties of blood and friendship are strong; I only have to think of my own family and of my sorority sisters to remind me of that. I half wish they were here now, to help me kick Rupert's massive ego into touch.

Alexander mouths 'Fuck' as I curse Rupert and myself. He saunters over with a smug smile and I find myself smoothing down my dress guiltily.

'I must say, Alexander, you're taking this international relations thing very seriously.'

Alexander's eyes glitter dangerously. 'Fuck you, Rupert.'

'Fuck *me*? Haven't you got the wrong person?'

'Tread very carefully.' Alexander's tone drips with danger.

All I want to do is leave. No, all I want to do is rewind to when I was reeling with Angus in the ballroom. Maybe rewind to the moment I rushed out of the welcome dinner and bumped into Alexander in the cloisters. A quick apology then, and I should have walked away, not stayed to fence with him. Not stayed to find out how much I wanted him.

'No offence intended.' Rupert holds up his hands in conciliation then shoots me a glance that makes my skin crawl. 'You seem a little flustered, Lauren.'

I dare not look at Alexander; I don't have to. I can feel the struggle he has not to retaliate. I hate Rupert knowing our private business. I hate the sneering way he speaks and the assumption that I've jumped into bed with Alexander. It's been a week since I arrived – less than a week, and already I have been sucked into a world that I despise.

'While I'd love to engage in scintillating banter, I'm going to find Immy,' I say.

'Lauren, wait.' Alexander's hand brushes my forearm.

'I expect I'll see you later.' I flash him the briefest of smiles before turning my back and heading for the ballroom. I wanted to keep my head down here and immerse myself in this amazing opportunity to study. Yes, I wanted to have a little fun, but I never asked for this: to fall in lust with a man who epitomizes a decadent, privileged world that will use any tactic to get its own way.

He doesn't come after me, of course, not that I want or expect him to. I don't even *know* what I want or expect any more.

And that, of course, is the problem.

Chapter Eight

'Forty—fifteen!'

Immy raises her arm, serves and the ball flies over the net. I may lose the match but I've got this point. People who don't play tennis much don't realize that you have more time than you think; the important thing is not to panic, but to slow down, prepare and *think*. The ball bounces in front of me, I swing my forehand at it – and my racket connects with fresh air.

When she said she can 'get a few balls back', she wasn't joking. The sweet, fun-loving Immy turns into a ruthless demon when she gets a racket in her hand and not even my Wilson can save me from a drubbing – again. It's Thursday of Second Week, five days since the party and, even though my ankle twinges when I lunge for a ball, I'm more than grateful for the distraction. It's been hard concentrating in seminars and although I've made a start on the research for my submission essay my mind keeps wandering to Alexander.

'Sor-rrry!' Immy calls cheerfully from the other side of the net, obviously embarrassed by almost doing a double doughnut on me.

'I'm the one who should be sorry. I can play a lot better than that.'

'Don't worry about it. You can beat me tomorrow if the weather stays dry.'

'You think?' I glance up at the schizophrenic sky. One half is benign and blue, the other steel grey and threatening clouds. As a metaphor for the conflicting emotions I've battled since the ball, it couldn't be more perfect. I zip up my top over my tennis dress, pick up my sports bag from the side of the court and swallow the lump in my throat. Immy's cheeks are pink and she's buzzing with adrenaline as we walk off court towards the Wyckham sports pavilion.

We hover in front of the drinks machine. 'Evian? Coke?' I ask.

'Definitely Coke. Full fat.'

I grab an Evian and we flop down on benches under the pavilion terrace as the first drops of rain fall on the roof. I had to open my bag to get some change for the machine, but I still haven't checked my phone. Alexander has now called three times and texted seven since Saturday night and I have ignored every single one. I have the phone set to 'meeting' and it must be exhausted by vibrating so often, for so long.

The rain comes in sheets now, driven by gusts of wind that were no more than a breeze while we were playing. As I watch the leaves eddying around the court, I come to the conclusion there is something austerely beautiful and melancholy about Oxford in the rain, as long as you're watching it from inside, that is, not squelching through puddles, shivering with cold.

Or perhaps that's purely my state of mind. Or does it remind me of Alexander?

That gorgeous shell around him, the sharp cheekbones, and the uncompromising way he speaks. Is it arrogance – or brutal honesty? He hates bullshitters, that's for sure.

An insistent buzz from the depths of my bag startles me. Immy sips her Coke as I keep my eyes on the rain, driving across the tennis courts.

'Aren't you going to answer that?' she asks.

'I don't think so.'

'It could be your parents.'

'Not this early.'

'Or Professor Handy?'

'I think he's lecturing this morning.'

'Alexander, then?'

The phone stops and I slump with relief, sipping my water as Immy drums her heels against the wooden deck.

My phone buzzes again and, mouthing a curse, I reach into my bag, check the screen, see the number on it and stab the off button.

There's a pause then Immy says quietly, 'You can't keep ignoring him, you know. He won't give up. He'll carry on going until he gets what he wants. That's what Alexander Hunt does.'

Is the reason for my irritation with the phone so obvious?

'He hasn't dealt with Lauren Cusack yet.'

'If you really want him to go away, you'll have to meet him face to face and tell him to leave you alone.'

'I'd have thought ignoring thirteen attempts to contact me might have given him the message by now.'

'Perhaps he feels the messages have been mixed so far.'

'What does that mean?' I sound a little snappy and it's not like me, more like something *he* might say. 'Sorry, Immy, I don't mean to gripe, and you're right. I shouldn't have gone off with him at the ball.'

'I knew something had happened, but you clearly didn't want to talk about it and I didn't want to push you.'

I raise an eyebrow and she sighs. 'OK. I *did* want to be nosy, but you clammed up so tight on the way home, that I knew I'd have to be patient and wait for you to tell me what went on. It's almost killed me.'

I have to smile, even in the midst of angsting over the situation.

'What went on? I'm not sure myself. Alexander and I, well, we kissed and things went further than I'd expected.' A whole lot further, but that would be way too much information.

'Did you shag him?'

I can't be angry with Immy for being so direct. 'No, not exactly, although we did almost everything but.'

Her jaw drops. 'Everything *but*!'

'Yes.' The image returns: Alexander taking off my dress, lifting me on to the billiard table, climbing on top of me. My body's response to him was about as direct as it could be.

'Oh. My. God.'

'You think that's crazy, that I almost had sex with Alexander Hunt and then stopped him?'

'Not crazy. I understand why you'd want to shag him. He is absolutely gorgeous and you won't need me to tell you that half the girls in England would kill to get him into bed. You must have made a very big impression on him. Huge, in fact . . .' She hesitates and bites her lip. 'I don't want to worry you, but I did try to warn you about him, not that I know him that well – I'm not sure anyone knows him that well, not even Rupert.'

'That's what worries me too. If his closest friends don't know him, who does?'

'Rupert says that Alexander doesn't get close to people. Not since his mother was killed.'

'What? His mother was *killed*? I had no idea!' I shudder and feel almost physically sick. Poor Alexander.

'Yes, she died in a car accident while taking Alexander back to school. I think he was thirteen and Emma, his sister, was in the car with them. I don't know exactly what happened, but Alexander and Emma were badly hurt and their mother died instantly.'

'That is truly awful. I can't bear to think of anything happening to my parents. I worry about Daddy as it is, with his public role.'

'My parents drive me insane at times, but I love them to bits. I don't think any of the Hunts have ever really got over it. Not that you get over losing someone, but there's more to it. Rupert says that Alexander's father blames him for the crash.'

'What? Why would he do that?'

Immy shrugs. 'Rupert's not sure but he says it wasn't Alexander's fault. Alexander's father is a shit. He's a general in the Guards and he wanted Alexander to join the same regiment. General Hunt makes General Tilney look like a pussycat.'

'So he went and joined the Paras . . .' I think back to the hints Alexander dropped about his choice of regiment and Immy's words make sense. 'It's complicated' doesn't even begin to cover Alexander. My stomach swirls. I wonder how losing his mother at that age – and, worse, being blamed for it – has affected his relationships with women. Then again, the more I hear about him, the more I think he should come with a danger sign and barbed wire around him.

Immy lowers her voice as a couple of guys in tennis whites stroll out on to the terrace. 'I can't tell you what to do about Alexander. I can understand the appeal. He's gorgeous, rich . . . and seemingly unattainable.'

'I never set out to attain him, that's the whole point, and his money doesn't impress me.'

'Hey, I know that and that's precisely why he's pursuing you so hard. The fact he's called Hunt is no coincidence.'

'That had occurred to me.'

'I'd hate to see you get your heart broken and if you're looking for an easy ride you couldn't have picked a worse person.' She glances away from me, perhaps a little guilty for offering advice – after all her own love life isn't perfect – yet I can't deny that everything she has told me fits with my own experience of Alexander.

'I wasn't looking for anything.'

'Which is precisely why Alexander has come along now. Doesn't it always happen like that? Fuck, it's bucketing down. I wish I could keep my Audi in Oxford during term time, but the parking for students is non-existent – unless of course you're Alexander and have your own garage.'

'So that was his house I went to? It's not rented?'

'I think it was his mother's when she was studying here, and it was rented out until Alexander started his degree. I'm not absolutely certain; the Hunts have a lot of property. Now, we have two choices, cycle home and get soaked or persuade that hotty over there from the Blues tennis squad to give us a lift back to college. What's it to be?'

The hotty, a tanned, lean blond who reminds me of Eric from *True Blood*, needs no persuasion to run us home once Immy works her charms on him. I spare a thought for Freddie as 'Eric', a.k.a. Skandar, scrawls his number on Immy's palm before we dash into the Lodge at Wyckham.

Back in my room, I dry my hair after my shower, trying to find answers behind the mirror. I crave Alexander like some kind of new drug that's been custom-made to give me my own unique high – and the fact that I want him that much only confirms my determination to go cold turkey.

The morning sun shines through the window as I scroll down through my notes on my iMac. We're nearing

Halloween and the rays don't even have enough power to warm my hands as I type. It's Saturday, Third Week officially starts tomorrow and I plan to get as much work as possible done today because a bunch of us are going to dinner at the Cherwell Boathouse on the river and tomorrow I'm heading for the V&A with a couple of people from my course. I went with Todd on his one and only visit to London, but he was bored within an hour and dragged me off to some pub.

There is so much I want to see there that I can't even begin to think about it, but the costume display is sensational. I'm disappointed that I missed the Fashion in Motion live catwalk events they held over the summer, but as a consolation there's a new exhibition of Photography and Truthfulness that's a must-see for me. If there's time, I'd like to call into Harvey Nicks while I'm in South Kensington tomorrow, but I guess I'm so close to London now that I can always go back another day.

I undo the catch on my window to let in some fresh air, and the chapel clock chimes noon. Last night, I lay awake thinking about the stuff Immy told me about Alexander's background and the car accident. The thought of what he and his sister went through makes me shudder even now. His father too; no matter what kind of pressure he's placed on Alexander, it can't have been easy for a man like that to raise two young children on his own, even with the help of the nanny I guess they had. Not that his family troubles are any concern of mine, especially as he hasn't called again since yesterday. Hopefully, he's finally given up hassling me.

And that makes you feel, how, Lauren?

'Arghhh.'

I cross to the window as if I'll find any kind of answer in the austere beauty of Wyckham's Jacobean front quad, where the statues of its stern founders gaze back at me through sightless eyes. Voices drift up from the path that skirts the quad, and I spot one of the younger porters walking through the arch that leads into our staircase. His footsteps thump up the stairs, growing louder and louder until they stop outside my door, and then there's a knock.

'Lauren Cusack?'

He knows who I am already, but I open the door and play along. 'Who wants to know?'

He grins. 'There's a courier in the Lodge with a parcel for you. Normally, we'd sign for it and we don't allow strangers into college, but he says he won't hand it over to anyone but you.'

The proverbial lightbulb clicks on in my mind. After the emergency trip to the ballgown emporium, I asked my mother to send over my Alexander McQueen dress in case I get invited to any more of these white-tie events.

'OK. I think I know what that might be. Sorry you had to trudge up here. I'll come down and collect it.'

Five minutes later I am in the anteroom of the Lodge, staring at the contents of the parcel, in shock. The package is not from my parents and it is not an Alexander McQueen gown. It is much smaller and it is from a different Alexander.

The Cartier necklace nestles in its box. It's a white-gold chain with a trilogy of pink diamonds glittering in the light. It is classy, understated and just about the most beautiful thing I have ever seen. I know from the design and the cut and colour of the diamonds that it must have cost tens of thousands of pounds.

And I cannot possibly accept it. Shutting the lid on the box, I dash out of the Lodge on to the street. The courier's van is still parked outside and he is climbing into the driver's seat. I run over and bang on the passenger window.

'I can't take this. You have to have it back.'

'Miss?' The window opens and he stares at me as if I'm a crazy woman, yet I know I'd be crazy to accept it. No matter how much I sympathize with what happened to his mother, the fact remains and always will: what Alexander wants, Alexander gets. He will do anything to get it. I feel as if I'm being hunted. I am his quarry. He never gives up. He has to win. He will do anything he can to get me into his bed. Including, it seems, buying me.

'Take it back to the store.' I drop the box on the passenger seat. 'Please.'

'Miss, wait!'

Too late. I'm running back to college, through the postern gate in the great oak door and along the quad to my room. By the time I've raced up the staircase, my lungs are about to burst, but I don't care. I lie on the bed, staring at the ceiling, wondering why.

What made him think he could buy me? Does he think I'm that easy to manipulate? I can buy my own jewellery; I don't need a guy to do it, yet the image of the necklace glittering in its box is seared on my memory. It was heart-stoppingly beautiful and also a symbol of how far apart we are in the way we view the world and our places in it.

I have work to do, but it proves impossible to concentrate over the afternoon. Every time I open a book or sit down at my iMac, my mind is filled with the necklace and why Alexander sent it. It was totally beautiful, a piece I'd have definitely picked out for myself if I could ever have justified the extravagance.

If it was simply to get my attention, then he has it. If it was a peace offering, it's had the opposite effect. Why does this happen now, when I finally got my chance to be independent and start again, free from the expectations of my parents and Todd's shitty behaviour? It feels as if Alexander Hunt has marched into my life when I *so* wasn't looking for him and now he won't leave me alone, like I'm some kind of challenge he has to conquer because he can or thinks he can. Even if I had been looking for someone, he's the very last man on the planet I'd have chosen, no matter how much he drives me insane with lust. *But*, comes the rogue, inveigling whisper in the corner of my mind, *he is the ultimate challenge for me.*

Now I am sitting on the edge of the window, looking out over the rooftops of Oxford. The dome of the

Radcliffe Camera is bathed in sunlight, with the finials and towers beyond pointing up to the sky. Bells chime, as they always do, and in the distance the fields and countryside dream under the sky. It is the classic idyllic Oxford scene that you can buy on a thousand post-cards around the city. It is *my* dream, so why do I feel so confused?

I think of calling Immy as soon as she gets back from her tennis 'lesson' with Skandar at the sports centre, but I don't want to play gooseberry and this is something I don't feel I can share with her until I've composed myself. How will Alexander feel when he finds out I rejected his gift? Angry, hurt, upset? It gives me no pleasure or triumph to cause him pain yet I still know I've done the right thing. The wind rattles the window and it's growing cold in here. I fasten the catch, and the bells are muffled. Everything is quiet as I sit on my bed, my knees hunched to my chest, before the peace is shattered by a barrage of thuds on my door.

Chapter Nine

'Lauren. Open the door, please.'

'Go away, Alexander.'

I hug my knees tighter as a brief silence is followed by more urgent taps.

'No.' His voice is louder now.

'You're wasting your time.'

'If I have to sit here all night until you let me in, I'll do it. I've spent the night in less comfortable places.'

I'm on the edge of the bed now, my heart beating faster.

'Then you'll have to sleep out there on the landing.'

His voice is loud through the wood. 'That's ridiculous.'

I jump up and hiss through the door. 'Me? Ridiculous? Keep your voice down. Everyone in college will hear you.'

'Good. Let them. I don't care.'

Immy will be home soon and I don't want her to hear this, or anyone else for that matter. Tentatively, I twist the Yale lock and open the door a few inches. Alexander paces the landing, grim-faced. The door squeaks and he rounds and stares at me like I'm an alien. Maybe he really didn't expect me to open it.

'You'd better come in before someone calls the porters.'

He gives a satisfied nod. 'About time.'

What? I wish I hadn't opened up, but it's too late now and I back inside as he pushes his way in. He's never been in my room before and, now he is, he seems to fill the space – although the walls, the floor, the furniture may as well not exist because Alexander has only one focus and that is me.

His blue eyes burn as he speaks in that quiet, unflinching voice. 'What do you think you're doing?'

'What do I think I'm doing? You're the one battering down my door.'

'A, I wasn't battering it down. Believe me, you'd have known about it if that was the case. B, you call racing off like that at the ball nothing? Ignoring my every call and text, nothing? Throwing that necklace back in my face, *nothing*?'

I am furious at this. 'You do know that your behaviour since the ball has verged on the stalker-ish?'

He grins as if I just handed him a huge compliment. 'I'll carry on stalking you until you see sense.'

'You call sending me that ten-thousand-dollar necklace sensible?'

'Actually, it was nearer twenty thousand.' His smile is wicked and sexy and so *wrong* as he adds, 'Pounds.'

'That makes it worse. You can't buy me no matter how wealthy or powerful you think you are.'

'*Buy* you? I sent you the necklace because I thought

you'd like it, and as for powerful? That's a joke when you have me calling you ten times a day, unable to concentrate on my work, lying awake at night thinking about you in that dress and out of it!'

My nipples peak under my top at the vision of him peeling off my ballgown and my throat is dry as I answer, 'Wow, I have to hand you full marks for frankness.'

'Actually, I always get full marks for everything.' The arrogant twist to his mouth drives me crazy in every sense of the word. 'Come on, Lauren, let's stop baiting each other and call a truce, although I have to admit the sparring is a massive turn-on.'

'You *get off* on me insulting you?'

'Oh, I get off on you all the time.'

His hands slip around my back and rest on my waist. Infuriatingly, I do not move. Even worse, I have an overwhelming urge to touch him back, but know that if I do there will be no going back.

'And here's me thinking that I've been driving you insane . . .' I murmur, balling my fists at my sides.

'You have, but not in the way you think. You surely can't deny that you want to find out what would happen if we do call a truce for a while? How exciting this could be for both of us? Because, Lauren, you strike me as a woman who doesn't back down from a challenge . . .'

My instinct ought to tell me I'm being sold a line, but the one instinct that truly matters is telling me to take the risk and embrace the danger – to revel in it My hands move to the waistband of his jeans, resting so lightly as I hover on the brink.

'You know what I think?' he says.

'I'm never sure what you're thinking, Mr Hunt.'

He laughs softly. 'I think that you think I'm some kind of player who uses his charm to get girls into bed and then leaves them.'

I burst out laughing. 'What charm?'

'Exactly.'

I shake my head as much at myself as him and my resolve is melting as fast as an ice cube tossed into a hot drink. 'All I've seen so far is a guy who's frank to the point of being brutal, a sarcastic, domineering egomaniac who thinks the world should fall at his feet.'

'I ought to warn you what will happen if you insult me again.' His eyes shine with sensual threat. 'I've never met a woman who's given me so many sleepless nights.'

I *want* to believe him . . . the same way I wanted to believe Todd so many times and that makes me wary.

'I'm not going to be flattered by that,' I say, yet my voice has softened, and I *am* softening.

'I can see that, but would you please tell me why you sent back the necklace?'

'Because . . . it felt as if you were trying to buy me.'

'I wasn't. I was simply giving you a gift. I wanted to make you happy and I'm sorry it had the opposite effect.'

'The necklace is truly fabulous, but you didn't need to spend that kind of money to impress me.'

'Lauren, of course I didn't have to. I'm well aware you can buy your own jewellery.'

What can I say? My other jewellery has come from

my family and my own occasional indulgence, but I'd never have dared splash out on a Cartier necklace.

'You *do* like it?' he asks, and the genuine doubt in his eyes is far harder to resist than his self-assurance.

I take a deep breath, knowing I probably just stepped off a cliff.

'I love it.'

There. I've said it out loud and there's no going back now. In seconds, he gathers me into his arms. His sweater is soft beneath my fingers as I push my tongue inside his mouth, longing to taste every part of him again. He deepens the kiss and it feels amazing, even better than at his house and at the ball. His fingers linger at the hem of my top and every nerve end tingles from my scalp to my toes.

'Take this off.' His voice is low and raw and my hands tremble a little as I slip my sweater over my head and toss it on the floor.

He sits on my bed and beckons me to stand between his thighs. I shiver a little as the cool air whispers over my skin. Alexander gathers me to him, his big hands settling on either side of my hips. When he rests his forehead on my midriff and inhales, as if he wants to breathe me in, the pleasure is so intense I tremble.

'You've driven me mad for two weeks.' His voice resonates against my ribcage. As he looks up at me again, I catch my breath at the intensity of desire I see in his eyes. 'Do you have to look like this?'

'Like what?'

He slides my mini over my legs to the top of my

128

thigh-highs. 'Like this. Sexy, maddening, so fuckable I've almost broken down your door every night since the ball.'

I exhale sharply as he hitches my skirt higher over my butt. His palms rest on my hip bones then slowly, agonizingly, he slides my panties down over my hips to the tops of my thighs. I can't hide how much I want him now and, more important, I don't want to.

Dropping my skirt, I push him back on to my bed and he pulls me down on top of him. Finesse has gone. We scrabble at each other's clothes in our lust to get to each other's bodies. A button pings off his shirt as I struggle to kick off my boots and panties. My bra's gone too and when he kisses my nipples, I cry out. Above the heat and weight of his body, I'm aware of my nakedness and complete exposure to him.

But I'm not going to stop.

And he knows it from my moan of sheer ecstasy as he presses down on my clit with the pad of his thumb.

'Good?'

'Oh yes.'

His gentle strokes on my swollen nub make me shiver and force whimpers of pleasure from my lips. My breathing is fast and shallow, but I don't care any more. When he trails his fingers through the stick moistness of my pussy, I buck my hips. I'm already on the edge of coming, right here on top of him. I don't have any doubts this time, or none I want to recognize now. I want Alexander inside me, filling me up.

The leather of his belt is stiff as I free it from the

buckle. My fingers struggle with the button fly of his jeans and his hand closes around mine.

'Wait.'

The single bed creaks as he climbs off it. Propping myself up on my elbows, I drink in the sight of him, stripping off his trousers and boxer shorts in front of my eyes.

My body spasms with desire for him. He's broad-shouldered and bare-chested and I realize it is the first time I have seen him without the barrier of clothes or uniform. His body has a restrained power, with its lean tight sinews and smooth skin stretched taut over muscles. He finds a condom from his wallet and sheathes himself while I imprint every detail on my mind, so I can recall the moment when I first saw him naked.

There are tan lines on his neck and arms. Dark springy hair dusts the centre of his chest and arrows down to his navel and groin. Broad shoulders balance a narrow waist, and the hard guns and ridges of muscle on his stomach testify to the life he leads that he won't tell me about. As does the puckering of white flesh, a thin angry line a couple of inches long, beneath his left shoulder blade.

No need for words. We both know what we want and I straddle him as he lies back on my bed. His fingers tighten under my bottom and he guides me on to his shaft. As the tip nudges inside me, I cry out. I can feel his thighs grow rigid beneath me and his cock swells and hardens until he's stretching me to the limit. I'm full of Alexander and it feels as if I've been waiting for this for ever. He slides in deeper until my bottom rests on his thighs and I moan as I take him all the way in.

His eyes cloud with concern. 'Is this OK?'

'*Amazing.*'

It's all he needs. He pushes upwards, his cock nudging at the very core of me. I have to brace my hands on the bed, clutching at the cover. He thumbs my clitoris, sliding through the wetness.

'Is that good? I want it to be good for you.'

'It's good . . . Believe me, it's good.' He carries on stroking me and I know I can't take much more because the tell-tale pulse of my climax ripples out from my sex. My climax starts to fizz through my limbs as the outside world recedes.

Springs creak, and the headboard bangs the wall as Alexander groans and lifts me off the bed with his hips. He has both hands around my thighs now, but I don't need him to touch me any more. I'm on my way and nothing can stop me as he thrusts into me hard and fast. Our breathing is a ragged mess, sweat pours off us and the whole room feels as if it might collapse as we fuck each other like we're fighting for our lives. The last thing I remember before his body goes rigid as iron is the intensity on his face. Then my own orgasm explodes through me, and feels as if it will go on for ever.

The bedcover is soft under my skin. The air is chilly over my breasts yet my arm and shoulder are hot and sticky. The sharp scent of sweat and sex clings to the air. I don't know how long I have been here, perhaps thirty seconds, perhaps a few minutes. I have no way of judging, but I know I am lying on my back, with Alexander's naked body pressed against me.

I turn my head and his face is inches from my hair, his eyes closed with faint shadows beneath. His breathing is rhythmic and steady. He's still and silent now yet the image of his face as he came inside me so violently is etched on my mind. It was pain, need, anger, release. Who knows? I don't think I ever saw that much intensity before. Have I done that to him? Was it release or triumph or aggression? I only have one other man to compare it to but Todd . . . deep down, I know there is no comparison and that *does* scare me and I don't know why.

The room is bathed in light of the darkest blue and I shiver as the unheated air licks at my sweat-sheened skin. The chimes of the clock filter through my window, muffled yet unmistakeable. There's a real world out there, beyond this room, beyond the cloistered walls of this college. Beyond Oxford. Fighting wars, killing, a dirty, bloody business, and Alexander is at the very heart of it. In entering his world, even at the fringe, those things have edged their way into my world now.

He opens his eyes. He isn't smiling but he looks at peace. 'What's the matter?' he asks me.

'Nothing,' I say. 'Absolutely nothing.'

'No regrets that you've screwed the enemy.'

'You're not my enemy.'

He rolls over on to his stomach and levers himself up

on his elbow. He touches my nose with his and whispers, 'Thank God, we got that one clear.'

He is naked, face down on my bed and I can't take my eyes from his body. His toes hang over the end of my single bed, and his calves are bunched muscle beneath a smooth curve of skin. Above the taut hamstrings, his butt is just awesome, sculpted and firm with big powerful glutes.

'What?' he demands.

'I couldn't possibly say.'

'You're checking out my arse, aren't you?'

I blush a little. 'Is it a crime?'

'No, but it's . . . a little disconcerting.'

'Well, I'm delighted to have finally disconcerted Alexander Hunt.'

Chapter Ten

Alexander washes in the vanity unit of my little closet and then dresses by the muted light of the bedside lamp. I am still naked, but he has pulled the cover over me to keep me warm and drawn the curtains to shut out the October evening. We could have stayed in bed all evening, but he's told me he wants to take me out to dinner 'to keep my strength up', he says, and I think I may humour him. I watch him shrug his shorts and jeans on and pick his shirt up from the rug by my desk

'Fuck.'

I feel a frisson of triumph as we both notice the missing button. It's halfway down the front of his shirt so he can't leave it open or tuck it in his trousers.

'Call it a war trophy,' I say.

'If you're going to wreck my clothes like this every time we have sex, I'll need to bring a spare supply with me.'

That phrase 'every time' does exciting things to my body.

Giving up on the shirt, he shrugs and swivels my office chair round to face me. It's one thing being naked while we're making love, quite another to display myself in front of him while he watches. He sits up straight in the chair, forearms resting on the arms, legs spread apart, and says, 'Your turn.'

Those eyes don't leave me for a second as I push back the bed cover and rest my feet on the boards. The polished planks are cool and smooth beneath my soles. I lost my thigh-highs to him the second time we had sex and I spot them now, one draped over the waste bin, the other next to it.

'Would you care to pass me my robe, please? It's on the armchair.'

He folds his arms. 'Not really.'

'I have to take a shower and get changed. I can't go to a restaurant in the nude.'

'Mmm. Perhaps not, but I'd like to see it.'

I'm laughing, but I'm also fizzing and wet again. We will both die of hunger if one of us doesn't get out of this room. 'Maybe I can get my thigh-highs back, then?'

He frowns then breaks out in a grin. 'Ah, you mean these?' He gets out of his chair and retrieves them from the floor. 'Thigh-highs? That's a much better description than hold-ups. I like it and you can wear these, with my blessing.'

'Why, thank you, sir.'

Once he's back in my chair, he watches me as I roll the stockings up my legs.

'Um. I need to put some fresh panties on before I go to the bathrooms.'

'Why?'

'Because . . .'

His blue eyes twinkle. 'I'd rather you didn't wear any at all.'

'What?'

'I'd like you to come out to dinner without any knickers on.'

My hesitation makes him smile. 'It's not a crime, Lauren, and only you and I will know about it.'

He pushes himself out of the chair. 'You can wear a top, if you must, but only because I don't want the rest of the male population seeing your incredible breasts.'

'You are outrageous.'

'Good. I'd hate to be predictable. And there's something else. I want you to wear this.'

He picks up his jacket from the floor and reaches into an inside pocket in the silk lining. Light glimmers as he pulls out the Cartier necklace I rejected. He holds it up and the diamonds sparkle in the lamplight.

'You kept it.' My voice is quiet.

He comes over to me, kisses the back of my neck. I am still naked except for the black thigh-highs and in the mirror above the washbasin, I see a girl with flushed cheeks and tangled blonde hair whose eyes shine with sex and happiness.

'You look like a Parisian courtesan,' he whispers. 'Will you accept the necklace now?'

'It's beautiful . . .'

'I know that. I spent an hour choosing it myself.'

'I'd love to accept it, not because it cost a lot of money but because you want me to have it. I can't believe you didn't return it to the store after I sent the courier away. Most men would have given up.'

His smile is slight and knowing. I should be annoyed at his nerve yet I'm only excited.

'*Vincit qui patitur*' he says quietly before kissing my neck.

'What's that? The family motto?'

'Of course.' His hands are on my breastbone, draping the necklace round my neck where the diamonds shimmer with a rosy fire.

'Oh, of *course*. And what does that mean? "Live long and prosper"?'

He shoots me such a look. 'You're laughing at me, Lauren.'

'I wouldn't dare . . . but what *does* it mean?'

'He conquers who endures.' His mouth quirks in a smile as he fastens the clasp on the necklace. It lies perfectly across my décolletage as if it were made especially for me.

'Wow. That's one hell of a motto to live up to, but thank you for the necklace. You must know how much I love it.' I turn round, resting my hands on his waist.

'I hoped you would. Thank you for accepting it and, please, never think that I'm trying to buy you again.' He trails a finger down my spine, resting his palm over one butt cheek.

'I'll try not to.' Standing on tiptoes, I kiss him.

'Much as it pains me to say this, you'd better get dressed or we may well be found by your scout in three weeks' time, dead of starvation.'

'But with smiles on our faces?'

He gives my bottom a sharp slap.

'Ow. That's outrageous and sexist!'

'It is, but I don't give a toss. Now get dressed, please, before I do something genuinely outrageous.'

In the end, I decide on a sapphire-blue silky top I bought last season but haven't had the chance to wear yet, teamed with my favourite black mini. It's a bit of a risk when I'm also going *sans* panties, but what the hell. While I've freshened up, brushed out my bed-head hair and applied a little mascara and gloss, Alexander has evidently made a few phone calls because a silver Bentley Continental with tinted windows is waiting for us on the street outside the Lodge.

'Is this your car?'

Alexander smiles. 'Not mine, strictly speaking, but I do have the use of it. Now, please get in before I cancel dinner and take you straight back to bed.'

Twenty minutes later, the driver, who needs no direction, opens the doors for us outside a manor house deep in the Oxfordshire countryside. Its honeyed stone facade seems vaguely familiar to me though I've never been here before. Alexander takes my hand and we walk up the gravelled path to the front door, then I see the name: *Le Manoir*.

'I've seen this place before, on TV. It's owned by a French chef.'

'That's right.'

'Don't tell me you know him.'

'Not personally, no.'

The door opens and a hostess greets us. 'Good evening, Mr Hunt, sir. Miss Cusack.'

He flashes her a smile that has her virtually melting on to the flagstones. 'Hello, Sarah.'

'So you don't know Monsieur Blanc but you know

the place well enough to get a table at an hour's notice,' I murmur as Sarah leads us into the restaurant. Alexander squeezes my hand and whispers back.

'I called in a favour.'

There's an ice bucket on a stand next to our table, which overlooks the moonlit gardens. Alexander pulls back my seat for me and I descend elegantly on to the chair. There's only the mini between me and the leather seat, and that makes me feel a dangerous combination of vulnerable and wanton.

Magically, a waiter appears. 'Shall I serve the champagne, sir?' he asks.

Alexander nods while the waiter extracts the bottle from the ice bucket.

'Is your seat comfortable?' His hand rests on my knee beneath the white tablecloth. I squirm a little, my bottom slipping against the chair. His fingers climb a little higher while the waiter's back is turned.

'Yes. Thank you.' I have that feeling, when you're itching to say something intimate and/or inappropriate to your dinner companion, but you're perched on your chair, trying to pretend you're as demure as a nun.

His hand creeps higher to the top of my thigh-highs as the cork pops gently from the bottle. The waiter hovers beside us, holding the bottle wrapped in a white napkin. I lick my lips.

'Would you like to taste it, sir?' the waiter asks.

'Taste it? Of course I do, unless Lauren wants to taste it for me. *Do* you want to taste it, Lauren?'

I smile demurely. 'Oh, I always want to taste it, Alexander.' Oh my, can you get arrested for coming in the middle of a Michelin-starred restaurant?

Taking the flute, I raise it to my lips. Alexander's hand is gone now and he's sitting opposite me, his expression as innocent as a baby. Bubbles burst against my palate, tickling my tongue. It's Dom Perignon and is every bit as divine as I'd expected; however I may not have noticed if my glass had held rocket fuel because my brain is full of the image of Alexander's dark head between my legs, tasting *me*.

'That's fine,' I say, putting down my flute.

The waiter tops our glasses up and Alexander nods. 'Thank you, we'll look after ourselves from now on.'

'I don't know how you dare do that,' I say after the waiter has gone, the imprint of Alexander's fingertips still burning into my skin. 'What if he'd noticed?'

He shrugs. 'He didn't.'

He sips his Dom but I'm left toying with the stem of my glass, mind working overtime. I'm here with Alexander at last, we've had sex and we're hopefully going to have a whole lot more. All the turmoil of the past two weeks has led to me giving in to him in the end. His face is briefly anxious and he reaches out and touches my arm.

'Still no regrets?'

I shake my head firmly. The shiver that runs through me at the thought of his hands on my body gives me my answer. 'No.'

'Good. I hope you don't mind me calling the car.

I wanted to take you somewhere special for our first proper date together.'

'Of course not. It's totally gorgeous here.'

'I like it too, not that I get the chance to come here very often.' This makes me wonder who else he has brought here, and Immy's Valentina comment springs to mind, but I push it away. It's over between Alexander and his ex. Immy told me and, more important, so has Alexander. Maybe he's had meals here with his father or friends. Maybe his mother brought him here, though he was so young when she died that I somehow doubt it. There are so many questions I want to ask about his family and his past, let alone his present, yet everything is so new between us.

He opens a menu and hands it to me. 'Hungry?'

'Mmm, ravenous.'

After we've made our choices from the menu and the waiter has left us alone again, Alexander says. 'So, now we've had sex, I suppose we'd better get to know each other a little better.'

I laugh. 'I'm surprised you need to ask me. You already seemed to know who I was at the pub. Incidentally, I still don't approve of you breaking that guy's nose. How did they not press charges?'

'Firstly, you'll be pleased to know it wasn't broken, only extremely painful for a day or so. Secondly, they're lucky the bar staff didn't call the porters or they might have been sent down. I hear they've already been in trouble for harassing women at their own colleges. One more strike and they'll be out.'

'And you? What if you'd been reported to college?'

He shrugs. 'I can't say I'm quaking in my boots at the thought of being hauled before the Master.'

That figures. I have to agree the Master would hardly hold much terror for a guy who's – allegedly – in special forces. 'So you wouldn't care if you got sent down?' I tease him.

'I'd rather it didn't happen, but I expect I'd survive. What about you?'

'Me? I can't think of any reason why I might be sent down but I'd die of shame if I was.'

'Why?'

He's so direct, so challenging, far worse than a tutorial with Professor Rafe. 'Because I don't want to fail.'

There's a flicker of something in his expression: recognition, empathy? I'm not sure. 'Or let down your parents?' he offers.

'No. I don't want to let *myself* down. Like I told you, they didn't want me to come here to do my master's, in fact they couldn't see any reason why I even had to leave the States. I think my father also worries about me . . . but he has no need. I wanted to come here to have the best tutors, and the galleries and museums on my doorstep. In fact, I'm going to the V&A tomorrow with some people from my seminar group.'

He frowns.

'Something wrong?'

'No. That sounds . . . thrilling.'

'You aren't convincing me you're an art lover.'

He feigns a hurt expression. 'On the contrary, I love

art. In fact, I think the V&A has a couple of watercolours on long-term loan from Falconbury right now. A Turner and a Ruskin. You might want to go and take a look while you're there.'

I am aware my mouth is open as the waiter brings our starters. Alexander picks up his spoon. 'Please. Don't let your velouté get cold.'

The food is beyond delicious, but I have to pass on dessert and cheese, no matter how much of an appetite I worked up earlier today.

We've talked a little about Falconbury, although he doesn't seem keen to go into detail. He's far happier to talk about Sandhurst and hear about my life in Washington. Alexander knows who my father is and he's very well informed on Dad's views on issues like gun control and the US economy. I'm not sure I agree with all his comments and I tell him so. At times, he can be forthright almost to the point of rudeness, but I can hold my own, and this is my territory.

Besides, I've realized I thrive on the tension and verbal foreplay between us. It makes me feel alive. With Todd, I think he thought I was there to tag along. Towards the end of our relationship, I felt as if I only existed to fuel his self-esteem, while he existed to erode mine. He wasn't a bad guy inside, only a hollow one. Whereas I sense a core of solid steel in Alexander – one that's wired up for electricity if necessary – that excites and disturbs me.

Squashing down the reservations that have begun to nag at the back of my mind again, I sip the last of the Pouilly-Fumé we'd ordered to go with the sole we both had for entrées. It's a clean, crisp, elegant drink that may match the food but is the opposite of the thoughts I'm having while he sits opposite me. Alexander is on to dessert, having related an outrageous story from his Sandhurst days that I'm still not sure whether I should believe. He looks more relaxed than I've ever seen him, apart from when we had sex, so I decide to seize the chance to ask about his family.

'So did you join the Paras to annoy your father?' I ask, as he finishes up his *clafoutis*.

He gives a snort of derision. 'Well, he was incandescent when I announced it, which was rather satisfying, but there were other reasons, some of which I'd rather not discuss over dinner.'

'Or any time?'

'Maybe it would be better not to.' He dabs the napkin to his mouth and smiles at me, but I know it's largely to distract me from a line of questioning that he's not comfortable with.

I try a new tack. 'I admitted I hate to fail. What about you? What do you call success?'

'Always being at the very top of my game.'

'The *top*? *Always*?'

'What point is there if you're not?'

'Is that at work?'

'That's a given, but in other things too. Sport, academically. I don't see the point of settling for anything less than your best.'

'Wow, and they say British guys are the masters of self-deprecation,' I joke.

'Only in Richard Curtis films. I find it a lot simpler to be a complete and utter bastard.' His eyes glint when he says it, throwing down the gauntlet to me again.

'That's not true. You just like playing a part.'

'Not at all. What you see is what you get with me. I go straight for what I want, no matter what it costs.'

'I had noticed. What if I hadn't opened the door to you earlier or thrown you out?'

'I knew you wouldn't,' he replies without hesitation. 'Coffee?'

'No, thanks.'

'Good. I don't think I can keep my hands off you much longer.'

That wicked sparkle is back in his eyes and I am more conscious than ever of my nakedness beneath the skirt. 'You'll have to wait until we get back to college unless you want the restaurant staff to call the police.'

'Ah.' He gives a grimace that I think is meant to be apologetic. Yet, somehow, I sense he's not the least bit sorry for what he's about to say.

'What have you done, Alexander?' My voice is wary.

'I'm afraid we're not going back to college. I booked a room here. I thought it might be a nicer place to spend our first night than your single bed or my place.'

A room? At an hour's notice?

Actually it's a suite, with a sitting room that's lined with some modern original artworks that I actually like. In the bedroom, there's art deco furnishing and a fabulous hand-painted closet. It's chic, stylish and understated, yet all of it pales in comparison to the bed or, more accurately, what is on it: a neat, Louis Vuitton case with a silver Kate Spade luggage tag with my name on it. In my handwriting. My heart beats a little faster as he walks over to me.

'If I'm not mistaken, that's my overnight bag.'

He lingers behind me, his breath warm against the nape of my neck. 'You're not and it is.'

'O-Kayy.' I stare at the bag, recalling the time he was on the phone while I went to the bathroom after we'd had sex. He must have packed and got my bag into the car and had it brought up here. That means he went through my closet and drawers, choosing clean clothes, underwear . . . He surely can't have been in my room earlier, that's not possible, and yet Alexander has as good as told me that he thinks anything is possible.

His lips brush the skin at the base of my neck .

'My God, I do believe you planned this whole thing,' I whisper.

I hear his voice at my ear, in a perfect imitation of my East Coast accent. 'I guess I did.'

I start to unfasten his shirt, stopping at the open front where he lost a button.

'I don't see an overnight bag for you. How are you going to manage without clothes?'

'I guess I'll have to cope somehow.'

'I guess you will.' I undo the final button and pull his shirt from his trousers, marvelling again at the warmth and solidity of his skin under my hands. The sight and feel of that chest and those abs has me in knots of desire and I close my eyes and press my face to his chest.

There's a soft whirr as he unzips the side of my mini and it falls to the floor, leaving me naked from the waist down. Alexander lets out a long slow breath and cups my butt with his hands.

'Do you know how much I want you?'

I tilt back my head and close my eyes. 'I'm getting there . . .'

He eases my top over my head and tosses it on to the bed, then unhooks my bra and throws it after the top.

'Look at yourself.'

He turns me round so that we're in front of the full-length mirror. All I have on now are the thigh-highs and my heels. Confronted with my nakedness, a sudden shyness overtakes me and my body tenses.

'What's wrong?' he asks.

'Nothing . . . It's just that seeing myself like this . . . it's pretty full-on.'

'It is and you look as sexy as hell.' His teeth graze my shoulder gently and then his voice is raw-edged as he murmurs. 'Touch yourself.'

His command goes straight to my core and makes me wet, but still I hesitate. I don't think I've ever felt this exposed – this bared – physically.

'Shall I help you?'

Alexander takes my hand and guides it downwards, pressing my fingers over the top of my pubis. The pressure of our two hands makes my muscles tauten sharply with need. I see my lips parted with desire and hear my breathing quicken as Alexander slides my fingers between my legs. Gently, he presses my finger against my clitoris. 'Touch yourself, like you would if I wasn't here. You have done that, haven't you, Lauren, because of me?'

His presumption – his ego – ought to make me mad, but it only makes me want him more. And it's true, of course, I've fantasized about him; even while I've hated him, I've craved him. I push my hips back against his erection and yelp with shock and pleasure as he moves his hand behind me and slips a finger inside me while I touch myself. Ripples of sensation radiate out from my core and I can't take much more.

'Good?'

'Yes, but I need you inside me.'

'Get on the bed.'

He moves to strip off his trousers and boxer shorts, so he's naked and hard for me. I lie down, opening my legs for him, and seconds later he enters me slowly, easing his length until I'm so gloriously full I don't think I can take it.

'More?'

Words fail me, but Alexander hears anyway and eases in a little more and starts to push in and out rhythmically. My muscles tighten around him like a ring of steel, and my orgasm rips through me. Nothing else matters, only this moment and everything else can go to hell.

Chapter Eleven

'So you finally shagged him, then?'

Immy dumps her bag on the bench at the side of the court and stands with her hands on her hips. We were going to play tennis before lectures this morning, but the courts were still coated in a layer of frost. It's Wednesday of Third Week and I haven't seen her since Alexander came round to my rooms on Saturday because she's been on a field trip. I tug the zip of my top higher and think back to last night, clutching at the pillows while Alexander went down on me, and I'm grinning so hard I can barely reply, so Immy does it for me.

'That would be a "yes", then?' She pulls her racket from her bag. 'I saw him in the library late last night. I don't know what you've done to him, but he looked totally knackered.'

'Oh, really?' My tone is cherubic, though I find it impossible to keep the grin from my face. The truth is that I've spent every spare second in bed with Alexander at his house. After breakfast in our suite at Le Manoir last Sunday morning, the Bentley arrived to whisk me to the train station and Alexander back to college. He wanted the chauffeur to take me straight to London, but I'd arranged to meet my course mates at the station so we could all travel together. I hate letting people down.

'You'll be the talk of college soon – Alexander has a reputation for being impossible to get.'

I pull my racket from my racket bag, feeling my cheeks heat. 'I think I was the one who put up a fight. As for college gossip, you're the girl who's dating two guys at the same time.'

Immy nibbles at her bottom lip then pulls a face. 'Well, not exactly. It's over with Freddie. I called him before I left for the field trip.'

'Oh, poor Freddie.'

She groans. 'He's a lovely boy and a fantastic shag, but we both know it wasn't going to work. I'd rather be honest with him and I didn't think I was upset, and he was all brave and philosophical, but I still cried buckets after I told him. I hit the Bombay Sapphire in a big way on the field trip. I can't remember much of the geology part of it, that's for sure . . . but Freddie will be OK; there's some girl in his tutor group who's been after him for months. She can console him . . .'

She hesitates, then taps her racket against her calf and runs on the spot. 'Come on before we both freeze to death. Let's see if you can take a set off me this time.'

I do take a set off Immy and though I still lose the match two – one, I feel pretty pleased as we cycle back to college for a quick shower. I'm going to dinner at Alexander's place tonight but before then I have a tutorial with Professor Rafe a.k.a. Handy. His role is meant to be pastoral, but he keeps telling me that I show 'exceptional promise' so he wants to have extra one-to-ones with me. Armed with Immy's warnings about him – and gossip I've heard at the faculty – I am now wary of him, but I can hardly refuse a tutorial with him. Besides, I'm confident I can give him enough 'busy' signals to keep him away from me.

The chapel bell chimes and my heart sinks a little because there's still fifteen minutes to go in my tute with Professor Rafe. We've spent the first thirty minutes discussing methodology, my specialist subject and the V&A's exhibition, but now he's moved on to American politics.

He brushes something off his knee where the cord is flattened and worn. Are they cookie crumbs? Why do so many of the girls here think he's sexy?

'I'm very impressed with your father's bold stance on gun ownership,' he says, launching into more of his opinions of our political system. All I can do is nod politely and agree with some of his views on our crazier politicians, but when he starts with the snide remarks about 'our colonial origins', 'religious extremists' and 'corrupt campaign financing', I really don't want to go there. I could, of course, give him the full benefit of my own opinions and point out that he's misinformed on a number of points, but you know what? I came here to study art history, not politics. And, yes, Oxford is about a rounded education and coming up against a wide range of opinions, but I'd rather not do any of that while some guy's hand is on my knee, as it now is.

'You know, I'd really like it if we could discuss these issues in more depth over a drink in the KA this evening?'

I shift my leg away from him and he gives my knee a brief pat. It feels spontaneous and *possibly* it's avuncular, but my thighs still close in automatic response and he takes his hand away.

'I'm pretty busy with my essay research,' I say, which ought to be obvious to him. I refuse to mention that I also have a boyfriend, because, frankly, it's none of his business.

'You know what they say about all work and no play?'

'Actually, I don't.' I spring up from the sofa, not caring that there's five minutes left of his tute. 'I have to go, Professor Rafe. I've got a doctor's appointment.'

'Oh dear. Nothing serious, I hope?'

'No. Just a routine check-up.'

'Aha, I understand.' His smirk makes my flesh crawl as I see his brain putting two and two together and possibly making a very creepy five. Actually, I have seen the doctor, as has Alexander. We both got checked out and I got a new prescription for birth control, but the thought of Rafe even suspecting those things makes me want to barf.

I grab my bag and back towards the door.

'Maybe another time, then?' he says, standing up and advancing on me. 'And I'll see you the same time next week, when you don't have a ... um ... medical appointment.'

'Yes. Next week. Bye.'

Outside, I suck a few lungfuls of clear cold air. What would he do if he knew my appointment was with Alexander, and that it may not involve anything medical, but it definitely will involve taking off my clothes? That thought fills my mind as I collect my bike and cycle to Alexander's house, resolving not to tell him about Rafe. First, I can handle the guy myself and, second, I don't want the police to find Rafe dumped in a trashcan minus the most treasured part of his anatomy. Not that I really think Alexander would physically harm Rafe, although he might scare the shit out of him. I'm going to have to be more assertive – a.k.a. rude – to Rafe and tell him straight out that his touching me makes me feel uncomfortable. It's not so simple, however, when I have to spend another two and half terms with the guy.

The fresh air lifts my mood a little. Since Immy warned me about Rafe, I've been hyper-aware of every comment he makes to me, and for ninety per cent of the tute he did confine his conversation to the subject or politics. It was only at the end when he asked me for a drink. Tutors do take students to the pub at Oxford; it's kind of a tradition and I know Immy's tutor does, but he's not trying to get in Immy's knickers, as she puts it.

Alexander opens the door while I'm chaining my bike to the metal railings outside his house. He's wearing jeans, but he has no shirt and is barefoot. My hands shake as they fasten the padlock. There is something raw about him like this, stripped of his armour of suit and uniform – perhaps even more raw than when he's totally naked. His hair is damp and his skin has that muted sheen that tells me he's fresh from the shower.

I rush through the door and he closes it quickly behind me. He touches my cheek. 'Your face is a little pink.'

'I raced here from my tute.'

'How was it?'

'OK. I don't really want to talk about it.'

'I'm happy not to talk.'

I exhale sharply as he pulls me against his bare chest and my hands seek the solidity of his muscled shoulders and back and press my hips against his jeans. I ease the zip down, slip my hand inside and meet soft hair and a hardening cock. 'Oh dear, Alexander, you appear to have forgotten your shorts.'

'My memory is terrible these days. I blame you.'

I wind my arms round his neck. 'I hope no one comes to the door and finds you like this.'

'Like what?'

'Minus your pants.'

'That makes two of us, then.' He lifts me up bodily. I wrap my legs round his back and he shuffles forward with me towards the stairs. My butt hits the step and I'm sitting on the stairway. My consolation is the view I have of Alexander stripping off his jeans, a feast for the eyes that makes me want to take him in my mouth right now. He's all hard-packed thighs and ripped abs, but it's the healed wound that adds a deeper layer of desire.

He's no pristine pretty boy: and his scars only serve to remind me his is a body that's been used and tested in real battle.

I shiver, part lust, part in the realization of what and who I have gotten myself into. But I don't care right now because I only want him deep inside me.

I push myself up off the stair tread so he can bunch my skirt around my waist. He clicks his tongue against his teeth, focusing on my legs.

'Tut tut. Hold-ups *and* kinky boots. Disgraceful.'

'They're not kinky, they're Prada, and also not easy . . . To ride a bike in, that . . . is.' My words are punctuated by sharp breaths because he's easing my panties over my ankle boots.

'I'm glad you risked life and limb for me.'

He parts my thighs and his dark head descends between my legs.

'Oh.' The rasp of his tongue on my clit makes me whimper like a baby. I hate him for reducing me to a keening mess yet I crave more.

His hands grasp my hips to steady me and he looks up at me. 'Keep still.'

'I can't.'

'It's an order. And open your legs wider.'

Using his mouth, he pays relentless attention to my pussy and clit with hot short breaths and cool laves of his tongue. He flicks at my clit with his finger and thumb, a shock of tiny pain that makes me cry out. Then he circles his tongue around the nub to soothe it. The muscles in my thighs are shaking and I'm clawing the flesh over his shoulders with my hands, on the very precipice of coming.

'Do I need to get protection or are you happy to go bare?' he asks.

His words are an extra push over the brink, when I was already teetering. 'Bare. Now, but quickly because I'm so ready.'

And he's on me, and I help him by pushing myself up from the step. His hips are between my legs so that I have to wrap my legs round his waist to allow him inside me. And then he is inside, his cock almost too large, hot. The feel of unsheathed flesh is beautiful and dangerous. He slides in and out of me, nuzzling my shoulder, his breath warm against my neck, whispering filthy things in that impeccable accent.

He thrusts harder and faster and my bottom bumps against the steps. It's not comfortable, and that turns me on even more. I pull him into me anyway, writhing against him, aching for my own climax as he seeks his. I feel the pulsing of his cock as he spills into me and I fall over the edge after him.

Chapter Twelve

One week later and judging by the knowing looks whenever I show my face in public the whole of Wyckham knows that I've shagged Alexander. I'm not sure word has got out into the rest of Oxford yet, but Immy has warned me we could end up in the student press gossip columns, which I'd hate every bit as much as Alexander.

I'm kind of hoping word hasn't spread to the American students' society, because tonight I'm at their Transatlantic Cocktail Party, which according to the invite is meant to be an 'informal themed mixer for graduate students'. After skipping the introductory party to go to the Rashleigh Hall ball I feel I ought to show up at this event. My mother sits on the same charity committee chaired by the mother of the organizer and while I haven't met Maisey before, from the tone of her email, I think she's following in her mom's footsteps. Looking around at the Anglo-American themed decor, canapés and cocktails, I suspect Martha Stewart herself could take a few tips from Maisey's party-planning skills.

'What the hell are you doing here, Lauren Cusack?'

A deep East Coast voice cuts through the throng of guests in the grad students union. Even if I hadn't heard Scott Schulze first, I guess I would have spotted his six-and-a-half-feet frame within seconds of him entering the room.

With an Amstel Light in his hand, Scott shoulders his way through the throng. I suppose it's not *that* surprising I should meet someone who knows Todd in Oxford. But Scott is his second cousin and that's a little too close to home for me right now. I wonder how much Todd told him about the break-up, or how accurate any of it was. I shouldn't be bothered any more, but I always liked Scott, and I do care what he thinks of me.

'So what *are* you doing here?' he asks when he reaches me. At five-seven plus a pair of Coach heels, I'm hardly vertically challenged, but he still has to duck low to kiss my cheek. I wonder if he's grown an inch or two since we last met.

I throw on a smile. 'Hey there, I could ask you the same thing. It's great to see you, but I had no idea you were planning to study at Oxford. You never mentioned coming here when I saw you at the Adlers' last fall.'

'That was before my rowing coach mentioned he knew a friendly Fellow at St Nicholas who happened to be in urgent need of a stroke for the college's First Eight. St Nick's is determined to beat Christ Church and be Head of the River this year.'

A few weeks ago, this statement would have gone over my head, but given Wyckham's obsession with rowing I now know exactly what he means.

'So you're studying rowing?' I tease.

'If only. My family think I'm doing a master's in

Water Science Policy, but, honestly, if I'd thought it would get me a place in the Blues boat, I'd have studied my own toenail clippings.'

'Is there a difference between the two?'

'Ouch. I'm hurt. Don't you know that water science is fascinating?' His 'hurt little boy' expression makes me smile and his sea-green eyes are alive with mischief. As we talk about Oxford's weird and wonderful ways, I realize why I liked him so much, although I guess I was always too caught up with Todd to recognize it. With that athletic physique and surfer blond hair, it's no wonder Scott had a string of girls after him at Harvard.

Soon Scott has me laughing out loud with some tales from his Blues training that I find so hard to believe that they must be true.

'Oh, come on. You must have made that one up. No one on the planet has a fifteen-inch penis! It's anatomically impossible.'

He winks. 'Don't you know by now that the more outrageous the story, the more likely it is to be true? This *is* Oxford.'

Since truly remarkable things have also happened to me in the three weeks since I got here, I can hardly contradict him. I sip my Bay Breeze. It's not quite how they make them back home, but the staff have done a pretty good job.

A waiter wafts by with a tray of canapés. 'Mmm. Interesting combination: mushroom polenta diamonds and mini Yorkshire puds,' says Scott, selecting a pudding.

'I guess Maisey thought it was symbolic. A fusion of our two great nations,' I say.

The canapé goes down in one gulp and he grimaces. 'So, are you here to snag a prince or make my cousin even more pissed than he already is? Why exactly did you guys split up? I thought you'd have been engaged to be Mrs Todd Adler III by now.'

The conversation has nose-dived and I'm obviously not quick enough to hide my discomfort because he screws up his face and groans.

'Shit. I think I overstepped the mark.'

'With the princes or the Todd thing?'

'Maybe both?'

His smile is rueful and I can't be offended by it. 'Don't worry about it. Besides, the princes appear to be taken and I'm not planning on being Mrs Anybody any time soon. Todd and I started to go downhill soon after his parents' anniversary and we've been history since midsummer. I'd already planned to come here to study and that didn't help. Todd wasn't happy, but this – the master's and Oxford – is what I've wanted for a long time.'

I keep it to that; the last thing I want to do is criticize Todd to his own cousin and drag up the whole saga of the shitty way he treated me. I flash him an ironic smile. 'You can make a remark about toenail clippings if you want and I can't even claim to be studying to get a place in the Blues boat.'

'It's OK, Lauren, you don't have to apologize for going for your dream. It's obvious you were passionate about your art and you've always seemed to be your own woman . . . Maybe I shouldn't say this, but I'm not totally devastated that you broke up with Todd even though you guys did seem serious. In fact, I salute you for having other, dare I say higher, ambitions.'

I'm not sure how to take his remark, which sounds sincere enough, but I'm also not sure what his definition of a higher ambition is. Suddenly, I become conscious of antennae twitching, mostly of the female variety. I can hardly blame them; Scott is handsome, loaded and single. The vintage clock above the bar tells me we've been chatting for almost half an hour and it must look like one or other of us is hitting on the other.

He seems to have picked up on my restlessness. 'Am I monopolizing you? I guess Maisey meant this to be a chance for the US grad students to interact socially, at least that's what her invite said.'

'You're not monopolizing me but maybe we should go mingle with a few others, if only for Maisey's sake. I'm sure I'll bump into you in between training and your water-policy studies.'

'You can count on it.' He lowers his voice and his expression becomes serious enough to set off tiny alarm bells in my head. 'I may be about to crash and burn . . . but we're going to be around the same small world for a year. How would you feel about going out for dinner one night?'

His ruggedly handsome features are softened by a disarming and slightly sheepish look. But for all the laid-back charm I can't help but compare him to

Alexander's icily polite veneer. Alexander would take it as a huge insult to be called charming. The very thought of it makes me smile to myself and all I have to do is tell Scott about him to end this, but can't see a way of doing it neatly or nicely.

'I thought you spent all your spare time down at the river? I'd hate to scupper your chances of making the Blues boat.'

'I don't think there's much chance of that and, even if you did, it would be a major consolation to know you were the reason I failed.'

It's so deft a compliment, that I'm wrong footed. 'At the risk of sounding boring, I have a lot of work. My tutor's a real diva and he keeps cracking the whip over me.'

He raises an eyebrow. 'My tutor's a demon too – some say she has scales under her gown.'

Scott has made me laugh out loud again. In fact, he makes me laugh a lot more than Alexander. But then I haven't exactly fallen for Alexander because of his comic timing. Plus, I *have* to put Scott out of his misery right now and tell him I'm seeing someone.

'You can't blame me for trying. You were always the sexiest girl in the state and, since I last saw you, well, it's like you've lit right up from inside.'

Heat rushes to my cheeks. This is way too much. 'Scott, I don't think –'

He holds up a hand. 'Don't beat yourself up trying to explain. I can see it might be too soon for you to think of dating again after the break-up, but it's only dinner and there's really no pressure. You know where I am – call into St Nick's any time or give me a call. Here's my cell number.' He pulls a card from the pocket of his Carhartt's and waggles it in front of my nose.

Just as he slips the card between my fingertips and I'm about to tell him about Alexander, Maisey's shriek reverberates in my ears.

'Lauren! I've been trying to get to you all evening, but people *will* keep talking to me. I am so happy you made it tonight. Do you know how many of the grad students have asked me to introduce you? You have quite a reputation already.'

'Are you thinking a Lindsay Lohan-type reputation or full-on Bernie Madoff-level of notoriety?'

Maisey's face registers a mix of confusion and dismay. Irony is obviously not her major at Oxford. She gives me a little push on the arm as Scott looks on, trying not to laugh. 'Oh, you're joking. Now, you must solve a little mystery for me. I heard a rumour you're dating a British aristocrat. I said it couldn't be true, so soon after you broke up with your fiancé. Everyone was so upset for you both. You seemed like the perfect couple.'

Can you get arrested for skewering people with a swizzle stick in the UK or is it considered a public duty?

'Well, I –'

'I knew it was a lie. I told Deanna Robeson – you remember her? Her father's running for the Ohio nomination?'

I don't, actually, but I already worked out that Maisey is the kind of woman who doesn't need a reply.

'I *said* I didn't believe you would be in a serious relationship with some British guy this soon.'

'Well, Todd and I weren't engaged and, as you pointed out, Alexander and I only met less than three weeks ago.' Oh shit. That didn't work, did it? Maisey's eyes pop out on stalks and Scott is failing manfully to show he's not totally pissed. Why do I feel guilty when I have no need to be? But I *should* have told him about Alexander before Maisey dropped the bombshell. I don't really know why I hesitated.

'I understand,' says Maisey, meaning precisely the opposite.

'But you *are* dating this aristo Brit?' Scott asks with great relish.

'I suppose we're kind of seeing one another . . .' Mostly naked, I think with a blush.

'Deanna said he was a duke!' Maisey's squeal is as sharp as a lancet.

I picture Alexander's face at the way she pronounces the 'u' as an 'oo' and thank God he's not around. 'Where did Deanna hear that?'

'Her house-mate's at Wyckham. You should have known you can't keep anything secret in Oxford.'

'Alexander isn't a duke. He's only a marquess's son.'

Scott raises an eyebrow. '*Only?* So, you decided to lower your expectations. The princes being taken, that is.'

A snarky reply hovers on the tip of my tongue, but I bite it back. 'Hey, well, sometimes you have to make compromises. Alexander's only twenty-third in line to the throne, but I can deal with that.'

The droplets from Maisey's cocktail wet my face. 'You have to be kidding!'

I back off a little to avoid further cocktail snorting. 'No. Didn't you see him at Kate and Will's wedding? Westminster Abbey? Second from the right, two rows back from Princess Beatrice's pretzel.'

Scott flicks Fuzzy Navel droplets off his jacket, looking about as impressed as a Westboro baptist at a Richard Dawkins tribute.

'So, it's not too soon after Todd, after all?' he asks mischievously.

Maisey lasers in on this comment. 'Oh. My. God. Was I interrupting something?'

'Not at all,' says Scott, and slurps down the last of his cocktail, eyeing me over the top of the straw.

'He's just joking,' I say through gritted teeth.

'If you're both sure? I'd *hate* to be a fifth wheel.'

'Oh, you're so not,' I say sweetly.

'In that case, can I borrow Scott?' She slips her arm through his. 'I've got a long line of women who are dying to meet him and I'm sure Deanna would love to hear more about your new boyfriend. Did you say he was called Alexander? So do you call him Sir Alexander or is he only an honourable?'

The USSoc party is now just a memory in the manic round of Oxford life. It's already the start of Fourth Week, and it's Formal Hall night at Wyckham. Somehow I've found time to do some studying, but the opportunities for distraction have been so many – and so pleasurable – I'm not sure I'm giving enough time to my work.

Alexander is talking to his tutor and looks hot in his MA gown with its red silk hood. Immy's gone to see a movie with Skandar so I brace myself as Rupert snags the space next to me at the dinner table. 'Oh, you've got me again. Goody, I've been dying to know how you finally wore down Alexander.'

'Actually, Rupes, he wore me down.'

'And I bet you loved every minute of it. I would have.'

'Would you? Sometimes I think that your interest in Alexander verges on the obsessive. There's something um . . . *classical* about it, if you know what I mean. You should commission a Greek mural featuring the two of you.'

It takes a second for him to register that I deliberately misunderstood his words. 'You are very, very funny, Lauren. I'll bet Alexander is smiling the whole time he's with you.'

'I do hope so.'

As Rupert swipes the wine bottle and fills up his glass, I remind myself that I'd fully expected this reaction from him. It's been almost a week since Alexander and I first made love and we've spent every moment together when we weren't studying – and some when we were supposed to be. We've had a wonderful time walking along the river to the Trout, and through the Parks and Christ Church Meadow, past the boathouses where the college Eights are practising for the end-of-term regatta.

We haven't spent too much time in my room because Alexander's house gives us more privacy. I think I'd curl up and die if we ended up as 'Couple of the Week' in one of the gossip columns and I can only imagine what Alexander would feel about that happening.

Over by the fire, Alexander is still talking to his tutor and I really hope he comes along soon. I can handle Rupert, but, frankly, I'm getting tired of his constant jibing. He's made it obvious he hates me seeing his cousin. Whether that's because I'm the wrong nationality, the wrong 'class' or he still hopes to screw me himself, I don't know.

Having been momentarily distracted by demanding a fresh bottle of claret from the waiting staff, Rupert turns to me again. 'I assume Alexander's Facebook status is now set to "It's complicated".'

There are a few sniggers from the other side of the table.

'Alexander would rather eat his own entrails than even look at Facebook, not that he has time.'

'So after a couple of weeks of shagging him, you know him as well as his friends and family, do you?'

'I do know he values his privacy and that includes not having his personal life discussed over the dinner table.'

'Should my ears be burning, Rupert?' Alexander has just taken his place on the bench beside me.

Rupert smirks. 'I wasn't thinking of quite that part of your anatomy.'

'Just fuck off.' Alexander tightens his arm round me. 'Now, what appalling crap are they serving up tonight?'

It seems strange to be sitting down to dinner with almost the same set of people as on my first night – yet this time to have Alexander by my side, and for everyone to know that we are dating. It ought to be fantastic and I've eaten in here several times since that night so I should feel comfortable. Yet somehow I feel more out of place with Alexander at my side than I did on my own.

I ask myself why that is as Alexander talks to Rupert and the other guys around us about some rugby game that's coming up on TV.

'I don't suppose we'll see you in Klosters over Christmas vac?' Rupert enquires in a louder voice, as if he wants our dinner companions to overhear this part of the conversation.

'I don't know yet.'

'Oh, so you'll be flying off to the States, then.'

In my fantasies, I could stab Rupert with my dessert fork but I stay quiet.

'I haven't made any plans that far ahead.'

'Really? Lauren may have.'

Alexander throws his napkin on the table. 'For your information, I really don't know what I'm doing at Christmas. I may well be . . . busy. If not, I doubt I'll be coming to Klosters anyway. One of the guys in my regiment wants to do some heli-skiing. I'd ask you, of course, but last time we went skiing, you ended up on your arse half the time and shagging the chalet girl for the rest.'

'Shagging the hired help is the best part of skiing so you can keep your army trip, Alexander. Will *you* be going skiing, Lauren?' Rupert's voice drips sarcasm.

'Actually, Rupert, I prefer snowboarding. Not that I'm any kind of expert. Usually end up flat on my back too, though I tend to leave the chalet staff alone.'

Alexander smiles. I can see he's enjoying me giving it back to Rupert, not that I need his approval or encouragement.

Rupert winks at me and lowers his voice. 'I'd love to see you flat on your back.'

'Trust me, you'll never have that pleasure.' I glance at Alexander, wondering what his reaction to Rupert's innuendo will be, but he's intent on his mobile, which is vibrating. His expression darkens and he stands up. 'Excuse me.'

'Is everything OK?' I ask.

'Nothing to worry about. I'll be back soon.'

After he's gone, Rupert points to the virtually untouched apple pie on my plate. 'Lost your appetite?'

'Oddly enough, round about the time you sat next to me.'

Rupert's thigh butts against mine and his breath is hot against my ear. He chose the garlic chicken for dinner. 'I'd like to get in close proximity to you, if Alexander would take his eyes and hands off you for a second. You do know that when we were boys we shared everything? I don't see why it should be any different now and I can understand why he's so smitten with you. Two reasons, in fact. Incredible.' He sighs. 'We've got a book running at the Club, speculating on your . . . um . . . assets. Most of the guys think 34B; I've got you down as a 32D.'

He stares right down my cleavage and gives a low whistle.

'Funny. Most of the girls in college have got your asset pegged at about two inches.' I wiggle my little finger. 'Though with the cold weather coming on, maybe that's being over-optimistic. One more reason for you to steer clear of the ski slopes, I guess.'

'Gosh, I'm flattered so many ladies are thinking of me in that way. But you know, Lauren, it'll never work between you, no matter how much you think Alexander is in "lurve" with you or what he says and does now.' His tone is laced with venom. 'In the end, he'll revert to his roots. That's what his father expects, what we all expect.'

'I may not have known Alexander that long, but the one thing he won't do is what anyone expects. Not his father, not his friends and definitely not you. Now, let go of my arm because you're making me feel nauseous and I'd hate to ruin another pair of your trousers.'

He releases his grip and curls his lip. 'Say what you like, but we both know the truth here. Where Alexander is concerned, you don't fit into the picture and you never will.'

'Whatever gave you the idea I had any intention of fitting anyone's picture? I plan on creating my own.'

All Rupert gets is the back view of me as I make my way out of Hall.

Alexander is pacing the flagstones at the bottom of the steps and shoves his cell phone into his pocket when he spots me. In the dark I can't quite see his expression, but there's a hunch in his shoulders that tells me he's on edge. He looks edible in his handmade inky blue suit, white shirt and silk tie. Add the formality of his graduate gown into the mix, and I could drag him off to bed right this minute, but I want to know what's bugging him first.

I also have no intention of telling him about Rupert, so I slip my arm through his. Moonlight bathes the grass in a silvery glow as we skirt the path around the quad

'Is everything OK?' I ask.

'Yes, of course.'

'So was it a, um, work call?'

'No, not work.'

'You looked a little concerned when you saw the screen . . .'

He gives a terse smile. 'Just some family business.'

'I see.' OK. I ran into a dead end there, but I decide to make a tactical retreat for now. We stop at the bottom of my staircase. 'Are you coming up?' I ask, half teasing, half soothing.

The look he slides me would melt a glacier. 'I'd rather we went back to my place. I have something in mind.'

Chapter Thirteen

Something in mind.

He sure has.

My eyes are shut, but I don't need to see anything, because every other of mysenses is stimulated. After we made love, Alexander left me in bed while he filled the huge white claw-footed roll-top with warm water and, whatever potion he poured in the bath, it smells divine: citrussy yet also spicy, like oranges studded with cloves or nutmeg. It's so delicious I can almost taste it. There's low-level mood lighting above the tub and candles flicker on the window, casting shadows on the walls as steamy tendrils rise from the bath.

He uses a sponge to trickle water over my breasts as I lie back against the solidity of his chest. 'Wow.'

'Good?'

'Uh-huh.'

The water tickles and tantalizes my skin. I open my eyes as he dabs a blob of foam on each of my nipples with his fingertip. 'The cherry on the cake,' he says. I relax back against him, feeling his erection stir against my bottom and his sigh resonates through my body. He's chilled, or as chilled as Alexander ever gets.

'Have I ever told you how much I love your breasts?'

'Um . . . you may have. Once or twice.'

He massages the foam into my nipples and they peak painfully under his fingertips. I can't help wriggling back against his erection. 'Alexander, I can't stand this.'

'That's the general idea.'

My sigh of pleasure as he slips his fingers between my legs is lost in an angry buzz from the pocket of his trousers on the tiles. His body stiffens.

'You should answer that.'

'In the bath?'

'Why not?'

'It'll wait.' He squeezes out the sponge, dribbling warm water over my back.

'No. Answer it.'

'A, I'm not going to speak to anyone while I'm naked in a tub with you and, b, I know who it is.'

'Care to share?'

The sponge pauses on my shoulder. 'It will be Emma again.'

'Emma?'

The sponge circles the top of my arm. 'My sister.'

'Oh . . . yes, Immy did mention her a while back. Is she OK?'

The sponge slides over my shoulder to the top of my breast as he gives the briefest of ironic laughs. 'Emma is . . . as she will point out to you ad nauseum, *virtually* seventeen. She is also infuriating and completely impossible.' His words are at odds with the underlying emotion. This girl may be impossible, but I can tell he adores her.

'You're close, then.'

'Who else has she got?' He drops the sponge into the bath and squeezes me tight into his chest. His hands rest lightly on my stomach and his damp chest hair tickles my back. 'Emma and my father don't see eye to eye on a number of things, one of the biggest being what Emma should do when she leaves school. She wants to go to Saint Martins to study theatrical costume design, but my father wants her to try for Classics at Oxbridge. That was her now, threatening to abandon her A levels and go to live in London with some French friends she met on a trip to Morocco.'

I have to smile at the frustration in his voice, almost as if he's Emma's father, rather than her older brother.

'At sixteen, Morocco and costume design sound a lot more exciting than Classics. I think I'd feel the same as she does. Is she at school now?'

'She was when she called during dinner. By now she may be on the train to London for all I know. She put the phone down on me when I asked her to see reason.'

He nuzzles my neck, his voice a low murmur. I wonder if this is the way his father speaks to Emma too.

'You don't think she'll seriously walk out right this minute?'

'Maybe. Maybe not. Emma always had her own way even when our mother was alive. Since she died, my father has found her impossible to deal with.'

'And you?' I try to twist to see his face but it's impossible. Maybe that's why he wants to have this conversation – when I can't read his emotions.

'Though Emma may not always believe it, I love her

and I want her to be happy more than anything. Occasionally she does listen to my advice, but it's getting harder as she gets older. She wants her independence, which I can understand, but she's convinced she doesn't need anyone else's help.' He pauses. 'I'll get you a towel.'

After he's helped me out of the tub, he hands me a fluffy white bath sheet. I already empathize with Emma Hunt, caught between a stern, domineering father who seems to have no clue how to handle his free-spirit daughter who's growing up fast, and Alexander, well-meaning yet with his own ideas of how she should behave. Emma isn't that much younger than me, but I know there's a big difference between sixteen and twenty-one – and a huge one between sixteen and twenty-five, which Alexander is.

While I pat my skin dry, I wonder if Emma gets her love of the arts from Lady Hunt. Was she creative too? Then I realize that Emma must have been very young when her mother was killed. Alexander goes out of his way to avoid speaking about her and closes down my every attempt to bring the subject up. Yet I wish I could have known her, and could meet Emma and the marquess to make my own judgement.

Alexander knots a towel low around his waist. The tanned torso, the ripped stomach, the muscular calves aren't the result of hours in the gym; they all testify to real-life battles and exertion. His hair is damp and tousled from the bath and I want to drag him straight back to bed, but there's something I want him to do even more.

I tuck my own towel above my breasts and put my

arms round him, my fingers pressing the damp skin around his spine. 'I have to say that I like the sound of Emma, the more I hear about her.'

'I think you two would get along very well.'

'I'd really like to meet her.'

The phone buzzes again, and he grimaces. 'I'm sorry. I ought to get this.'

In the bedroom, I'm getting changed and trying not to listen to his conversation through the open door, while also trying *to* listen to it. Yes, it's wrong to eavesdrop, but I'm curious about his family and background, and tired of having to interpret his silences and evasions. I know it's part of his job to be discreet, secretive even – but it also frustrates and disturbs me. I don't expect him to 'open up' to me or do anything 'soul-baring'. Most guys would rather die than do that anyway, but Alexander is buttoned up so tightly at times it seems impossible to find a way to the man underneath.

No matter how much I try to ignore what Rupert said at dinner – and what Immy warned me about earlier – I do worry about not being part of Alexander's 'picture'. The wealth, 'class' thing and cultural gulf: these are things I should laugh off, but they still niggle at the back of my mind.

Now I can't help but hear him because his voice is raised as he remonstrates with his sister. The words come in snatches, often indistinct, but I can chart the ebb and flow of their conversation as he veers from grudging patience to bursts of frustration.

He strides into the bedroom, phone to his ear, while I'm rolling up my thigh-highs.

'I'll come down to see you at the weekend, Emma. Don't do anything stupid before then unless you want Dad coming to the school.'

The phone lands on the bed beside me with a thump. 'Jesus.'

'So she's not walking out?'

He shakes his head. 'Not today anyway.'

He sits down on the bed next to me, picking at the quilt.

'I don't want to interfere or sound trite, but it must have been awful for Emma, losing her mother so young. What was she? Eight?'

'Barely four. I was thirteen.'

'That must have been hard on you both.'

'*Hard?*' He echoes me, and I can't for the life of me work out how he feels about what I said. Angry? Upset? Annoyed I dared to drop a pebble into the dark pool of the Hunt family angst?

'I can't imagine what it would be like to lose my mother or father in that way.' This feels like tiptoeing over eggshells in a pitch-black room.

'Then don't.'

He dives on top of me, tipping me back on to the bed and giving me a kiss that's so far from tender or empathetic it rips the breath from me. It's a savage kiss, because as far as he's concerned the conversation is over for now and for good.

He jerks my dress up and yanks my panties down my thighs, running his fingers lightly over my clit. He plunges a finger inside me and the sound he makes is guttural and primeval. I'm wet; I was from the moment he pushed me on to the bed, but, still, this is fast, hurried, desperate.

He shifts his weight from me a little so he can rip my panties off my ankles. The towel falls from his waist and I inhale sharply as I see his cock, already thick and hard. I'm excited and alarmed by the urgency of his need to take me like this: without finesse.

He pushes my knees apart and plunges into me.

'Ohhh.'

My moan forces a gruff, 'OK?' from him and a drawn-out 'Mmm' from me and he sinks in deeper, spearing me up to the hilt. He's like a leather glove that's too tight yet when he shifts his hips from side to side I stretch a little further to fit and the discomfort eases to a glorious fullness.

'Touch yourself.'

At his guttural command, my fingers move to my clit, and I'm flicking and teasing myself as his eyes lock on mine. It feels wanton and forbidden to pleasure myself with him watching me, but his eyes are glazed with a kind of savage delight so I don't want to stop. When he pulls his tip out a little way then slips inside me again, I moan to the air and press my fingers harder to my clit. My fingers work on the bud, the sensation radiating outwards through my limbs.

'I have to come.'

'I want to watch while I'm inside you. You're so tight I won't last long.'

I hesitate. His expression is so intense he looks in pain.

'Do it. Look at me while you do it.'

His voice is jagged and I rub my tender, swollen clit as those blue eyes burn into mine. He moves inside me, in and out, rhythmically, the feeling of being full to the core and beyond, sending me to the edge.

'Let go, Lauren.'

His thrusts are harder, more urgent and I can't last now. I can't look at him either and I close my eyes and drop my fingers and feel him thrust into me hard. I let go and there are seconds when I don't know anything; I'm only waves of sensation rippling out from my centre as Alexander lets go too. His body goes rigid and as I open my eyes his are shut tight, his neck stiff. He's out of whatever troubled world he inhabits and I'm glad that I took him there.

'No! God, no!'

I'm having a nightmare; a terrible dream where someone is in the bedroom, throwing the furniture around the room. I know it's not real but I'm still battling to wake up as some unseen presence lifts up a chair high into the air and launches it at me.

It hurtles through the darkness and I scream but no sound comes.

My breath comes hard and fast as my eyes open to the room. It's lit only by a sliver of dim light from the streetlamp outside the window and there's no one there. My heart feels as if it's trying to escape from my chest.

'I'm sorry!'

Just in time, I see Alexander's arm scything through the air towards my face and I roll out of the way. 'My God!'

His arm crashes down onto the mattress. 'I didn't mean it! I didn't!' His voice rings out through the silent room as he thrashes the space where I lay, his head rolling from side to side.

It wasn't my nightmare, it was his – fighting its way from his mind into my sleep.

He sits bolt upright in bed, his eyes still screwed tight shut. 'I'm sorry. I'm so sorry. I didn't mean it to happen.'

Standing at the side of the bed, trembling with cold and shock, I feel completely helpless. Should I try to wake him? Leave him be? Comfort him?

Sweat prickles his forehead and glistens on his torso. His face is contorted in agony. What horrible things is he seeing or doing? What's brought on this awful nightmare? Is it something from his work? Or linked to his mother's death? I remember Immy telling me that his father blamed him for causing the accident, but how I don't know.

'Alexander . . .' I reach out and touch his arm and he flinches away.

I wrap my arms around myself then realize I'm still naked. My robe is on the chair so I wrap it round me and stand a few feet from the bed as Alexander lies down again, mumbling words I can't understand but know stem from extreme anguish.

'Shhh.' I step closer. 'It's all right. You're OK.'

Warily, I let my trembling fingertips rest on his bicep and this time he doesn't flinch. His eyelids flutter a little and he looks at me. I heave a sigh of relief that he's freed himself from whatever hell he was in. I climb on to the bed beside him and stroke his hair.

'It was only a bad dream,' I say as he looks at me.

'I'm sorry. Forgive me.'

'Of course . . .'

'It wasn't my fault.'

His eyes are open, but when I wave my hand in front of them he just keeps staring ahead. He isn't free; he's still locked in some dark and terrifying place and I can't do a thing about it.

His hand clamps round my arm and I wince. 'I'm sorry!' His plea is desperate and savage – it can't possibly come from the self-assured, controlled man I thought I knew. Slowly, as I watch him, his fingers unclench, his hand drops to the sheet and he sinks back against the pillow, breathing softly.

Now all is calm – on his half of the bed. On the opposite side, I lie stiff and tense, expecting him to cry or lash out at any moment.

Chapter Fourteen

I don't know how long it is before I open my eyes to find the room still in a state of gloom. Is that dawn on the way or my wishful thinking? The floorboards creak softly and my body stiffens as I reach for Alexander and find the sheets next to me cold. My eyes refocus and a sliver of light reveals him standing in front of the window, holding the drape aside. He drops the drape but the gap leaves enough light to see his face by.

'Alexander? What's the matter?'

He turns sharply. 'Nothing.'

'Can't you sleep? Are you sure you're OK?'

'Of course I am. I just got up for a glass of water. Go back to sleep.'

I lie on my back, staring at the ceiling for what feels like hours and then fall into a doze.

When I finally wake, it's to the aroma of coffee and baking and the sight of Alexander by the bed, track pants sitting low on his hips. He holds a tray containing freshly squeezed juice for me, an espresso for him and a plate of pastries. The autumn sun, filtering through the blinds, seems to have chased away whatever demons found him during the night.

He smiles warmly, yet I have the impression he's only doing it to fend off any questions.

'To what do I owe this honour?' I push myself up the pillow, going along with the pretence. Because I'm not sure which is best, ignoring the dreams or confronting him about them.

He sits on the bed next to me. 'Does there have to be a reason?'

'You tend not to do anything without a purpose.'

'I don't see any point wasting time on things that aren't productive.'

'What about poker? Skiing? Sex?'

'I can see you're going to be trouble today. Shut up and eat your croissant – you're going to need your strength.'

I do as I'm told, in the hope, but not expectation, I'll find out more about last night's episode. All morning, he's been acting about as close to amiable as Alexander ever gets. I'm half wondering if I really did dream last night's episode – which, of course, is what he wants me to think.

After we've made love, and forced ourselves to do some work, we take a walk over Port Meadow to the Trout for lunch, and wander back, chatting about our coursework, friends and Emma – everything but the dream. Before I know it, we're back in the city and walking down Broad Street.

'Hey, can we stop here? I need to go into Blackwell's to pick up a book I ordered. Do you want to go back to college while I get it?'

He squeezes my hand. 'No, it's fine. I'll come with you. Who knows what might happen if I leave you in there on your own.'

'Like I might get kidnapped by a crazed Klimt fanatic and you'd have to take him down?'

'It would certainly be more interesting than writing an essay on international political economy.'

'I thought you were passionate about your subject.'

'I am, but I'd rather conduct an in-depth study of something else this afternoon. I'm not sure I've paid enough attention to your right breast yet and there's a little dimple at the top of your bottom that needs more of my time.'

Warmth rises to my face. 'If this is some kind of D. H. Lawrence fixation, I'd rather you saved it until we're not out in public. Right now I have to pick up this book and go back to work. And your mind should be on higher things in a store like this.'

His palm travels to my butt, curving round the denim of my jeans. 'Sadly, my mind has descended even lower.'

'Lauren! Hey there.'

The familiar deep voice makes me turn sharply. 'Oh, Scott. How are you?'

'I'm good. How's things?'

'Good. They're good . . .' Shit, why do I feel suddenly guilty?

'And this must be Alexander?' He folds his arms.

'Yes, of course. Scott, meet Alexander Hunt.'

Scott thrusts out a hand. 'Scott Schulze.'

Alexander takes it and I'm grateful not to be a part of the bone-mashing contest that I suspect is going on.

Scott grins in a super-friendly way. 'It's good to meet you at last. Lauren's told me so much about you.'

Alexander seems puzzled. 'Has she?'

'Oh yes. I feel I know you already.'

Despite wanting to strangle Scott, I laugh. 'Don't believe a word he says, Alexander, he's trying to bug me. Scott's a cousin of Todd's and we met at the US Grad Soc cocktail party last week. I didn't know he was in Oxford so it was a big surprise.'

'Really?' It's at this point that I might expect Alexander to politely tune out but there's a gleam of interest in his eye that I'm not sure I like.

'We were just about to go into the bookstore,' I say, aware that Alexander's arm has snaked round my waist.

'Are you an art historian, then, Alex? You must know that Lauren's very talented.'

I cringe but Alexander seems encouraged by this statement. 'She definitely has hidden talents but I can't describe myself as an art historian.'

'Alexander's doing an MPhil in international relations, Scott.' I turn to Alexander. 'Scott's supposed to be studying water policy, but he's really here for the rowing. He's training with the Blues squad.' Shit, I sound like I'm setting up two people on a date, though I suspect it may turn into something more like a duel.

'International relations, huh? I have to say you don't look like a diplomat.'

'I'm not.'

'What do you do when you're not doing international relations, Alex? Do you row?'

I wince at the shortening of Alexander's name again, but he answers like a lamb. Which worries me a lot.

'I'm afraid not.'

Scott raises his eyebrows. 'You don't say? A big guy like you? You look in shape – you should try out for the Blues squad. Do you play any other sports? Soccer? Tennis?'

'No.'

'Surfing, maybe?' asks Scott with an air of innocence that defies belief.

'Not these days.'

I feel compelled to defend Alexander, even though I'm itching to get into the safety of Blackwell's. 'Alexander likes winter sports,' I say.

Scott's interest in piqued. 'Oh, where? I do a bit of snowboarding in Aspen. Have you been?'

Alexander smiles. 'Not yet, but I may go heli-skiing over the Christmas vac.'

Scott whistles. 'I'm impressed.'

'Please don't be.'

I can't believe what I'm seeing. I've never seen guys conduct a fight by sheer politeness. Scott's superpower is obviously suffocating bonhomie and Alexander is relying on cryogenic civility.

Scott grins. 'I've an old college buddy who runs a heli-ski operation out of Whistler. Where are you going?'

'The Kamchatka Peninsula.'

'Mmm. Can't say I've heard of it.'

'We tend to go places people haven't heard of.'

Scott whistles. 'We? Is Lauren going with you? I didn't know you were into extreme sports, Lauren.'

'Not as a rule,' I say, unless dating Alexander counts. 'And I'm going to be home in Washington. Alexander's going with his army buddies.'

I see the cogs whirring in Scott's brain. 'So you're in the military? Lauren didn't mention that.'

'She didn't mention you at all.' Alexander gives him a smile, the kind a crocodile is supposed to give before he swallows his prey whole. Oh, fuck.

I check my watch ostentatiously. 'Look, boys, you can stand around chatting all day if you want to, but I need to track down this book and get back to work on my essay. Professor Rafe wants to discuss my progress in tomorrow's tutorial.'

'Well hey, I wouldn't want to keep you both from your studies.' Scott doesn't actually bracket the word 'studies' with his fingers, but no one could miss what he's implying.

For once in his life, Alexander seems lost for words so I jump in. 'Scott, I really *have* to go. I'll see you around.'

I know Alexander is *so* going to make me suffer for this, but for now his fingers rest lightly on my lower back, lightly but proprietorially.

'I'll look forward to bumping into you, Lauren.' He turns to Alexander. 'But that's not a bad idea about a chat. Alex, here's my card. If you want to have a beer some time, give me a call.'

Without glancing at the card, Alex slips it in his jacket pocket and says crisply, 'Thank you. I may just do that.'

The book still lies in its bag on Alexander's coffee table. I haven't mentioned Scott and Alexander has waited until we are back at his house – and until I am naked – to say anything. I have a sneaking feeling this may be some kind of special-forces tactic.

'So, my ears should have been burning the other evening. Funny, you never mentioned Scott. Is he an ex?'

I shift in his lap, the denim of his jeans under my bare butt. 'No, he is not. He's a distant cousin of Todd's and I haven't seen him since the Adlers' silver anniversary party.'

'Really? He seems to know you very well.'

'Not as well as you're implying.'

'I'm not implying anything, Lauren.'

I run the edge of my fingernail down his chest, pretending to be intent on his pecs. 'So, are you going to take Scott up on his kind offer of a beer and a chat?'

'Would you mind if I did?'

'Hey, far be it from me to come between a budding bromance.'

He treats me to a scowl, but it's such a sexy one it only makes me want him more.

After we've had sex, he's sleeping peacefully beside me, moonlight dappling his face. His eyelashes flutter on his cheek and he looks boyish, beautiful even. I find it hard to imagine that this is the same man who last night had such violent dreams or the one who has done and seen things that haunt him.

'There you go.'

I plonk a drink on the table in front of Immy, who sighs with something approaching ecstasy. A few days after the Scott–Alexander bout, we've retreated to the G&D ice cream cafe on St Aldate's after trying out a new contemporary dance class.

'Is that right? A double espresso with ice cream, whipped cream *and* M&Ms?'

'Absolutely.' She takes a large sip of the drink and smacks her lips. 'God, I *so* needed this and it would be even better with a couple of shots of Stolichnaya in it.'

And I *so* needed the distraction and relaxation of the class. Not that I'll tell Immy, but last night Alexander had another dream. I was tired out after a tennis, session, a jog and an early-morning essay crisis, but his cries still woke me. By the time I came round properly, he was sitting on the edge of the bed, his head in his hands. I pretended to be asleep and saw him get up, go to the bathroom and splash water on his face.

Immy surfaces from her drink. 'Who knew that prancing around was absolutely knackering?'

'Prancing? Is that what you were doing?'

Her pink tongue captures a smear of cream from her lip. 'I certainly felt – and probably looked – like a Lipizzaner.'

'*That* elegant?'

She bats my arm. 'Hey, I didn't look that bad.'

Despite the cool shower and the make-up, I have to admit she is still a little red in the face. 'Maybe I can find a little colour corrector in my purse?'

'You're enjoying every minute of this, aren't you?'

My smile almost hurts my face. 'I'm only joking – you look fine – but I did love the class. I'd forgotten how much I love dancing and I really appreciate you coming along. I know it wasn't really your thing, but it makes up for all the times you thrashed me on the tennis court. Are you sure you won't come back next week?'

'If you don't mind, I'll pass. I think I'll have to accept I'll never be a dancer. Thank God.' She pulls a face. 'Did you say Alexander's coming to pick you up?'

'Uh huh. We're going up to London for the night. He said we'd go straight from here so I can't wait around too long.'

'It seems to be going well for you two.'

My lemonade sorbet tastes sharp in my mouth. 'It seems like it. Are you seeing Skandar later?'

'Yes. We're going to a club.'

'I'm glad it's going well for you too.'

Her eyes shine. 'So far, it is, I have to confess. We didn't get much sleep last night, which may explain my crappy dancing. Or not.'

Immy is making her way through a choc-chip cookie when Alexander appears outside the window. When he spots me, his face lights up with pleasure and he breaks into a smile.

Immy's voice, low but wicked with glee, reaches me. 'Lauren?'

'Uh huh?' I say as Alexander rounds the corner into the cafe.

'What the fuck have you done to Alexander Hunt? I could be mistaken, but for a nanosecond there I could have sworn he looked happy.'

Whatever I'm supposed to have done to Alexander, I hope I can keep on doing it. Since the night before my dance class, there have been no more nightmares and I don't want to spoil what has been, apart from the bad dreams, a truly magical few weeks.

It's the start of Seventh Week – the last one in November – and the time since I arrived at Wyckham has been the most intense of my life. I arrived here determined to study and to start a new Todd-free life. Now, against all expectation and judgement, I think I may have fallen for a guy who is the antithesis of what I would have chosen: arrogant, privileged, titled and dangerous.

Despite all my misgivings, I've never been so happy. We've walked through the Parks and Christ Church Meadows in sunshine and showers. We've been out to dinner at Brown's on our own and with Immy and Skandar. I feel I can concentrate on my studies now we've finally admitted we don't, in fact, hate the sight of one another – the opposite, in fact.

But I'm not about to confuse this relationship with security. I feel safe with Alexander in the physical sense, of course – but emotionally? Not a chance. He's too guarded, too closed up, too much like an unexploded bomb to ever feel secure in that sense and, besides, I'm self-aware enough to realize that the excitement and danger are heady drugs that keep me craving more.

Today is Sunday and we've taken a punt up the river. Huddled inside Alexander's down jacket, which he's made me wear over my DKNY pea-coat, I watch the pole slide through his hands and feel the punt slip effortlessly through the black water. He guides the boat steadily upstream from the punt station at the Cherwell Boathouse to our destination: a pub called the Vicky Arms where we've got a table reserved for lunch. Even now, as the tip of my nose reddens with cold, I'm imagining toasting my hands by the log fire and the tang of wood smoke in the bar.

Alexander is concentrating hard on steering, which gives me the opportunity to drink him in. I don't think I'll ever grow tired of that fluttering in my stomach when I see him. Now and again he smiles at me or points out something along the bank or in the water, but largely he's quiet, either absorbed by the task in hand or perhaps lost in his own thoughts.

He pulls the pole from the river, water dripping from his fingers. Along the bank, the willow trees are bare now, their branches like spiky fingers trailing in the eddies. The river, I'm told, is like a motorway in the summer, but not today. Only a few hardy or crazy-in-love souls like us were prepared to break the ice skins in the bottom of the punts.

After a couple of failed attempts to push him about his family, I haven't tried for a couple of weeks. Emma is still at school; in the end, Alexander didn't have to rush off and see her. She said she would stay, but she's still dead set on applying to Saint Martins and I back her to the hilt in that. Alexander says he doesn't mind what she does as long as she's happy. I know we haven't known each other long, but I also suspect I'm being kept away from her.

'We're here. Can you give me a hand?' He steers the punt towards the mooring stage on the bank below the pub. I scramble up from the bottom of the boat and it wobbles alarmingly as we near the muddy bank.

Alexander jumps on to the landing stage, forcing me to grab the sides as the boat rocks.

'Watch your hands!'

His warning's a second too late and a squeal escapes me as the punt scrapes the wall, trapping my fingers, briefly, between concrete and punt. It's hardly life-threatening, but the pain makes me feel nauseous for a few seconds. Tears spring into my eyes and now I'm beyond embarrassed. He pulls me out of the punt by my other arm.

'Let me see your hand.'

'It's nothing. It's OK.'

'You're crying.'

'No, I am *not*.'

Carefully, he peels my suede gloves from my throbbing fingers while I grit my teeth, trying hard not to wince. 'They're not broken, but you'll be bruised.'

I frown down at my red and skinned middle fingers. 'Shit. It's my right hand.'

He smiles. 'No tennis for a few days or you'll have to play left-handed.'

He makes me smile even though my fingers throb like crazy. 'It may well improve my game.'

He puts his arm round me. 'I think this is the perfect excuse for a medicinal brandy.'

Inside the Vicky Arms, I watch him queuing at the bar. Getting to know Alexander is like dismantling one of those Russian dolls: you take off one layer and there's another underneath. The moment I – or he – hints at anything to do with his family, he either clams up completely or deflects the focus on to me.

By the time he returns from the bar with two Rémy Martins, the pain in my hand has eased and the fire has warmed my chilled bones.

Alexander slips his arm round me. 'Better?'

'Yes, thanks. The medicinal brandy is working.'

He kisses my lips and I tingle all over. 'Maybe we should skip lunch?' I say.

'Maybe, but do you want to look at the menu first?' He smiles but there's an edge to his voice that sets off an alarm bell in my head. Only a faint one, but it's there all the same. Maybe I'm being paranoid but he seems a little distracted.

After lunch, he tops up my glass of red wine and we relax back against the old settle. The combination of the fire and his body have lent me a delicious glow, both inside and out. The pub is packed with friends and couples laughing and chattering. There are posters up asking people to book their Christmas parties and suddenly I'm hit by the realization that it's Thanksgiving next week and that this will be the first time I've missed the day, but it's the same for all the US students here.

I wonder if Alexander has sensed my mood because he squeezes my un-squashed hand. 'Lauren?'

'Uh-huh?'

'I'm going to be away for a few days this week.'

This wasn't what I was expecting him to say, but I manage to stifle my disappointment. 'Oh, OK . . . Is it for work?'

'Yes. I'm sorry.'

'It's, uh, fine. Absolutely. To be honest, it might be a good idea if I actually got some sleep this week.'

His thigh butts against mine. 'In that case, I'd get some while you can. I should be home by mid-week and I promise to have you up all night, every night.'

'I'll look forward to it.' I pause, then ask, 'How does your family feel about you going away like this? Does Emma know?'

'No. She has no idea that I leave Oxford. I don't tell her anything unless I have to.'

'What about your father?'

'He probably guesses, but I don't volunteer anything.'

'Do you think he's so keen that you quit the service because he's worried about you?'

He shrugs. 'If he is, he never shows it to me. We've never been close and after my mother died things took a turn for the worse between us. He views me as some kind of custodian of Falconbury, the same as any other member of staff, apart from the fact that I have no choice whether to join the firm or not and no say in the terms or conditions.' He hesitates and then adds, 'And, of course, he blames me for my mother's death.'

'What? How could it be your fault?'

'Because I was arguing with her. It was on our way to prep school, I'd been teasing Emma and my mother had told me to shut up so many times and she took her eyes off the road to shout at me . . .' He pauses. 'That's how he sees it and maybe he's right. I really don't give a fuck any more.' He makes a point of checking his watch. It's one of those wind-up ones with a gold bracelet and it has to be a family heirloom. I know instinctively that he's already said more than he wanted to. I think he definitely still gives a fuck, and a whole lot more, but for now he just gets up and says, 'Come on. We need to take the boat back before it gets dark.'

We punt back downstream to the boathouse, past frost-sheened willow branches shimmering in the wintry afternoon haze. Alexander is mostly silent and intent on getting the boat home as fast as possible and my mind keeps wandering to other things. While I'll hardly be sitting in my room waiting for his return – Professor Rafe is cracking the whip over me (an image I wish I hadn't allowed into my mind) and I could be at a drinks party, faculty event or clubbing almost every night if I wanted – I wouldn't be human if I didn't wonder what Alexander might be doing while he's gone. And, just occasionally in the darkest corner of my mind, if he might not come back at all.

It's also impossible for me to understand the gulf that exists between him and his father. My mother drives me nuts at times, and Daddy's so over-protective that sometimes I used to fantasize about walking out myself – but I know that's because we all care about and love each other and we're not afraid to show it. If that accident had, God forbid, happened to my mother, even if I'd been shouting and screaming in the car, would my father have blamed me? The answer is loud and clear in my mind: no.

But I might have blamed myself.

Is that Alexander's real trouble: that he *does* blame himself? I can't do anything about that, but I find it hard to forgive his father for making his teenage son feel he contributed to the death of his own mother. What kind of a man must General Hunt be? Does he really live up to the image presented by Immy and Alexander – and even Rupert? I don't care how intimidating the man is, I'd sure like the opportunity to judge for myself.

By the time we tie the punt up at the boathouse, I'm numb with cold and no matter how much I've tried to think of all the amazing things about being in Oxford and being in love with Alexander, I'm missing home just a little. Back at my room, Alexander follows me inside and I draw the curtains to shut out the darkening afternoon.

He sits on my bed. 'Is everything OK? You've been very quiet on the walk home.'

'I've been thinking of my family. It's Thanksgiving next week.'

'Of course it is. I'd forgotten – it's Thursday, isn't it?'

'Uh-huh. The USSoc is hosting a Thanksgiving Lunch. I was thinking of going along.'

He frowns, then says, 'You should do that. I was hoping to be back by Thursday but please don't rely on me.'

I'm far from doing that, I think, but instead I toy with the buttons of his shirt front.

'It's hot in here,' I say.

'It is . . . Will Brett be at this dinner?'

My fingers pause on his top button. 'It's not Brett, it's Scott, as you well know, and, yes, he might be at the dinner. Does that bother you?' There's no change in his expression when I pop open the button.

'Why would it bother me?'

'I don't know, Alexander.'

He regards me steadily. 'That's because there is no reason. It was merely an enquiry.'

He opens his legs so I can kneel between them. As I free the next button, a sprinkling of dark hair appears. 'Because . . .' I slip my hand under the cotton and flatten my hand over his pec, where his skin is deliciously warm under my palm '. . . *Because*, if I didn't know you better, I could almost believe you were jealous.'

'Then you'd be wrong, but if it amuses you to think I might be jealous I wouldn't dream of spoiling your pleasure.'

'It doesn't amuse me – it intrigues me.' I withdraw my hand, but only to unfasten another button.

When I blow lightly on his bared chest, my reward is

his intake of breath and the raw edge to his voice as he replies. 'Then enjoy being intrigued, but I'm afraid I'll have other things on my mind over the next few days.'

'So will I . . .' I flick the bottom-but-one button. 'And it won't be turkey.'

His expression is unreadable as he meets my eyes without flinching. 'Lauren, undo any more of my shirt looking like that, and I won't be responsible for what happens next.'

'Looking like what?'

'Hot as hell and totally shaggable.'

I pop the last button and tug his shirt from his waistband. 'Hey, I must remember to put that on my resumé.'

Chapter Fifteen

So, should I laugh – or cry?

The Skype window disappears from my screen and I sit back in my chair with a sigh. After I'd got back from the USSoc lunch, I spent the past hour or so chatting with my family while they enjoyed Thanksgiving dinner. Maybe, in the circumstances, I'm allowed to have mixed emotions. Outside, darkness has descended on the quad and there's a low mist wreathing around the Lodge tower. I'm used to the time difference now, but it feels weird to see the sun streaming in through the windows of our dining room in Washington while it's past supper-time here.

My mother, father and three of my grandparents were all gathered around the table at our house in the time-honoured way. My paternal grandfather died when I was small, but my Grandma Cusack and my mother's mother still come over to help with the turkey and pumpkin pie.

Everyone wanted to know how my studies were going and about the social life here and I showed them around my little room, which was quite surreal. My grandfather teased me a little, hinting about 'new special friends', but I side-stepped that one. Now I realize that I haven't told them about Alexander and I ask myself why. Is it simply because it's easier for me to keep my life private now I'm so far away? No, it would be too complicated and I can't face the inevitable grilling from a distance. My mother would *definitely* want every last detail about Alexander's family and Falconbury. She'd be on Debrett's in a flash, and as for my grandmothers they'd never leave me alone – ever again.

There's a knock at my door and my heart pitter-patters.

'Hell-oo!'

It's Immy. It may not be who I'd expected, but just what I needed, and there's a huge grin on my face as I open the door to her.

'How are you? Happy Thanksgiving!' She holds up a bottle of Cristal in one hand and a ribbon-tied gift bag in the other.

'Wow. You shouldn't have.'

'Why not? It must be horrible to be in this hole when you could be at home with your family . . . and with the Great Alexander away too, I thought I'd try and cheer you up.'

'You just did.'

'I hope you like it,' she says, nodding at the bag.

Nestled in the blue tissue paper is a turquoise gift box that I recognize immediately. The Kate Spade Silver Street keepsake box inside has the word 'Stowaways' stamped on the lid.

'I thought you could keep your bits and bobs in it.' Immy's voice sparkles with excitement.

'It's gorgeous and I totally love it – thank you, but I

thought you were going to Brown's with Skandar tonight?'

'We are after he's finished training so I can't stay long, but I thought you might need a little company tonight – and any excuse to drink Cristal.'

As I give her a hug, I have a horrible moment when I think I might cry, but Immy pretends not to notice and chirps: 'Shall I open the champagne before it gets warm?'

While Immy twists the cork out of the Cristal, I find a couple of glasses and we sit opposite each other on the bed, sipping fizz.

'So how was the Thanksgiving Dinner?' she asks.

'The real one or the virtual one? I'd just got off a Skype call to my family when you knocked.'

'Were they having fun?'

'Always. You know I love them all, but sometimes I used to find the whole family thing at Thanksgiving a little wearing.'

'Oh, same here. I lose the will to live by Christmas afternoon. Can you believe that my parents still expect me to watch the Queen with them?'

'I can't imagine, but . . . I really did wish I could have beamed over to be with them for the day. The USSoc dinner was fun and the staff had tried really hard to recreate the food and the atmosphere . . .'

'But it wasn't the same?'

'I hate to say this, but it almost made me feel further apart from my family and –' I sigh '– Professor Rafe was co-hosting it.'

'Oh for fuck's sake! What was he doing there?'

'Apparently, a few of the Fellows always make an effort to attend so I guess there's nothing unusual in him being there, and the Senior Tutor joined us too. A couple of the girls were hanging all over him, but I'm maxed out on Rafe. You know I told him I don't feel comfortable with him touching me in tutorials?'

'I remember you saying, but you should have reported him to the Dean or kicked him in the nuts.' There's a wicked gleam in her eye. 'Or both.'

'Maybe, but it seems to have worked. Since then, he's kept his hands scrupulously to himself, though he keeps asking me if I'm "comfortable with his proximity".'

'I hope his dick shrivels up and drops off.'

'I can handle it, but I've also seen him outside of tutes and lectures three times this week. Twice might be a coincidence, but the last time was in a boutique on the High.'

'What the fuck?'

'My thoughts exactly. I told him I was surprised to see him and he said he was looking for a gift for a god-daughter.'

She shudders. 'Ewww. Yuk. Have you told Alexander what's going on because he'll probably want to waterboard him or something.'

'That's why I haven't told him, and, also, I'm more than capable of dealing with it myself.'

'Alexander does like to do things his own way and subtle isn't part of his vocabulary. When's he back?'

'He was vague about it, but I'd really thought he might be back today. He doesn't share that kind of thing with me.'

She sips her Cristal carefully. 'Mmm. I did warn you what you were taking on.'

'He doesn't say much at all. He did tell me a little about his sister and the accident with his mother, but when I pushed him he clammed up. I think it would be a good idea if I met Emma and General Hunt so I can make up my own mind.'

She grimaces. 'Emma's cool, a bit of a wild child, but who can blame her with the ogre for a father. I'm sure you'd like her, but I wouldn't be in any kind of rush to meet General Hunt.'

'Surely he can't be that bad?'

'I've only met him once and he clearly considered me beneath his notice, which was fine by me, but from what I hear he's an appalling snob. I'd thank your lucky stars that Alexander hasn't taken you to Falconbury. Now, can I top your glass up?'

After Immy leaves, I try to settle down to read some online papers for my essay, but my mind keeps wandering to Alexander and his threat to keep me up all night. I hear footsteps thudding up the staircase, and put down my pen and notebook. I expect them to stop on the landing below me, because there's only my room and Immy's up here, but they continue, rounding the top flight and ending right at my door. I'm out of my chair and flinging open the door with indecent haste.

'Alexander!'

'Not Alexander. I'm sorry to disappoint you.'

'Scott! No, you haven't. It's – uh – lovely to see you.'

He peers over my head into the room. 'Not interrupting anything, am I?'

'No, no . . . I'm on my own.'

'No Alex, then?'

'He's, um . . . out of town.'

'On Thanksgiving? I thought he might want to celebrate with you.'

'Like I said, he's busy and I went to the USSoc Thanksgiving lunch. I thought you might have been there, as a matter of fact.'

'Like this?' In my surprise at seeing him, I hadn't registered that he's in his Dark Blue kit of hoodie and trackpants, a rucksack slung over one massive shoulder. 'I've been busy too. Aren't you going to ask me in?'

'Oh, sure . . .'

In my room, he immediately focuses on the bottle and glasses on my desk. 'You've been celebrating the day in style.'

'My friend Immy brought me the champagne as a Thanksgiving gift, but she had to go before we finished the bottle.' I hesitate, unsure what to do next, wondering if I should offer him a glass or not.

'I must admit it was a long shot. I had no idea if you'd even be in, or if you'd be holed up at Alexander's. I heard from Maisey that he has his own place in Oxford. In fact, she said, his folks own the entire row of houses down there.'

'My God, news travels fast. I expect the whole of USSoc know his shoe size and favourite pizza topping by now.'

'He didn't strike me as the pizza type of guy.' Scott grins and I can't help but be amused too. 'Besides, he wouldn't mind an old friend dropping by to wish you happy Thanksgiving, would he?' He kisses me on the cheek, smelling shower-fresh, and adds, 'Alexander Hunt doesn't have the monopoly on the best-looking girl in Oxford, does he?'

I roll my eyes at the flattery, but it's sweet of him to call, and he's right about one thing: why should I mope around here, waiting for Alexander to materialize? He only said he might be back today. I've had no text or call to say he's on his way – and, yes, I'll admit a niggle about where and how he might be has been lurking at the back of my mind.

'Whether he minds or not, I can have a drink with a friend and meet who I like. Would you like a glass of champagne?'

His handsome face lights up. 'My coach would probably go ape-shit but I guess it is Thanksgiving . . . Oh to hell with it, why not?'

'I'll go get a clean glass.'

When I return with a spare flute from a box in the back of my closet, he seems to be checking out the discarded tissue and ribbon on my bed, but drops them when he sees me.

I hand him a full glass, but he looks disappointed. 'I hope you're not going to let me drink alone.'

'No, of course not.' After tipping the remaining champagne into my flute, I raise it high. 'Happy Thanksgiving!'

'Happy Thanksgiving.'

He takes the office chair, while I sit on my bed. 'So what was so important that you couldn't make the USSoc party.'

'As you say, it's just another day here, and there was a selection trial at the Boathouse. If I'd missed it, I could have kissed goodbye to my chances of being in the extended squad.'

'That's a shame, but I understand why you had to go.'

'It's only one day and I did pretty well on the test so I'm through to the next stage.' He raises his glass again. 'Another reason to celebrate.'

'Congratulations. I'm sure you'll make the final cut.'

Once again, I see him glance at the wrapping paper on my bed. 'As it's the season, and you're receiving gifts, I've bought you something too.'

Fuck, this is awkward. 'Oh, Scott, I didn't expect . . .'

'Aren't they the best kind of presents? The ones you didn't expect?'

'I guess so, but I haven't got you anything.'

'You didn't know I was going to turn up, did you? If you had, I'd have expected at least a gift-wrapped Porsche, now that you're dating Lord Hunt.'

He laughs at my indignant face, opens his rucksack and pulls out a small parcel. 'Here you go. Don't expect diamonds.'

My hand goes to my throat. I wore the necklace to

the lunch. Maybe it was a little too much for daytime, but I hate the thought of something that beautiful lying in a drawer all the time.

'So, are you going to open it?'

Nervously, I lift the lid on the small box. I really hope he hasn't spent a lot of money and that it's not jewellery. I wish he hadn't bothered at all, but then I see what's inside the box and burst out laughing in relief and delight.

'You like it?'

I lift out the object. 'It's very, very cute.'

'Be careful. It cost a fortune.'

'I'll treasure it.' When I hold the snow globe aloft and shake it, a glittery blizzard swirls around the tiny model of the White House inside the dome. It's the height of kitsch, but I can't stop smiling. 'Where did you get this? They don't sell these in Oxford, as far as I know.'

Scott comes to look at the globe. 'My sister has one at home so I ordered it from the White House online gift shop. I thought you might appreciate a reminder of home today. Classy, isn't it?'

'It's a true work of art. Thank you.' I get up and hug him briefly. Immediately, I feel guilty, not because of what Alexander might think – I don't care about that – but because I might be giving Scott the wrong idea. But, to do him credit, he looks perfectly comfortable. He really is a lovely guy; he deserves someone super-nice.

'So what are you doing for the rest of the evening?' I ask, when we've finished the champagne and chatted a little about his rowing training and my course.

'Eating the contents of my fridge then I ought to get some rest. The trials have almost finished me off and we're back on the river at seven a.m. What about you? Will Alexander be back tonight?'

'Um . . . I don't know. He might, or he might not.'

Scott seems distinctly unimpressed. 'Why don't you come out for a quick drink? I'm starving.'

'I thought you said you were tired.'

'The champagne has worked wonders. Look, you said yourself that you aren't going to wait around for the guy, and if he chooses to have better things to do what can he expect?'

'It's not that simple.'

He folds his arms. 'Really?'

'Trust me, it isn't,' I say firmly, knowing I can't tell Scott where Alexander is, not that I have any idea myself. Alexander said he'd call to let me know when he'd set off for Oxford, so I'll have plenty of time to get back here or meet him at his house. I pick up my keys. 'I guess a quick drink would be fun and it *is* Thanksgiving . . .'

Some time later, I walk back up the stairs, mellow with champagne and the two glasses of mulled wine we shared outside, warming ourselves by the old-fashioned brazier in the courtyard of the inn. We talked about Washington; apparently Todd got a promotion in his father's law firm and is dating a girl from the office. A month ago, that would have had me lying awake wondering whether to be relieved or hurt. Now, I just don't care. I check my watch, to find it's past nine p.m.

'Happy Thanksgiving.'

Above me, Alexander leans over the banister and my heart-rate picks up as I hurry up the final flight.

'Alexander . . . how long have you been back?'

'A little while.'

I climb the last few steps, feeling disappointed and irrationally guilty – and annoyed with myself for feeling bad that I was out when he finally got here. Under the harsh light of the landing, he's even more gorgeous than I remember, but there are dark shadows under his eyes and, is it my imagination, or are his cheekbones a little sharper?

'How was Thanksgiving?' he asks, waiting for me in the centre of the landing.

'Better than I expected . . . You know, I kind of expected you to call and let me know you were on your way.'

'I wanted to surprise you. Is that OK?'

'Of course it is.'

'Then come here.'

His kiss is deep enough to blot out the world. It's also kind of prickly because I don't think he's shaved for days. I could swear he's holding on to me a little tighter than he normally does, and as I renew my acquaintance with his body again the shivery feeling I get tells me I've missed him more than I'd ever admit.

He squeezes my fingers. 'Your hands are cold,' he says.

'I forgot my gloves.'

Where have you been?'

'Just to the pub with a few friends. I'd have made sure I was back, if I'd known you were on your way.'

'Like I say, I wanted to surprise you.'

I haven't told him about Scott; it's not important but I get the feeling Alexander might make a big deal out of it and, right now, I just don't want the drama.

'You have.'

'Good. Now, I'd like to go home. I need a shower, a shave and some decent food, but first I've got a surprise for you.'

Within minutes we're back at his house and for the third time today I get to open a gift-wrapped package – which Alexander is 'helping' me to try on. A fire burns in the hearth and the thick curtains are drawn against the dark night, yet I'm shivering, partly because the house has been empty for a few days, but mainly because I'm naked except for a pair of Saint Laurent pointed pumps with black satin ribbons that tie round the ankle, and the Cartier necklace.

'Is the bow perfect yet?' My calves wobble a little as the five-inch heels spike the Persian rug.

'Not quite.'

Kneeling at my feet, Alexander adjusts the knot of the satin bow on my right shoe. The left one took an age until he was satisfied.

'Surely it will do?' Impatience tugs at my voice combined with a burgeoning sense that if I stand here any longer, with his hands caressing my ankles, I will want to drag him down on to the sofa.

He gives the bow a tiny tweak and glances up at me.

'You've clearly never been to Sandhurst. I was made to do two hours' drill in the pouring rain once because the toothpaste on my brush wasn't the regulation length. Since then, the phrase "It'll do" has been absent from my vocabulary.'

'If you hadn't noticed, I'm not at Sandhurst.'

'I'm delighted to hear it. Everyone would be court-martialled if you walked into the mess looking like this. However, I'm aware it's a little cool in here, so for now I'll allow you to pass.'

As he gets up, his strong fingers glide up the backs of my calves and thighs.

I wobble a little. 'And how am I supposed to walk in these?'

'You're not. I'll get my driver to drop us right outside Covent Garden. I hope you like *Giselle*?'

It's one of my favourites. 'I suppose it will do,' I tease, still amazed that he has arranged tickets to the ballet tomorrow evening as a Thanksgiving gift and, I suspect, compensation for being away from me. I haven't been to Covent Garden on my previous trips to London and I can't wait.

He stands up and assesses his handiwork.

'Now, are you satisfied?' I ask.

'I'm never satisfied, Lauren, you should know that.' Taking my hand, he helps me drop to the rug so that we're face to face.

I run my fingertip over his now-smooth chin and he grimaces. 'Sorry about earlier. I managed to grab a shower, but I didn't have time to shave.'

'I don't care if you'd walked in here straight from some battle ground.'

'Oh, believe me you would, but I wanted to get to the shoe shop before it closed.'

'Now, that is a phrase I didn't think I'd ever hear from Alexander Hunt's lips.' I push him back on the carpet, sitting astride one thigh, my wet sex pressing into the iron-hard muscle. He grips my hips and shakes his head, as if he can't believe I'm here – or he is.

'You look sensational, Lauren. I've wanted this for the past five days.'

'Ditto.'

He exhales sharply when I unzip the fly on his trousers and tug them down over his hips, as he realizes what I'm going to do to.

I enjoyed this with Todd, mainly because *he* enjoyed it, but I never craved to do it like I do now. 'I have to taste you.' My fingers circle the base of his shaft and I lower my head and close my mouth around the head of his penis.

He's so aroused that his cock is almost too big for me but I love the heat and taste of his flesh inside my mouth and his groan of pure animal delight as I suck gently on the crown. I press my damp sex against his thigh, rubbing my clit against the muscle. I slide my lips from his penis and circle it tightly at the base. Alexander tangles his fingers in my hair, tugging gently at the roots while I flick my tongue along his hard shaft. It hurts a little but the sharp little tugs turn me on even more.

'Do you know what you do to me?' His voice is fractured, unlike him. I love tearing down his defences and his thighs grow rigid as I touch my tongue to the purple head. 'Fuck, stop!'

I lift my head up. 'You're not enjoying it?'

'God, yes, but I want to shag you even more.'

He helps me to my feet and drags off his shoes and trousers. Then we're up against the sofa, my hands braced on the arm, my calves taut as high-wires in the heels, the ribbons cutting into my calves. He pushes me down over the sofa and his fingers slide between the cheeks of my ass. Briefly, I tense up, thinking he's going to take me from behind like Todd once tried to. I hated it, and with Alexander the thought scares me too – yet also makes my gut clench with irrational lust.

His finger slides between my lower lips and into the slick heat of my body.

'You're so ready.'

I whimper my response as he withdraws his finger and massages my clitoris with my own juices. He slides in easily, yet still he's so full and thick and hot. I wriggle back against his thighs to take in his whole length. 'Lean back.' I straighten and he stimulates my clit with his fingers, pushing the feeling out from my bud throughout my pelvis. Everything tightens around my nub until I'm swollen and desperate.

'Close?'

'Mmm.'

My pussy ripples spasms around him and he starts to thrust harder. I slap my hands back on the couch arm as he drives in faster and harder. My climax builds, until I want to scream for release. Alexander slams into me, my fingers dig into the couch and I come, a shuddering, whimpering mess, holding nothing back from him.

It's a crisply beautiful Saturday morning at the start of Eighth Week, with a cloudless blue sky. A light sheen of frost lingers in the shadows on the front quad lawn. My run has gone great, the sex I had with Alexander this morning has left me with a smile on my face, and as for the ballet last night – that was all I'd dreamed of and more. Only the prospect of the looming vacation at the end of this week clouds my mood. I'm so looking forward to seeing my parents again but that also means I'll have to be without Alexander for six weeks.

Despite this, not even the sight of Rupert strolling up to me can ruin my morning.

He smirks when he spots me walking in through the Lodge. 'You look fit,' he says, and by now I've been here long enough to recognize the double entendre.

'You should try it some time,' I shoot back between breaths.

'Alexander not joining you on your run? Or have you worn him out?'

I grit my teeth. 'He's working on an essay.'

'I suppose he's got a lot of catching up to do with all his extra-curricular activities. I really don't know where you both find the energy.'

'If you ran, Rupert, you might find you have the

energy. But I can't stand here chatting to you in the cold – I need to take a shower.'

'If you want company, you only have to ask. I know you get lonely when Alexander's away.'

'Not that lonely.' I start walking towards my room.

'I suppose I'll see you next weekend at Falconbury.'

His voice stops me dead in my tracks and I turn back. 'What?'

'At the Falconbury hunt, of course.'

'What hunt?'

Rupert frowns. '*The* hunt. The one the marquess holds annually on the Falconbury estate. I would have thought that Alexander had already mentioned it to you. Everyone's going down to the house on Saturday morning, although you'll already be there, I presume, knowing how Alexander likes to arrive a couple of days early?'

Through my clouds of breath, I see Rupert grinning at me like a troll, his eyes glinting with delight. I realize that I have been lured into a trap and swallowed the bait whole. The only thing I can do now is try to call the bastard's bluff. 'Oh that . . . Alexander mentioned there was some kind of event this weekend, but I didn't connect it with the hunt.'

'Of course you didn't . . . but I'm delighted Alexander has "mentioned" it to you.' He brackets his fingers round the word. 'It would have been very strange if he hadn't because I can't imagine why he wouldn't want to show Falconbury to you and introduce you to his father.

I'm surprised he hasn't taken you before, but now's your chance. You *do* hunt, don't you?'

I paste on a smile. 'I'll see you there, Rupert, *if* you have the energy.'

Turning away from his smirking face, I walk towards my room as if nothing is wrong. Inside, my mind is whirling like a fairground ride. Alexander hasn't so much as hinted about the hunt or the weekend.

Yet Rupert said that 'everyone' was going down to the estate on Saturday.

Everyone, it seems, except me.

Chapter Sixteen

Why?

That is the question which has occupied my mind since I left Rupert smirking in the quad yesterday morning. Why hasn't Alexander asked me to his home, to the biggest event of the year at Falconbury? The event that, if Rupert is to be believed, *everyone* has been invited to?

It's Sunday lunchtime and Alexander still hasn't said a word about the weekend. Last night, we went for cocktails at the Duke of Cambridge with Immy, Skandar and some of the tennis Blues, and then made love in his house until the small hours. It has killed me not to ask him anything, but I want the invitation to come from him; it *has* to come from him. Until now I have kidded myself that he has been too busy working to discuss it or that he wanted to keep it a surprise for Saturday night, but as the time ticks by that hope – that delusion – has ebbed away.

He is acting super-nice to me, but I feel as if it's not his hand in mine as we stroll along the gravelled drive through Christ Church Meadow towards the river. I feel as if it is not him walking at my side as we turn out of the avenue of trees and on to the bank of the Isis, but a stranger.

'Would you like to go somewhere for lunch?'

His words cut into my thoughts. I focus on a lone sculler sweeping past on the river, which is black under the louring skies. 'I don't care.'

'You don't *care*?'

It was a bratty reply and unworthy of me, as he might say, but I'm not sure I can hold back much longer.

'I meant that I don't mind.'

'We could go to Quod,' he suggests as we walk along the riverside path. 'Or I can drive us out to the Trout or the Mole at Toot Baldon if you fancy getting out of Oxford. I know how claustrophobic this place can be.' From the edge in his voice, I'm certain he guesses something is wrong.

'I guess I'm not hungry today.'

He stops by the bridge that leads to the college boat-houses. 'Lauren, what the hell is the matter with you?'

'I'm –'

'Please, don't insult my intelligence by saying "fine".'

'Oh, I wouldn't dare insult the intelligence of the great Alexander Hunt!'

Birds scatter in the tree above our heads and a middle-aged woman purses her lips at our raised voices, as if to ask how we dare ruin the tranquillity of this beautiful place. Alexander touches my elbow.

'What's the matter with you? Is it something I've done?' His voice bristles with irritation.

'Why would it be something you've done?'

'Because you wouldn't behave like this for any other reason. Unless you've had some bad news from home?'

'Nothing like that.' I take a deep breath. 'I just want

to know why you think it's OK not to ask me to your home next weekend.'

There's a pause that lengthens before he finally murmurs, 'How do you know about that?'

'From Rupert. Unless you were going to ask me today? Is that it, Alexander? You were waiting to surprise me?'

Guilt is stamped on his face. *Good.* 'No, I wasn't waiting to surprise you.'

My stomach clenches sharply. 'So you weren't going to tell me about it?'

'Of course I was going to tell you about it and I'm sorry you found out from Rupert. He should mind his own fucking business, as usual.'

'What else did you expect? He assumed I'd been invited and why wouldn't he? I pretended you *had* mentioned it because I wanted to give you the chance to ask me, but I was obviously wrong.'

His back stiffens as he retreats inside his armour. 'I should have told you I was going to be away this weekend, but I kept putting it off.'

Words almost fail me at the shock of realizing he had no intention of including me in the weekend, but then they burst out, without restraint.

'I'm flying home next week and it was going to be our last weekend together. You knew that!'

'Lauren, you've got things completely wrong. This is the hunt, remember, and I know you'll hate it. The whole thing is tedious and full of liggers, hangers-on and social climbers who you'll probably loathe on sight.

I wouldn't go back to Falconbury myself, but I have no choice.'

'Why not?'

'Because it's a tradition,' he says with icy patience.

'Tradition? Oh, in that case, *of course* you have to go. Don't let me get in the way of tradition.'

'Oh, for God's sake, grow up.'

His armour slips and I stare at him open-mouthed. I walk off the bridge, trying to stay calm, but he catches me in a few strides and grabs my arm.

'Let's discuss this like adults.' He sounds so stiff I feel as if a chasm has opened between us.

'Are you embarrassed by me and that's why you don't want me to come?'

'*Embarrassed?* Is that honestly what you think?'

'What else should I think when you refuse to ask me to what's clearly the biggest occasion in the social calendar.'

He snorts in derision.

'It *is* important to you, though, isn't it? Rupert might be a top bullshitter but he did say that "everyone" was going.'

'Not everyone. He's talking out of his arse as usual – and winding you up – and as for me being embarrassed by you, that's the very last reason I haven't asked you.'

'I don't buy that.'

We face up to each other, both daring the other to back down. Alexander glares at me, then sighs. 'I'm embarrassed by my family, that's why, and some of my friends. I wasn't lying when I told you you'd hate them.

As for my father . . . he's an awkward bastard at the best of times and I can't guarantee he'll be any different because I've got company. In fact, he could be worse.'

The words tumble out as if he's physically hurt by saying them.

'But won't Emma be there?'

'She may be – it depends on her end-of-term plans, but really it will be almost exclusively hunting people – and Rupert of course.'

I feel as if he has mentioned Rupert as an added dissuasion, but I refuse to take the bait. 'I can understand that you can't get away from your family, but if you loathe these people so much, why do you invite them to your home?'

'I don't loathe all of them – most of them, I admit – but I didn't invite them, either. My father decides the guest list now, and my mother did it when she was alive. They're all hunt people we've known for years, centuries in a couple of cases, and,' he adds contemptuously, 'nothing changes at Falconbury. My father sees to that. The Falconbury meet and the ball afterwards are traditions that have been going on for generations.'

'There's a *ball* too?'

He glances away from me guiltily. 'Yes, it's on the Saturday evening after the meet but . . .'

'But what?'

'Well, if you *really* want to come, then I'm happy for you to be there, but . . .' He pulls me into his arms and I stand, stiffly, as he looks at me seriously. 'You can come on one condition, that you believe me when I say that I'm not ashamed of you in any way. I was only trying to protect you by keeping you away from my bloody family and friends for as long as I could.'

There is such fierce passion in his voice that I have to believe him, even though I'm still confused and reeling from his admission that he wasn't going to invite me. 'I wish you'd told me this sooner instead of me having to hear it from Rupert. You don't have to protect me from people – whether they're idiots in pubs or your own family.'

'You haven't met my relatives.'

'You're forgetting I'm a politician's daughter. I think I can handle a few awkward family members and I certainly don't need to be wrapped in cotton wool. I had such a battle to persuade my parents that I wanted to study over here, but I stood my ground, so I can deal with your father and anything these so-called friends of yours throw my way. You know, I bet they're nowhere near as terrible as you think they are.'

I sound more confident than I feel and, far from reassuring me, Alexander simply murmurs, 'Let's hope you're right.'

'My God, is this the new distribution centre for Net-a-Porter?'

Shaking her head, Immy glances up at the clothes piled on my bed, hanging from the doors and hooked over the picture rail. God knows, I've probably spent more time packing for this weekend than I did for the whole eight-week term. I tried to ask Alexander what

I should take, but couldn't get more than a muttered, 'Whatever you wear I'm sure you'll look beautiful,' out of him. In truth, I've hardly seen him since Sunday because we both had so much work to do to meet deadlines for our end-of-term essay projects. When I have seen him, he's been on edge and snappy.

In the end I asked Immy round, though I felt guilty because she hadn't been invited.

'I don't know what to take for the weekend. I wish you were coming to Falconbury.'

She snorts. 'Me? No way.'

'Why not?'

'Because I don't hunt and I don't want to. I love riding and I've been to meets a couple of times, but all that outdated silly ritual does nothing for me.'

'But they don't hunt foxes now, do they? They only follow trails.'

Immy raises her eyebrows in response.

'I wouldn't dream of going along if they did,' I declare. 'I hate cruelty to animals.'

'Don't let them hear you say that. However, that's not really the point of a Falconbury meet these days. Some of them are there for the thrill of the sport, like Alexander, but the rest love the socializing, the drinking and, most of all, the being seen to be invited into the Hunt social circle. If you think you've seen social climbing, you've seen nothing until you experience a Falconbury hanger-on. Some of them would trample on their grannies to get an invite.'

'You haven't been to a White House fundraiser. It's white tie and crampons.'

'I'd be happy to hone my climbing skills there.'

Even though I laugh, I'd be lying if I didn't admit that the weekend was making me feel increasingly nervous. Alexander's touchiness isn't helping one bit. He keeps saying that he's glad I'm coming now, but I can tell how tense he is about it. Can his family and friends really be *that* unpleasant?

'So, what do you think I should take?'

'Mmm.' She circles the room, chewing her lip. 'Are you actually going to ride out with the hounds on Saturday morning?'

'No, but I might go for a ride with Alexander at some point. I bought a new tweed hacking jacket, jodhpurs and boots for that.'

She sighs with relief. 'Thank fuck for that. You would not believe the etiquette involved in hunting turn-out – almost as bad as the rituals here – and the Falconbury lot are sticklers for it. Wear the wrong colour coat or forget to give the Master his due deference and you can kiss goodbye to being asked back. I hate the whole ridiculous charade personally, but it's an unbreakable Hunt fixture and I know Rupert adores the whole thing. Don't let this weekend drive a wedge between you and Alexander.' She runs a finger reverently over my Donna Karan cocktail dress.

'So, what do you think? I need something for drinks and dinner with the Hunts on Thursday evening.'

'Oh, lucky you.'

'I thought maybe I'd wear this?' I hold up the sleeveless black Twiggy studded silk-crepe dress I splashed out on in Harvey Nicks.

'That's perfect. Chic and edgy. However . . .'

'Yes?' I ask anxiously.

'Falconbury is probably glacial. These places always are and General Hunt probably considers it a blood sport to keep his guests shivering. Have you got anything to put over the top of it?'

'I bought a silver shrug from home.'

'Perfect. What about the ball? Will you wear the dress you bought for Rashleigh Hall?'

'I thought I'd better try something different so I got my mother to send over a couple of things.' I show her the Alexander McQueen purple chiffon gown and a Calvin Klein dress similar to one I saw Kristen Stewart wearing to the Met Gala.

She strokes the teal velvet. 'My precious . . .' she purrs, and I burst out laughing. 'I bought it while I was dating Todd, but I haven't worn it yet. I hope that's not an omen.'

'They're both stunning and either would knock everyone dead and –' she grins wickedly '– that's probably what you'll want to do by the end of the weekend.'

'Lauren!'

It's Thursday morning and Rafe's voice echoes under the vaulted roof of the Lodge gate. My heart sinks but I have no choice but to stop.

'Oh, hello, Professor Rafe.'

'I'm so glad I caught you. How are you?'

I manage a smile. 'OK.'

He frowns. 'You don't look it. You're very pale, if you don't mind me saying. Not going down with fresher's flu, I hope?'

'No, nothing like that. I was going out for some, um . . . breakfast.'

Rafe raises his eyebrows and I realize just made a big mistake. The truth is I've had very little sleep, partly because Alexander and I spent half the night having sex before he left at dawn to get some work done. I was hoping to do the same before I head off for Falconbury this afternoon.

'A late one, eh? Well, it's never a good idea to skip breakfast.'

'No, of course not.' I'm itching to get away.

'Actually, I've been meaning to catch you before our tutorial tomorrow morning. How's the essay going? I'm looking forward to hearing your thoughts on Klimt's involvement with the *Wiener Secession*.'

Oh fuck. I'd forgotten about the tute. Tomorrow I'll be at Falconbury. I daren't tell him.

'Oh, yes. I mean, of course. The essay's going pretty well.'

'Good. I shouldn't say this, but I dread some tutes; however, you're different. You always have such, ah, original ideas that I relish our times together. You're also so reliable and punctual, unlike some people I could mention. I really want to discuss the vacation reading list and our plans for next term before you go back to the States.'

My head swims a little. I'm going to have to tell him I can't make it tomorrow after all, but what excuse can I give? I feel uneasy at missing a tute, even for Alexander.

'You *do* look rather pale. Why don't we go and get a bite to eat? Blackwell's coffee shop is only two minutes away. Perhaps I could treat you to a pain au chocolat and cappuccino in there. Neutral territory and all that.'

He gives a wry smile that makes me feel ever so slightly guilty for having been so blunt about him touching me in tutorials. Though God knows why because he did make me feel uncomfortable. In fact, everything he does, even when he seems to be genuinely nice, like now, puts me on edge.

'Um . . . well.' My stomach rumbles and he laughs softly.

'You look as if you're about to pass out from starvation.'

Going for a coffee with him now is the last thing I want, but I can hardly refuse when I plan to bail out of his tutorial so I nod politely. 'Not quite, but maybe I could use a cup of tea.'

A short time later, I'm sipping a cup of Earl Grey as Rafe returns from the counter with two pains au chocolat and an espresso for himself. He pushes the pastry towards me and empties a sachet of sugar into his coffee. I don't want to refuse the pastry and, anyway, I won't have time for lunch now; I'll have to work right up until Alexander calls for me.

'I must say I'm impressed that you still plan on making the tute when there are so many other temptations in Oxford, as I'm sure you've discovered.'

The pastry sticks in my throat.

'The Falconbury Hunt is a huge social occasion, isn't it? I hear Alexander is travelling down tonight.'

I swallow. 'I'm – um – not sure I understand you.'

'Really? But you must have been invited. Alexander wouldn't leave *you* off the list, now would he? In fact, I'm very surprised you still plan to come to my tutorial. Maybe I've got things completely wrong, but I can't help having noticed that you've got into his group. You *are* seeing him, aren't you?'

'Yes, but . . . how do you know about the hunt?'

'I've been around Oxford for years; the hunt and ball are legendary among people who care about such things, not that mere mortals like me get invited, of course. Not that I'd go if I was; the Hunts – and hunting people in general – are not people I'd choose to socialize with, and obviously I'm bitterly opposed to blood sports.'

'So am I. I despise cruelty to animals, but it's a drag hunt now.

'So he has asked you.'

'Yes, he has.'

He holds up his hands. 'I apologize. You want to go, understandably. It's none of my business, of course, and you have every right to ignore me, but if the relationship affects your studies then I wouldn't be doing my job as your tutor not to bring it up.'

It really *isn't* any of his business and I could and probably should tell him that, but he is my tutor and I am supposed to be here to study as well as enjoy myself.

'It isn't affecting my studies. I've tried not to let it.'

He gives a little sigh. 'I know. Your coursework has been exemplary and . . . as I said at the start of term, you're an outstanding prospect, Lauren. I really think you could go on to do a DPhil here if you wanted to and if you applied yourself. I would hate to see you throw all that potential away by getting distracted.'

'I've no intention of getting distracted by anyone.'

'I must say I'm very relieved to hear it. Also it's very creditable that you plan on staying here for the tute, and not sending me some excuse afterwards about being ill.'

I tear off another piece of pain and shove it in my mouth. Rafe may be a creep but he's also very clever. He knows exactly what he's doing here.

'I'm happy I'm wrong and you decided your end-of-term work was more important.'

My mother told me never to speak with my mouth full so I nod, panicking inside. Now I'll have to make some excuse tomorrow – or come clean now.

He checks his wrist and grimaces. 'I really should be leaving. I'm having lunch at a friend's in Summertown.'

'Of course. You don't want to keep him waiting.'

'Her,' he says with a smile. He gets to his feet and to my horror I find *my* hand on *his* arm. 'Professor Rafe, wait.'

He glances down at my fingers, as if he's astonished

I actually touched him. Heat rising to my face, I pull them away, but it's too late. He smiles and sits down again.

'I expect my friend won't mind if I'm a little late, not if you've something important to ask me. You do have something to ask, don't you, Lauren?'

'I –' Oh God, what am I doing? 'After what you've said about my studies and me being reliable, I shouldn't ask this, but I would very much like to go to Falconbury this evening. Alexander has asked me to dinner with his family and I had agreed. I'd hoped to find a time to ask you if we can reschedule the tute and kept putting it off. Now I know it's too late unless you can see me later today?' I ask hopefully.

'Unfortunately not, but in view of the fact you've been honest with me I've got half an hour now. We could have a quick chat about next term's work load and reading list and you could email your essay to me.'

'That would be great,' I sigh in relief.

Half an hour later, I'm trying to pay attention to his thoughts on the Hilary schedule, relieved that I got off so lightly. When we've finished, he checks his watch again. 'Well, I could chat to you all morning, but I really have to go now. I hope you have a good time at the hunt and ball, but, please, be careful.' He pats my hand. 'I'd hate to see you get hurt.'

'Why would I get hurt?'

He shakes his head. 'Nothing. None of my business.'

'Please, Professor Rafe, say what you need to.'

I think I raised my voice a little because a couple of people glance up from their books and tablets, but instantly return to their own private worlds.

'My dear, I'm sure I don't know anything about Alexander beyond what you've worked out for yourself, but I would hate to see you ruin your studies over him – or worse, get hurt very badly.'

'I can look after myself,' I say, yet my stomach is fluttering. 'But, now you've started, go on.'

He gives a deep sigh. 'I hate pigeon-holing people – it goes against everything I believe about the complexity of human nature – but I know Alexander.'

Hastily, I swallow down my pastry. 'Sorry, but you *know* Alexander?'

'Of course I know him. He did his undergraduate degree at St Merryn's College. I was his pastoral tutor there before I joined Wyckham. You are aware of his background and circumstances, of course?'

'Of course I am, and I'm not influenced by it in any way.'

'I knew you wouldn't be. You're not one of these naive young women who would be seduced into thinking a man like Alexander would see them as a long-term commitment. He may act like a cavalier maverick, but when it comes to family he'll marry within his circle, as his kind always do.'

I'm so pissed by the sexism of this statement, I can hardly reply. 'I can assure you I've no intention of marrying him. We've not long started dating.'

'Then I won't have to worry about you any more.'

Rafe gathers up his laptop bag. 'Now, my dear Lauren, I really *must* go. I'll email you with some more information about next term's work and, if you need me, please don't hesitate to give me a call. My only concern is your welfare and happiness – and, of course, helping you to achieve that wonderful potential. Don't let anyone take that away from you.' He pats my arm. 'And have a wonderful Christmas.'

Chapter Seventeen

'This bloody weather. If it rains again tomorrow, the hunt will have to be called off.'

Alexander switches the wipers on to max and they thrash across the screen. It's been raining since we left Oxford, and forty miles and over ninety minutes later water is still pouring down the windscreen as we turn off the main road on to a lane that seems barely wide enough for the Range Rover.

The Thursday-afternoon traffic combined with the rain has conspired to make it a tedious journey largely conducted at a snail's pace. None of the roads seem big enough to cope with the volume of traffic and Alexander has spent most of the journey drumming his fingers on the wheel, concentrating on the road or staring moodily into space. Now we're on the way to what I assume to be the Falconbury estate, it's hard not to clutch the grab handle as the hedgerows whizz past at dizzying speed.

'Jesus Christ!'

The screech of brakes cuts through me. In front of us, a Porsche 911 has stopped in the road, inches from the grille of the Range Rover.

'If he thinks I'm backing up, he's mistaken. There's a farm gate behind him. He can pull into that.' Alexander revs the engine, forcing the enemy Porsche to reverse back along the twisting lane. The driver flinches first, tucks in against the metal gate and the Range Rover flashes past, the scrape of twigs on our paintwork setting my teeth on edge.

'Idiot!' Alexander seethes as we roar off again. Closing my eyes, I say a silent prayer that we get to Falconbury before I throw up.

Ten minutes later, he swerves the Range Rover between two pillars topped by what I think are griffins. It's hard to tell in the afternoon gloom and rain, and the griffins are so weathered by age, who knows . . . then the headlamps sweep briefly over a sign that reads FAL-CONBURY HOUSE.

I sigh with relief that the journey is over and hope both Alexander and I can relax a little now we're finally here. I've tried not to give Professor Rafe's comments any credence, suspecting that they were another way of manipulating and undermining me – this time without touching me. Yet I wouldn't be human if I didn't wonder if there was a tiny grain of truth in them, or have thought something similar myself once or twice.

The gates may have announced our arrival at Falconbury, but the driveway from gates to house seems to go on for ever. I'm sure I catch a glimpse of eyes glinting under the trees as we drive along. Maybe it's a fox, I think, and say a silent prayer that it won't be chased all over the countryside on Saturday. The drive rolls on and on until the trees stop and meadowland opens up in front of us, with dark shapes dotted across the fields.

'Are those deer?'

Alexander keeps his eyes on the road. 'Yes, there have been deer on the Falconbury estate for eight hundred years.'

Eight hundred? By any standards, that's impressive. I realize now that I could have Googled the place and wonder why I haven't. Partly because it seems a vulgar thing to do, and in the past week my mind has been focused on the weekend itself, but now I wish I'd prepared better.

Too late.

Just in time I bite back an 'OMG' as we drive round a bend.

Immy wasn't joking when she said that Rashleigh Hall was small in comparison to Falconbury. We sweep on to the forecourt and Alexander brakes hard, bringing the car to a halt in a spray of gravel.

While he climbs out and opens the tailgate, I slump back in my seat, taking it all in. Through the rain-spattered window, Falconbury looms above me. It's hard not to find the place a little forbidding on a foul December afternoon like this, but the sheer grandeur of it eclipses everything else.

It's far bigger than Rashleigh Hall and completely the opposite in character. Rashleigh was built in creamy stone, all neoclassical elegance. Falconbury is full-on gothic revival, channelling dark medievalism with turrets and gargoyles. I'm guessing it dates back to the mid-nineteenth century, but Alexander said there had been a deer park here for eight hundred years so I assume there were earlier buildings on the site. With the rain lashing the facade, I almost want to laugh at the gloomy splendour of the place.

The tailgate whispers down and Alexander appears at the door. 'Let's get inside, shall we?' His voice is still gruff but a little softer now and I wonder if he's regretting his earlier loss of temper. 'Please, let me give you a hand, and mind the puddles.'

A guy hurries towards us and as he gets close up I almost do a double-take. I'm sure he's wearing some kind of butler's uniform.

'Good evening, sir. What a dreadful night.'

'Hello, Robert, and yes, it could be better.'

Alexander shakes hands with him and breaks out the same warm smile he used on the elderly salsa dancer who tried to help me when I fell after my run. The same smile he uses to me, when he's not glowering or brooding.

'Please, let me take those, sir.' Robert nods at the bags on the gravel.

'I can manage, but I'm sure Miss Cusack would be glad of the help.'

'No really, I'm OK.'

Politely ignoring me, Robert picks up two of my bags, while Alexander carries the other two and his leather holdall. I brush the rain from my face as we hurry under the porte-cochère with its gabled tower and oriel windows.

The door is open and a petite blonde woman, who I guess is in her early fifties, beams as we reach her.

'Good afternoon, sir. How was your journey?'

'Not too bad, Helen. I hope you're well?' He kisses her on the cheek.

'Very, sir, and it's wonderful to have you home.' The warmth in her voice tells me Helen means what she says. I'm guessing she's known Alexander a long time, maybe since he was a baby, which means she must have been here while he's been serving in the army – and while his mother was alive.

His smile is tight and I can tell he's a little embarrassed too. 'How are the grandchildren?' he asks as I hang back, unsure what to do or say.

Her eyes shine with pride. 'Very lively and growing up far too quickly.'

'Good.' I feel his hand slip over mine and my heart rate picks up. It's possibly the first sign of real warmth I've had from him for a few days. 'Helen, this is Lauren Cusack.'

'Good to meet you, Helen.' I hold out my hand.

'You too, miss.'

She takes it briefly, but I'm not sure I did the correct thing. 'Please, call me Lauren,' I say, more in hope than expectation.

'Whatever you wish.' Helen's smile is polite, but I can see the discomfit beneath.

'I'll have your bags taken up to your room, sir,' says Robert. 'We thought Miss Cusack might prefer the larger room above the porch.'

My antennae twitch. I have my own room, so I'm not sharing with Alexander. I should have realized, but I'm still taken aback, yet he nods as if it's all expected and perfect. 'Thank you. Is my sister home yet?'

'Lady Emma is staying on at school for the end-of-term party, I believe.'

238

'And my father?'

'Lord Falconbury has been in town today, but he should be home soon. He asked if you and Miss Cusack would be joining him in the sitting room for drinks before dinner?'

I hide my disappointment; I'd have loved to have met Emma, and sense she might be some kind of ally.

'Of course we will.'

'Do you want to go to your room now, sir, or shall I have some tea served in the sitting room?'

'We'll go up.'

Helen smiles at me. 'I expect Miss Cusack would like some tea sent up?'

'I'd appreciate that.'

'Can we take your coats?' Gratefully, I hand my damp pea-coat to Helen while Robert takes Alexander's Barbour. Another guy, not in uniform but in a shirt and tie, is already carrying some of our luggage up the red-carpeted oak staircase to the first floor.

Suddenly a dark shape shoots out of a door to the side of the stairs and a volley of deafening barks drowns out everything.

'Benny!'

A black Labrador hurtles along the hall, his claws clattering on the polished floor, and launches himself at Alexander like a guided missile.

His face lights up. 'Hello, boy! I wondered where you'd got to. Have you missed me?'

Benny's answer is to leap up at Alexander and lick his face. He laughs and strokes the dog's ears. 'OK, OK, settle down, boy.'

Ignoring him, Benny weaves his way round my legs, almost knocking me over.

'Down!'

At his master's command, Benny drops to the floor, panting hard and gazing up at me as if he'd like to lick me to death. I crouch down, stroking his silky ears.

'He's adorable! I didn't know you had a dog.'

'I've had him since I was at university, but I don't get to see him often enough, do I, boy?'

Benny rolls over so I can tickle his belly, his tongue lolling to one side in happiness.

'Ignore him. He'll do anything for attention.' Alexander crouches down beside me, scratching the dog's belly.

'Buddy used to do that,' I say, and suddenly there's a huge lump in my throat. Oh shit.

I renew my efforts to tickle Benny into submission.

'Buddy?' he asks.

'He was a schnauzer – we had to have him put to sleep while I was at Brown. We used to take him with us for summers on the Cape. I loved him.' My throat is scratchy with emotion. It must be the end of term, Thanksgiving and this weekend getting on top of me.

Alexander either hasn't noticed the moisture on my cheeks or is pretending not to. 'He sounds like a fine dog. I'm sure you miss him, like I do this rogue when I'm away.'

I straighten up, managing to hold it together.

Benny twists back to his tummy, eyes fixed adoringly on Alexander.

'I promise I'll take you out for a walk later,' he says, then holds out his hand for me to go ahead of him. 'Shall we go up?'

The walk up the staircase serves to reinforce my impression of the scale and opulence of Falconbury. The walls are panelled in oak, with a lofty, carved arched ceiling. We pass dozens of portraits of people I assume to be Falconbury ancestors. As we reach the first floor I stop, unsure whether to turn left or right down the landings on either side of the staircase.

'We're in the West Wing, at the end.' Alexander points to the left.

Halfway along the corridor, two women about my age bustle in and out of rooms. Both of them smile at us briefly and say, 'Good evening,' and Alexander responds with a nod, but they're clearly not part of the Hunts' inner circle of loyal retainers. That's six staff already and we haven't even reached our room.

I don't know why it surprises me so much that the Hunts have staff. My mother has help with the cleaning and hires in caterers if she throws a big party. Logically, it's obvious that an estate this huge has to be managed and run, but there's an air about these people that you don't see in employees. I can only describe it as deference – and, in the case of Robert and Helen's response to Alexander's arrival, I have to admit there's genuine warmth and affection too.

'This is it.'

He opens the door for me and stands back so I can go in first.

'Wow.' My coolness deserts me as I walk inside.

My bags stand at the foot of a four-poster bed, with brocade hangings and a canopy that seems as if it touches the ceiling. Immediately, I picture us making love on the silk bed throw and my anxieties about this weekend melt away temporarily.

Then I focus on the rest of the room. Opposite the bed is a huge window with leaded panes and stained-glass coats of arms. The walls are panelled to half-height, with antique red wallpaper above and an elaborately carved cornice. It's a Gothic dream – or nightmare, depending on your point of view. The wardrobe, dressing table and drawers are huge pieces, polished to perfection. A stunning arrangement of fresh roses stands in the centre of a table in the window, their delicate scent perfuming the room.

'Alexander, I had no idea.'

'About what?'

'This house, the staff, the estate. It's on a different scale to anything I expected.'

'It's not my house,' he says, crossing to the window. 'It's my father's.'

Joining him, I peer out into the darkness, which stretches on and on, uninterrupted by any lights that might signify neighbouring properties. The moon peeps out briefly, revealing the shadowy figures of deer at the edge of the woods. Suddenly I feel very small and insignificant.

There's a knock at the door. Alexander opens it and Helen comes in with a huge tray of tea and cookies.

She sets the tray down on the table. 'I've made a pot of Darjeeling and one of Earl Grey because I wasn't sure which you preferred, Miss Cusack. There's milk and lemon.'

'Thank you, and also for the flowers. They're beautiful.'

'It's a pleasure, but don't thank me. Alexander asked for them to be waiting in your room. Is there anything else you need?'

'No, everything's great.' Apart from not sharing a room, that is.

Helen smiles, obviously waiting to be dismissed by Alexander. The subtleties of dealing with the staff are so nuanced that I don't think I'll ever get to grips with them.

'Thank you,' says Alexander.

After Helen has gone, I take another look through the window, still unable to quite believe that Alexander spent his childhood in this place; it feels so little like a 'real' home in some respects. The rain is lighter now and there are headlights wavering along the road that leads through the parkland.

His hand is on my shoulder and I turn. 'The flowers were a lovely gesture. Thank you.'

'I'm glad you like them. I wanted you to feel welcome . . . Will they do?' he adds, almost anxiously.

'They're perfect and this suite is magnificent, but I still wish we were sharing a room.'

He sighs. 'So do I, but it's traditional for unmarried couples at Falconbury to have separate rooms. I know that's incredibly old-fashioned, but it's simpler to leave things as they are rather than have a battle over it. If I'd insisted to Helen that we share, my father might have made life hard for her.'

'I'd hate for that to happen. Robert and Helen seem like lovely people. I guess they've worked here a long time.'

'They've been here since I was born. Robert started out as an assistant to the old butler and Helen worked in one of the estate offices. She's a housekeeper and staff supervisor now.'

'And now he's the butler?'

The word is so at odds with the modern world, though I know that they're popular with some of the Asian and Middle Eastern dignitaries we've met back in Washington.

'Of course.'

'I'm not really sure that Helen likes calling me Lauren, but I'd feel a lot more comfortable if she did. Robert too.'

He holds me. 'I may be able to persuade Helen to use your first name, but Robert won't have it. I'm afraid you're going to find some of the things we do here archaic.' He shakes his head. 'My father's determined to cling on to the past.'

'Stop worrying, it's been great so far.'

Voices and the slamming of doors draw our attention to the forecourt below the window. A Bentley has drawn up, the same one that whisked us to Le Manoir and the ballet.

Alexander presses his lips together and it doesn't

take Sherlock to guess that the middle-aged man stepping down from the rear is his father. A large black umbrella is held over his head by Robert and his face is obscured from view.

Alexander says nothing and pulls me away from the window and sharply to him. His mouth comes down on mine, hard and insistent. When he's finished kissing me, he tugs the front of my wrap dress away from my cleavage, exposing my breast. The flick of his tongue over my nipple draws a whimper of pleasure from me and I let my eyes drift shut to savour the warmth and wetness of his mouth suckling my swollen nipple.

'I know we have to be ready to go down at seven, but that still gives us plenty of time to christen the bed,' I whisper.

He lifts his head from my breast and runs the edge of his thumbnail idly over my exposed nipple, like it's a juicy plaything to him. 'There's nothing I'd like more . . .' he sighs, then his tone hardens. 'But I have some things to do before everyone starts arriving for dinner. I'll be back well before seven, but can you manage on your own until then?'

I try to keep the disappointment from my voice. He may want to talk to his father before the other guests arrive. 'Of course. I'll have a bath and get ready.'

He brushes his lips over mine. 'Good. Relax and enjoy yourself. I'll be back soon.'

Relax, he said. Easier said than done.

In the end, I have to rush to be ready. He said the

dress code is 'smart casual' – the worst dress code ever invented because ten to one you jump the wrong side of the smart or casual. I've spent far too long wondering what to wear and after changing three times, I decide the studded Twiggy dress is a little *de trop* for tonight's 'informal dinner' and go for the Donna Karan I wore for the Wyckham welcome dinner. It's a favourite piece of mine and I need all the confidence I can get tonight. Teamed with a pair of nude slingback heeled pumps from my go-to brand, Kate Spade, I think I'll do. I've left my hair down in what I hope is a Kirsten Dunst-chic-but-natural way, and kept my make-up low-key. I'm also wearing the Cartier necklace, of course.

As well as dressing, I've been busy online. In fact, I only switch off my phone when I hear the bedroom door open. I wouldn't want Alexander to know I've been Googling Falconbury to find out a little of its history. There's no official website because the place isn't open to the public, which tells me the Hunts must be able to afford to run it from other sources of income without resorting to such vulgar practices. After that, I checked the Debrett's website in the hope I won't make faux pas tonight.

From that I found out that, as heir to Falconbury, Alexander himself has a courtesy title, as Immy mentioned. He is, in fact, Earl of Sledmere, which it's very tempting to tease him about – but maybe not tonight.

I've been checking my watch every few minutes and as it passes the eleven, my door opens and he marches in with a muttered 'Sorry'.

I'm glad I erred on the side of smart because when

Alexander arrives he looks molten in an immaculate dark navy suit and pale blue Oxford shirt. He hasn't bothered with a tie, leaving the top button of his shirt undone, giving a glimpse of his tanned chest with its crisp dark hair. His hair is still a little damp and if we weren't in so much of a rush I'd like to take off his suit and try out the four-poster right now. But there's no chance because from somewhere far below, a bell rings out, followed by hurrying footsteps and shrill laughter.

Alexander checks his watch. 'We'll be late. Are you ready?'

He glances up at me, finally noticing me since he rushed in here. He smiles at me, possibly for the first time since we left Oxford. 'You look absolutely beautiful.'

'This will do, then?' I touch my dress. 'I don't want to let you down.'

'You could never do that.' He holds out his hand. 'But I'm afraid it's time to face the enemy.'

I manage a laugh in reply, but get the impression he's not joking.

'Alexander, what do I call your father?' I whisper as we hurry downstairs. I found out that a marquess is the second most senior rank in the peerage: below a duke but above an earl. I heard Robert refer to him as Lord Falconbury but that seems incredibly formal if we're eating together.

'"Awkward bastard" should do nicely.'

I grab his elbow, stopping him sharply. 'I'm serious. Help me out here.'

He curls his lip. 'His name is Frederick but most people call him "General Hunt". The staff will call him "sir". You don't have to do that.'

'Oh, really?' I say sarcastically. 'So I don't need to call you, "my lord"?'

He takes my hand firmly in his. 'That won't be necessary during dinner. Later perhaps . . .' The look he gives me scorches my skin and diffuses the tension a little before he sighs and reverts to full-on gloom. 'With a bit of luck, you can avoid my father as much as possible. I asked Robert to sit us at the other end of the table from him at dinner. Shall we get it over with?'

My stomach flutters as we walk across the hall and through one of the doors at the opposite side from where there's a low buzz of conversation and the odd clink of glasses. As we walk in, Robert is pouring drinks, wearing a butler's jacket and striped trousers.

There are only two people here, one of whom I recognize though I've never met him. General Hunt is an older, greyer, stockier version of Alexander. Imposing though he is, he's eclipsed by the woman chatting to him as if she's known him for ever. No one could fail to miss her, because she is probably the most stunningly beautiful woman I've ever seen in my life.

Chapter Eighteen

Alexander's expression switches from grim to thunderous and back again to something I can only describe as frozen.

'Alexander, *amore*!'

The girl sashays across the room to us in strappy heels so high she must need oxygen. Ignoring me completely, she throws her arms round his neck and kisses him on the lips. His hands move to her waist as if to fend her off, but she entwines her arms round him then lets out a dramatic gasp.

'*Tesoro*, you look so tired! What have you been doing while I've been away? Look at these dark circles . . .' She runs a scarlet nail down his chin. 'And you are so pale under the sun tan.'

My stomach knots. *Tesoro? While I've been away?*

'There's absolutely nothing wrong with me, Valentina.' He unwinds her arms from his neck and stands back. She pouts.

'Alexander, I know you are being brave. Your father says you've been away a lot and he worries about you so much.'

'Then he shouldn't.'

'I worry about you too, *tesoro*.' Her long, slim fingers rest on his sleeve and she stares into his eyes.

I may as well not exist as General Hunt looks on, a broad smile on his lips. Valentina clearly by-passed the smart part of the dress code and has gone straight for no-holds-barred runway glamour. Her skin-tight black jersey and leather dress has to be couture. The long sleeves and high neckline only draw attention to the hemline, which ends mid-thigh, exposing her endless tanned legs.

She flicks her jet-black hair over her shoulder and captures Alexander's hand in hers again. 'I am being impolite. You have a guest with you. Aren't you going to introduce us?'

'If I ever get the chance,' says Alexander crisply. 'Lauren Cusack, this is Valentina.'

'Valentina di Cavinato. So happy to meet you.' She swoops down on me, brushing one cheek then the other with a kiss. Her perfume fills my nose; exotic, sophisticated and heady. 'Come and meet Alexander's father. He's told me how much he's longing to meet Alexander's new girlfriend.'

Valentina's entrance is as showy as a firework display and I'm reeling from the spectacle as she threads her arm through mine and escorts me to General Hunt. Alexander follows; I can't see his face, but I can sense the indignation and discomfort bristling from every pore.

As we reach General Hunt, Alexander steps in and grabs my hand. 'Dad, this is Lauren Cusack, Lauren, my father, General Hunt.'

General Hunt holds out his hand. '*Lauren*. Delighted to meet you.'

He says my name quickly like it might explode in his mouth, and drops my palm like a hot potato. I have to say, I never saw a man less delighted to meet me in my life.

Valentina bats Alexander's arm playfully. 'So this is your new American girlfriend? Your father has mentioned her to me. Yes, I cannot wait to hear all about you too, Lauren. How did you two meet?'

'At Oxford,' says Alexander in a clipped tone.

His brusqueness rolls off her. 'Are you an undergraduate? I hope you don't mind I say it, but you look very young.'

I do mind she say it, but I keep my cool and smile politely. 'I'm twenty-one, actually, and I'm doing a master's in art history.'

She narrows her eyes. 'How interesting! I own a gallery in Positano and it amuses me to acquire new pieces when I visit my parents' villa. I expect you will enjoy studying the paintings at Falconbury while Alexander and I are out hunting on Saturday. Unless you ride to hounds?'

'No, I don't, but I'm coming to watch the hunt.' You try stopping me, I think.

'You will love it, but I hear it is not the same since the ban, is it, Alexander?'

Alexander opens his mouth to speak, but his father bulldozes in. 'Bloody interfering politicians. These people have no idea of what we do in the country.'

Valentina sneers. 'I agree, Frederick. They should not poke their dirty noses into our business.'

'Surely you can still get the thrill of the hunt and the social side of it by following a trail?' I ask.

Valentina laughs. 'It's not the same as chasing the live animal, as you would know if you'd been born and bred to Falconbury ways.'

I notice Alexander has sloped off to the drinks table, where he's pouring himself a large whisky.

Valentina rolls her eyes. 'All this talk of cruelty is ridiculous, and cooked up by people from big cities who have no idea what they're talking about.'

'Really? I thought the ban had huge popular support. It was reported in the US.'

General Hunt manages what I take to be a 'pshaw' before declaring, 'Sentimental nonsense. Foxes have to be kept under control.'

I'm stung into a response. 'Aren't there other ways of doing that?'

General Hunt snorts. 'Rubbish.'

'There is some debate about it,' Alexander cuts in, returning with an Aperol spritz for Valentina and a glass of champagne for me. It's his attempt, I think, to save me from a verbal roasting by the general, but I won't back down.

The general goes on: 'There is no other way. Foxes have been hunted in Falconbury country for three hundred years and, if I had my way, they still would be.'

'But you can't, of course, since they passed the Hunting Act, because that would be illegal.' I try to keep the smile off my face.

Valentina sneers. 'There are plenty of ways of getting around this ridiculous ban and if some silly fox gets in the way you cannot blame the hounds for "accidentally" picking up his scent instead of the trail.' She brackets her nails round the 'accidentally'.

'That's not likely to happen tomorrow, though, is it, Valentina?' Alexander says, glaring at her before taking a sip of his whisky.

She shrugs. 'As you know all too well, *tesoro*, anything can happen in the heat of the chase. Hunting is unpredictable and dangerous.'

'Do you mean you might fall off?' I ask innocently.

Her eyes are incredulous. 'Me? Fall off? I was born in the saddle!'

'That must have been tricky for your mother.'

Alexander struggles to hide a smile, but Valentina's eyes are feline as she glares at me. 'I am an expert horsewoman. I have never taken a fall, no matter how hard the ride.'

'And you always pick up the scent?' I add wickedly. 'Having a nose for the chase, that is?'

Alexander gulps down his whisky as Valentina simmers like a boiling kettle. 'I have been hunting since I was three years old. There is no one out in the field with more experience, not even Alexander!'

The general cuts in. 'We had the grooms take him out on the lead rein on his fourth birthday.'

Alexander answers lazily, 'You know, I really can't remember when it was.'

'Of course you damn well can. You fell off twice and screamed the bloody place down.'

Valentina rests her slim fingers on the sleeve of

Alexander's jacket. 'Poor *tesoro*! You told me your mother didn't want you to hunt so young.'

'She didn't, not that anyone took any notice of her.' Alexander's comment is obviously directed at General Hunt and I hold my breath as he and his father exchange glances of undisguised enmity at the mention of Lady Hunt's name. I fully expect his father to lash back a reply, but instead he takes a gulp of his whisky and mutters, 'He was perfectly safe, and it hasn't done him any harm at all.'

Valentina strokes Alexander's arm again. 'Of course no harm was done. Look at him now. Alexander adores hunting and is always at the top of the pack. He never misses the Falconbury Hunt, although it is such a pity we are no longer allowed to chase foxes, is it, *tesoro*?'

Alexander smiles and downs the rest of his whisky before replying. 'I can't say that I cared much either way beforehand, but now it's in place I don't really see that it makes any difference to my enjoyment of the day.' His reply is aimed squarely at his father, whose face turns almost puce with fury.

Valentina claps her hand to her mouth in mock shock. 'How can you say that? You don't mean it. You must want the ban repealed. You must think that a law like that, cooked up by . . . by –'

'Peasants?' I murmur.

Valentina's tone is like a scrape on a violin: '– by tin-pot politicians and ignorant little people goes against everything that Falconbury stands for! Alexander, you must be furious.'

Alexander shrugs. 'As long as I can still ride out, I really don't give a flying fuck if I have to chase after a rag on a stick and if other people want to have a tantrum about it that's their problem. These days I tend to have slightly more pressing matters to consider, like am I and, more importantly, my men, going to get shot to pieces or blown to fuck.'

General Hunt slams down his glass on the table. 'This is not the barrack room and I will not have that kind of language in my house, Alexander. Is that clear?'

'Perfectly,' says Alexander, his voice laden with contempt. 'Excuse me.'

Blood sports might have been outlawed here, but I still feel like a spectator at one. The animosity between Alexander and his father is rabid. Valentina's hostility and snobbery I can handle, but it's not so easy to ignore the fact that she's obviously been incredibly close to Alexander and wants me to know it.

Alexander stalks off towards the door into the hall, past Robert. I hear Robert whisper to General Hunt, who sighs but walks out after Alexander, leaving me alone with Valentina, who sits down on the sofa, her elegant legs posed to one side.

She lets out a long sigh. 'It is such a shame. Alexander is under such terrible pressure in the army or he would not have insulted the hunt and his father. So, will you be joining us in the field on Saturday?' she asks as I perch on the end of the sofa.

'I haven't decided yet.' It's true. I can't decide whether I can stand spending my day trailing after Alexander's hunting friends if they're all like Valentina. However, the alternative is to leave him to her and I don't want to do that.

'Some people, true enthusiasts, love to follow, but those who are ignorant of our ways can find it boring.'

I flash her my sweetest smile. 'Don't worry, I know *exactly* what's going on here.'

She arches an eyebrow. 'Well, if you decide you can't stand the pace, perhaps you'd be better off taking Alexander's precious dog for a walk or going shopping while we are out together, although the shops here are so parochial and dowdy compared to Roma and Milano. I flew back to our apartment in Roma especially to buy my autumn wardrobe. Have you been to Italy?'

'I've been to Milan with my father when he made a trade visit to Italy.'

She pats her mouth with her hand as if stifling a yawn. 'Oh yes, I remember now. Frederick mentioned to me that your father was a liberal politician.'

'He's not a liberal, he's a Democrat.'

She shrugs. 'It is all the same to me. Politics bores me.'

'Really? I can't think of anything more exciting than to be in a position to change the world and make ordinary people's lives better.'

She curls her lip at me. 'Ordinary people bore me too.'

Alexander enters, followed by General Hunt. I don't know if they've been arguing but the general is very red-faced and Alexander looks like a pan about to boil over.

'So you're an old friend of Alexander's, then?' I ask Valentina.

'*Santo cielo!* Friends? Hasn't Alexander told you? We were engaged.'

My stomach flips over and over like someone pushed me down a hill in a zorbing ball and my words tumble out before I can stop them. 'You were his *fiancée*?'

'Of course. We were together for two years before we broke up this summer. It was in July before he went up to Oxford. He was under incredible pressure at work or I don't think it would ever have happened.' Her dark-brown eyes glint. 'I cannot believe you did not know about me.'

I knew Alexander had broken up with his ex, but I'd had no idea they were actually engaged. Finding out from Valentina herself is a bit of a shock, to say the least.

'I, uh . . . no, he hasn't mentioned you, actually.'

'Really? Perhaps he did not want to worry you,' she sneers.

I sip my champagne. 'Why would I be worried? I'm sorry it didn't work out for you, but I knew he was in a long-term relationship before he met me.'

She shrugs. 'You know, I think Alexander has struggled horribly to get over our break-up . . .'

She leaves her remark hanging presumably so I can ask her about the split.

'. . . and his father was heart-broken.'

'I expect he couldn't bear to see his son hurt,' I say icily.

'Perhaps. Frederick worries so much about Alexander; he is a brave and exceptional man, but Frederick wants him to give up the military and take his rightful place in society.'

'And what is his rightful place?' I ask. 'In your opinion?'

'Here of course and I do agree with Frederick. Alexander is the heir to Falconbury and, as you can see, the estate is large. A son's duty is to take over the burden and start preparing to be Lord Falconbury with all the social responsibilities that go with it, not racing off round the world playing games with his army friends.' She hisses in contempt. 'Any woman who truly loves him would recognize that and encourage him to live up to the role he was born for.'

'I've only been seeing him for a couple of months; I'm not quite ready to direct his life choices.'

Her beautifully arched brows meet in confusion, then she tosses back her hair and ploughs on. 'You could not be expected to understand this because you are not from the nobility. My father was the Conte di Cavinato and Alexander's mother was my godmother, so you see I have a *very* special link to the family.'

'I don't like him going away either, but anyone can see that it would kill Alexander to be forced to leave the army.'

'It will kill him if he stays. He's already been shot once, even though it was only a flesh wound . . .' She crosses herself and even I suppress a shudder at her revelation. 'You must have seen the result.' She reaches over her shoulder and touches her back where Alexander has his scar. 'How could you miss it? You must have seen it when you are fucking him.'

Oh my God, did she really just say that? I find it impossible to formulate a coherent reply and I'm not sure what's shocked me most, the news that Alexander was wounded or the unbelievable reference to our sex lives. 'I wasn't sure it was a bullet wound,' I mumble.

She nods in satisfaction. 'Oh yes, he got it dragging one of his men from a bombed-out house, but he only talks about it to those closest to him. Alexander is a very private man.'

Maybe he heard his name spoken because Alexander is now watching us intently. He carefully replaces his whisky tumbler on the mantelpiece.

'In that case, I'm sure he'd hate us discussing him now.' I put down my glass on the marble table and get up as a bell rings in the hall. 'Is that the dinner bell?'

As we walk into the dining room, Valentina leads the way on General Hunt's arm, with me following with Alexander. In front of us, her voluptuous bottom sways from side to side, accentuated by her spray-on dress that also emphasises her tiny waist. Alexander takes my hand in his and I feel the lightest pressure on my fingers as if he's reassuring me, but I can't bring myself to squeeze back. I'm still stunned by the revelation of their former engagement. Even allowing for her blatant bitchiness, she wouldn't dare to lie about that, knowing that I only have to ask him about it. Which, I guess, is exactly what she wants.

Robert and some other guy pull back our chairs. Valentina sits opposite me, with General Hunt at the top of the table and Alexander at the far end. That's four people at a table made for twelve at least, meaning that any conversation has to be conducted at full volume.

I force down some soup and bread, but when the fish course arrives I find I can barely eat a morsel. Valentina toys with hers and when the main course is served, a filet of beef, waves Robert away. '*Oddio!* No! I will get so fat!'

Alexander rolls his eyes.

'You look all right to me.' General Hunt growls this but I think he means it as a great compliment.

Valentina laughs. 'You are sweet to say so, Frederick, but I have put on so much weight since I come to England. The food is so stodgy. I am on a diet now.'

I wonder how this is possible because she must be a US size two at the most.

Robert offers me a dish of potatoes and, while I'm really not hungry, I smile enthusiastically. 'Yes, please. They look delicious.'

I accept a healthy portion of vegetables and force down a mouthful as Valentina tinkers with a green bean.

Alexander attacks his beef like it is still alive, while his father chews savagely. In between mouthfuls he starts asking me about US foreign policy and criticizing Obama's fiscal strategy.

'I heard your father's speech about Afghanistan on

Radio 4. Well-meaning but misguided. Your father's partially sighted, isn't he?'

Just in time, I bite back 'And you think the two are connected?' and reply coolly, 'Yes, he is.'

Alexander cuts in. 'I thought Senator Cusack was pretty spot-on with his anaylsis.'

General Hunt ignores him. 'Attacked by some thug, wasn't he?'

I put down my fork. 'Yes, he was.'

Now I know the meaning of the word harrumph, which is what the general does in reply. 'That's the trouble with America. Lunatics running loose all over the place, and all of them armed to the teeth.'

'He wasn't shot,' I say, trying to be patient. 'He was attacked on his way to a drug store by a guy with a base-ball bat.' It still makes me feel sick to say this, even though I was ten when it happened. In my lap, I realize I've scrunched the napkin into a tiny ball.

'I had no idea.'

I look up from my plate to find Alexander looking at me, his eyes full of concern. I ought to be touched, but I hate it. I don't want to be the centre of the conversation because of what happened to my father, but he goes on. 'What happened?'

'He'd driven out to get my mother some migraine medication and I still remember the police coming to the house to tell us and my mother in shock. My father was in the ITU for three days and we didn't know if he'd come through it, let alone what kind of brain damage he would have afterwards. In the end, I guess he was lucky to keep some of the sight in his left eye.'

Alexander frowns at me. 'I'm sorry.'

'He got over it,' I say. 'We all have.'

Valentina shudders. '*Oddio!* This is why I never enjoy travelling to the US. I feel safer in Nicaragua or Cape Town or even Manchester than there!'

'It's not that bad. We're not all gun-toting maniacs. Some of us are almost civilized,' I snap back.

She makes a moue with her lips and reaches over the table as if to pat my hand. 'Of course, if you are used to this kind of violent lifestyle, you must become hardened to it. I could not bear it.'

'Italy's no idyll, Valentina,' says Alexander sharply.

'Maybe not, but I do not live in places with guns and men with baseball bats. Even if I did, I have bodyguards who protect me at home and in the city. I am surprised your father's bodyguards did not save him.'

'Incompetent fools should have been sacked,' rumbles General Hunt.

'He doesn't have any bodyguards,' I say, feeling like a pressure cooker about to burst. 'Not then and not now. My father refuses to live in fear.'

Valentina gasps. '*Cielo!* A man of his standing with no security? You will be telling us next that you have no staff in your home!'

'We don't.'

'Ah, no. Now, I know you are joking with me.' She waggles her fork at me then spears a sliver of carrot on the tines. 'Alexander, *amore*, would you pass me some water, please? This talking of baseball bats and guns has made me feel a little faint and you know how sensitive I am.'

That's it. I pass on dessert, and sit through the cheese, which no one eats anyway except General Hunt, who attacks the Stilton like it might rise up and bite him. My head has started to throb and I'm longing for the opportunity to leave without it seeming too obvious. Alexander and his father are in a heated debate about the tenants on the estate while Valentina regales me with stories about her family homes on Lake Como and Rome, and her 'vacation' apartments in Paris and London – and how she only ever travels by private jet.

'Alexander, do you remember when we went to St Bart's for our first anniversary? It was so wonderful; we stayed in an old plantation house owned by my cousin.'

Turning briefly from their conversation, Alexander mumbles something in reply then immediately turns back to his father. General Hunt's face is like thunder and their voices are growing louder by the second.

'It was the most exclusive location, right above the ocean, with so many staff I don't know what they found to do there.' She sighs. 'I've never seen Alexander so happy, although we might have gone anywhere because we barely saw the scenery all week, did we, *tesoro*?'

Alexander turns and answers sharply. 'What?'

'I am telling Lauren about our special week in

St Bart's. Alexander needed another vacation to get over it,' she purrs.

I *cannot* believe she said that over the dinner table – and in front of Alexander's father.

Alexander seems unable to formulate a reply and General Hunt coughs. 'We'll have coffee in the library. Will you ladies join us?' he asks.

'I would love to. I am dying to hear all about the plans for the hunt ball, aren't you, Lauren?'

I drop my napkin on to the table. 'I'm afraid you'll have to excuse me. I have a bit of a headache so I think I'll go to bed.'

Valentina sighs. 'What a shame. I was so enjoying your company.'

I throw her my sweetest smile. 'Ditto.'

As I get up from the table, Alexander gets to his feet and the general rises with somewhat less enthusiasm.

'I'll come up and see how you are,' says Alexander.

'How sweet,' Valentina simpers.

'There's no need to come up yet. I'll be fine with a couple of Advil and a good night's sleep. Thank you for dinner, General Hunt.'

I think he grunts in reply, but I don't know and don't care because I'm on my way out of the dining room as fast as I can.

Chapter Nineteen

From my window I can see that the rain has stopped and a shaft of moonlight has broken through, silver beams sparkling on the frosty lawns. An owl hoots and, I watch the deer silently wandering towards the woods in the meadow beyond the ha-ha.

It's the picture of carefully managed tranquillity, yet I'm still processing the fact that Valentina has been the one to break it to me that she and Alexander were together for two years and actually engaged. It crosses my mind to slip downstairs and take a walk outside but where would I go? I'm trapped at Falconbury. But immediately I remember that I did practically force Alexander into bringing me here. Now I know why he was so reluctant to invite me in the first place. His father has been frosty at best towards me and it's clear that he doesn't want Alexander to get involved with anyone other than Valentina. It's occurred to me that General Hunt has the hots for her himself, but that's surely secondary to the fact that he's made it patently clear that she would make the perfect mistress of Falconbury.

And you know what? He's right. She's sophisticated, well-travelled, speaks around half a dozen languages and is already so at home she's part of the furniture – a very expensive, very beautiful piece at that.

My head really is thumping so I pop a couple of Advil, take off my dress, slip on a robe and lie down on the four poster. I turn off the lamp, hoping the pills will work their magic and I'll fall asleep. The bed may look inviting, but it's as hard as nails and I can't seem to get comfortable.

I don't know how long I've been tossing and turning and thumping the bolster pillow, but I must have drifted into a troubled doze, one in which Valentina is mounted on a stag and chasing me over the front quad at Wyckham. Just as her stag rears over me, I jolt awake to find a figure looming above my bed.

A man is silhouetted in a shaft of moonlight through a gap in the drapes. Rubbing my eyes, I blink awake.

'Alexander!'

He flicks on the lamp. 'I'm sorry. I didn't mean to frighten you. I did knock, but there was no answer so I came in.'

He sits on the edge of the bed as I back up to the bolster, screwing up my eyes. 'I came to see if you were OK. How's the headache?'

'Much better,' I say grudgingly, my nose responding to the peaty scent of whisky as he shifts closer to me.

'Good, and if it had something to do with my father I apologize for him.' He walks his fingers up the bed-cover to my waist.

'I'll admit he isn't the easiest guy to talk to, but I can handle that. It's Valentina who's difficult to deal with. I'd have appreciated it if you'd warned me you'd invited her . . .'

'I *didn't* invite her.' He toys with the ribbon at the top of my Victoria's Secret cami. 'Your idea of pyjamas is interesting . . .'

My nipples tingle as he tugs the loop free, but I won't be distracted. 'Then what's she doing here?'

'I have no idea, but I can only assume my father asked her to come. She's been invited to the last five Falconbury hunts so I expect he thought it was only polite to include her this time.'

'Even though he knew I was going to be here too?'

'He didn't know about you until a few days ago because, if you remember, you hadn't decided to come until last weekend.'

'Only because you hadn't asked me!'

'Well, now you know why! I didn't *know* that Valentina would be here, but I'll admit I knew there was a *slim* possibility that she might be invited. But at no time did my father actually inform me she was on the guest list. I was as shocked as you when we walked into the sitting room, though after you left she did let slip that she was asked two weeks ago. I assume my father forgot to let me know.'

'How convenient.' God, was that my voice dripping with jealousy and sarcasm? This place seems to have brought out my worst side.

His voice cools. 'I'm as happy about her turning up as you are, but it's not that surprising. She is my mother's goddaughter and whatever you may think of her, the link between us goes back to when we were both born. My mother and hers were . . .' he hesitates '. . . very close. They met at finishing school in Switzerland and they've remained family friends since then. Valentina has been coming to the hunt for several years. I expect my father couldn't simply cut her off just because we've split up. The contessa would have considered it a personal insult.'

'How dreadful!' I exclaim, all mock horror. 'And I already knew her mother and yours were friends. Valentina was keen to let me know that, and about her noble heritage and her various homes around the world. I believe a private jet was also mentioned.'

'I thought you'd take all that crap with a pinch of salt. Can't we forget this, there are so many more interesting things we could be doing right now . . .'

Before I can stop him, he climbs on to the bed beside me, leaning on one elbow.

'She *is* very beautiful. You can't deny it.'

'I won't deny it, but why does it surprise you,' he says, pulling my cami open to expose my cleavage, 'that I love fucking very beautiful women.'

Before I can tell him he's an arrogant bastard, he's on top of me, caging my wrists above my head. Lying above me, with his thigh over my legs, he's bone-hard through the cloth of his suit trousers. Briefly, I respond as he takes control of my mouth in a fierce and desperate kiss.

He pushes my cami aside, baring my breast and I can't help arching my hips to meet his erection. He slips his thumb in his mouth then rubs the damp tip over my nipple which puckers and aches in response. Then he transfers it to the other nipple.

'You like that?'

'Uh-huh.'

His hand glides down from my breasts to my shorts and slides inside the waistband. He slips one finger inside me and my sex tightens around it, eager to take him.

His voice is hoarse with lust. 'You see. Why waste time arguing when there are so many better things to do . . .'

Physically, I hunger for him but I know 'Let's not argue' means 'Let's not *talk*'. Making love to me now is his strategy to ignore and avoid the pain and anger that's simmered between us since I found out he lied about this weekend.

'Wait!'

It's like pulling the emergency brake on a speeding train and either he hasn't heard or refuses to because he pulls my pyjama shorts down my thighs. Even now, while my palms push futilely against his shoulders, my body betrays me. My nipple puckers and hardens inside his mouth.

I suck in a breath and breathe my words against his ear, quiet and slow. 'I said, stop this. Please.' The pressure on my body eases and he rolls off me, lying by my side but not touching. I can't see his face because I'm focused on the underside of the bed canopy.

'I don't think this is a great idea, just now.'

'Why not? I got the impression you were enjoying yourself.'

'I was, you know how much I was, but having sex now would be a smokescreen for the way we're both feeling.'

'Great. Just exactly what is the bloody problem? I'm listening now.'

'I want to know why you didn't ask me to come to the hunt. *Really* why you didn't ask me, not some bull-shit about being embarrassed by your friends.'

'It's not bullshit. It's true. You saw my father; you heard him. He has one path in life for me and Falcon-bury is it and anything or anyone who gets in his way is the enemy. Including anyone I care for.'

'I agree he's been a little frosty,' I say acidly.

'*Frosty?* You have no idea and this ... this row between us is exactly the reason I wanted you to keep away. I'm used to my father's behaviour, though I hate it, but you shouldn't have to deal with it. I warned you about this, Lauren, but you insisted on coming.'

I sit up, rounding on him. 'Then why have *you* come, if you hate the whole thing so fucking much! I'd have thought you of all people would have the courage to stand up to your own father and friends. Or have I got you completely wrong?'

There's a brief silence, during which he looks at me like I'm an alien, then he shakes his head and gets off the bed. 'This is my life and if you can't understand what that means, then there's nothing more I can do. I'll see you in the morning.'

The first thing I realize when I wake is that the sun is streaming in through the gap in the curtains. Then I remember Alexander storming off out of my room, leaving me lying awake in a fury until I finally heard Valentina and General Hunt come up to bed.

Then I remember cooling down and kicking myself for losing my temper. Shit!

Double shit, because the old-fashioned alarm clock on the night stand tells me it's past nine a.m. I bet I've missed breakfast, and that must be a major faux pas.

Which means I'll have to face Alexander and Valentina and the general en masse. I can picture them sitting around the table, finishing their coffee, the general bristling with outrage, Valentina sly with triumph and Alexander stiff with embarrassment at my tardiness and maybe pissed off with my snarkiness last night.

Maybe if I hurry, I can make it. As I grab my robe from the bedcover, there's a soft knock at the door. I can't have the staff catching me like this.

'Hold on, please. I won't be a minute.'

'It's Helen, Miss Cusack.'

I tie up my robe and open the door.

Helen holds a tray with a pot of tea, a plate of pastries and a pale pink rose that I suspect came from one of her own arrangements in the hall. 'Would you like some breakfast, Miss Cusack?'

I open the door. 'Thank you . . . but I thought young unmarried ladies weren't allowed breakfast in bed in country houses.'

Helen sets down the tray on the round table. 'Oh, I think that rule went out of the window some time ago. I heard you had a headache last night and when you didn't come down to breakfast, I thought I'd bring up a tray.'

'That's very kind of you.'

'Are you feeling better now?'

'Yes, much . . . Um, does Alexander know I'm having breakfast in bed?'

'Not as far as I know, Miss Cusack. He breakfasted with his father and Valentina. Do you want me to tell him you're eating in your room?'

'No, don't worry about that. I'll be down after I've had this, and thanks again.'

'A pleasure.'

After Helen's gone, I draw up a chair, pour out a cup of tea and nibble at a croissant, trying to work out what to say when I see Alexander again. I had hoped he might have come in to my room by now. Was I really that spiky with him last night? A few of my words come back to haunt me, particularly the phrase that had finally driven him out of the room: *'I'd have thought you of all people would have the courage to stand up to your own father and friends.'*

I push my plate away and cross to the window, where the full grandeur of the Falconbury estate is laid out before my eyes, reminding me of how different my life and Alexander's are. I have to admit, I wouldn't fancy having to run this place either.

There's another knock at my door and this time I know it must be him.

'Come in.'

The door opens and he walks in, tall and stiff. It's

immediately obvious from his demeanour that he's still pissed about last night.

'How's your head this morning?'

'It's fine.'

'Good.'

He hovers, but makes no attempt to kiss me or touch me. I think he's still simmering. He glances at the breakfast tray. 'I see Helen's looking after you.'

'Yes. It was a bit of a surprise . . . I'm sorry, I didn't get to sleep until late and then I woke up too late for breakfast. Am I in a lot of trouble?'

'Do you want to be?'

'I didn't mean to say some of the things I did last night. I wasn't feeling one hundred per cent and it was a bit of a shock finding out about Valentina.'

'I've told you she's in the past, and that should be enough.' His tone is granite hard.

'OK . . .' I reach out my hand to touch his.

He wavers, then says in a slightly less chilly tone. 'When you didn't turn up to breakfast, I half thought that you might have left.'

I have to smile. 'And just where would I have gone in the middle of the night?'

'I don't know. I've wanted this weekend to go well for you – for us – against all the odds, and don't think I'm naive. There's a lot about Valentina that I don't like, but, as I said last night, my mother and hers were very close. The contessa used to bring her here for visits and my mother occasionally took me and Emma to their villa.'

'Are you saying your parents actually planned for you to get married to each other?'

'I'm sure our mothers did, but that's not the only reason we got engaged – although I wish I hadn't let family expectations influence me. At the time, I didn't think they had, but now I suspect I was giving in to the pressure, however subconsciously. I thought I was in love with her at the time.'

'Then why did you split up?'

'Because in the end I couldn't stand the drama and the constant rows any more, and because Valentina insisted I give up the army and come home to help my father run the estate.'

'Why?'

'Because she's old school, like my father. She's always loved the lifestyle here, the country sports, hunting, managing the estate, and she thinks I should take what she sees as my rightful place in society.'

It's on the tip of my tongue to say that I also think Valentina would kill to be Marchioness of Falconbury, but I don't.

'I honestly don't think she can conceive that there's any other kind of life out there beyond our wealthy privileged world, despite the fact she's travelled so much. She hated my army friends and couldn't understand that, despite all the danger and hardship of combat, I enjoyed spending time on ops with the men in my command. She gave me an ultimatum to quit or lose her, and I chose the army.' He hesitates. 'Like I

274

said, she's no more than a close family friend now, like part of the Falconbury furniture, if you like.'

I try to picture Valentina as a solid oak wardrobe or a dining table. No, can't do it. But I guess I *can* see that she's an important link to Alexander's past and I do feel better. After all, this is only a weekend. I have Alexander now and Valentina doesn't. It's clear to me that she will do almost anything to get him back, even if Alexander doesn't want to recognize that.

'Don't let her hear you say that.'

'Perhaps I'd better not. Now, come here, I've got a proposition for you.'

'Sounds interesting.'

'Two propositions, actually. The second is that, later this morning, we go for a ride together.' He pulls the lace trim of my cami away from my cleavage.

'I'd love that but you'd better be gentle with me. I haven't ridden for months.'

'Oh, I'll break you in gently, don't worry about that.' My skin tingles deliciously as he blows gently down the gap between my breasts.

'And the second?' I ask through half-closed eyes.

He lifts the hem of my cami and pulls it over my head. 'I can break you in gently for that too, if you like.'

Some time later, we reach the stable block behind Falconbury House. The route through the house and out past the kitchens, laundries and offices at the rear has made me realize the scale of the place. As we walked,

I got Alexander to give me some details of the history of the house. It turns out there's been a building on the spot since William the Conqueror invaded, starting with a Norman manor then a medieval priory, the remains of which are still in the grounds.

The magnificence of the house is window dressing compared to the sight of Alexander in fawn jodhpurs that leave nothing to the imagination, black leather riding boots and a short Barbour jacket that's all the more sexy for having seen some action.

'I had Talia saddle up a horse for you. I think you'll like him.'

Alexander curves his big palm round the seat of my jodhpurs. At this rate we won't get out of the yard.

The clatter of hooves announces the arrival of a magnificent bay stallion who has to be almost seventeen hands high, and snorts and stamps his feet while Alexander tries to soothe him.

'Here's Hotspur, sir, as lively as ever.'

'Excellent.' Alexander keeps a firm hand on Hotspur's reins, while stroking his neck and shhh-ing him. Shoes ring out on the yard and there's louder snickering as a stable boy leads a sparky grey into the yard. Alexander glances up and frowns hard. 'Why is Calliope here? I thought I asked for Harvey to be tacked up for Lauren.'

Talia bites her lip. 'I did get him ready, but Valentina has taken him out.'

'Valentina took Harvey? You are joking?'

'No, sir. She went off on a hack early this morning.'

'When will they be back?'

'She said she'd be gone most of the day.'

Alexander hisses in frustration. 'What about Jupiter, then?'

'I'm afraid he's a little lame, sir, or of course I would have brought him out. In fact, the vet's on her way now.'

He presses his lips together angrily.

'Alexander, don't worry. Calliope will do me just fine. She looks magnificent.' I walk forward and take her reins and the grey mare backs away a little, her eyes flicking nervously about her.

'She is magnificent, but she can also be a bitch.'

That sounds so much like someone else I know that I have to bite my tongue hard, but I laugh. 'I'm sure that's not true, is it, girl?' I pat the horse's muzzle and she rears her head.

'She *can* be as quiet as a lamb, if she's in the mood,' says Talia. 'But if Alexander thinks she isn't suitable we can wait for Valentina to bring back Harvey. *If* he's in a fit state after that, of course.'

'I think we both know he'll have had enough.' He turns to me. 'I think we'll have to forget the ride for today, Lauren, and go for a drive around the estate instead.'

'Go for a drive? After Talia has got both horses ready? You have to be kidding. I'll be totally fine with Calliope. She sounds a really fun ride and it's not as if I'm a novice. I go to the stables every couple of weeks back home.'

This is an approximation of the truth. I used to ride

every week – until about a year ago. I haven't been on horseback more than half a dozen times in the past twelve months and not at all in the past three. I also don't like the nervy look in Calliope's eye at all, or the way she seems to flinch whenever I try to touch her. But there is no way on the planet that I am letting Alexander, Talia – and especially not Valentina – know any of this.

'She's not good with strange riders,' Alexander continues, 'and she spooks easily. I'm not entirely comfortable with you taking her.'

I raise my eyebrows. 'Don't you trust me?'

'Oh, I trust you. It's Calliope I'm not sure about.'

'If I'm worried, I promise to let you know. Now, do you think we can get started on this ride before dusk?'

I see him hesitating, then he nods. 'Talia. Can you hold Hotspur while I help Miss Cusack mount, please?'

'Whatever you say, sir.'

Alexander ignores Talia's doubtful face. I find it more difficult as Alexander shoves two hands under my boot and boosts me up on to Calliope, who whinnies shrilly and stamps her feet as I lift my leg over her quarters.

'It's an English saddle, miss; we do have a Western but Alexander said you're from the East Coast so I guessed you'd be used to the traditional style?'

'I am, thanks, Talia.' I take the reins, relieved that Calliope stands quietly enough as I get comfortable. Next to me, Hotspur's breath mists the chilly morning air, his hooves ringing out on the yard as Alexander mounts him, shhh-ing and steadying him.

With a tight hold on the reins, he throws out a smile to Talia. 'Thanks.'

'A pleasure, sir, as always.' There's a definite edge of irony in her voice and she sashays back to the stables, her bottom wiggling in her mud-spattered jodhpurs. It occurs to me that she and Alexander might have . . . before I dismiss such suspicions as my imagination working overtime.

'Everything good with Calliope? I hope she won't give you any trouble,' he says as we walk slowly out of the yard.

'She's good as gold,' I say. The tang of woodsmoke fills the air and ravens cry as we ride past the end of the stable block on to a rutted track that skirts the woods. I imagine a fox trembling in the thicket and suppress a shiver at the thought that the hounds might pick up its scent tomorrow, by accident or otherwise. I don't care how naive anyone accuses me of being, I'm entitled to my opinion and I'll fight my corner again if I have to. For now, all seems peaceful and idyllic, as our horses settle into the gentle rhythmic thud of hooves on earth. Alexander is thoughtful beside me.

'Are you riding Hotspur to the hunt tomorrow?' I ask.

'Hotspur? God, no. I've got an ex-steeplechaser for that.' He pauses, then says, 'Would you like to see the whole estate?'

'If you're sure we'll be back before dark?'

He shakes his head at my teasing. 'It may be touch and go whether we have to stay out all night.'

'Sounds terrible.'

He smiles and kicks Hotspur's sides. 'Come on.'

A few hours later, my fingers are numb despite my gloves, my nose is pinched with cold, but there's a glow inside me. I know I'm going to be stiff tomorrow, but it's so glorious to be out together that I feel as if I could ride all day. Alexander has taken me on a tour around the estate, skirting the woods and deer park, then through muddy fields and along a river bank, the reeds dusted with frost, melting in the late morning sun. Then we headed out into the lanes beyond, the rhythmic clop of hooves strangely soothing. After her initial flightiness and a nervy encounter with a tractor, Calliope has lived up to her 'lamb' reputation. I suspect Alexander of being over-protective and I'm really glad I didn't let myself be spooked into giving up the ride. I can't wait to see Valentina's face when I get back.

'Enjoying yourself?'

'It's fabulous. I'd ride more often if I had time, but my free time in the States has always been taken up with my art and dance classes. It was Mom who wanted me to have riding lessons, partly for social reasons, but also because she'd secretly love to have an Olympic show-jumper for a daughter.'

He laughs out loud and I realize that I've rarely seen him so happy. He's in his element, no matter what he says about wanting to leave Falconbury, but I'm not going to point that out now.

'Shall we go back past the old priory?' He reins in

Hotspur at a gap in a stone wall that must lead back onto the estate.

'A priory sounds very dramatic.'

'It's been in ruins since the Reformation so don't get too excited.'

He sounds so terribly British that I can't help but laugh. 'Oh, I wouldn't dream of it.'

A kick of Hotspur's flanks and he's off to a brisk trot. Feeling more confident, I decide to see what Calliope can do when a sound like a gunshot rings out from behind us. Ravens scatter, screaming into the air, and before I can steady her Calliope bucks and rears. I try to rein her in, clinging to her with every muscle, but there's another shot, then another and she takes off.

Oh God, I'm flying through the air, clinging on to her neck for dear life. My heart's thumping and I can't even find the breath to cry out as she hurtles towards a wood. Dark trunks and spiky branches race towards us, but all I can do is hold on with every ounce of strength. I try to see Alexander and I think I hear him shout, but the thunder of hooves and the rush of wind is too loud.

I know I'm going to fall or be thrown. I pray that it's soon on the muddy field, not in the wood. Think, think . . . what did they tell me in training? Use your seat to brake? God, what if I lose the stirrups. I think I hear Alexander shouting. I could steer for a high hedge, a really high one, too high to jump. But what if Calliope does jump it and throws me off – or she might forget about jumping at all and just plough through it.

Oh, Jesus . . . My heart's racing and my thighs scream as I hang on, with the trees racing towards us.

'Pull one rein. Make her turn!'

Alexander's voice reaches me but I can't see him.

Make her turn. Make. Her. Turn. Heart hammering, I pull on one rein and make a grab for the strap over her withers. The thicket seems almost on top of me.

Calliope swerves. My feet part company with the stirrups and I hear a scream. My scream, because I know I'm going to fall and then . . . the thicket moves away to my right because she's turning. And slowing. Just a little, then a lot and then I get my feet in the stirrups again and I'm slumped over her neck, gulping in air like a drowning woman as she comes to a stop.

Finally, she stands still, breathing hard, clouds of steam rising from her body into the frosty air. Sweat glistens on her neck and she's snorting and blowing hard. Underneath me, she's breathing so heavily I feel like I'm on a choppy sea. There's mud spattered over my boots and jodhpurs, and the same sort of silence you get after a car crash.

The silence is shattered as Alexander reins in Hotspur at my side. 'Lauren! Are you all right? Christ, I thought you were going to come off in the trees!'

'I'm OK. See? She's quiet as a lamb now.' I pat her damp neck.

'I kept calling at you to turn her.'

'Funny, I found it hard to hear for a while.'

'Well, thank God you haven't been hurt. I warned you about Calliope, but you insisted on riding her.'

'It was either that or be chauffeured around like the Queen!'

He hesitates and then suddenly his deep laugh echoes in the still air. 'Believe me, I can't think of anyone *less* like the Queen than you.'

I don't know whether to hit him or burst into tears, then I think better of any dramatic actions while Calliope is between my thighs.

'I'm delighted you think it's funny, Mr Hunt.'

'I don't. Not really. I'm simply admiring your balls.'

'Now that really *would* be funny.'

Sliding down from Hotspur, Alexander shakes his head and takes Calliope's reins from me. 'Let me help you down.'

He takes my gloved hand, and I'm glad of it, because when my feet touch terra firma, my knees are distinctly wobbly. Wisps of steam rise from me too, and I realize I'm soaked in sweat. I imagine what I must look like and cringe.

Keeping one hand on Calliope's reins, Alexander pulls me to him with the other arm as Hotspur stands obediently by.

'You know,' he says softly, 'you did pretty well to stop her. Most people would have gone flying over the withers. You're lucky she took straight off with you under her, and didn't whip round when she heard that bird scarer.'

'I don't think "lucky" is the word I'd use, but you needn't have worried, I had everything under control.'

'Sure you did,' he replies in a terrible East Coast accent.

'You know that doesn't sound the least bit like me.'

'Sure it does.'

'OK, you do, but I wouldn't give up the day job yet, if I were you.'

'Perhaps, I won't. How about we walk the horses to the priory, although I don't think Calliope will be spooked again. That bird scarer is miles back now. I ought have known it might go off.' Now he tells me, but it's with the utmost reluctance that I wriggle free from his embrace because, sweaty, shaken and stirred, I could still rip down his jodhpurs and make love to him this instant.

He grins and pats Hotspur's neck. 'The priory's in the middle of the wood in a clearing. There's a path, but be careful.'

Leading our horses, we pick our way over roots and fallen branches, the dead leaves crisp under hooves and boots. The trees are a mix of bare-branched oaks and dark spruce and yew, and the sharp tang of damp hangs in the air. Ahead of us, I glimpse pools of pale sunlight where the clearing opens up and, all at once, we are at the priory. 'This is it.'

He was right: the priory is a roof-less shell of tumbled stones, smothered with green moss and rusty lichens. The muted colours, myriad textures and the sense of melancholic timelessness seem to cry out for a Turner painting and make me want to return with my own sketchbook or watercolours. Next to the ruins a small stone-walled building stands apart under the trees, perhaps the only building that was spared by Henry VIII's 'reformers'. Its roof is certainly a few centuries younger than the decayed and shattered building in front of us.

An old fence post makes a convenient place to tether Hotspur and Calliope, now behaving like an angel. Clambering over a mossy rock after Alexander, I let out a low groan as the strained muscles in my thighs and butt remind me of my wild ride.

'Aches and pains?' he asks.

'I think I used muscles I didn't even know I had.'

'I like the sound of that.' His sexy glance shoots lust through me. I have a feeling this visit to the priory has nothing to do with Alexander wanting to share the Hunt family history.

'I expect you could do with a drink?'

He produces a silver hip flask from his pocket, unscrews the top and offers it to me.

'Thanks.' The brandy scalds my throat and my coughs shatter the silence in the clearing. Alexander smiles as I splutter and takes a few gulps of the brandy himself.

'More?' he asks.

'Mmm.' Sipping slowly this time, I stand next to him in front of the ruins. Alexander places his boot on one of the stones.

'How long has the priory been here?'

'Nearly nine centuries, give or take. It was built after the manor house at Falconbury as a distant outpost of the abbey at Tewkesbury. The ruins stretch further beneath the trees, along with the old family vaults.'

'Are your ancestors still buried here?'

'Most were exhumed when the new house was built, and taken to the family vault in the new chapel.'

Despite the brandy warming my veins, I shiver. Is that where Lady Hunt was laid to rest? Thankfully, Alexander hasn't picked up on the nuance and takes my hand. 'There's something else I want you to see.'

He leads me through the broken walls to the far side of the ruin towards the stone hut.

'What's this for?' I ask when we stop outside.

'It's a woodsman's hut's but it's hardly ever used now. Shall we take a look inside?'

The wooden door demands a firm push before it shifts from the damp frame. Inside, my eyes take a second or so to adjust to the dimness. The stone walls are lined with shelves, all largely empty except for a few rusty tins and ancient tools. Stray shafts of sun pierce through holes in the roof and cast light on the floor. The hut may rarely be used, but today it has been spread with fresh straw topped with horse rugs. On the workbench, a bottle of champagne is wedged in an ice bucket, alongside a small wicker hamper and two crystal glasses.

'Hmm. I guess the woodsman was expecting guests?'

'I guess he was.'

Hands on hips, I shake my head in amazement. 'When did you do this? Was it before we made up this morning?'

'Does it matter?'

'Yes. I'd hate to be that predictable.'

'You're not. I asked Talia to drive out here while you got dressed.'

'You mean she knows you were going to bring me here for sex?'

His fingers trace a line from my temple to my neck, where my pulse beats thickly. 'You think I'm going to have sex with you here?'

'You know damn well you are, you bastard.'

The champagne stays on ice because we're on fire. Alexander backs me up against the workbench, flattening his hands on the worktop. I clutch his buttocks, kneading his glutes though the skin-tight fabric. He crushes his erection into my pelvis as we kiss, snatching at each other's mouths. He unzips his jodhpurs and shoves them down his thighs together with his shorts, and his cock nudges my thighs. I circle the base with my fingers and he groans a primal cry.

Somehow, I wriggle my jodhpurs and panties down my legs and there's a clatter as my elbow knocks God knows what off the workbench on to the floor.

His hands grip my hips and almost lift me off my feet as he plunges inside me. I'm not quite ready so he feels tight, but I dig my fingers into his glutes anyway and urge him in deeper. It's a hot, dirty coupling that makes me feel craved-for, wanted, *desired*.

And that's exactly what I need.

As he thrusts inside me, nothing before or after this moment matters. Alexander increases the speed of his thrusts, almost taking me off my feet as his thick shaft slides in and out of me. I'm wetter by the second, but he's still huge and hot, almost hurting me, but the soreness makes me know I'm alive.

His thrusts are urgent now. I wriggle so I can rub myself against the head of his cock.

'Yes. Yes. Fuck me! Fuck me!'

My cries drive him over the edge, and he stiffens. I'm not ready to come yet, but I have the pleasure of seeing him climax, eyes lifted up, every tendon, sinew rigid as steel. The power to take him so completely out of this world, and watch him lose control, is intoxicating. His climax seems to go on and on before his body relaxes, he groans and gathers me to him.

'So you have a stately home and an estate and you decide to take me in a hut. Is this some kind of Mellors role reversal?'

I'm lying in the crook of Alexander's arm on the blankets, covered in quilted rugs. We still have our clothes and boots on. Although I lie here quietly, my sex is swollen and aching for its own release.

'If it is,' he says, stroking my hair, 'you should be threading daisies through my pubes.'

'There are no daisies in December.' I walk my fingers over the crotch of his jodhpurs and his cock stirs again at my touch.

'True.' His voice softens. 'Sorry for being selfish back there. I couldn't wait.'

'You can make it up to me.'

'Oh, I intend to.'

His words are laden with sensual threat and he

removes his arm from under my head, lifts the blanket, and scrambles up.

'May I take your boots off, my lady?'

'Do I have a choice?'

'No.'

He tugs off the boots and my jodhpurs and panties follow, so I'm lying, naked from the waist down, with him kneeling between my bent legs. The straw tickles the soles of my feet through the blanket as Alexander scoops up my bottom with his hands and lowers his head between my legs.

'Oh God.'

I twist the blanket in my fingers as his tongue makes a long slow sweep from my clit all the way to my entrance.

He lifts his head and slowly and deliberately runs his tongue over his lips. 'Mmm. Your cunt is delicious, my lady. I must taste it again.'

'My God, you are filthy.'

His eyes gleam wickedly. 'You have *no* idea.'

My groan rents the air as he licks me again and sighs with pleasure. OK, Todd was willing to go down on me, but Alexander savours me like I'm the rarest delicacy. Every nerve ending sizzles as he flicks his tongue over my clitoris and then blows on the nub, and flicks and blows again. It's the gentlest of sensations, but leaves me whimpering as if I'm in pain.

'Yes. Do it.'

'Manners.'

'Do it, *please*.' I have no problem with begging.

'That's better.'

His hot, wet tongue circles my clit relentlessly as I clutch his back and moan in ecstasy. I can't keep my hips still any longer and buck them towards his face. My climax is so near, my sex pulses. There's a fullness as he pushes two fingers inside me and withdraws them, holding them up, glistening with my juices.

'You're ready this time.'

I hear the zip on his jodhpurs rasp down, and he edges the tip of his cock inside me. He slides into me, gliding easily through my wetness to my core, and it only takes a few thrusts before I come hard. Alexander comes soon after, and collapses beside me, eyes shut, a smile of sheer bliss on his face.

The chill soon dries the sweat on our bodies and above me the first few drops of rain start to drip on the ramshackle roof. The champagne still rests in the bucket, untasted, but we don't need it. Despite General Hunt and Valentina, and the whole culture shock that is Falconbury, I honestly don't think I've ever been happier in my life.

Chapter Twenty

I wake at eight thirty the next morning to the sound of hushed but urgent voices in the corridor outside my room. It's the staff and they sound pretty stressed. Through the window, I hear the crunch of gravel and get out of bed.

Or rather I hobble – my day in the saddle, and almost out of it. I think my butt must be bruised, my thighs still ache from gripping the horse and there's a stiffness across the back of my shoulders from trying to rein in Calliope's head. When I do make it to the window, the staff are already buzzing about the front of the house, setting up trestle tables. Benny is sniffing around them, tail wagging furiously, as if he knows something big is happening.

After Alexander and I left the hut yesterday, we rode back for lunch at Falconbury without further drama of the equine variety or otherwise. General Hunt was out, which I have to say was a huge relief. Valentina, presumably, was still hacking Harvey around the lanes because he wasn't in his stall when we took the horses back.

Frankly, I was hoping we *would* bump into her; I'd like to have found out if she deliberately took the only safe horse in the stable, knowing I was due to ride.

Alexander, on the other hand, seemed happy she wasn't around.

In the afternoon, he took me to do some Christmas shopping in Henley-on-Thames, where they had a few cool boutiques in the narrow back streets. I bought some gifts for my parents and a couple of friends back home, and tried to ignore the mixed feelings I have about the holidays. I can't wait to see everyone, yet I know it means being separated from Alexander over the long vacation. As well as his skiing trip, he mentioned some vague plans to return to his regiment for a few weeks, which takes care of most of the time we have apart.

But Henley was still bliss. Alexander had also booked a table in a great little bistro overlooking the river – presumably so we could spend the evening away from Valentina and his father. Away from Falconbury, he let down his guard a little; when he's there, he puts on a suit of emotional body armour as if he's preparing for battle, but whether that's with his father or Valentina – or both – I'm not sure.

I can't say I relish the prospect of spending the day alone while he hunts today, and I still haven't decided exactly what to do until they return; whether to follow or get a cab out of Falconbury until they get home.

But, as we only have three more days together before my flight home on Monday, the last thing I want is to start today by missing breakfast again, so I dress quickly and knock on Alexander's door. When there's no answer, I hurry down to the breakfast room, hoping I'll find him there alone. I walk in to find no one at all, although a place is laid and the warming dishes are still on the sideboard.

Robert follows me. 'Good morning, miss. Would you like tea or coffee?'

'Coffee, please. Am I late?'

'Not at all, but Lord Falconbury and Lord Sledmere are eating at the hunt breakfast. Miss di Cavinato had coffee taken up to her room.'

'Oh. Where are they now?'

'Lord Falconbury's with his guests, Lord Sledmere said he was going to the stables, I believe, and I think Miss di Cavinato is in her room getting ready for the hunt. Please, help yourself to breakfast, but if there's anything else you need, ring the bell and one of the staff will come. I'm afraid I have to go now; people have started arriving. The main hunt breakfast will be served outside at nine.'

'Thanks, Robert.'

His tight smile and quick exit tell me how stressed he is. I guess it's the biggest day of the year for him and the team, with scores of people arriving for the hunt breakfast and over a hundred for the ball.

I grab a coffee and bolt down some fruit and yoghurt, unwilling to stay out of the action for too long. Before Calliope decided to go AWOL, I had thought of riding out with the hunt, but I've had second thoughts. I'm not sure I can handle the kind of horse I'd need to hunt all day, and the last thing I want is to end up on my butt – or worse: in some ditch with Valentina and Alexander's horsey friends sniggering at me.

By the time I head back up to my room, the hall is swarming with people and full of bags and suitcases. Robert and Helen seem to know them all and are busy allocating rooms. I change into Calvin jeans, my Burberry wax jacket and a pair of Emma's Hunter wellingtons that Helen found for me, and head outside.

There couldn't be a greater contrast between last night, when I looked down on the silent moonlit lawn, and now. The grass is almost obscured by people, horses and hounds. Above the baying and yelping as the hounds swarm between the red-coated hunstmen, the air is filled with people calling 'Good morning' to each other across the clear, cold air. It sounds bizarrely formal because these people have obviously known each other for years, but I guess it's part of the ritual.

Some people are waiting in line at the trestle tables where the kitchen staff are handing out bacon rolls and glasses of port, whisky and, judging by the steam rising from the glasses, Glühwein. The driveway is full of horseboxes and swarming with grooms and staff coaxing horses down the ramps from their trailers.

More and more horses gather at the front of the house, until I can't see the gravel for equine magnificence. There are people in dark jackets, but they only serve to make the bright red coats of the hunt master and seasoned members stand out even more. I spot Rupert in a red hunting coat, laughing with General Hunt. No one speaks to me, yet I can't help but feel their eyes on me as I head to the stables to find Alexander.

As I round the corner from the house to the yard,

I spot Valentina outside the stable block. I stop in my tracks before she sees me. She's in a black coat, her fawn jodhpurs shrink-wrapped to her bottom and thighs and her glossy mane fastened in a black net. There's no sign of Alexander, but Talia is there, and I see Benny running around the yard, sniffing madly at anything and everything.

Valentina mutters something to Talia, then points at the stables with her riding crop. Talia, who looks thunderous, nods and heads off to the stables. While she waits, Valentina paces the yard, swishing her crop at the air and checking her watch. Benny lollops up to her and sticks his muzzle at her crotch.

'*Oddio!*'

I almost fall into the wall when she brings the crop down sharply on the dog's back. He yelps pitifully and I clamp my hand over my mouth, bile rising. It's not in my nature to hate anyone, but I just came within a whisker of feeling that way towards Valentina.

Benny slinks away and I want to run up and hug him, but I feel too angry to leave my spot. I'm worried I'll say something I really regret if I confront her now.

Talia emerges from the stable, carrying a silk hat. 'Did I hear Benny just now?'

Valentina twitches the snowy-white stock at her throat. 'I have not seen him. It must have been one of the hounds. They make such a noise.'

'It sounded like Benny.'

'I said you are mistaken.' Valentina snatches the top hat from Talia. 'Bring Artemis to the front of the house.'

With a face like fury, Talia marches off as Alexander rounds the corner. He looks incredible in his hunting gear, but also strange and alien. He stops beside Valentina. I can hear their raised voices, but cannot make out exactly what they're saying, then I realize that some of it is in Italian.

They seem to be arguing, judging by Valentina's wild gesticulations and shrill tone. Alexander switches to English and I hear mention of Harvey and 'fucking dangerous', but I can't be sure he's directly confronting Valentina over taking the horse out. I hope he isn't because I'd rather fight my own battles. I'm thinking of doing exactly that when Alexander throws up his hands in frustration and turns away. Valentina dives after him and cracks her riding crop hard across his behind.

'Fucking hell!' He rounds on her furiously while she stands with her hands on her hips, shrieking with laughter.

'I don't see you complain before, *tesoro*.'

They're only a few yards away now so I shrink behind the wall, holding my breath.

Rubbing his butt, Alexander snaps, 'For God's sake, come on or we'll be late for breakfast.'

I hurry back to the lawns where Robert and his team are still dishing up hot food from silver warming dishes, although most people are mounted now. Everyone seems to have a role and a purpose, even if it's only to do some serious networking, which I suspect may be the main aim of the day for most. Hovering at the edge, with a glass of mulled wine for company, I feel like a spare part.

Talia and one of the other grooms arrive with two horses. Alexander mounts a magnificent stallion, who's even bigger than Hotspur. Even with my limited equine knowledge, I can tell from his sleek, powerful lines that he's a thoroughbred, but boy is he feisty. He looks very highly strung, but also as if he'll go all day.

Valentina's on a sparky grey mare, an Irish draught, I think. Admiring eyes turn in her direction, the sea of riders parting to let her and Alexander through. I hear someone muttering 'such a shame', which I take as a reference to their broken engagement. Though it hurts to admit the fact, from a distance Alexander and Valentina appear to be the perfect couple. Two beautifully matched aristocrats on magnificent mounts with the mere mortals orbiting round them. Around us, the chatter grows louder. Horses snort and stamp, and the yells of the pack rise to fever pitch.

I gulp down my mulled wine, burning my mouth in the process. I'd love to speak to Alexander, but there are so many people I don't think I can get to him. Briefly, he catches my eye over the throng and smiles at me, but then more horses and riders hide him from view. It's like being thrown a lifeline in the middle of a stormy ocean, then having it snatched away.

Suddenly Rupert looms beside me on a massive chestnut gelding. 'You managed to wangle an invite, then,' he says, sneering down at me. 'And haven't decided that there are more interesting things to do back in Oxford?'

'Like I told you, Alexander had already asked me.'

'Of course. I forgot. So you're not going to follow the hunt?' He casts a contemptuous glance at my wellingtons.

'I went for a hack with Alexander yesterday, but I'm no hunter.'

'You could have fooled me.'

The bastard. He's implying that I'm some kind of gold-digger, but I manage to keep my cool and hold a hand to my ear. 'Sorry, I can hardly hear you above the dogs barking.'

'They're not dogs, they're hounds, and they don't bark, they give tongue.' When he licks his lips, he reminds me of a lizard devouring a fly. 'It'll be lonely all day here on your own ... you know, I *could* stay here and give you some tongue, if you wanted. We'll be quite safe. Alexander will be too busy with Valentina to notice.'

I shudder. 'Rupes, that's terribly kind of you, but if I wanted to spend my time surrounded by crap I'd help Talia muck out the stables.'

There's a blast on the horn and the hounds bay like crazy. Some of the horses start stamping their feet and have to be reined in.

'Hadn't you better go play with your friends?' I say.

He laughs. 'You'd better enjoy Falconbury while you can. You won't get another chance now Valentina's got her claws back into Alexander's arse.'

Still laughing at me, he wheels away. The noise of hooves ringing on the ground is almost deafening, and they're off, trotting up the drive and out of the park, with Valentina's top hat bobbing at the head of the followers.

People set off after them on foot and in Land Rovers and Volvos until there's only the staff left – clearing away the debris of breakfast – and me.

The baying of the hounds in the distance reminds me of poor Benny and I think I'll try to find him to see if he's OK. He'd slunk away from the stables, so that's where I head now and find Talia walking across the yard. Spotting me, she comes to meet me, a smile on her face.

'Can I help you, Miss Cusack?'

'Oh, for God's sake call me Lauren!'

Talia holds up her hands. 'OK, OK.'

I groan in embarrassment. Valentina and Rupert have really got to me and that makes me even madder. 'I'm really sorry, Talia. I didn't mean to snap. I'm just not used to all the deference and formality around here.'

She rolls her eyes then laughs. 'You should try working here. Alexander's OK, of course, and to be honest I was only winding him up yesterday by calling him "sir". We're all on first-name terms when Robert's not about.' She bites her lip and her eyes twinkle. 'Did you enjoy your picnic in the woods by the way?'

Heat races to my cheeks. 'Um, yes, it was delicious. Thanks.'

She laughs. 'No biggie. I'm glad Alexander's found someone normal.'

This is one of the biggest compliments I've had since I landed at Heathrow, what seems like an age ago. 'Thanks.'

'I could be sacked for saying this but I can't stand Valentina; none of us can apart from Robert, who thinks the sun shines out of her pert arse. Lady Falconbury loved her, but she didn't live long enough to see what a bitch the woman has turned into. I don't know what Alexander sees in her.'

'She *is* stunning,' I say, unwilling to say anything that might get back to Alexander.

'So is a cattle prod.'

I can't help laughing out loud, and joyful barks fill the air as Benny hurtles into the yard. I bend down and bury my face in his silky ears. Talia crouches beside me and tickles his tummy.

'She's cruel to Benny when she thinks Alexander isn't looking. I heard him yelping while she sent me to fetch her bloody hat this morning though she denied he'd been here.'

'She hit him with her whip. I was, uh . . . passing by and saw it happen.'

'Fuck, what? The bitch!'

'I think he spoiled her turn-out by drooling on her jodhpurs.'

Talia ruffles Benny's ears. 'Well done, boy!' She smiles at me. 'I'm sorry she left you with Calliope yesterday. I did try to stop her from taking Harvey because Alexander had asked me to tack him up for you, but Valentina turned up at the crack of dawn and demanded to have him. She swore you and Alexander wouldn't mind and I could hardly tell her to knob off. I hope Calliope didn't give you any trouble? She can be really skittish, but you seemed confident and Alexander was with you, so I thought it would be OK.'

'She was good as gold,' I say, too embarrassed to confess the truth, and also not wanting my unscheduled flight to get back to Valentina. 'But thanks for thinking of me.'

'That is *such* a relief. Shame she didn't kick off when Valentina was on her yesterday, and it would have served her bloody right because poor Harvey was traumatized when she brought him back. God knows where she took him. Hey, I've got a couple of hours off to follow the hunt – do you want to come along? It would be nice to have the company. I've been up since four, and the other grooms are going to hack out the fresh horses to the field later.'

'You mean they have two horses?'

'The general, Alexander and Valentina always do, but I'm done for the day.'

'I don't want to spoil your day off.'

'You won't. We can take Benny if we keep him on a lead. I wouldn't want him to get among the hounds or under anyone's hooves, if you know what I mean, though I'd love to see Valentina fall flat on her arse.'

Not smirking at this comment is one of the hardest things I've ever done, but I manage. 'In that case, I'd love to.'

'Great. Let's get his leash and we'll take the Land Rover.'

Benny barks joyously as he jumps into the rear of the car and we head off out of the yard and up the lane. I can see the pack in the distance, galloping across the fields. Talia steers the Land Rover expertly through a mile or so of narrow lanes till we reach Falconbury village. A cluster of honey-stone cottages, a church and a post office mark the centre. Talia parks the four-wheel drive in the car park of the local pub. As we jump down, the inn sign, with its faded coat of arms, creaks in the wind.

'Not the Falconbury Arms?

She grins. 'Of course, what did you expect? They own everything for miles around. In fact there's no need to even go off their own country to hunt.'

We climb on a gate and balance on the bars. Horns and high yelps in the distance signal the arrival of the pack and the dull rumble of hooves swells to a thunder. The hounds race past, barking and yelling, and disappear into a wood.

'They've gone into the covert. This should be good.'

In half a minute, the lead horses fly past, Valentina and Alexander at the front. Even from my perch on the gate, I can tell he's having the time of his life. Valentina's hair has come loose from its net, and streams back in the wind as she urges Artemis towards a hedge separating the field from the covert.

'Oh God, I hope she's not going to try and jump that. Artemis isn't up to it. She'll refuse.'

'Alexander's behind her, look.' I point.

'He's on Rasputin. He'll be fine. Jesus!'

Valentina raises her whip and slaps Artemis's flank and the horse leaps, scattering loose twigs.

'Poor Artemis!'

Alexander clears the hedge a second later and is off after Valentina, followed by the rest of the riders. I'm left breathless, both at the spectacle and the sight of the two of them leading the rest of the hunt. As we walk back down the lane, with Benny let off his lead for a sneaky run, we pass a horsebox in a lay-by. The trailer is swaying and I can hear muffled thuds and squeals. Talia pauses and rolls her eyes.

'Is that what I think it is?' I ask.

'Yup. It's Binky Peters's trailer. Jesus, I wonder who she's with.'

'I could be mistaken because everyone went by so fast, but I didn't see Rupert in the pack.'

'Neither did I, but Binky wouldn't . . . she's almost old enough to be his mum! Then again, Rupert would shag anything with a pulse and Bink's husband is away working in Dubai . . .'

'But in the middle of a hunt?'

'With the adrenaline pumping and the booze they're necking, almost anyone looks great in hunting clothes. At some meets you can't pass a trailer for people shagging, and this one's not called Fucking Falconbury for nothing.'

There's a creak and the trailer rocks alarmingly.

'And I thought they came for the sport.'

'Yes, all kind of sport!' She sees my horrified face. 'Oh, don't worry! Valentina wouldn't try to shag Alexander while they're in the field. She's too busy showing off what a great rider she is.' Talia sighs. 'She's like a demon when she gets at the top of the pack and she never gives up until they blow the horn to leave the field. *Nothing* gets in her way.'

None of this is reassuring and there's another shriek from inside the trailer.

Talia grimaces. 'Eww. This is too much. Let's drive to the other side of the river. The pack should be heading that way next, if I know the trail layer.'

We climb in the Land Rover and rattle off the pub car park. 'Are you going to the hunt ball tonight?' I ask, although I think I know the answer.

'Me? You are joking? That's for the hunt members and the family's inner circle, but I wouldn't want to go anyway. I waited on tables once for some extra money and it was an eye-opener. If you think this lot are obnoxious in the field, wait until tonight.'

She glances over to me, almost swerving off the road. 'Don't worry. I'm sure it won't be that awful, and Alexander will want you to have a good time. He never got me to turn the hut into a shag pad for Valentina, that's for sure.'

Chapter Twenty-one

From below me in the courtyard, the sounds of hooves and laughter has me hastily closing the cover of my sketchbook. Talia had to go home after lunch so I came back to the house. There are about a dozen people staying over at Falconbury, including Rupert. Only a handful are leaving their horses here; Talia says the rest will be taken home in trailers or have been hired from hunt members.

While the house was empty apart from the staff, I spent an hour checking out some of the works of art, with the help of a catalogue Helen found me from the library. I went to my room, intending to do some research on one of the artists, before washing my hair ready for the ball, but the view from my window was so beautiful I got out my sketchpad and pencils instead.

Although it's barely past three, the sun is going down, turning the sky pink and orange. I really need to capture it in watercolours when I get back home, but I tried to portray the stark beauty of the deer park, the meadow and the copse beyond. I was sketching in the church spire when I heard the horses returning.

Despite Talia's company, it's been a long day and a strange one. Alexander's face as he thundered past with Valentina was joyous. This weekend might have been a 'duty' for him, but today he was definitely in his element.

Now I can see him, trotting up the drive, with Valentina and Rupert by his side and a dozen or so other people following. Abandoning my sketchpad, I pull on my coat and run downstairs.

The riders are dismounting on the drive, where a small army of grooms is waiting to lead them back to the stables. Alexander's fawn breeches are spattered with mud, his face glowing. As I walk down the steps, he takes off his riding hat and ruffles his hair. Valentina says something and both Alexander and Rupert roar with laughter. To my shock, Alexander taps her behind with his riding crop. It's only a playful swat, but she shrieks with delight.

'Hello.'

Alexander's still laughing as he turns round. Valentina looks at me like I'm a beetle she found in her soup. Rupert smirks as he watches us. I refuse to be wound up by any of this, but it's not easy.

Smiling, Alexander strides forward and kisses me briefly on the lips. 'Hello. Had a good day?'

'Good, thanks. You?'

'Fucking amazing.' His eyes shine.

'*Magnifico!* The best day ever, wasn't it, *amore*?'

'Anything had to be better than last season. The weather was an absolute bastard,' Rupert cuts in.

'*Oddio*, yes, it was terrible, but we still managed a few good meets, didn't we?' She slips her arm through Alexander's. 'What a shame you couldn't join us today,

306

Lauren. I hope you enjoyed your little hack on Calliope yesterday?'

Alexander stiffens a little, but he doesn't remove her arm.

'Thanks, I did. In fact, Calliope was magnificent; it's such a pity that you didn't feel confident enough to take her out – I'm sure you would have been fine.' Valentina's mouth gapes open as I push breezily on. 'Talia and I were talking about it this morning when we followed in the Land Rover. In fact, we saw you ride past the village.'

Her dark eyes flash with fury. 'Then you must have seen me clear that hedge? No thanks to my horse, but I suppose it was the best I could expect from the stables here. I have my own thoroughbred at home, of course.'

'Artemis is a good mare.' Alexander withdraws his arm.

Ignoring Valentina, I speak directly to Alexander. 'Is there another Falconbury meet?'

'There's a smaller lawn meet here in February, but the local hunt meets three or four days a week in the season.'

Valentina snorts in derision. 'The Falconbury meet should be held on a week day. There are far too many people who are too slow and boring here on Saturdays, and far too many farmers.'

Alexander tears off his gloves impatiently. 'Farmers are the lifeblood of the hunt, Valentina.'

She curls her lip. 'A pity.'

Rupert interrupts with his lazy drawl. 'Last season was shit. The one before was the best ever. I managed twenty-two days on twelve horses with nine different packs. Not as many as I had wanted, of course, because I had to bloody work most of the week.'

'Only twenty-two? You lightweight, de Courcey! I did twice that many a few years back.'

Rupert rounds on a blond guy I don't know. 'Bull-shit!'

Alexander roars with laughter again. Everyone's pumped up, laughing and telling stories about people and events that I don't have a clue about. I'm glad to see Alexander so happy and relaxed, but I also can't miss the puzzled, and occasionally pitying, glances aimed in my direction, presumably because I've missed out on the fun. Hey, I have my pride and there's no way I'm going to hang about like a spare part again. With Alexander and Valentina the centre of a laughing knot of people, I slip quietly back up to my room. We're all meeting in the drawing room for drinks before the ball at seven and I need to shower and do my hair.

A short while later, darkness descends and the drive is once again empty; the house guests have retreated inside to get ready for the ball. A rap on my door heralds the arrival of Alexander, who walks in before I can answer.

The sharp kick of lust deep in my stomach over-rides my disappointment at being sidelined earlier. His breeches mud-spattered and the once-shiny boots have left a trail of earth on the carpet. He's also radiating pure sex.

He strides straight over, takes me in his arms and claims a fierce kiss.

'So it was as good as it sounded?' I ask, when I finally have the breath.

'Awesome.'

'That still doesn't sound like me, but I have to admit you do look happy. Almost as happy as when you've just come, although I don't think I can live up to a climax that's lasted all day.'

'Now that would be worth trying.'

'I think I'd be saddle-sore.'

He raises an eyebrow and murmurs, 'I'd hope so. So . . . how's your day been? I do hope you haven't been too bored.'

'Not at all. Talia and I followed you for a while . . . we took Benny.'

He squeezes me to him and I can tell he's happy to hear it. 'I hope he behaved.'

'*He* did.' A tiny emphasis on the 'he' is as close as I dare come to telling him that Valentina hit his dog. We've talked about her enough and I won't say anything this time, but if I see her hurt Benny again I won't be responsible for what I do with my riding crop.

He leans back and searches my face. 'Lauren, you have that look on your face; you're upset about something but too cool to tell me what it is.'

'I do not!'

'I'd show you a mirror if I could. What's happened?'

'Nothing. Really, I had a great day. I enjoyed Talia's company, and in my opinion you should make sure she gets a raise.'

He laughs. 'Believe me, I would do it instantly if I was in charge here, but failing that I'll drop a big hint to Robert. Now, let's hear the "but" that was coming after you said you had a nice day.'

'No "but". I came back here and took a look at some of the art collection and I'm seriously impressed.' I toy with one of the brass buttons on his coat. 'I visited the orangery and the library, I did some sketches –'

'Sketches? You?'

'Is it that surprising?'

'Not at all. Let me take a look.'

Shit. I walked into that one. 'No way!'

'Why not?'

'Because they're not great.'

He gives me the laser-stare treatment. 'I don't believe that. What did you draw?'

'Only the view from the window. Nothing worth seeing, honestly.'

Twisting out of my arms, he scans the room, looking for my sketchpad.

'Alexander, no. You can't!'

'Oh, I think I can.'

It takes seconds for him to spot the pad on the window seat. Though I dash forward, he whips ahead of me and snatches up the book.

'Hey!'

It's too late. He flips back the cover and I see his lips

part in surprise. All I can do is hang back, my hand over my mouth.

'So this is the view from your window, is it?'

My cheeks are burning with shame. 'I asked you not to look at them. I never meant for anyone to see them.'

'I'm glad about that.'

'Oh God. They're not that awful, are they?' I peer through my fingers as he turns the pages slowly, frowning with concentration.

'Well, they're not da Vinci . . .'

He may be right, but I have my pride. 'They aren't meant to be. They're purely for my own pleasure.'

'Your pleasure? I'm very relieved to hear that.'

I feel his hand prise my fingers from my eyes but I can't look at him.

'Lauren. They're not bad at all; in fact, they're pretty good and you shouldn't be so hard on yourself. My only objection is that I'm in far too many of them.'

I open my eyes. 'Oh, fuck.'

He picks up the sketch pad, flicking to a charcoal study of him standing above me in the punt, staring into the distance as he steers us down the river. His face is serious as he studies the picture. 'I had no idea,' he says.

'You were concentrating.'

His brows knit together in the exact expression I tried to capture. 'Clearly. Is this really how I look?'

'No. It's just my very badly executed impression of you.'

He turns the page again and I want to melt right through the rug.

'From memory, I'm guessing?'

Nodding my head, my heart sinks as he holds out my sketch of him lying naked in my bed.

'I must say, that sheet is strategically placed.'

My toes curl with embarrassment. 'I . . . um . . . couldn't bring myself to draw that part of you.'

'Didn't feel you could do justice to it?' He turns to me with a teasing smile that irrationally makes me want to jump him even more.

'Have I ever told you that you are beyond arrogant?'

'Frequently.' He lays down the sketch pad and holds out his hand. 'I'm glad you found something to amuse you while I was out. I was worried about you.'

'You didn't *look* worried,' I shoot back, recalling the exhilaration on his face during the hunt.

'I was. I did try to get to you at the hunt breakfast, but there were too many people.'

I remember the loss I felt as he was sucked away from me by the tide of strangers this morning, but I don't want him to know how isolated that made me feel. I also won't tell him about Rupert's taunts or the remarks I heard as he and Valentina rode to the top of the hunt this morning. Nothing else is going to spoil tonight or our last weekend.

'I've been fine, but this is all so . . . alien to me. You have to admit it's a pretty arcane world to those of us who aren't part of the club.'

'But you *are* part of the club, Lauren.'

'I'm not sure everyone would agree with that.'

'I agree with it and that's all that matters.'

'Thank you for saying so.'

My fingers graze the muddy streaks on his cheek and his mouth twitches.

'Sorry, I'm absolutely filthy.'

I throw him a crooked smile. 'That suits me.'

'You really want me like this, after I've spent all day in the field?' Salt makes my lips tingle as I taste his mouth. My body responds to the sharp scent of clean sweat and testosterone.

'Yes, I do.'

His jacket is rough and damp against my cheek. How can I tell him that I want him like this, with the exhilaration still pulsing in his veins and clinging to his skin? That it's my way of sharing in his world? He wouldn't understand; *I* don't understand – I just know I want him now.

'Look what you've done to me,' he whispers, guiding my hand to the bulge in his breeches.

His cock, already hard, stirs and swells beneath my fingers. 'That's only the thrill of the chase.'

'In that case, you don't want to deny a man when his blood is up.'

'And what will happen if I do?'

His hands cup my bottom, pressing me harder against his pelvis. 'I can't answer for that.'

I let my fingers drift to the white silk stock at his throat. 'Then perhaps it's time for you to get out of these dirty clothes.' Carefully, I draw out the gold pin that's holding the silk knot in place and hold it up in front of me. Lamplight glints off the metal. 'This is beautiful.'

'My mother gave it to me.'

'I'm sorry.'

'For reminding me about her? You don't have to be.' He holds out his hand, palm upwards, fingers calloused from the day's hunt. I drop the pin into his hand and he places it on the table next to him.

'Why so tight?' I ask, struggling with the knot of the stock.

'To save me from breaking my neck, of course, and to use as a makeshift bandage if I do.'

'You're joking?'

'No. Obviously, it wouldn't have been much protection in a bad fall, but a century ago that's all they had.'

'And here's me assuming you only wear it to make you look hot.'

When he laughs, his throat ripples beneath my fingers. '*Hot?* You really think?'

'Uh-huh.'

He loosens the knot so I'm able to free the silk band from his neck and drop it on to the floor. The silver buttons on his scarlet coat are easier to unfasten, and he shrugs the jacket from his shoulders and throws it on the bed. I bury my face in the cotton of his shirt, feeling his chest rising beneath my cheek. Taking my time, I work my way down the buttons of his collarless shirt, savouring the slow, delicious revelation of his firm pecs and hard abs.

'Enjoying yourself?' He breathes the words into my hair.

'Uh-huh.'

I drag his shirt from his breeches and he pulls it off his arms. Wow. The sight of him, bare-chested, in his muddy breeches and boots makes me fizz from the top of my scalp to the tips of my toes.

'I'd better take my boots off.'

He sits on the edge of the bed to pull off his boots and socks.

He pops the fly buttons on his breeches one by one. There's hunger in his eyes, his nostrils flare and my pulse quickens. I'm the watcher, but I've no illusions; it's me who's being stalked and hunted. Sure enough, in two quick strides, he springs off the bed, catches my hand and pulls me hard against his torso.

'I want you naked now and I need a shower and there's only one answer to that.'

Stumbling over his discarded boots, I'm dragged towards the ensuite bathroom. He shuts the door and strips off his breeches and boxer shorts while I pull my sweater over my head and unclasp my bra. My jeans and panties follow the rest of our clothes on to the tiles.

In seconds, we're packed inside the shower cubicle and the door slides shut.

My shriek is snatched away by the jet of cold water hitting my body. He hugs me to his body as the heat finally hits the shower head and takes away the stinging shock. I'm still struggling for breath, but Alexander plunges his mouth on to mine as water thunders on to our heads. I lean back out of the spray. 'You're filthy.'

'I know. Do something about it, then.'

I reach for my shower gel and squirt it on to his pecs,

rubbing it in with my palms, sliding my fingers through the hair around his dark nipples and down over the ridges of his stomach. My hands slip lower, through his wet pubic hair and along his penis. I cup his balls in my hand, holding their weight in my palm, squeezing gently. My reward is his moan of undiluted ecstasy and his erection prods my stomach.

'Turn around,' he orders over the deluge of water.

'It's tight in here.'

'Oh, I'm counting on it.'

I shake water from my eyes and he works a lather between my shoulders, down my spine, across my buttocks and between them. My nipples stand to attention, but I have to close my eyes. This is so intimate, more intimate than being bathed, because he's soaping my behind thoroughly, his roughened palms rubbing my soft skin. I tense my butt as his index finger drifts slowly down the cleft between my cheeks. My throbbing clit tells me I want him to go further, but my mind backs off. I want him to touch me *there* with his fingers and more, but I can't do it. Sensing the tension in my muscles, he withdraws his hand and turns me round to face him.

Through the haze of spray and steam, his expression is laden with sensual threat. He knew what he was doing, hinting at what will come between us, if not now then sooner or later, and that I'll be thinking about it every time we make love from now on.

Maybe that's why I'm trembling a little as his teeth graze my shoulder, but I buck against his erect penis.

The nip was short and sharp and shot fire right to my sex. He massages my clit with his fingers. Skin on skin, our bodies slick, we devour each other's mouths. The water roars in my ears as he backs me up against the cool polish of the tiles. His big hands scoop my thighs up and lift me. Braced against the wall, he holds me up, biceps shaking with strain and slides me down on to his rigid shaft.

My arms cling to his neck, hands locked across his shoulder blades as he thrusts upwards into me. I'm sliding up and down his shaft, my butt slipping on the tiles, his face almost obscured by steamy mist that fills my nostrils and eyes. His penis grazes the core of me and I rub my clit frantically against his abdomen, seeking my climax. Then Alexander's muscles tauten like wet cord as his cock pulses deep inside me. He's still holding me up, his head thrown back, his eyes screwed shut, in an agony of release.

I'm on the edge myself, but then I find my soles touch the tiles and I'm lowered.

The spray dwindles and the silence is startling. Alexander folds me softly against him, like I'm some fragile treasure. His body is soft, his face pressed to my shoulders, water droplets glistening on his back and buttocks. Still not quite there, I press my hips against him to let him know what I need.

It's enough of a hint and his fingers find my clit, feathering it. Craving more, I part my legs a little to give him access to my pussy.

'I love baring you,' he whispers.

'I love to be bared. Oh my . . .'

The words die in my mouth as he draws a line from my clit through my labia with his fingertip, resting it at my entrance. One, then two fingers plunge inside me and my muscles clamp around them. I grip the muscles of his shoulders as he pushes his fingers in and out of me and presses my clit lightly with the thumb of his other hand. I've no resistance against this twin assault, only greed for my release. I'm half aware of my nails puncturing the flesh of his back when my desperate howl echoes around the cubicle.

All is dark, quiet, steamy mist. When I open my eyes, I'm still holding on to his waist, my clit pleasantly swollen, my limbs soft as water.

He pushes a sopping strand of hair out of my eyes and leans back to see my face. Those ice-blue eyes glow with pleasure, his face is relaxed. 'Good?'

'Mmm.'

The corner of his mouth quirks. 'I aim to please.'

'No, you don't. You don't aim to please anyone. You're Alexander Hunt; you do what you want and screw the world.'

He laughs. 'I want to please *you*. The rest of the world can go to hell.'

I shake my head because we both know this isn't true. He can't and won't upset Valentina – nor Rupert, nor the people coming to this ball. He's a creature of his upbringing, no matter how much he wants to play the rebel.

'I can't change,' he whispers, and I'm not sure if it's a statement of fact or apology.

'I don't want you to. I wish that things could stay like this, just you and me here right now.'

He slides back the cubicle door, and a blast of cool air licks our bodies. 'Me too, but I'm afraid that duty calls.'

Chapter Twenty-two

'Duty calls.'

I'm still mulling over Alexander's remark when a sharp rap on the door is followed immediately by the sound of him striding across the boards of my bedroom. I turn round from my seat in front of the dressing mirror to find him standing a couple of feet away. Once again, he's wearing mess dress rather than white tie or hunting dress. Is it purely out of pride or one more way of winding up his father?

He glances at his watch.

'Am I late?' I ask.

'No, I'm a little early.'

His smile can't erase the tension etched on his features and it's clear he sees tonight as an ordeal he has to get through.

The fabric of my gown shimmers in the bedroom lamplight when I stand up. Pleasure flickers in his eyes and he pulls me to him. 'You look good enough to eat and that's exactly what I'd love to do right now. In fact, I've some plans involving a very rare bottle of my father's single malt and your amazing breasts.' He kisses me and my lipstick must be all over the place, but I don't care. 'You look, smell and feel fucking incredible.'

'Well, hey, you're not so bad yourself, but you won't *quite* do.'

I tweak the Para wings on the lapels of his mess dress until they're perfectly symmetrical. Whatever his motives for wearing the uniform this evening, I'd forgotten how handsome he looks and the way it makes him seem even taller than his six feet three inches. His pride is evident in the way he stands even more upright in it, with his shoulders back and his chin held high.

His hands span my waist and he smiles. 'So, you've no regrets about accepting the necklace now?'

My hand strays to the delicate stones at my throat. 'It's gorgeous.'

'Only because of the wearer.' He drops a kiss on my shoulder and my exposed skin tingles in anticipation of his touch.

'I'd love to ditch the ball and spend the evening naked with you,' I whisper.

Almost idly, he lifts a strand of hair from my cheek. 'There are a lot of things I'd like to do with you, but we have to get through tonight first.'

I search his face, looking for clues as to how he really feels. 'Alexander, is everything OK?'

'Of course. Why wouldn't it be?'

'You seem a little on edge.'

'I just want to get it over with. Are you ready?'

The swirling in my stomach tells me otherwise, but I give him a confident nod. 'I think so.'

I take his outstretched arm and the realization hits me. I'm the special guest – the partner – of the heir to

Falconbury. Twice before, that role must have been taken on by Valentina; twice before, Alexander must have come to her room, told her she looked beautiful and led her down to the ballroom.

I don't need to ask how she must feel tonight, knowing that I have taken her place. I'd be lying if I said I feel sorry for her; she's made it clear she'd rather roast in hell than have my pity, yet the thought of taking on her role makes me fizz with nerves. While I might have stayed anonymous in the melee and mayhem of the hunt, I'm hyper-aware that every eye will be upon us when we walk into Falconbury's ballroom. Faced with that prospect, I'm not sure if I'd not rather melt into the crowd again. My hands tighten on Alexander's arm.

'Relax. They'll love you,' he says, as if he can read my mind.

I don't need them to love me, respect will do . . .

I shake my head and give him a wry smile in return. 'You think?'

'I do. Come on.'

He gives me that smile; the one that sparkles with tender warmth and sexiness, the one I glimpse occasionally and would love to see more often. My legs wobble a little, not only due to the teetering silver heels I have on. Exhilarated by a day's hunting and resplendent in his uniform, I don't think I've ever wanted him more. It really is a *very* big thing to be his partner for the evening, but that's not what makes my heart rate speed up. It's the way I feel about him right now, the lurch of unexpected emotion that seizes my throat and chest that really scares me; but I have to swallow it down and keep it for another time, another place. As he says, we have to get through tonight first. What lies beyond – and on the other side of the long Christmas vacation – I'm not ready to contemplate.

The velvet of my gown rustles on the boards as we walk out on to the landing. I decided to give the Kristen Stewart dress its first outing tonight. The deep V-neck plunges lower than I normally wear, but I thought it was OK when I checked myself out in the mirror. I had to do my own hair, so I went for a simpler version of the style I tried for Rashleigh Hall and added a vintage marcasite clip my grandmother gave me for my twenty-first. The antique design seemed to fit the occasion, and it feels like a small but comforting connection to my family.

The buzz of chatter swells in volume as I walk downstairs on Alexander's arm. Below us, I can see the tops of a dozen or so heads as the staff take coats and wraps from guests. The sudden draught from the open front door chills my skin. As we step on to the black and white tiles in the hallway, the strains of a string quartet drift out of the ballroom, underlying a rising tide of excited voices. Although I recognize a few faces from the hunt earlier, the vast majority of the people are strangers to me. They nod and smile deferentially at Alexander and regard me with mild surprise, like I'm some exotic animal they didn't expect to find here. Though I've thrown on a confident facade, I can't help wish Immy were here, or that I could beam down my friends from Brown.

My arm tightens on Alexander's when we reach the double doors into the ballroom. 'Good evening, sir, Miss Cusack.'

Robert is presiding, of course, in white tie no less, and he beckons to a waiter with a tray of champagne. I'm so busy taking in the room that it's a few seconds before I realize Alexander's arm is gone. While I'm more than capable of managing without him by my side and would hate him to think I was clingy, I can't help feeling I've been cut off from my lifeline in a stormy ocean.

It's only a social event. Smile, Lauren.

Laughing at my own paranoia, I take a glass from the tray, and marvel instead at the transformation that's taken place in the ballroom since I made my tour of the art collection this afternoon. Back then, the portraits of Alexander's ancestors stared sightlessly down on the white-clothed tables that had been set up for dinner. The only sound was my own footsteps on the parquet floor as I skirted the room, gazing at the aristocratic faces, searching for some resemblance to the present-day Hunts.

And now? It feels as if I've stepped into another dimension, as if the people in the pictures have come alive again, ready for this feast. The tables are laid with snowy white linen and silver cutlery. Candelabras sparkle and the scent of exotic flowers fills the air from the table centrepieces and decorations.

Alexander has reappeared at my side after a brief word with an older couple.

Taking a deep breath, I exhale. 'Wow.'

'Hmm. Although it pains me to admit it, Falconbury scrubs up well when it needs to.' He sips his champagne and seems a little more at ease now we've actually taken the plunge and made it into the ballroom. Then General Hunt carves a path towards us and the clouds descend on his mood again. My heart sinks at the expression on the general's face. I'm predicting ice storm versus hurricane, but I'm determined not to be intimidated.

'Good evening, General,' I say.

He barely spares me a nod before launching into his son. 'You deigned to attend after all, then?'

'I always intended to.'

The general snorts. 'Then why did you allow me to think otherwise? Determined to be bloody awkward as usual, were you?'

'I wonder where I get it from?'

Dying with embarrassment at being dragged into another family war, I feign a great interest in an imaginary mark on my dress.

'Damn you, Alexander. If your mother were alive, she'd weep to see the disrespect you show your home and family.'

'If my mother were alive, she'd probably have left you by now.'

Jesus. I can't imagine talking to my father like that and can't help but try to intervene. 'Alexander . . .'

My words draw a fierce scowl from the general and are completely ignored by Alexander, who takes my hand and practically drags me away to the other side of the room.

He stops by a French window and murmurs obscenities under his breath.

'What the hell was that about?' I ask.

'The usual. Me staying here and doing my duty instead of pissing around with my mates. If he only knew –'

'He's a soldier too. Are you sure your father doesn't know exactly what you're doing and this is his way of trying to protect you?'

He curls his lip and for a split second I'm blasted by a glare of contempt that rivals his father's. Then it's gone and he murmurs, 'Take my advice and keep out of this. I know you mean well, but you can't possibly understand.'

'Maybe not, but I'd like to try. I knew there was something wrong when you called for me. I guess you two had a row earlier.' I may be stinging at his brusqueness but I'm determined to keep my cool.

'A row? All-out war is more accurate, but I'm done with him.' He calls over a waiter and swipes a glass of champagne from the tray. 'Bring me a whisky. A large one.'

Alexander knocks back his fizz in two gulps then spots a group of hunting friends from earlier, of which, to my dismay, Rupert is at the centre.

'Come on,' he growls. 'If I have to be in the same room as my father, I'm at least going to make the evening fucking bearable.'

Rupert greets us with a raised eyebrow and a theatrical glance at his watch. 'So, Alexander, you made it down here, then?'

Alexander allows himself a small smile. 'Eventually.'

My face heats up, but at least I get the satisfaction of his fingers brushing the small of my back. Still, this wasn't how I'd hoped the evening would go: once again, I'm ammunition between Alexander and his family and friends – his father, Valentina, Rupert. A weariness overtakes me though it's only the start of the evening. Why can't things between us be simple? Why is there always a battle?

An older couple of about forty butts into our little group and the man seizes Alexander's hand. 'Alexander. How the devil are you?'

He greets the man's wife with a kiss and then she looks at me with an amused twist of her lips. 'And this must be your new friend?'

'Aunt Celia, this is Lauren Cusack, Lauren, meet my Aunt Celia.'

She shakes my fingers limply for a second as her husband claims Alexander.

'Good to meet you,' I say.

'Oh gosh, you really are an American!'

'I'm afraid so.' Oh shit, I hope that didn't sound sarcastic. Oh shit, it probably *did* – probably because I meant it to. 'Even worse, I'm from Washington.'

Celia raises her eyebrows. 'How . . . interesting. We went to the Bahamas in January. There were a lot of Americans there.'

'You don't say?'

'Gosh, yes, hordes. You couldn't get to the buffet in the hotel for them.'

'That'd be us. Always first in line for the food.'

Her husband interrupts. 'Celia, can't you persuade Alexander to stop playing soldiers and come back to Falconbury? His father needs him.'

I hold my breath as Alexander fixes a rigid smile to his face and mutters something about having to circulate.

The smell of whisky almost overpowers me as Rupert sidles up to me. 'That's a nice dress you don't have on, Lauren.'

'Thanks. I see you couldn't get a red coat to fit.'

'These are drinking pinks, but you couldn't possibly be expected to know that . . . Ah, Alexander, your glass is empty and we can't have that. I do hope Lauren is going to let you off the leash tonight? I must admit, I'm surprised she didn't find far more appealing things to do back at college.'

This is a moment when I really wish that spontaneous combustion actually existed because it would be wonderful to see Rupert go up in a puff of smoke, but Alexander shakes his head.

'What the fuck are you on, Rupert?'

'The same thing you ought to be on. Take the poker out of your arse, mate. You're supposed to be enjoying yourself.' Clapping his arm round Alexander's back, he snaps his finger at a passing waitress. 'Whisky for Lord Sledmere and make sure it's a bloody massive one. He needs it.'

Alexander laughs. 'I already ordered one.'

'So what? Unless you're scared of what Lauren thinks. She disapproves of hard liquor, you know.'

'Actually, Rupert, I disapprove of assholes.'

He winces. 'Ohhh, I'm cut to the quick.'

Alexander shakes his head. 'You're lucky she didn't kick you in the balls, you arse. Now, tell me where you were for half the day because oddly enough I can't find anyone who saw you after lunch until we met up back at the house.'

He has his arm round Rupert's back in a guy kind of way and I can't help thinking he's trying to steer him away from baiting me. Within no time, a group of young guys in pinks bears down on us and Alexander is the centre of a bunch of braying testosterone of which I want no part. There's no way I'm going to hang around the edges like some groupie. I see not one but two waiters approach with whisky tumblers. Nearby, in a room off the side of the ballroom, a small army of catering staff fusses over the buffet that's due to be served soon, when I can reclaim Alexander. After that, there will be dancing so we'll be together again.

With a fresh glass of champagne in my hand to steady my nerves, I skirt the room, an observer again, like I was from the window of my bedroom. Normally I enjoy people-watching; it gives me ideas for sketches and some small insight into the minds of real artists. I've always believed you have to be an outsider to create great art or literature and it's good to step out of the herd.

You could also look at it another way. I'm not an observer; I'm an outcast – an interloper into this exclusive, tribal club of which Alexander is king. No amount of money or manners or education could buy you a ticket into it. Unless you're born and bred among them, you might be tolerated, but you'll never be truly welcome. Oxford seems a soft, nurturing world in comparison.

I'm not far from the doors of the ballroom now, and I can see a flurry of movement. Is it coincidence that the musicians strike up Handel's 'Arrival of the Queen of Sheba' as Valentina makes her entrance?

Though it hurts me to admit it, she looks incredible. The boned bodice of her scarlet column dress shoves her breasts together like two apples in a basket; and if I thought my dress was low, hers barely covers her nipples. Her hair is a black silk veil shimmering in the light from the chandelier, her skin as smooth and brown as latte.

Waving away a waiter with a flick of her hand, she cuts a swathe through the crowd of guests near the door. It seems as if every head turns in her direction as she glides among the masses to the centre of the room. The women stare with a mix of admiration and envy while the guys of all ages are drooling so much I'm surprised the staff haven't got floor mops out. Even General Hunt's eyes are popping as if he's about to have a heart attack.

'Good God! I can't stand the woman, but she knows how to make an entrance, I'll give her that.' The distinctly horsey tones come from a woman behind me. I sip my champagne, hoping to calm the nervous fizz in my bones.

'Yes, if that dress was any lower, you'd be able to see her navel. Why did Alexander split up with her?' It's another voice, older and deeper.

'I heard she demanded he leave the army or it was over between them. General Hunt wanted him to come out too, but you know Alexander. He'll go out of his way to do anything that annoys his father.'

'Including an American?'

I freeze, feeling my pulse quicken.

The older woman tsks. 'That's naughty, Stephanie, but I think you're right. The general must be apoplectic that his son and heir is shagging one of our former colonists. Did you know she was from Los Angeles or some equally appalling place? I expect she's an aspiring actress on the make.'

'I don't think so, Mummy. He met her at Oxford. She's from New York and her father's something to do with politics. I think they have family money too.'

'What from? Oil or coal or some other unspeakably dreary activity, I expect. My God, that's hardly any better, is it? Poor Frederick! No wonder he's even more miserable than usual and Grace must be turning in her grave.'

Stephanie intones dramatically: 'Are the shades of Falconbury to be thus polluted?'

Mummy's whinny almost deafens me. 'That is *very* wicked of you!'

Stephanie giggles. 'She is *quite* pretty, though. I love her dress and I'd love to know where she gets her highlights done.'

Turning, I smile politely at the women, a girl with a nose to rival Calliope's and a middle-aged matron with a face like an old saddle. Genes can *so* deal you a rough hand.

'Enjoying the ball?'

Their faces are pictures of frozen horror. 'Yes, thank you.'

'Full of dreadful Americans, though, isn't it? I can't think who let them in.'

Stephanie giggles nervously. Perhaps she thinks I have a Smith & Wesson concealed under my gown.

I raise my empty glass to them. 'And actually, Stephanie, they're not highlights, they're natural.'

With my flute trembling in my hand, I walk off towards the windows, trying to maintain a dignified demeanour. That's not easy when my blood is boiling. These people go beyond any degree of snobbishness I've encountered before and that's saying something. It's not like me to be outwardly rude, but they damn well deserved it. But it's a Pyrrhic victory; it only makes me more dispirited that I sank to their level.

A frisson of apprehension prickles my flesh. A few yards away, the flash of scarlet draws my eye. Valentina has wasted no time hunting down Alexander and is holding court among his friends. That's it. I won't be sidelined any more – I'm going to fight my corner. But as I grow near, I stop and my heart catapults to my mouth.

While everyone laughs at something she's said she lays her hand on Alexander's behind. I expect him to move away, but he stays where he is. She squeezes his butt and he turns to her, yet not to object as I expected, but with an indulgent shake of his head and a smile. Then as she transfers her hand to his arm his fingers rest for a nanosecond on her perfect bottom. It's the lightest of touches, almost unconscious, then he breaks away to chat to Rupert.

Next to me, the French doors to the terrace are open a little. I down my glass and swipe another one from the nearest waiter. It's hot in here and I feel a little light-headed.

But not light-headed enough not to recognize what I just saw. Alexander had his hand on her butt, for God's sake! OK, maybe it was only a brief gesture, the kind of thing that could easily happen between two people who were once lovers – more than that, two people who were once engaged to be married. I've only known Alexander eight weeks; Valentina has been part of his life for twenty-five years and that kind of connection can't be dissolved quickly – if ever. They are always going to share a bond and he *is* a man and she *is* completely stunning.

It's naive of me to expect him to ignore her, *but*.

My stomach clenches violently as I remember my vow never to be taken for granted or treated with the casual cruelty that Todd did. Fuck them.

My glass abandoned, I slip through the open French doors. Cold air hits my lungs and chills my bare shoulders. The lawns and clipped box hedges are crisp with frost, the tranquil gardens a sharp contrast to the heat and tension inside the ballroom. Catching my breath, I try to calm my racing pulse. Should I tough it out and tackle Alexander later, or simply ignore him touching Valentina? What the fuck is going on here and with him? Hugging my body, I glance to the sky where the moon glows mournfully down at me.

'*Buona sera*, Lauren.'

Keeping my eyes on the frozen garden, I answer, 'Valentina.'

'You liked the hunt?' she asks, taking her place by my side.

'I followed for a while.' Finally, I meet her eyes and she gives a sharp laugh.

'Followed? You should have been there with Alexander and I at the top. There is nothing like the thrill of the chase for me.'

'Then it must be so disappointing for you when you've no chance of catching your quarry.'

Her dark eyes flash with anger and her voice is a hissed whisper. 'How do you know that I haven't caught it? The chase has only just begun and I never give up until I get what I want.'

'Good luck with that.' My tone is as chilly as the night air.

She tosses her hair over her shoulder. 'I don't need luck. Alexander is in love with me; he always has been and he always will be.'

My God. Her sheer nerve robs me of a reply.

'Let's not beat round a bush. This thing you have with Alexander cannot last. When you go home to your parents next week, he will soon forget all about you.'

'You really are a very sad and insecure person, Valentina. Have you thought of getting some therapy?'

'Therapy? I do not understand you. I do not need therapy. I know what I want and what everyone here wants, his father, his family and friends and mine. They want Alexander and I to marry. It's what is expected of him and, no matter what he tells you, Alexander will do his duty.'

I shake my head, because I genuinely believe she's pitiable, but my bravado is crumbling. 'He also knows his own mind and he won't be manipulated. By you, his father or anyone. The more you try to hound and pressure him, the more he'll follow his own course.'

She pouts. 'Poor little Lauren. You really have no idea of what keeps a man like Alexander happy, do you?'

'What do you mean, a man like Alexander?'

'I mean that he may want to fuck you all the time now, but he'll soon grow tired of what's on offer from his tame little American. He needs more than that. He likes a challenge and the thrill of a battle too. Did he pursue you at the start? Call you? Text you? Batter down your resistance until you gave in and opened your legs for him?'

'Jesus. You really are disgusting.'

'I think you mean "exciting". That's what Alexander loves: he lives only for competing and winning. You saw him at the hunt today; nothing else mattered but getting to his goal before anyone else. Nothing else keeps him happy. That's why he loves the army and all the dangerous sports, because he wants to feel exhilarated and alive. Since his mother died, Alexander will not let anyone near this part of him.' Her fingertips press on the spot where most people have a heart. 'Except me; because I know how to keep him chasing and wanting me. He needs me, and he will always come back to me.'

Even while I know that she wants to wound me, her bitchy words stick like barbs in my heart because I have a horrible feeling that in some ways she's right about Alexander's need to win at all costs. There's still no way I'm giving her a single inch.

'If he was really anything like you say, he'd be a monster and you'd be welcome to him, but you're wrong,' I say.

She snorts. 'He *did* pursue you, didn't he, like a hound after a fox? Rupert told me you got the full Alexander onslaught.'

I recoil like I would from a cockroach as she lifts my necklace. 'Did he give you this?'

'It's none of your business.'

She lets it drop on to my chest and nods in satisfaction. 'I guessed he did. I have something like it. Not Cartier, that is not my taste. Bulgari is what he had sent to me. He makes it his business to know what his women like.'

'*Women?* So you're not the only heinous bitch he's dumped then?' As I lash back my reply, I can imagine my mother's gasp of astonishment – and the cheering from my sorority sisters.

She arches a slim eyebrow. '*Oddio!* Lauren has claws after all.'

'Believe me, you ain't seen nothing yet.' Inside, I feel physically sick. I'm determined to give as good as I get, but I hate being dragged down to Valentina's level, which is somewhere south of Hades.

'Lauren?'

Alexander is silhouetted against the French doors and my heart skips a beat. I'm so relieved to see him, but at the same time reeling from Valentina's comments. She greets him with a dazzling smile.

'Alexander, *tesoro*! Lauren and I were wondering where you had got to.'

He steps between us, his hand at my elbow. 'Lauren, I've been looking for you everywhere.'

'*Everywhere?* Really?' I can't keep the edge from my voice.

'Yes. The food's being served. Valentina?'

She pulls a face. 'All that fat and carbohydrate. Urghh.'

'I would have thought the hunt would have given you an appetite,' I cut in.

'Not for English food.'

'Let's go in. Valentina, are you coming?' he asks impatiently.

She blows him a kiss. 'For you, *amore*, always.'

The buffet is a Valentina-free zone; she spends the time flirting with General Hunt while we sit down at a table with some of Alexander's friends. I've simmered down a little, but my own appetite has deserted me. Alexander has moved on to more champagne and he isn't drunk, exactly, but he's definitely louder than I've ever seen him before. I've tried to cut him some slack. His father is determined to do battle with him and almost everyone here must remember the days of Lady Hunt, so it's hardly surprising the younger ones still regard Valentina and Alexander as an item.

Her comments have also shown me how desperate she is; and how threatened she must feel. I should take some comfort from that fact, but I'm determined not to get into a catfight over Alexander, no matter how much she provokes me.

Alexander dances with me a couple of times, but now he's laughing with his friends again. That's fine; we're not joined at the hip and I don't think it will do any harm to show him and Valentina that I'm not some clingy ingénue who needs to hang on his every word. So when Angus invites me for a reel I don't say no. Two dances later, I'm dizzy and exhilarated from being whirled around the floor. I love dancing, and the endorphins are pulsing through me as the music finally stops. Angus and I stroll back to our drinks, laughing and chatting.

Then I see Valentina again. Does the woman never give up? I can't help staring as she hangs on to Alexander's arm. He's laughing with a group of hunting friends, and may not even have noticed. Then – Jesus! – she curls her fingers round his behind again. Pangs of jealousy stab me and I curse myself because this is clearly what she wants – maybe she knows I'm watching. Valentina lets out a shriek of laughter that draws attention from the people around her and then she throws her arms round Alexander's neck and kisses him full on the lips.

Chapter Twenty-three

I knock back the rest of my wine savagely. Why doesn't Alexander move away from her? Why does he simply stand there while she hangs on to him like a limpet? Does she know I can see them? Is that what she wants? Now she's stroking his bicep like he's some kind of furry pet.

The band strikes up some folksy tune with a fast tempo and there's a buzz of recognition from around me. Seems like everyone's well past the stage where they don't care about making a fool of themselves.

'Oh, let's have another dance!' I say. 'What about another reel?'

There's a brief look of total confusion on Angus's face, then he laughs. 'Well, this is hardly reeling music, but why not?'

'Come on!' Grabbing his hand, I haul him back on to the dance floor, aware that Alexander has torn his attention from Valentina and is now watching me with a look of incredulity on his face that I believe is described over here as 'gobsmacked'.

In seconds, his face is a blur because Angus is whirling me around the ballroom. We bump into someone, but there's no time for apologies because we're off again, hands crossed, skipping down the middle of the floor.

When the music stops, I can hardly speak. Angus leads me from the floor, and I flop down at a table. I scan the room for Alexander, expecting to find him watching me, but he's nowhere to be seen – and neither is Valentina. A kick of panic hits low in my stomach, making me feel faintly nauseous.

'I need a drink. What can I get you?' Angus asks.

'More champagne, of course – or, better still, a bottle?'

He laughs. 'I can ask, but I'm not drinking tonight. I'm on call.'

'On call? Oh, yes, I'd forgotten. That's tough.'

'Just the way it is, but don't let me stop you . . . Are you sure you don't want to share this drink with Alexander?'

'I don't know where he is. Maybe playing poker? Sliding down the stair banisters?'

Angus laughs. 'I'll be back as soon as I can.'

Another dance tune strikes up and I tap my foot against the floor, waiting for Angus to return. There are now so many people at the bar that I can't see him, but what I do notice is Alexander, drink in hand, talking to Rupert. He doesn't look at me, and is intent on what Rupert is saying.

Two more dances later, there is still no sign of Angus.

'Hello. You must be Lauren.' A blond, almost white-haired, guy stands opposite me, holding a bottle of champagne in one hand and two glasses in the other. I think he was one of the people baiting Rupert after the hunt, which puts him up a notch in my estimation.

'Here's your champagne,' he says.

'I thought Angus was going to get me one . . . but I'm not sure where he is.'

'He had an urgent phone call from the hospital and sent me over with this.' He puts the bottle and glasses on the table and takes the seat next to me. 'I'm Henry Favell, by the way. I've been waiting to be introduced all night and, frankly, I didn't think Alexander was going to let you out of his sight, but I see he's been distracted.'

He turns slightly to Alexander, who is now intent on something Rupert is saying.

'Has he? I hadn't really noticed. How do you know Alexander?'

'I was in his house at Eton.'

I raise my eyebrows. 'Really? I bet you know all of his bad habits. Why don't you tell me about them?'

While he pours me a glass of fizz, he laughs. 'I don't think we've got that long, and who wants to waste time talking about Alexander when I could hear all about the most stunning girl in the room.'

As if he heard his name mentioned, which is impossible, Alexander has turned towards us and is making his way over. I angle myself towards Henry. 'Flattery will get you everywhere.'

'Hopefully . . .' he says.

'He's a nice guy, Angus . . .' I say, feeling Alexander's eyes burning into my back.

'He is. But me, I'm a different matter.'

I rest my chin on my hand. 'Uh-huh?'

'And if you're seeing Alexander, I suppose nice guys aren't really your thing.'

I raise my voice a notch. 'Bastards appear to be.'

'Then I think I can help. Do you want to dance?'

'Love to.'

Henry takes my hand and leads me to the dance floor past the astonished figure of Alexander, who must have heard our conversation. Good, I wanted him to. As Henry's hands settle on my waist, the band plays some cheesy eighties ballad, but I hardly care. There's no mistaking now that I have Alexander's undivided attention. He's standing at the side of the dance floor, rigid with fury – and his aren't the only eyes intent on me. General Hunt, Valentina, Aunt Celia and assorted other stiff-assed relatives are all staring at Henry and me as we shuffle around the floor.

I half expect Alexander to march in and haul me off the dance floor like he did at Rashleigh Hall, but he doesn't. Not that I'd go with him. He can go to hell.

When the music stops, my head seems to take a little while to catch up with my feet.

'Whoa . . .' Henry steadies me and keeps hold of my arm. 'Do you think you should get some fresh air? Why don't I take you outside?'

I glance at him and then to Alexander, whose face is a mask of suppressed fury.

'No, really. I'd rather go upstairs.'

'So would I.'

Then it registers what he's said and how close he's

leaning in to me. I shake off his arm. 'Thanks for the drink, but I'm going to bed. On my own.'

Still a little light-headed from the booze and from throwing myself round the floor, I march past Alexander and towards the ballroom doors.

'Lauren, wait.'

Oh shit. Henry has followed me. 'I'm just going to the bathroom to wash my face,' I say. 'Why don't you wait out on the terrace for me?'

With a leer, he heads for the doorway – while I dash in the opposite direction, past the cloakroom door and out towards the orangery at the other end of the house. From my tour earlier, I know it's been a long time since the place was heated. Now it's just a summer room and the chilly atmosphere hits me the moment I walk into the moonlit interior.

I walk to the glass French doors, looking over the side of the house towards the gardens. The cool air has helped my dizziness, but I know I've had far too much to drink as a wave of nausea hits my stomach. I sit on one of the white ornate benches and put my head in my hands.

'Lauren!'

I take my hands away from my face and Alexander glares down at me. He has no jacket on now and the two ends of his bow tie hang down his collar.

'Good evening, Alexander. How nice to see you again.'

'Just what the fuck do you think you're doing?'

'Enjoying myself. What about you?'

'Is that what you call being all over Angus and Henry Favell?'

I sputter with laughter. 'I'm surprised you noticed, as you've spent the evening surgically attached to Valentina.'

'Don't talk bollocks.'

'You were touching her butt, if I recall.'

'What?'

'Didn't you even notice you were doing it?'

'No, I didn't – unlike you, who knew exactly what you were doing when you jumped on Angus and then let Henry Favell stare down your cleavage.'

'I was only being nice to your friends – wasn't that what you wanted?' I sneer. 'And you were otherwise engaged with Valentina, or maybe that's the wrong choice of words.'

'Everyone noticed you flirting with Favell – they couldn't fail. Do you realize what a fool you've just made of yourself?'

'*What* did you say?'

'Was this some plan to get my attention?' This is too close to the truth for comfort, but I'm so mad at him for calling me a fool that there's no way I'm going to back down.

I laugh in his face. 'Don't kid yourself. Look, this is pointless. I'm going up to my room.' I get up but he bars my way.

'I should have known better after what happened while I was away.'

His words stop me dead. 'What?'

'That evening I got back from Helmand. I know you'd been out celebrating with the all-American hero.'

Turning, I see the flicker of frustration in his eyes as he realizes the secret he just let slip, but he carries on as if nothing happened. 'Rupert saw you and Scott cosying up in the Turf.'

Rupert? I didn't see him at the pub but he, the snake, must have seen me and probably exaggerated what he saw by a factor of ten. I lift my chin. 'Not that it's any of his business, I *did* go for a drink with Scott before you got back. So what? It didn't mean anything.'

'Then why did you lie to me about going out with some friends?'

'Scott *is* a friend. And you said you'd phone me when you were on your way home. You didn't and I felt like getting out of college. I'm not going to sit and wait around for you to call me, Alexander.'

'I never asked you to,' he snaps back, then his voice quietens. 'I knew something like this would happen if you came to Falconbury.'

'Something like what?'

'Us. The rows. This place always brings out the fucking worst in people.'

'Maybe it brings out who you really are. Who we both really are.'

'And who do you think I "*really* am"?' He brackets his fingers around the last words. 'Go on, Lauren. I'd love to hear.'

'OK, then. Let's start with Troubled, Guilty, Defensive,

Emotionally Stultified.' I count off the fingers of my hand. 'Shall I go on?'

He folds his arms, his voice mocking. 'Please do. I'd hate to stop you now you've started.'

I realize I've backed him into a corner and made him angrier than ever, so I soften my voice, trembling a little now. 'I just think . . . that this weekend has shown how far apart we really are.'

'Then why don't you go and find someone who's closer to your ideal?'

My heart thumps away. 'Alexander . . .'

'Breakfast's at eight thirty,' he says coldly. 'I expect I'll see you there.'

Can it rain any harder? Could I get any wetter? Will the sun ever show its face or has it finally abandoned this soggy, gloomy country with its repressed and class-obsessed citizens for good? With a shiver that shakes me to my bones, I retreat a little deeper inside the little stone shelter opposite the gates to Falconbury House and clap my hands together. Water droplets fly off my gloves into the dank air and my head throbs. With three bags to carry, I couldn't use my umbrella and every inch of me that wasn't covered by the Barbour is sodden.

It's still better than the cab arriving at the magnificent door of Falconbury.

And way better than another confrontation with Alexander.

I didn't sleep after we parted in the orangery last

night. How could I? I lay awake for the rest of the night until I made my decision: that no matter how much I want Alexander, it's never going to work for us and that the differences between us are fundamental.

So, I looked up the name of a twenty-four-hour cab company from my phone and asked them to pick me up from outside the gates of Falconbury at first light. I'd rather they met me at the end of the drive, even if I had to walk up there in the gloomy dawn, because I didn't want the cab pulling up outside the house and the staff answering the door. I think one of the early shift did spot me as I crept downstairs and across the hall, hoping that Robert or Helen wouldn't catch me. It was like escaping Alcatraz, and just as wet.

The walk to the end of the driveway was maybe no more than a mile but felt like five as I lugged my bags through the driving rain. A front from the Atlantic – from home – must have gathered overnight and I know it's crazy, but it seems as if even the weather is telling me I'm doing the right thing, because all night I've been afraid that in fitting in with Alexander's world, socially – emotionally – I have become someone different to who I am. I don't do that for anyone. Period.

Wiping my watch face on my sleeve, I pray the cab is on time; almost immediately the rumble of a diesel engine makes my pulse beat a little faster. Briefly, my heart is in my mouth in case it's the Range Rover with Alexander, darkly sexy, begging me to stay, wearing me down as he has before and changing my mind about leaving.

I don't want the drama – my mind is made up – and to my relief my cab stops and the driver gets out to help me load my bags into the trunk. He pulls away from Falconbury and I stare out of the window at the retreating gates, thankful now that my rain-spattered face hides the tears streaming down it.

It's nearly nine on a Sunday morning and apart from the chaplain I saw scuttling through the showers in the front quad, Wyckham is as quiet as the grave. Most of the undergraduates were picked up by their parents yesterday, although I know Immy wanted to stay on for a week or so with Skandar. She's probably in bed with him now, sleeping it off after a night, or maybe shagging him, which is why I haven't dared phone her. I mean, who would phone someone on a Sunday morning at this hour?

I put my ear to Immy's door, but I can't hear anything. Immy, where the hell are you?

It's no good. I'll have to wait until I hear her surface . . . but she may not be in there at all; she's probably at Skandar's house and, anyway, what could she do if I do call her?

No one can help me except myself and my mind is already made up.

So why am I sitting here contemplating the remote possibility that I might want to keep my relationship with Alexander Hunt going?

I turn the key in my lock and walk inside, almost treading on an envelope that someone has slid under the door. Immediately, I recognize Immy's handwriting and open it up to find a Christmas card.

Sorry I missed saying goodbye. Have had to rush home because George is in hospital. He's had his appendix out, poor thing (!) and is doing OK now but I really want to see him and my parents need me. Hope you had a fabulous time at Falconbury. Have texted you but guess you are far too busy having fun to reply. Call me when you get back, am dying to hear all the gossip & have a good journey home. Can't wait to see you next term — Skype me if you get chance.

Hugs, Immy xxx

PS Happy Holidays!

Maybe I can call her from the airport or perhaps I should wait until I get home; she has enough to worry about right now. And I have things I need to do too. The airline customer line crackles into life and I take a deep breath. 'Hello. I'd like to make an amendment to my flight.'

Though I was supposed to be flying back tomorrow evening I checked out the schedule and found there's a flight leaving tonight with a space in Business Class. I'll get a car to Heathrow and I'll be in plenty of time to check in. Yes, I know it's crazy. Yes, I know it will cost a fortune, but I've got my own money and don't care any more. The sooner I get out of here the better, and now I can be in Washington for breakfast.

Ten minutes later, it's all rebooked. Another call and I've arranged a cab to come pick me up this afternoon, leaving me hours to kill – hours in which Alexander may or may not turn up on my doorstep. I drag a suit-case from the closet and start tossing in pants and sweaters, and sweep a couple of dresses off the rail and throw them in on top. The lid closes on a crumpled melee of designer clothes that would make my mother weep if she were here to see them.

As I hang my ballgown back in the closet, it smells of perfume and faintly of cigar smoke. I'm reminded of the time last night when I took Alexander's arm and we walked down to the ballroom and of how happy I was. Although it's only been a couple of hours since I crept out of Falconbury, it seems like an age. I imagine Rupert, Valen-tina and the other house guests crawling down to break-fast, if they make it. Is Alexander with them, wondering why I haven't surfaced? Or is he, even now, knocking on my bedroom door, bursting in, finding me gone . . .

By the time I've finished packing and sorting out my room, it's nearly eleven. The printer churns out my new flight ticket while I stare at my phone, lying dead on a draft of my essay. My fingers itch to turn it on and find out if there'll be texts from Alexander or frantic mes-sages demanding to know where I am.

There's no way I want to waste my time and energy confronting him so I may as well get out of here. The rain has stopped so I button the funnel neck of my coat, pull on my gloves and lock my room. The sky is a dirty white with grey clouds chasing across it and the damp clings to my face. It may be Sunday, but the streets of Oxford are bursting with students, tourists and Christmas shoppers. No one gives me a second glance and that's exactly what I want. The Bodleian, the Radcliffe Camera, All Souls' College – I walk past them all, and they remind me why I came four thousand miles to this esoteric world, of why I stood up for all I want and hope for my future. It definitely wasn't to fall so hard for a man like Alexander Hunt.

Over the other side of the High, I push through the iron turnstile and out into the meadow that leads to Christ Church Meadow and the river. The open fields provide no shelter from the wind that's cutting through the city and the river is granite coloured. Tiny wavelets ripple the surface, giving the scullers and Eights a hard time. I come to a halt near the boathouses, hugging my body in the bitter air.

'Lauren! Hey there!'

'Scott. Oh, shit.'

'That happy to see me, huh?' Wearing track pants and a dark blue padded jacket, he treats me to the warmest of smiles despite my greeting.

'I am happy to see you. In fact, if I had to see any-body right now, I'd rather it was you than anyone else.' Then I add, because perhaps I'm over-compensating, 'I guess my social skills are on life-support this morning.'

He peers at me closely. 'You do look upset.'

'It's been a long term and I can't wait to get back home tomorrow. Are you going back soon?'

'Not yet, I'm staying on here for a while to train with

the squad. You caught me on my way back to college after an erg test so I'm beat. What are you doing here?'

'I decided to have a walk before my car comes to take me to the airport. I'll be sitting around for the next twelve hours so I thought I'd get some fresh air.'

'You're kidding me? Not spending your last day before the vac with Alex? You know, he never did call me to arrange that beer. Maybe it was something I said?'

'Maybe.' I bite my lip.

'So where is he? Saving the planet? Crossing swords with some villain?'

My voice is a whisper, almost smothered by the wind, because I can hardly bear to say the words out loud. 'We broke up last night.'

He blows out a breath. 'Fuck me and my size thirteens. I am sorry, Lauren. I really mean that, and it's crappy that it happened right before you have to go home.'

'Shit happens. At least I have the vac to get over it.'

'Sure you do, but it's still a horrible thing to happen. At the risk of sounding like a Hallmark card, do you need a hug?'

'Thanks, but I don't think that would be wise. I don't want to blub all over your nice Blues jacket.'

'Screw that. Come here.'

And he puts his arms around me and hugs me to him and the tears are hot as they finally spill out. My chest heaves and I can't stop and don't want to lift my face from his chest and see the people around me averting their eyes in that British way while desperately trying to see what the fuck is going on.

But then I have to stop because I know Scott's coat will be snotty if I don't. Dashing my hand over my face, I break away from him.

'Here.' He hands me a fresh Kleenex from his pocket. 'Sorry, no crisp white handkerchief. I'm no gentleman.'

'I don't want you to be.'

'Want to tell me about it?'

After I've wiped my eyes I take a deep breath. 'No, I don't think I do.'

'Want me to walk with you back to Wyckham?'

I nod. 'But I don't want to go back to Wyckham yet. Can we just walk for a while?'

He frowns then says, 'OK. Whatever makes you feel better.'

As we wander along the riverside and back through the narrow lanes of the city, we talk about home, about our work – or Scott's lack of it – anything except what's happened with Alexander. I don't want to share any of it with anyone; I just want to go home and try to put this term behind me. Even as I tell myself that fact, I know it will be almost impossible because Alexander Hunt has left an indelible mark on me: for good and bad.

The belfry of St Nick's comes into view and I glance at Scott. I can't say I feel much better, but I'm grateful for his presence. He's a calm, friendly oasis – a hint of home – in a world that this morning seems cold, repressed and alien.

When we reach the medieval doorway of St Nick's, I touch his arm.

'You can leave me here. You must be tired after training.'

'Not that tired and I could leave you, but I won't. I'm taking you all the way back to Wyckham, no arguments.'

I certainly don't want any arguments, and if I don't feel any better I can at least make Scott feel better – so I walk beside him. Finally, we round the corner, the Bridge of Sighs arches above our heads and beyond that, the tower of Wyckham.

I stop Scott with my hand on his arm. 'It's OK now, I'll go on from here.'

'I'm not comfortable with leaving you here and I know it's none of my business, but what happened with you guys? Did he cheat on you or did you dump him?'

'Let's just call it irreconcilable differences.'

He puts his arm round me. 'I'm genuinely sorry, but I must admit he seemed a pretty uptight kind of guy, and I never had you down as the sort of woman to hang out with an upper-class Brit. I didn't say so at the time but you were a little on edge at the pub on Thanksgiving. I put it down to you working too hard and missing your family, but you were pretty cagey about him not being around.'

'It had nothing to do with that, trust me; I just decided things were never going to work out.'

'So where is he now? Did you walk out of college to get away from him? Because if he's hassling you I'll make sure the bastard backs off.'

Oh God, a fight between Alexander and Scott would be like two freight trains crashing into each other, and although Scott's bigger than Alexander I really don't fancy his chances in hand-to-hand combat.

'There's no need for that. It would only make things worse and, as far as I know, he's still at his family in the country. I was there for the weekend, but we had a big bust-up and I left early this morning without telling him.'

He rests his hands on my shoulders and looks down at me with concern. 'Are you sure you're OK? If he's making trouble for you . . .'

'He isn't and he won't. Trust me; you don't need to ride to the rescue,' I say, fully aware that trouble is Alexander's middle name. 'Thanks for, um, being around this morning. I'll see you next term, maybe?'

'Definitely, but I'll call you when I get back to the States.'

My throat clogs with emotion because the reality that Alexander and I are history has finally slammed into me. 'OK, see you.'

'Hey there. Don't cry.'

Scott's arms are around me and my eyes blur with tears. Before I know it, his mouth is on mine. It's a tender, warm kiss that goes on longer than it should and is something more than comforting, but I don't know *what*. Oh hell, after this weekend maybe I don't know anything about myself any more. He pulls away the same moment I do and I shut my eyes and rest my forehead on his chest. 'Oh, Scott.'

'Did I just complicate things?' he whispers, keeping his hands on my arms.

'No, but I don't think we should do it again right now.'

He pushes my hair from my face. 'It was selfish but can you blame me? It's killing me to see you wasting tears over this guy. You deserve better.'

'I'm a grown-up. I walked into Alexander's world with my eyes wide open. Now, I really have to go.'

I wriggle away from him and then I see the man on the corner of the street watching us. Alexander stands right in the middle of the narrow pavement, so that people have to step into the gutter to go round him. His collar is buttoned up against the wind and he buries his fists deep into the pockets of his reefer coat, like he's making a massive effort of will to hold himself back.

And as I step forward and open my mouth to speak, to say something – anything – that tells him this wasn't how I wanted things to end between us, he quietly turns his back and walks away.

He just wanted a decent book to read ...

Not too much to ask, is it? It was in 1935 when Allen Lane, Managing Director of Bodley Head Publishers, stood on a platform at Exeter railway station looking for something good to read on his journey back to London. His choice was limited to popular magazines and poor-quality paperbacks – the same choice faced every day by the vast majority of readers, few of whom could afford hardbacks. Lane's disappointment and subsequent anger at the range of books generally available led him to found a company – and change the world.

'We believed in the existence in this country of a vast reading public for intelligent books at a low price, and staked everything on it'
Sir Allen Lane, 1902–1970, founder of Penguin Books

The quality paperback had arrived – and not just in bookshops. Lane was adamant that his Penguins should appear in chain stores and tobacconists, and should cost no more than a packet of cigarettes.

Reading habits (and cigarette prices) have changed since 1935, but Penguin still believes in publishing the best books for everybody to enjoy. We still believe that good design costs no more than bad design, and we still believe that quality books published passionately and responsibly make the world a better place.

So wherever you see the little bird – whether it's on a piece of prize-winning literary fiction or a celebrity autobiography, political tour de force or historical masterpiece, a serial-killer thriller, reference book, world classic or a piece of pure escapism – you can bet that it represents the very best that the genre has to offer.

Whatever you like to read – trust Penguin.